THE
BOOK
OF
STONE

JONATHAN PAPERNICK

BEDFORD, NEW YORK

Published in the United States by Fig Tree Books LLC, Bedford, New York

www.FigTreeBooks.net

Jacket design by Strick&Williams
Interior design by Neuwirth & Associates, Inc.

Library of Congress Cataloging-in-Publication Data Available Upon Request

ISBN 978-1-94149-304-5

Printed in the United States
Distributed by Publishers Group West

First edition

10 9 8 7 6 5 4 3 2 1

TO MY DAD,
WHO SAYS I'M A LUCKY BOY.

"... how false the most profound book turns out
to be when applied to life."

—WILLIAM FAULKNER, *Light in August*

THE
BOOK
OF
STONE

1

Matthew Stone opened his eyes and looked down onto the street. People in twos and threes moved languidly in the pale yellow haze as if constrained by a barely discernible gauze. A whisper of breeze on his face brought him back into his body, his hard-beating heart. It convulsed in a sudden, discordant two-step that left him gasping for air. The sleeves of his father's robe hung beyond his wrists and flapped like wings as he leaned over the rusted railing, the street five stories below vertiginous, noisy. A bus roared past, a trail of vapor shimmering in its wake.

Stone pulled the robe tight around him, binding his chin against his chest. He smelled his father's scent, the sour odor of his tobacco. It was ironic, he knew, that he would seek comfort beneath his father's robe. After all, the exact article of clothing that had drawn his father away from Stone during the Judge's lengthy trials was the very same robe that embraced him when the endless empty space around him was too much to bear. As a boy he snuck into the Judge's closet, awed by his father's tremendous bulk, and pulled the majestic robe—which forever smelled of the stale smoke of Nat Sherman Originals—from its heavy wooden hanger. He would drape the robe over his slight body and feel full, as the vast emptiness around him closed up like a slamming door. In an instant he felt like a superhero, like Batman, or the Caped Crusader. Anything was possible.

But that was a long time ago.

It was hard to believe that morning the Honorable Walter J. Stone had lived and breathed and existed. He had still been reading a book at five o'clock in the morning, as if preparing for a lecture later in the week. Now he was what? An empty vessel? Food for worms? Nothing. Forever is impossible to conceive until it's upon you: the realization that forever is forever is forever. The Judge was gone and Stone was alone in the world.

As an only son, Stone faced the overwhelming task of selecting his father's burial accoutrements. The body was barely cold and the funeral director, a thin arrow of a man with jet-black hair and a weak chin, who introduced himself as Mr. Ehrenkranz, had asked whether the Judge would enter eternity in a muslin shroud or a linen one, Israeli or one handmade here in America? It had never occurred to Stone that some-body actually had to make such a decision, as though picking out a Father's Day tie at Macy's. He didn't care. His brain fired blanks.

He let Ehrenkranz decide.

"You'll note," Ehrenkranz added, handing Stone his father's beloved school ring—yellow gold with a glittering blue sapphire in the center, bracketed with the words COLUMBIA UNIVERSITY, "shrouds have no pockets to carry man's material possessions into the next world. How-ever, it is customary for the deceased to be wrapped in his prayer shawl. Do you happen to have it with you?"

The pigeons cooing on the ledge below sounded almost human, a choir full of sorrow and regret and loss, unintelligible, but almost human. Stone threw one leg over the railing, feeling dizzy exhilara-tion, a vein jumping in his wrist. He stood on the street side of the railing now as the pigeons chattered, beckoning him forward. You can fly like us, the pigeons teased, you have wings. Stone spread his arms wide and knew the black robe could just as easily be his own burial shroud; all he had to do was step forward, and the pain would be gone in a pure act of erasure. He could fill the empty space below him in an instant.

Instead, he pulled a pack of matches from his pocket and lit a loosely rolled joint. As he inhaled, the heat of the burning tip near his skin, he was reminded of the elemental power he held in his trembling hand. He dropped a match onto the street, lit another match, held it for a five count—nearly burning the tips of his fingers—and dropped it. A cluster of pigeons rose into the sky and scattered, a pungent rush of air blowing past on the updraft. A few streets over, a car alarm wailed.

Looking across the river toward the city and the fading pink sunset, he could see from the monolithic Twin Towers and the crenellated spires of the Woolworth Building all the way to the Chrysler Building halfway up the island, rising like a stainless steel rocket ship from the dissonant chaos of Midtown. He took another hit of his joint, pondering. This squat, ordinary apartment house set against a backdrop of brown brick tenement buildings was exactly the sort of end he deserved. As the smoke filled his lungs, his father, vibrant with life, appeared before him floating in the air, wearing a three-piece suit and half-moon glasses, a paragon of scholarly civility, shaking his colossal bald head in disapproval.

"Do it," his father said, with characteristic cruelty. "You're nothing but a coward, Matthew. You're not even a shit stain in my shorts."

"Would it make you proud?" Stone said aloud, his voice weak.

But the Judge vanished as quickly as he had materialized.

Now, in the cool air of the rooftop, a pigeon alighted on the railing beside Stone, strutting with stupid avian bravado; a challenge. He flapped his wings and disappeared into the sky. Stone spread his arms, the fabric fluttering in the wind. A single green iridescent feather floated in the air just out of Stone's reach, taunting him.

"I can do it if I want to," Stone shouted to the sky. It was strange how foreign his voice sounded to his ears in the thick evening air. "But I won't. Because you want me to."

He slumped against the railing, breathless, realizing he had made up his mind to live. For now. Stone might have nodded off because the sky was dark, full of heavy black clouds rolling in high on the wind as eerie yellow lights came on in the streets between his tenuous perch and the river. Brooklyn looked somehow more lurid now that night had fallen, its low buildings more shabby. Its windows were filling with broken silhouettes of WIC-assisted poor bent over dinner plates in the blue glare of their televisions; rooftop water tanks hunched like wild things about to spring; disembodied renegade shouts filled the

air, the streets below burning with anger freed by the cover of darkness. Manhattan, too, looked different, its jagged spine illuminated,
lights flaring along the length of the island like torches lit by primi-
tives in another age.

Stone heard footsteps at his back, and then: "What the fuck are you
doing?" It was Pinky. Stone had almost forgotten, amid the bewil-
dering whirlwind of emotions, that he was staying with Pinky now; his
father's Midwood apartment was no longer safe. "You look like Count
Dracula in that thing. Get off there before someone gets hurt."

Stone had come up to the roof to get away from Pinky, who
understood death and loss the same way a twelve-year-old boy understands sex by gawking at pictures in a *National Geographic* magazine—
distant, exotic, virtually impossible. But Pinky had phoned at the right
moment, with Stone in a panic at the state of his father's apartment; he
had come right away and filled a white cube van with Bankers Boxes
of the Judge's belongings and loaded them into his street-level apartment. Pinky had offered Stone a mattress and a bare room, but he
offered no comfort aside from empty platitudes and a firm handshake.
As soon as the last box was stacked in the middle of Pinky's living
room, he cranked up his stereo, subwoofers pulsing, blasting some
hideous, bass-thumping rap music that threatened to split Stone's
head in two. Pinky produced a nasty resin-filled bong from a kitchen
cabinet and presented it to Stone with a be-my-guest gesture meant
to be comic, but that only made Pinky more of an insensitive jackass.

His father had just died, and this was what he was left with.

All Stone's childhood friends were gone. Danny Green was in med
school in Baltimore; Alan Grinstein, Harvard Law; Alvin Zuckerbrot,
Stanford Law; Jay Coopersmith head chef in a Michelin-starred restaurant in Amsterdam; Mickey Zin was married, lighting out for the
suburbs of Westchester County; Ami Alfasi, dead two years in the
Security Zone in Lebanon and buried on Mount Herzl in Jerusalem.

Only Pinky, Michael Pinsky, the schmuck who dropped out of
twelfth grade to try out for the Yankees, who got genital herpes from
a prostitute in Paterson, New Jersey, who believed Jack Ruby was
a great American Jew, only Pinky remained. He was a friend, but a

friend of habit more than desire. They had known each other a long time and they were the last two childhood friends left standing. It was hard to believe they had once had so much in common, but passion for baseball cards, bike riding, and ding dong dash was a flimsy foundation for an enduring bond.

"It's time to come inside, bitch," Pinky said, offering a hand to Stone as he climbed back over the railing. "We've got a funeral tomorrow."

Stone returned to the apartment reluctantly, wordlessly, and he and Pinky descended the stairs. When they were back inside, Pinky asked Stone if he wanted to play blackjack or something, but Stone didn't answer and locked himself behind the bathroom door. He hung the robe on a hook and turned on the fan. Then he sat down in the cool bathtub and lit a cigarette. Stone unbuttoned his pants, pulled aside the zipper, and found the pale white of his upper thigh. It had been a long time, but the skin called to him now. His skin was nothing more than a tight-fitting body bag anyway. He took a deep drag on the cigarette. His hand shook as he maneuvered the cigarette toward his thigh. An old purple scar in the shape of the letter C smiled at him, beckoning. The hair burned first, then the skin. His vision went white and his blood began to calm and, soon, he closed his eyes.

THE MORNING SKY was a bright Dodger blue and the glare of the piercing sun was sharp and pricked Stone's retinas like needles. Dressed in his only suit, a modish single-breasted number he rarely had cause to wear, he asked Pinky if he had an extra pair of sunglasses. Pinky disappeared inside the apartment, leaving Stone alone on the sidewalk. His chest was tight, as if filled with cement—some invisible force had been crouching on his chest all night long, whispering in his ear, whispering something in a strange language he could not understand. He wanted to go back inside and close his eyes, but he was even more afraid of sleep than he was of facing the real-life nightmare of his father's funeral.

A long black limousine idled in front of the apartment. The neighborhood homeboys, who had been throwing dice on the pavement and laughing when Stone arrived yesterday, now gathered around the limo, faces pressed to the tinted windows in curiosity. Stone could not imagine ever laughing again. For some reason, he had an overwhelming urge to shout something terrible at them, something sharp and biting, like a broken bottle to the face, something he would later regret. He just wanted to be alone with his anguish, and the shouting and hollering before him made him feel as if he were losing his sense of reason.

"Take your pick," Pinky said, tossing Stone a Bloomingdale's shopping bag. There must have been a dozen new pairs of brand-name glasses, still in their original packaging. He fished out a pair of dark Ray-Bans and slipped them on.

"Lookin' good," Pinky said.

"What's with this?" Stone asked.

"I figured we should ride in style. You really want to gypsy cab it to your old man's funeral? Don't worry. I've got you covered." Then Pinky turned to the homeboys and said, "Nothing to see here. You think Biggie's back from the dead? Well, he ain't."

They drove in silence out to Queens, that inimitable borough of escape, of airports and cemeteries, as Stone imagined the unimaginable, the fact that he would be burying his father so soon, before he himself had accomplished anything in this life. Stone had no job, no advanced degree, no skills. Nothing. He would be alone, no wife, no girlfriend, no children, no mother, no aunts, no uncles, no friends to share his burden. Just Pinky.

How could his father die so young? There were ex–Nazi executioners still living into their eighties, unrepentant killers on death row eligible for Social Security, and his father, a fit sixty-three, was gone. His father had been a force of nature, molded out of pure brass. Even pale and faded, his father struck Stone as awesome, frightening. Even when the cancer had ruined his voice, withered his body, his will was radiant. It was clear the Judge didn't believe he was going to die, lying in bed with his half-moon glasses perched on the end of his nose, reading to the end, a book propped on a pillow before him. Then yesterday morning, not long after sunrise, with the swiftness of a sudden summer storm, they both realized he was going to die.

The limousine passed a ragged handful of protesters by the cemetery gate, waving handmade signs announcing: ABU DIS & RAS AL-AMUD = PALESTINE! and ARAB BLOOD FROM ZIONIST STONE. Stone had become so used to his father's divisive cult of personality that the clownish activists barely registered in his mind. The ride out had numbed him with a sort of vestigial comfort, the light humming of the road soothing his nerves, and he drifted in and out of consciousness. But he was awake now, as Pinky rolled down the window, flipped them the bird, and called out something crude.

Stone recalled the time his father brought him to Montefiore Cemetery as a boy to pay respects to his hero Ze'ev Jabotinsky. Of course this stern-faced man with the cruel expression and round rimless glasses, whose framed picture his father kept on his desk, meant nothing to Matthew. He remembered the brutal black granite slab platform set in the center of a limestone plaza. His father handed Matthew a small stone and asked him to place it on the grave, and, rather than doing as his father asked, he said, "Why?"

"Jabotinsky was the creator of the first Jewish army since the time of the Romans—" his father began.

"I know," Matthew said. "But why the stone?"

"It indicates someone has visited, and a stone, unlike flowers, lasts for eternity."

Eternity is forever and death is for eternity.

Stone was shocked to see how many people had come to pay their respects to his father. There were hundreds upon hundreds of men gathered, some dressed in the customary black of the ultra-Orthodox, bearded and black-hatted, others wearing knitted skullcaps, typical of militant Zionists, many of whom spent time studying or living on the West Bank.

"Quite a shit-show," Pinky said, lighting a cigarette. "You sure this isn't the great American beard-growing contest?"

"Put it out," Stone said. "It's disrespectful."

Overcome by swirling vertigo, he leaned against the side of the limousine for balance. Who were all these people? He knew his father had achieved a lot in his life. He had accomplished good deeds but also suffered his share of controversy. Somehow, when Stone had imagined the funeral as he tossed beneath the thin sheet on Pinky's bare extra mattress he was certain had fallen off the back of a truck, he'd seen only himself, alone with his father, saying good-bye. He had imagined a poignant moment after his father had been lowered into the ground in which he would close the book and move on with his life.

"There you are, Matthew. I was worried you were going to be late." It was Ehrenkranz, the funeral director. "You might want to clip this on to your garment to show you are grieving. Near the heart, if it feels right to you." He handed Stone a small black ribbon, torn at the corner, which Stone slipped into his pocket. Ehrenkranz led Stone by the elbow through the throngs of mourners toward the graveside. "This is a very nice turnout," Ehrenkranz said. "You should have seen the Lubavitcher Rebbe's funeral. Thousands of mourners. Absolute chaos. Trust me, you don't want that."

Stone did not recognize one single soul, not one familiar face, as strangers reached out and blessed him and wished he be comforted among the mourners of Zion.

When they arrived at the grave, Ehrenkranz asked Stone if he was all right.

"All right is entirely relative," Stone said. "Especially here."

Ehrenkranz gave an avuncular laugh and patted Stone on the shoulder. "Here comes the *shomer*."

A watery-eyed old man stepped forward with a solemn expression on his worn face. "Your father was a great man and warrior, a friend of Israel and of Jews everywhere. The Chofetz Chaim says, 'The sign of a great man is the closer you get, the greater he seems.'"

These past months, Stone had been as close to his father as he had ever been, physically—tending to him like the good son he would never be, taking him to his appointments, making sure his medication was right—but still he barely knew him. His father had treated him with scorn, as if he were some sort of servant not worthy of conversation. He knew people believed his father to be great, but to him, the Judge was just distant, cruel, and unforgiving.

The old man fished into his jacket pocket and produced a small, battered prayer book. He handed it to Stone. "It is *tehillim*," the man said, "as a keepsake."

"The book of Psalms," Ehrenkranz said. "It is the duty of the *shomer*, or watcher, who stays with the body so it is not alone, to recite psalms to comfort the departed. It is a wonderful tradition to know a body is never left alone like a piece of lost luggage at a bus station."

Stone thanked the old man for the book and approached the grave.

He looked down into the empty hole in the ground. The soil was damp and black like coffee grounds, minuscule roots protruding from the earth here and there, life springing up in the midst of death. So, this is where it all ends; in the dark, in a box, underground. The thought terrified Stone, and he gasped for breath to compensate for the certainty that he, too, would one day arrive at this point. Would his father approve of his neighbors? Would it matter that Mr. So-and-So's son had married a *shiksa*, or that Mr. Such-and-Such with the extravagant tombstone had been a social climber in life with no substance to speak of? It didn't matter now, but at the same time, it did. It was a pleasant spot, however, open to plenty of sunlight, with tall shade trees standing nearby.

Someone behind him clapped a hand down onto his head. For a moment, Stone was afraid he was going to fall into the grave, but he held his balance and turned to see a bearded man in a black hat and long gabardine coat, his deep-set eyes sepulchral, empty.

"You must cover your head."

Stone realized now the man had placed a kippa onto his head, one of those satiny vinyl jobs old men tended to wear, propped high on the crowns of their heads like tents.

He didn't want to, but this was no place to make a scene. The man, perhaps sensing Stone's reticence, grabbed him by the shoulders and said, "You will wear the yarmulke and honor your father."

He would honor his father whichever way he chose, and thought for a moment of tearing the thing off his head, but when he saw Pinky pulling faces behind the man, with his own kippa clipped to his gelled hair, he realized this was not a fight he needed to have. He placed the kippa back onto his head, looked the man in his empty eyes, and said, "Satisfied?"

"You are in mourning?"

"My father is dead," Stone said.

"Then you will rend your garment as an expression of your grief for the loss of a loved one." Before Stone had the chance to consider the man's words and what they meant, the man had torn the pocket off Stone's jacket with a swift yank, so the fabric flapped down below his heart. "Now, you are among the mourners of Zion," the man said, stalking off into the crowd.

Stone was among no one. This was his only suit, and the man had ripped it with such arrogance and entitlement because of some meaningless tradition that did nothing to comfort Stone. Who were these people? And how could his father have tolerated them? Stone was not part of this world, and for that he was glad.

Stone scanned the crowd to distract himself from the unpleasantness at hand. He began to count in his head, by fives, how many people were in attendance. He doubted he knew half a dozen people who would care enough to pay their respects to him if it were all over now. The thought depressed him, and an immense empty space opened up around him. Somehow, in the blazing spotlight of the sun, he shivered in his suit. He had reached a hundred and fifty when he saw, standing on a small grassy hill beyond the last ragged group of mourners, a slim dark-haired man, face pressed to a camera, its enormous telephoto lens a giant eye out for a day at the circus. Why couldn't the media just leave this one alone? His father was dead, nothing mattered anymore. The story was over, the funeral a final parenthesis on a complicated life that had ended too soon. He imagined the photograph the next day in one of the local tabloids, the ghoulish headline punning on their family name for the final time. But something caught Stone's attention: the way the man tilted his head from side to side, as if trying to work out a crick from having slept badly. Among all the black-clad mourners chatting in a noisy mélange of English, Hebrew, and Yiddish, this man was different.

Stone failed to notice the casket arrive at the graveside. A rabbi was reciting prayers. The prayers meant nothing, repeated by rote in an ancient language that had no relevance at all to Stone. As the casket descended into the ground, he imagined his father wrapped in the white shroud and prayer shawl the Judge had told him he had received at his bar mitzvah over fifty years ago.

Stone had been so ill at ease at the funeral home that when Ehrenkranz asked him whether he had his father's prayer shawl with him, he had taken the opportunity to leave at once to go find it. He had left his father's apartment only a few hours earlier, but when he arrived he saw the lock had been jimmied and the door left ajar. Stone felt as if he had been dipped into a pool of freezing water as he called out, "Hello!" He heard no answer and entered the apartment, half expecting to see his father still in bed, reading. He called out again, heard nothing, and now, filled more with anger than with fear—who the hell would rob a dead man?—he slammed the door behind him and pulled the deadbolt.

The apartment was trashed. His father's precious books, yanked from the shelves, lay scattered around the floor; his drawers were overturned; keepsakes and *tchotchkes* lay smashed on the ground. A panicked fist of anxiety gripped his throat and he fought to gain his breath. Something told him not to call the police, not to report the break-in. He was alone, had never been so alone before. But, gathering one of his father's books from the floor, a yellowed paperback copy of Viktor Frankl's *Man's Search for Meaning*, Stone realized no, he wasn't entirely alone. He discovered, as he flipped through the pages, that his father had underlined pertinent passages and made marginal notes throughout the book. He paused for a moment at a passage his father must have marked years ago with a graphite pencil: "<u>Everything can be taken from a man but one thing: the last of the human freedoms—to choose one's attitude in any given set of circumstances, to choose one's own way</u>."

Frankl had survived the Nazi death camps but had lost his parents, his brother, and his pregnant wife and had the strength to write those words. Stone was barely a quarter-century old and had suffered no such tragedies. And yet he was overcome by such loss and emptiness.

In a blind fever he began to gather the books and stack them up in towering piles, nearly as tall as himself. The Judge collected rare books, from "In the beginning . . ." and his eighteenth-century reprint of the Gutenberg Bible through to the Spanish Inquisition and the Jewish mystics, from biographies of the American presidents to the voluminous writings of Churchill and Freud, to Carl von Clausewitz and Ze'ev Jabotinsky. Each one was underlined, marked, or annotated to some degree, and, in this way, his father was still alive. The impenetrable mystery of his father lay in those books. The Judge was speaking to Stone, guiding him, as he discovered in book after book, in sentences as bright as gems meant to show him how to navigate his path forward. Stone continued stacking thirteen volumes of Rashi's Torah commentary, smelled the pages and ran his fingers over the Hebrew words his father had read. More religious books: the Tanach, bound in green leather; the Gemarah; and the *Shulchan Aruch*, Joseph Caro's code of Jewish law. The religious books were unmarked, but the soft pages had been read again and again.

Just yesterday, in the hours before his father had slipped away forever, the Judge had, with monumental effort, motioned to a thick book on his bedside table. Stone had propped it on the pillow for him and opened it. The Judge moaned. Wrong page. Stone flipped to another page and then another, until finally the Judge was calm. His father's eyes moved across the page. Stone thought his father was reading out of habit now, barely registering the words. Soon he drifted in and out of consciousness, his voice destroyed by the cancer, muttering the words of the Shema and "God Bless America," the languages mixing and blending. Stone went to move the heavy book from his father's chest, but the Judge gripped it with surprising strength and Stone relented. And now the Judge, alert for the last time, recited the Aramaic words of the Kaddish, enunciating every syllable of the ancient recitation with crystalline clarity before slipping back into delirium.

Stone wanted to call someone, anyone, to fix what was happening to the Judge. A chill of panic rushed up and down his spine, but then he realized there was no cure for death, and it was making its appearance at last. As if scrolling through the major players of his life, the

Judge called out the names Daddy, Bunny, Abi, and Matthew, three generations of his family. He also called out the name Henry, a name Stone did not recognize. When he asked the Judge, "Who is Henry?" the Judge did not answer.

Could it be that Walter Stone had had another son Stone did not know, a son who had not failed to disappoint? Stone figured anything was possible, but why the insistence, and why now, when he had never said the name Henry out loud before?

Soon Stone no longer understood what the Judge was trying to say, as if he had already passed over into the other world and was speaking its timeless language. He muttered "Seligman" in his sleep and awoke with fright in his eyes, repeating the name, "Seligman, Seligman," and then in the same breath, "Henry."

When Stone asked again, "Who is Henry?" the Judge mumbled some words, something about "the numbers."

He asked, "What numbers?"

"Which, which," the Judge said with difficulty, and Stone realized to his horror that even now, with communication so tenuous between them, the Judge was correcting his grammar. He dabbed water on his father's lips for the last time, and the Judge said with difficulty, "Seligman. Seligman."

Then the Judge was silent, and Matthew Stone was alone with the corpse of his father.

He stared in awe for a moment, barely comprehending that his father, speaking just moments earlier, no longer existed on the earth. Stone reached for the book spread open on his father's chest. It was volume two of Edward Gibbon's *Decline and Fall of the Roman Empire*, open to page 1,613, the section discussing the succession of Greek emperors of Constantinople. The words at the top of the second paragraph were underlined in red. He read out loud, as if they had to be spoken to be understood: "After the decease of his father, the inheritance of the Roman world devolved to Justinian II; and the name of a triumphant lawgiver was dishonored by the vices of a boy."

■ ■ ■

THE GRAVESIDE PRAYERS were over now, and someone handed Stone a shovel. His father's casket looked so small and inconsequential down there in the ground as he hefted a shovel full of dirt into the air. He tossed the first clots of earth onto the plain pine casket and it sounded like his own bony knuckles knocking on the door of eternity. It was almost impossible for his mind to accept this was happening, like comprehending with absolute certainty there was no God and we were alone in the universe, and it struck Stone with a sudden panic. He was sick; he knew for certain he was sick in the mind, sick in the body, his blood feverish with approaching death, his nerves vibrating with the contagion of his condition. He thought about climbing down into the hole and throwing his arms around the casket and embracing his father at last. Instead he shoveled, and shoveled and shoveled, until Ehrenkranz placed a soft hand on Stone's, bringing him back to the world. Ehrenkranz took the shovel from Stone's hand and Stone realized he had been crying.

"It's all right," Ehrenkranz said. "There will be a time when you will understand the purpose of your pain. Right now, you need to find a place to put the pain."

As the crowd dispersed, Stone shook hands with dozens of strangers, deaf to their words, blind to the pitying expressions on their faces, embarrassed, not for his tears, but for the fact that his only suit was torn.

A young bearded man in a knitted kippa approached Stone and offered his condolences. Stone responded automatically and turned to head back to the limousine where Pinky held court, cracking up the driver with some inappropriate joke.

The man was in his early twenties, squat and pear-shaped with a patchy ginger beard. "Matthew, wait a second." He held a cellular phone in his hand and offered it to Stone. "Someone would like to speak to you."

Who could possibly be calling him at this moment? He did not recognize the pear-shaped man, and his blank expression told him nothing. Stone took the phone in his own hand and sucked in a deep breath. "Hello?"

"Matthew," the familiar voice said, "I am so, so sorry for your loss."

In an instant, Stone was gasping for breath, suffocating: his father's voice. He was silent. Was he losing mind? This could not be happening; his father was dead and buried in the ground beneath his feet. But his father, so competitive, so driven, could not bear the thought that his useless only son had outlived him. He had focused his incredible will, gathering all his rapidly dispersing energy to make this phantom phone call, to destroy his only son, who had wept at the grave like a weak child.

The voice continued, "It is never easy to lose a parent. But your father will be the first in line when redemption comes. *Baruch Hashem*."

It wasn't his father's voice. The voice was similar, Stone realized, but it was not the same; it reflected similar upbringing, similar age. It was Seligman.

"Matthew, are you there?"

Stone was silent again for a moment. His father's old friend had not made the trip from Israel. It was natural he would call to offer his condolences.

"Uncle Zal," Stone said. It had been a long time since he had called him that, a long time since he had considered Seligman with anything other than revulsion.

"I understand you will not be sitting shiva for your father. But you should not be alone at a time like this."

"I have no place to host."

"I understand, but it is important that you say the Mourner's Kaddish for your father." Seligman's voice, thousands of miles away, digitized into bytes and codes through fiber-optic lines, reconstituted as a ghoulish facsimile of a man's voice, free of any warmth or humanity.

"As the only surviving son, it is your obligation, your duty. You understand your responsibility, don't you? Now tell me, where will you be saying Kaddish?"

Stone's worst fears had been realized. Seligman was an emissary sent by his father from the other world to belittle him and make him feel small, the way the Judge had done his entire life. The finish line was always being extended, just out of his reach. He would never be free.

2 Alone in Pinky's apartment, surrounded by cardboard boxes filled with his father's most prized possessions, Stone tried to mouth the words of the Kaddish prayer. He hated Seligman for shaming him, especially for the manner in which he had done so—close enough to plant the seed of misery but distant enough to provide no comfort whatsoever. Stone would be reciting the ancient chant only out of guilt; useless obligation, carried along through generations of blood, minted onto his DNA like a brand, the need to soothe the irresistible force tormenting him. But he was not a good son, and could never be a good son. His father was gone—he had missed his chance. Stone could barely form the words of the Kaddish. Burning skeins of acid rose up his throat; his eyes filled with tears. He stopped, trembling in fear, his chest heaving, scarcely human sobs bursting from his open mouth.

Later, after night had fallen, he stared at the boxes that seemed somehow as mysterious as the pyramids of Egypt. Who was his father, after all? Stone knew the broad strokes, the highs and the lows, the triumphs and disgraces, but he did not know why the Judge had been so distant, shattering, in his dismissive treatment of him. He did not understand why he was lionized by so many or what he had still planned to do before the cancer struck him down. An accomplished life, Stone thought, but incomplete.

His father, Walter Joseph Stone, would be forever remembered as the "jurymandering judge," the New York State Supreme Court justice who had presided over the controversial Court Street Riot trial and been forced to resign over improprieties regarding jury selection. When Stone was younger it had felt like sweet revenge, his father devoured by the hungry media out for blood, but now he was left with nothing but sadness for his father's tarnished legacy. Stone finished off his joint and mused: Would things have turned out differently if he had, instead of celebrating his father's disgrace, done something to help ease it?

He knew his father had been born in Brownsville, Brooklyn, son of the notorious gangster Julius Stone. His father had enrolled in Columbia College at the age of fifteen after graduating at the top of his class at Brooklyn Technical High School, and completed Columbia Law School at twenty before becoming the state's youngest assistant district attorney at the age of twenty-two. He had even been honored by Mayor Robert F. Wagner in a public ceremony for his exceptional service before joining the army's branch of the Judge Advocate General's Corps during the Vietnam War.

It was remarkable how different his father was from Julius Stone, reputed trigger man for the crime syndicate Murder Incorporated. It couldn't have been easy for the Judge to escape Julius's toxic influence, the violence, the intimidation.

Stone slipped the Judge's robe on again and closed his eyes: an entire life in thirty-six boxes. He leaned against a stack of boxes, knees pulled to his chest, rolled another joint, and lit it. As the weed took hold of him, Stone knew he wanted to do something, even if it only meant walking down the street to buy a newspaper. He wanted to get up off the ground, to put on clean clothing, to stand up and shout, but his voice would not come. He wanted to do something important, but he was frightened. Stone had even been afraid to open the boxes to learn what was inside—he knew there were old photo albums stacked between the books, photos of him as a child, his father as a young man and then, later, as the force of nature he had become. Perhaps his mother was in those albums as well. He had forgotten what her face looked like; it had been such a long time. Stone wanted to see those faces again, familiar faces in the proper sense, alive with the possibilities of a future they could not imagine.

The first box opened with a sigh, as if the books themselves were glad to be freed from their confinement. Stone stacked them in neat piles along the wall, his fingers blackening with dust. He opened a second and a third box and stacked the books, washing his hands of grime as he went. By the time he had emptied ten or eleven of the boxes, he finally paused, sweating, flipping through a hardcover biography of Orde Wingate, the eccentric British general credited by many with creating modern guerrilla warfare. Something akin to a shiver seized his body; not cold, but electric, as if he had stuck his finger into a light socket. He was not alone. Somebody stood just over his shoulder, reading the words before his eyes, breathing in his ear. "Who's there?" Stone called and spun around, but there was no one in the room. The books whispered to him. It was a whisper, an actual whisper, but it came from inside Stone's head. He did not so much read the words as the words read themselves. The Judge had underlined Wingate's call to arms: "<u>Today we stand on the threshold of battle. The time of preparation is over and we are moving on the enemy to prove ourselves and our methods</u>."

His father had been reading that book back in the spring when Stone had first arrived. The underlining was new, done with the blue Uni-ball pen Stone had given his father from his knapsack. Stone closed his eyes, and the words remained before him, illuminated, shimmering in the darkness. "I am so fucking high," he said out loud and began to laugh before he heard four successive gunshots ring out somewhere down the block. He froze in place, waiting for the police to come, but he never heard any sirens.

Stone unboxed *The History of Nations*—all sixty-eight volumes, reprinted from the London edition, encapsulating the histories of all nations from Greece to Rome to Persia to France to England—his father had bought as a student at an old antiquarian bookshop on 104th Street, according to the stamp inside the cover of the books. More histories: Josephus, Churchill, Thucydides, Gibbon, a three-volume set called *History of the Jews in Russia and Poland*. Biographies of Moses Montefiore and the Rothschilds, the writings of Israel Zangwill and of Ze'ev Jabotinsky, his father's hero, fluent in eight languages, writer and translator of Dante and Poe, a lawyer by training, a journalist, and above all the most eloquent and forceful voice in Zionism. He found Lincoln; Hitler; Stalin; Machiavelli's *Prince*, the pages edged in gold leaf; Clausewitz's *On War* in the original German; a signed, personalized copy of Hannah Arendt's *Eichmann in Jerusalem*. He found a first edition of *Altneuland* by Theodor Herzl, published in Leipzig, Germany, and then slim, elegant volumes of the poetry of Ibn Gabirol; the tales of Nachman of Bratslav; the works of Maimonides; the Harvard classics, all fifty-one volumes; Faulkner's novels; Tolstoy; Dostoevsky; Shakespeare; the Greek tragedies—all rare or first editions in English.

IT WAS HARD to imagine just weeks before his father died, a man had knocked on the door offering to purchase the Judge's entire estate: his books, papers, furniture, even his clothing. How did this vulture even know the Judge was dying and that his belongings might soon be available? He could have the furniture and clothing, but these books were the Judge's children after all, more important than Stone had ever been to his father. Stone at least owed him the respect of taking proper care of his books.

It was true, there were ghouls out there looking to make an easy buck, and Stone, under different circumstances, had no objection to making a sale, but the Judge wasn't really dying, was he? He'd be needing those books before long. He wasn't dying, he wasn't. The inexplicable appearance of this shady merchant of misery was enough for Stone to slam the door in the man's face, but he deftly slid his foot across the threshold and said, "I won't take but a moment of your time, Mr. Stone."

This was the first time anyone had ever called him Mr. Stone, and he realized that one day, like it or not, he would be the only Mr. Stone. He opened the door and the man, seeing the living room lined entirely with floor-to-ceiling bookshelves, smiled and said, "Quite a collection." He produced a wad of cash from his pocket. "I'll give you fifteen grand for everything. Including any personal papers or documents." He must have been in his early thirties; he was slim and wore a nondescript blue windbreaker and a Mets cap pulled low over his eyes so they were nothing but shadows. He had the makings of a beard on his angular face and did not offer his hand. There was something familiar about him—his greasy arrogance, his presumptuousness—but Stone could not place him. He'd lived too long in the heart of Connecticut and was afraid he'd begun to think that all Jews looked similar.

"Not for sale," Stone said.

There were no remaining documents, and the books meant everything to his father. When Stone had arrived in the spring and found the Judge's filing cabinets emptied out, he had asked the Judge what happened, and his father had told him there were no papers, there never were any papers, and to mind his own business. But Stone had found a receipt on the kitchen table from an information management company named Iron Mountain. One afternoon, overcome with curiosity, he had phoned the company only to learn his father's papers had all been securely shredded.

"Everything is for sale for the right price," the man insisted, peeling off some more crisp bills. "Think what you can buy with twenty thousand dollars." He slipped the money into Stone's hand and it felt like freedom.

Stone considered leaving Brooklyn behind forever, starting out anew on the far side of the world. There was nothing here for him, nothing at all.

"What makes you so sure he's dying?" Stone asked after a moment.

"Only Hashem knows for certain," the man said. "But I am making an offer now."

Stone heard his father stirring in his bed, clicking the morphine drip, and he suddenly felt the violent need for the man to be gone.

"You have to leave," Stone said, pressing the bills back onto the stranger. "Get out."

"I'm here to help you."

"He's not dying, he's not dying. He's not."

Stone managed to push the man into the hall, but he was certain he heard through the closed door the words, "I'll be back, Matthew."

Stone retreated to his father's room, furious at himself for even

considering the money. What kind of son could do such a thing? His
father was going to get better, he was going to survive this. But there
in his sickbed, his father looked like a stranger, a pale withered husk
of what he once was. His eyes were closed and Stone observed movement behind the lids, a sign of life. And then his eyes swung open, icy
blue and pitiless, and he said, "You are smart, but not so smart." After a
long pause in which he never removed his eyes from Stone, he added,
"Everything is in the books."

Stone knew for certain his father was calling him through these
books. The Judge was gone, but his eyes had tracked these pages, his
mind had been shaped by the words written before him. Somebody
was in the room with him, just over his shoulder, there but not there,
whispering the words in English as they appeared on the pages, overlaid at the same time with that other strange and ancient language.
He found a leather-bound copy of *One Thousand and One Nights*;
Churchill's *A History of the English-Speaking Peoples*; Rashi's commen-
taries; a colossal book on the origins of the Spanish Inquisition; religious texts; legal texts; two books on gematria; the complete works of
G. K. Chesterton; a silk-bound copy of *Othello*, with a tasseled bookmark that tickled Stone's wrist.

When he finally reached the box in which he had placed the photo
albums, Stone took a deep breath, expecting to be consumed by emotion. This was the life behind his own life, a blueprint to himself, which
would go a long way toward explaining his future and what he might
become. The albums were heavy and bursting with black-and-white
pictures of his father as a child on Ocean Parkway: young Walter and
poor Aunt Bunny playing on the front lawn, her broad mongoloid
face shining beneath a frilled bonnet; his father lacing up a brand-new
pair of PF Flyers, the corner of his tongue poking from his mouth in
concentration; his father, missing his two front teeth, mugging with
a baseball mitt in the stands at Ebbets Field. Stone's father was small
like he was, with a full head of hair and easy smile. He saw his father as
a shirtless, happy teen, hair cropped short in the military style, leaning
carefree on an oar beside some nameless lake. What an impossible
image, that this smiling teen was his father. Stone had rarely seen him

smile, and when he did there was a deep cruelty behind his calculating eyes as if he were taking pleasure in someone else's misfortune. And then, deeper into the album, something changed in his father: he'd grown into the six-foot-three clean-headed giant that he was, a full six inches taller than Stone had ever grown. What a drastic change he had undergone, from an ordinary midcentury American boy into something almost mythic. He no longer resembled his son in the least—he looked like a different man.

In another album Stone found pictures of himself as a child, at birthday parties, Passover seders, Thanksgiving dinners—all the usual events at which a camera ordinarily appeared to document the moment for posterity. There was nothing unusual about these pictures—he might have been any one of ten million American boys the same age—except nearly every photograph had been defaced. Where Stone's mother would have been, smiling as he opened his fifth birthday present or crying on his first day of school, there was nothing but a scratched-out spot as if somebody had taken a razor to the glossy sheen and rubbed it down to the raw photographic paper. Again and again his mother had been eliminated from each photograph, scratched out or excised with a pair of scissors, eliminated and thrown down Orwell's memory hole.

Stone had little sympathy for his mother, who had disappeared without a word when he was twelve years old. But he had hoped he would see in these photographs a family as yet unbroken, happy, ignorant of the future that lay ahead. He wrapped himself in the robe and took a deep draft of the fabric, but instead of his father's scent all he smelled now was the stink of his own marijuana.

A wrinkled manila envelope slipped out of the back of the album, scattering old scallop-edged black-and-white photos about the floor.

"Papa Julius," Stone said, snatching up a photo. The Judge had never referred to him by name, but Stone's mother had insisted her son call him Papa as a sign of respect—an early suggestion of the rift yet to come. The name had felt right on the tip of Stone's young tongue despite the fact that he had not met the man and was forbidden to speak his name aloud when his father was near.

He was surprised the Judge had kept pictures of Julius; he had not seen him, as far as Stone knew, since he had moved uptown to Columbia over forty years earlier. But there was Stone's grandfather, faded against the yellowing photographic paper, smiling, his foot on the running board of a black Oldsmobile. Another shot: under the sign for Ratner's Deli, the Williamsburg Bridge in the background, Julius laughing as he pulled a hat off Meyer Lansky's half-turned head.

"Meyer fucking Lansky!" Stone said, laughing. "Holy shit!" This was history, he thought, with a flash of pride. He had met his grandfather only once, just before he died, and had been trained by the Judge to act as if he had never existed. But if his grandfather had never existed, it would mean his father had never existed, which in turn would mean that he himself could never have come into being. But Stone was here, and he belonged to them; he'd inherited their genes, shared the same strands of DNA, climbed a similar whirling double helix like a magic ladder to his past and future at the same time.

There were dozens of photos of Julius Stone from his days with Murder Incorporated. Stone studied the photos. His grandfather did not look like a killer. He had intense eyes, sure, but there was a playful glimmer in them, as if he were about to tell a joke. He might have been a vaudeville comedian or a magician with those mischievous eyes. Stone was amazed how similar in build he was to his grandfather, the wild-haired killer, one hundred and twenty pounds of dynamite set with a short fuse.

Stone had to pee and stumbled his way to the bathroom. He caught a glimpse of his face in the mirror as he passed. His image swam in and out of focus as he looked into his own eyes, bloodshot and coated in a sickly film, and saw no sparkle, just pools of sorrow.

A strange thought occurred to Stone as he slipped out of his father's robe. He looked so much smaller now, pale and gaunt, his body like a plucked bird, like some depilated mammal waiting to be snatched in predatory jaws. But he knew he was not helpless; he stood on the shoulders of two powerful men whom one crossed at one's own peril. His fingers were slim and tapered—musician's fingers. He had let his father down giving up on piano as a boy even though he had shown some brilliant sparks of talent. His father had wanted him to be the next Vladimir Horowitz or Arthur Rubinstein, but he had no interest in playing just to please his father, so he quit and never played again. Now, he formed the delicate fingers of his right hand into the shape of a pistol and pointed them at his own image in the mirror. "Reach for the sky, or I'll fill you full of lead." Stone laughed for the first time in months, shouting, "Bang, bang, bang, bang, bang."

"What the fuck is going on back there?"

Pinky must have returned home while Stone was emptying the boxes. He fell silent, neither shamed nor embarrassed, just irritated he had been interrupted.

Pinky was at the bathroom door, smelling of cheap cologne, his gelled hair brushed forward on his head to form a severe widow's peak. "I'm telling you, it's not good for you to be alone right now. I'm buying you a drink."

"I'm not thirsty," Stone said.

"My house, my rules. You're going to drink with me."

IT WAS A cool September evening, with a soft breeze off the river. Stone's high was fading fast, his misery rolling back in like a black tide. Somehow he knew leaving the apartment, leaving the books and photographs behind, would lead to his premature destruction. He would be run down by an errant driver, shot by a stickup man, mugged by a neighborhood kid for the lint in his pockets. Nothing good could come of this. They walked in silence past the tangle of graffiti tags on the wall of Pinky's apartment building. Pinky's shadow bounced jauntily ahead of Stone's, his head blackening the paint-scrawled words YOU LIFE IS NOT SO GREAT. Three young black men hung out in front of the Tip-Top Deli and Grocery, crowding the pay phone, waiting for it to ring. They passed a vacant lot and then a small storefront Brotherhood Ministries church where one of the Reverend Randall Roebling Nation's preachers shouted from a basement pulpit, "Jesus gonna bring ya on home . . ."

Stone could still hear the parishioners clapping their hands and stamping their feet when he and Pinky reached the overpass of the Brooklyn-Queens Expressway two blocks away. A livery cab drove past honking its horn, a Puerto Rican flag waving from its antenna.

The whole world was full of static, chaos, random vibrations of noise filling the air to the point of rupturing the invisible seams of the universe. "I need to go home," Stone said, feeling dizzy. "Before something happens."

"Nothing is going to happen," Pinky said. "It's the weed got you paranoid. Nothing a couple drinks can't fix."

"No, listen," Stone said, "I need to go home. Now."

Pinky grabbed him roughly by the shoulders and said, "You don't have a home without me. Remember? A couple drinks, that's all."

Under the damp belly of the Brooklyn-Queens Expressway they walked with the flow of traffic along the length of a rusted chain-link fence. They turned left at Washington and stepped out from underneath the BQE onto a one-way street that dead-ended a few hundred feet away at the Navy Yard, sleepless Manhattan lit up beyond. This tiny stretch of urban decay looked like the last battlefield of the Industrial Revolution. Forklifts were parked in a crazy array on the sidewalks, some with their silver prongs still raised. Twisted metal lay hunched in piles against the old graffiti-covered warehouses. An oil drum burned on the corner. Despite the late hour, an ice cream truck played a mournful children's song somewhere in the distance.

For some reason, some presentiment itching at the back of his skull, Stone turned toward the overpass, where he saw, through the glow of the oil drum fire, three figures moving out from under the shadow of the expressway, dressed in black, their hats propped on their heads like smokestacks. He heard garbled mutters of Yiddish. Jesus Christ, he thought, remembering the man who had torn his suit at his father's funeral. He couldn't get away from them. Walking through the blighted streets of Pinky's neighborhood, it was easy to think this was another planet, of graffiti, dice games, institutionalized poverty, and urban decay, but it was still Brooklyn, and Stone realized the farther he got from Midwood, the closer he got to the ultra-Orthodox of Williamsburg.

"Well, this is it," Pinky said, gesturing like the emcee of some third-rate road show.

A small stairway lit by a single bare bulb led to the basement of a boarded-up redbrick building, remnants of smashed windows shining on the top floors. A stenciled sign on the door read, HIT SIGN. WIN SUIT. Music played from behind a battered steel door.

"How did you find this place?"

"I found it is how I found it," Pinky said. "After you."

The Catbird Seat was little more than a repurposed fallout shelter in the basement of an abandoned bottling plant, torched by arsonists in the seventies. The brick walls had been painted in vivid purple and gold and hung with garish abstract paintings bracketed by candelabra fashioned from parts of industrial machinery. They entered the low tin-ceilinged room, blue with cigarette smoke. A group of students, wan artist types, sat laughing around a long table beneath an antique billboard that read, ASTRAL OIL: "SAFE AND BEST." One of the students had thick sideburns shaped like the state of California. Another wore an army jacket with the word CRASS scrawled in black marker on the back. A girl with blonde pigtails and glitter on her cheeks laughed. The room was lit only by candlelight. Stone took a seat at a small table nearby and noticed in the flickering yellow light the drawn faces of the students. A GREAT INDUSTRIAL CITY, another vintage sign read, and Stone imagined they were the great industrial workers worn down by coal dust, asbestos, ashes, and gas.

"I'll get you a double from the well," Pinky said, lighting a cigarette.

This was not a good idea, Stone thought. These people looked like the walking dead themselves. Dry-mouthed, he wished only for a glass of water. Pinky lingered at the bar, leaning close to the red-haired bartender, whispering something that would have been drowned out by the music.

As he sat alone at the table, Stone's thoughts drifted back to his father, to the funeral, to the horrible sound of the dirt clots rattling against the coffin lid. It was past one in the morning, and the Judge would still be there in the ground, all night long and all the next day, and all winter long, and all year long, and there he would remain, or, at least, his remains would remain, until he was completely forgotten, mourned by no one. The thought was almost too much to bear, and Stone gasped for air. He wanted to go home, but Pinky was already making his way over to the table, a crooked smile on his face.

He slid a glass of clear liquid across the table and raised his own. "*L'chaim*. To life!" he said, and emptied the glass in a single gulp.

Stone did the same, but whatever rotgut Pinky had brought him rushed back up his throat. He swallowed it again, eyes watering, empty stomach burning. "What the hell is this?"

"Vodka, my man," Pinky said. "Not the top-shelf stuff, but it does the trick."

"I think I'm going to throw up," Stone said.

"You really are a pussy." Pinky laughed, but Stone didn't think there was anything funny in Pinky's words. "Put on your man pants and take it." When Stone managed to regain his composure, Pinky ruffled Stone's hair and said, "Straight up, no chaser. That's the way to do it, my friend." Pinky was no friend but Stone, hit hard by the double shot of vodka, felt maudlin, the urge to talk overwhelming his desire to leave Pinky and rush back to the relative comfort of his bare mattress.

"Have you ever imagined what happens to you when you die? Really thought deep on it?"

"Honestly?" Pinky said. "No." He fiddled with his thick gold chain, tucking and untucking it from his New York Jets shirt.

"I was there when he died," Stone said. "He was there, and then he was not. Something and then nothing. I was with him, and then I was alone. It is almost impossible to understand how one can be and then not be. Do you know what I mean? He was alive. He lived. And now . . ."

"I hear you, brother," Pinky said. "But seriously."

"Seriously what?" Stone said.

"I mean, I get it, like life is an illusion and we don't know if we're here or we're not here, like maybe we're all somebody's dream or the earth is just some cosmic giant's ball of snot flying through space and we're like ants or something just running around like it matters when it don't. We all die in the end. That is the capital-T truth."

By the light of the candle, Pinky's sallow, pasty-white complexion was even more repulsive than it was under the bright light of day. Stone wanted to pity him but he knew the unexamined life was a contented life, and for a moment he wished he could switch places with Pinky to know what it felt like to be a happy idiot preoccupied with only the basest concerns. He stared at Pinky in disgust for a long moment, but he needed to talk, just to hear the words out loud, to make them real, to find a proper place to put his emotions.

"You know he died—just like that. The Judge. His heartbeat was replaced by a rattle in his throat. You know the death rattle is real? And then the rattle stopped. He looked the same at first, except the eyes maybe, but he wasn't in there. And soon, I don't know how long, he was just gone. No life at all. Where does it go?" Stone said. "Where does it go?"

"I don't fucking know," Pinky said. "You want answers, go see a priest or professor. I'm here to show you a good time."

"I'm not much of a good-time guy right now," Stone said, regretting his attempt to open up to Pinky.

"You'll feel better. Just give it time," Pinky said, craning his neck around and pointing toward a skinny girl with red, bee-stung lips. "Check out fuck-mouth over there. Why don't you start with that?"

"I want another drink," Stone said. He didn't care what Pinky brought him; he just wanted to be alone again with his thoughts.

"Okay, but the next round is on you," Pinky said, rising from the table. "I'm just bustin' your balls. It's on me, buddy."

The dark, flickering room pulsed like a heartbeat, bodies pressed so closely together that Pinky was quickly lost to Stone's view. Every mouth burned like an orange star as cigarettes were drawn and then exhaled. A song by Nico, which Stone had listened to on repeat one weekend with his girlfriend as a freshman at Wesleyan, played from the darkness. It was an acoustic song, sad and beautiful, the simple strumming of the guitar, her voice breaking and dropping, that accent, low and full of disappointment, then rising with hope through the strings. Not ten feet away, a tall skinny girl in a green wool hat and dark sunglasses mouthed the words. Points of ginger hair poked out of the bottom of her hat against her pale cheeks. She was almost flat-chested, wearing loose black peasant pants and a ripped gray cardigan. Stone thought she looked like a boyish elf when she sucked her cheeks in to draw on her cigarette. The girl danced almost without moving, a molasses-slow gyration. Her eyes were closed behind her dark glasses, but she was singing to him.

It would be obscene, vulgar, to pursue a woman now, considering all the things his father would never do again.

"Mind if I join you?"

Stone had not noticed the man approach, and without thinking he told him he was welcome to sit. The bar was packed, after all, and it would have been rude to refuse him a seat. The man wore a suit that looked out of place in the Catbird Seat. He was ten or fifteen years older than Stone and of a trim, sturdy build—he must have been an athlete once. He wore a neat goatee and had an olive complexion with a dark circular birthmark high on his right cheek. His battered nose appeared to have been broken numerous times. His eyes were small and brown and intense. Stone turned away. But the girl was gone now.

"Looks like you blew your chance there." The man neither smiled nor frowned, his face inscrutable, blank. But there was something in the way he moved as he lit a cigarette off the candle, tilting his neck to one side as if he were working out a kink, which brought him into focus for Stone. The man had been at his father's funeral, on the grassy knoll, telephoto lens pressed to his face. He had been too far away for Stone to make out his features, but the way he kept stretching his neck was his signature.

"What were you doing at my father's funeral?"

"I'm sorry for your loss," the man said. "I truly am."

"You're a journalist?" Stone asked. He didn't look like the typical rumpled newspaperman. His suit was pressed and neat and his Windsor knot, even at this hour, was still tight and sharp, as if he had just slipped the narrow tie around his neck.

"Let me buy you a drink."

"I have nothing to say," Stone said. "And if you think a drink is all it takes to make me dish on my father, you are sadly mistaken."

"Suit yourself," the man said, sucking on his cigarette.

Stone scanned the bar for Pinky, wishing he would return with the drinks, but Pinky was nowhere to be seen. Stone thought about picking up and leaving rather than suffer the awkward silence of the stranger. But he was curious. Why had the photographer followed him here if he had just seen him at the cemetery? What could he possibly want?

The man was enjoying the uncomfortable silence as if he knew Stone would be the first to break. He blew some smoke into the air, winked at Stone, and took another long satisfied drag.

"All right," Stone said at last. "Are you going to tell me who you are?"

Wordlessly, the man placed a small rectangular business card on the table between them. In the top right corner it read: FEDERAL BUREAU OF INVESTIGATIONS. And then, centered in capital letters: LARRY ZOHAR— SPECIAL AGENT—JOINT TERRORISM TASK FORCE.

The vague uneasiness Stone had been feeling all night gathered in his chest and though he tried to harness his voice to respond, he could not. His premonition of doom had been correct. Stone felt a queasy swirling in his gut. Something big was about to happen, something he was not at all prepared to deal with.

"Now Matthew, let's be clear," Zohar said. "You are not in trouble. I just want to ask you a few questions."

Stone managed to say, "And what if I don't want to answer?"

Zohar laughed and said, "You have nothing in the world to worry about. I just want to ask you a few simple questions. This is not a big deal. Relax."

"I have nothing to say about my father."

"You seem quite certain I'm interested in your father and not you. You see, you've already told me something."

Stone rose from the table, but Zohar grabbed him by the wrist and he sat again. "Maybe you'll just listen then. Can't hurt to listen, right?"

Zohar sipped something through a clear straw, placed the glass on the table, and looked Stone in the eyes. "You understand history, you're well-read, educated, aware. You know the old cliché: those who forget history are doomed to repeat it. There is something to that.

You were born the day eleven Israeli athletes were murdered at the Olympic Village in Munich. That's right, I know your birthday is in six days. Quite a violent welcome to the world. Of course you don't remember, but you were told later, how your father spent the entire day watching Peter Jennings report on the massacre for ABC, and it wasn't until the next day, when all the hostages were dead, that he came to see you resting in the maternity ward nursery."

Stone was still, unmoving. The Judge had not even cared enough to visit his newborn child. Stone did not question how Zohar knew this, because it was consistent with the way his father had behaved his entire life. He tapped a cigarette out of his pack and lit it. His hands were shaking and the smoke failed to calm him.

"You didn't know he was too preoccupied to see you?" Zohar said. "I'm sorry."

Stone did all he could not to respond, channeling the strength and will of his father, but he could not restrain himself. "You're lying."

"So now we have a dialogue," Zohar said, smiling. "This is progress."

"I'm not saying another word."

"It would explain a lot, wouldn't it? Your father never had time for you. Not even from the beginning."

"It's not true."

"Who can deny it?"

"This is harassment. I've done nothing wrong. Can't you see I'm in mourning?" Stone's breath grew shallow again, barely pulling the smoke-filled air into his lungs.

"Let me tell you a story," Zohar said. "To put things in context, so you know where you stand."

"I don't need to hear a story from you."

"Oh, really?" Zohar said. "Did you know your grandfather and Meyer Lansky contributed large sums of money to the Revisionist movement, money which was funneled directly to the paramilitary organization the Irgun, money which paid for the bombing of the King David Hotel?"

"So what? That was a million years ago, if it actually happened. Why are you telling me about my grandfather? I only met the man once. Whatever he did or didn't do in his twisted life has nothing to do with me."

"Because this relates to your father," Zohar said. "You know the saying: like father like son."

"Don't be absurd," Stone responded. "My father upheld the law, fought against organized crime. He was a lawyer and a judge. He hated Julius."

"Just like you hate your father?"

"I'm not talking about him," Stone said, his stomach awhirl.

"Your father was also a proud Zionist, a member of the Betar youth group, co-founder and chairman of the Eretz Fund. He served as an advisor to the Israeli Supreme Court, helping to extradite and prosecute suspected Nazi war criminals, most notably John Demjanjuk, thought to be the infamous Ivan the Terrible at the Treblinka death camp. Demjanjuk was extradited to Israel in 1986 and sentenced to death. The sentence was later overturned as the Israeli Supreme Court rescinded its earlier judgment and returned Demjanjuk to the United States, citing misconduct on the part of overzealous prosecutors."

"I see where this is going," Stone said, overcome with rage at this callous intrusion into his most private grief. "And I've heard more than enough. Can't you at least show some humanity and let me mourn in peace?"

Stone pushed back his chair from the table and stood up. Run, run, he thought. But his legs had gone numb and he waded into the swelling crowd of hipsters. Stone brushed past the skinny girl who had been singing to him, and she said, "Don't look so sad, darling. Life is crazy for everyone."

Zohar followed him, hot breath at his ear. "During the infamous Court Street Riot trial, your father's impartiality was impugned again when he allowed a member of the jury who was sympathetic to the killer Isaac Brilliant to stay on after the Judge became aware of the juror's own anti-Arab sympathies. There is no doubt Brilliant killed the sixty-three-year-old Palestinian-born shopkeeper Nasser Al-Bassam. There is even video of him bashing the man's head in with a brick. Yet Brilliant went free."

He was going to lose his mind, Stone thought, wrenching his arm from Zohar's grip and making for the exit.

"Your father was always trying to destroy those he considered his enemies. He was a punitive, spiteful man with a biblical hunger for revenge. Let me tell you, he was no better than Julius Stone."

"That's enough," Stone said, bursting out the door and into the street, his voice wracked with broken sobs. He was prepared never to speak a word aloud again.

"Tell me one thing," Zohar persisted. "That warehouse across the street. Are you familiar with the Crown of Solomon Talmudical Academy? Weren't you on your way there tonight? Don't lie to me, Matthew."

"I have no idea what you are talking about."

"It may be a legitimate Torah school, but I know the organization your father ran funds one hundred percent of its operation."

"I can't help you," Stone said, his mind blank with panic.

"Matthew, I have reason to believe the school is a front for a terrorist cell connected to your father's former colleague Rabbi Zalman Seligman. People's lives may be at stake," Zohar said, grabbing Stone by the shirt, his sour breath turning Stone's stomach. "I need to know what is going on inside there."

"This interrogation is over." Stone tore himself from Zohar's grip and sprinted up the street at a dead run.

3 Stone crossed under the BQE without checking for traffic, Zohar's footsteps fast at his heels, pursuing him. This was his executioner, Stone thought. He would be the end of Stone, but Stone would never speak a word. He stumbled on a curb, righted himself, and continued to run, never looking back. All his organs and muscles and bones worked in tandem now, his nerves vibrating with the pure, uncut rush of adrenaline. The invincible fear was back with greater force than it had been in years. But, Stone thought, if he could just outrun Zohar, just shake him now, he would never again be haunted by anything.

The keys to his father's red 1980 Thunderbird jangled in his pocket, and he knew what he had to do as he crossed silent Myrtle Avenue with its fried-chicken joints, check-cashing windows, and grim bodegas. He needed to drive, to drive, to drive, to get away, to put everything behind him, to drive and drive and drive and leave his past and everything he ever knew behind. This was not death, this was life, and he was rushing toward it in a breathless sprint. With a furious leap, he reached his father's car, found the lock, tore the door open, and slid inside. Stone started the ignition and floored the gas, cutting across the sidewalk, nearly knocking over a battered mailbox. Yes, he thought, yes, breathing in his father's smell on the soft upholstery, so magnetic, so powerful, so redolent with life he was overcome. As he turned right onto Washington Street, green ailanthus and syca-more trees flickering past, he saw in the rearview mirror the face of his father, his unforgiving eyes flashing through his half-moon glasses. He knew he was speeding. His father had never had a ticket in his entire life, and he was showing his displeasure now, but Stone could outrun anyone, didn't his father know that?

On his right, he passed the abandoned Graham Home for Old Ladies, its windows shuttered like coins on the eyes of the dead, and the skeletal jungle gym in the empty playground. Stone pressed his foot on the gas, passed under the giant cruciform shadow bleeding from the roof of Christ: Light of the World Church, and raced through a red light at Lafayette.

His father was stuck in the mirror, and Stone needed to get him to stop hiding in the glass, certain he was going to step out and devour him whole. "Forgive me, forgive me," Stone shouted.

The red neon hands of the clock atop the golden-domed Williamsburg Savings Bank tower read some hour that looked like a crooked V for victory, and he raced on, singing the Columbia fight song his father had taught him with his first words. He sang as he drove, crossing from neighborhood to neighborhood, lights off now, a knife cutting through the darkness. He had shaken Zohar but the Judge remained in the mirror, fragmented into a mosaic of expressions—joy, sadness, disappointment, fear, all mixed as one. He continued to sing "Roar, Lion, Roar!"—the fight song of his father's alma mater, a school Stone had refused to attend just because. *Davka*, as his father would have said. And Stone sang and he sang and he sang but his father would not join him and would not go away until, finally, Stone wrenched the rearview mirror off the windshield and tossed it out the window.

Stone's adrenaline had flamed out. No sense of victory buoyed him, just deep exhaustion. All he wanted to do was sleep, but he was lost. He drove in a fog of confusion until he could not drive anymore and he shut the car down, sprawled out across the front seats, and fell into a restless sleep.

■ ■ ■

WHEN HIS FATHER was selected to preside over the Court Street
Riot trial, during Matthew's junior year of high school, Matthew was
unimpressed; his father's accomplishments had long ceased to mean
anything to him, serving only to draw the Judge farther away. He
became even more silent and introspective, rarely uttering a word.
He locked himself in his study for hours at a time and slept at his
desk. Matthew thought his father was selfish, self-absorbed, and dull,
his ceaseless immersion in legal texts and documents antithetical to
life. As the trial came closer and protests became louder, calling for
the Judge's ouster, Matthew hid from reporters and sometimes stayed
out all night with one of the girls impressed by his newfound celebrity. One girl asked Matthew whether the Judge would go easy on
a landsman. Seeing his father on the nightly news, Matthew realized the Judge did not belong to him but to the state, the public, the
media—he was his father in name only. It was ridiculous to think this
man, larger than life and vibrant on television, was the same silent,
moody pile of nerves who holed up in his study as if it were a defen-
sive bunker. But, sometimes, Matthew missed his brooding presence
at home, and he went to the Kings County Supreme Court building
in downtown Brooklyn. The Honorable Walter J. Stone sat at the
front of the courtroom beneath the engraved words: LET JUSTICE BE
DONE THOUGH THE HEAVENS FALL, his half-moon glasses pushed down
on his nose. He spoke with a firm tone, questioning both lawyers
at length. This was the man Matthew knew, the man who had been
absent around the house for so many months. He spoke with force
and confidence and authority. Sitting there in the courtroom, Matthew arrived at the absurd realization that the Judge was father to all
those people present—no wonder he had no time or tenderness for
his son.

The defendant, Isaac Brilliant, was slim and wiry in his black suit,
slouched in a chair beside his lawyer. Matthew did not remember
the jury or the makeup of the spectators, but he did remember the
exhausted *New York Times* reporter slumped next to him, doodling in
his notebook, again and again, around the words that would constitute
his lead paragraph in the next day's paper. Quoting Oliver Wendell

Holmes, the words read, "The world's great men have not commonly been great scholars, nor its great scholars great men."

Not long after, when the selection of jurors exploded into a full-scale controversy and the word *jurymandering* entered the New York lexicon, Matthew believed his father had gotten what he deserved for his cold arrogance in overriding the prosecution's challenge to the defense's jury choice. It was the first time in his life Matthew had seen his father wounded, battered by a world he strode through like a giant, brushing aside problems with ease. The Judge was questioned many times by the district attorney's office, walking the humiliating media gauntlet, passing signs reading BLOOD IS ON YOUR HANDS and BASSAM DIDN'T ASK TO DIE as the clutch of TV cameras pressed in on him. The Judge was composed and stoic as he walked, but Matthew realized he had lost control of his personal narrative, his carefully constructed mystique smashed to pieces, when he heard the young television reporters begin each day's coverage with, ". . . son of notorious gangster Julius Stone . . ." It was then that Matthew finally allowed himself to feel sympathy for his father. Papa Julius had laid this minefield long ago, and only now was the Judge forced to confront it.

A man and a woman from the district attorney's office rang the Stones' doorbell one night after dinner. They both showed their DA badges and asked Matthew to answer some simple questions. They related to the Judge's character and were general questions he finessed with ease—he said nothing of substance. The thin, crane-like woman asked point-blank, "Did your father, Walter Stone, knowingly approve, as a member of the jury at the trial of *Brilliant v. State of New York*, a man he knew would not be able to fairly render a decision considering the facts presented to him?"

"I don't know," Matthew said.

"Is that your answer?" the woman asked.

"I don't know," Matthew said.

"Can you repeat that, please?" the man said, taking notes. "Did your father, Judge Walter Stone, knowingly approve—"

"I don't know."

"Thank you," the woman said.

The Judge walked in the front door as the pair from the DA's office was leaving.

"What are you doing in my home?" the Judge said to the man, who was fiddling with his briefcase.

"Just asking a few questions. We're leaving now, Judge Stone."

He stepped up close to the man and said, "Get out of my house." Then, turning to the woman, he added, "This is my private home. If you want to speak with me, you know where to find me, but leave my family out of this." He spoke in a measured tone, belying the irritation he must have felt. "Now," he said. "Good-bye."

When they were gone, Matthew sat frightened at the foot of the stairs. His innards steeled themselves, hardened with fear. The Judge lit a cigarette and held the smoke a long time before expelling it into the air. "What did they ask you?" he said, turning to face Matthew.

Matthew told his father everything he remembered, and as he did so he watched the Judge's face to make sure he did not slip up.

"Is that all?" the Judge said, a long gray ash hanging at the end of his cigarette.

"They asked if you knowingly approved a juror who would not be able to render a fair decision."

"What did you tell them?"

"I said, 'I don't know.'"

The ash fell to the floor.

"'I don't know'?" the Judge said, his voice rising. "When the district attorney's office asked you if your father knowingly approved a juror who was dishonest and corrupt, your only answer was 'I don't know'? What is the matter with you, Matthew? Don't you have a brain in your head?"

"Dad, you don't understand."

"Matthew," the Judge said, cutting him short. "I don't think you understand how serious this is. You're graduating from high school soon—you're going to be a man. You have to know these things."

After a moment, Matthew said, "I made a bad choice."

"Blood is not a choice, Matthew, yet somehow, somehow you managed to circumvent thousands of years of genetics, biology, and history in one fell swoop." Turning away and speaking as if to a private audience, he said, "He's a modern miracle, a revolutionary wunderkind. He's stormed the Bastille and brought down the ancien régime."

"I made a mistake," Matthew pleaded.

"Matthew, have you ever read a play called *Othello* by a man named William Shakespeare who had the answer to everything? I suggest you read it. Particularly act 2, scene 3, lines 281 to 284."

"I made a mistake," Matthew sobbed.

"No mistakes," the Judge said, walking toward the open door of his study. "There can be no mistakes."

MORNING ARRIVED LIKE a hammer to Stone's head, and he was wide awake, animated with pain through every quarter of his body, little more than a flaming nerve, as if he had no skin at all. He had slept the entire night sprawled across the front seats of the Thunderbird. His clothing was sodden with sour sweat. The new day promised worse than the day before. His logical mind said he had not seen his father, he had been overtired and his imagination had played tricks with him, his unconscious desires and fears manifesting themselves as vivid hallucinations.

It was then he realized where he was. He had, as if guided by an invisible hand, returned home to his father's apartment, parking in the street right out front. The Judge's bedroom window was lit up, and Stone was seized by terror, his throat clenching in a stifled scream, until he remembered Pinky had refused to turn off the light when they had left, saying it didn't fucking matter since nobody was paying for it anymore.

The Judge had worked so diligently to drill into Stone the ideals his hero Jabotinsky had preached: the concept of *hadar*—beauty, respect, self-esteem, politeness, faithfulness. Stone displayed none of these qualities. He had willfully made himself ugly in the eyes of the Judge. He had spent his life ignoring the wisdom of his father, chasing after disastrous sexual entanglements, clutching the sinking lifeboat of hopeless relationships and cheap marijuana highs. He believed in nothing. He was nothing. Slumped in the front seat of his father's Thunderbird like a homeless thing, he realized he was in danger of becoming less than nothing, an absolute unexalted negative clinging to this world simply through the vagaries of biology and a deep-seated stubbornness. But there he was in front of his father's apartment, and he knew he had arrived there for a reason. Stone had been so distressed about the state of the trashed apartment that all he had wanted was to gather up his father's precious books and keepsakes and leave as quickly as possible. But this was not a random breaking-and-entering. Simple vandalism was not the goal. Nor did the man in the Mets cap have anything to do with this. He had money. He was no second-story man. The fact was, he had wanted the books and yet the books remained. The answer was so clear now—the break-in was about his father's meds. The Trinidadian hospice nurse, Mavis, who had been coming twice a day for months to check the Judge's vitals and to ensure his morphine drip dosage was correct, had begun pressuring the Judge to move to a palliative care clinic to receive round-the-clock attention. "Judge Stone, your quality of life will be greatly improved with a team of specialists working to make you comfortable. It will be the best for you."

If Stone knew one thing, he knew the Judge wanted to live on his own terms, surrounded by his books; he would never submit to any form of institutional care. The Judge, furious his reading had been interrupted by her repeated requests, beckoned Mavis over to his bedside and said, "I won't have some community-college-educated mammy tell me what is best for me."

"But Judge Stone, you are not well," she said.

"And you are not welcome."

She left immediately, never to return. But in her haste, she had left behind the lockbox in which the Judge's medications were stored, his IV dilutions, his pills—benzodiazepines, fentanyl, morphine.

Stone still had the apartment key in his pocket and he opened the front door, afraid not of what he would find but of what he wouldn't find. Mavis had hugged Stone good-bye and wished him the best, but he was certain now that her friends from East Flatbush, eager to even the score and make a nice profit, were the ones who had broken into the apartment. The place smelled of stale sickness and sounded hollowed out, echoey without the walls of books to absorb the noise. All the mirrors had been smashed, and Stone picked up a fragment, saw the state of his face, wrecked by grief and exhaustion, and dropped the shard to the ground. He was afraid to go into his father's bedroom, and had asked Pinky to gather anything worth saving so he wouldn't have to enter the place where his father had breathed his last breath, but now he had no choice if he wanted to find the lockbox of medication.

A deep sense of unease penetrated him, and he froze at the doorway as if some psychic force were preventing him from entering his father's room. But the pain throbbing behind his eyes, his nerves electrified with hurt, was so oppressive he forced himself to enter—one foot first, then the other—and he was in. The ceiling light glared against the bright morning sun sifting in through the windows, and he flicked the light switch off.

Stone recalled the times he had seen his father drift away as the morphine entered his system. For the longest time, the ever-stubborn Judge had been loath to take anything that would affect his mind, keep him from his reading, but during the last weeks he could no longer sleep without the morphine drip. He had seen his father's face soften, his eyes rolled back in his head, and Stone had seen something like joy. Now he wanted to go to that place, to float away on a river of light where pain was nothing but a rumor.

The lockbox had been smashed open and tipped on its side, but Stone was surprised to find none of the medication was missing. The intravenous bags of morphine sulfate had all been cut open, their contents puddled on the floor, but the prescription bottle was not damaged at all and it was still half full with orange 60 mg tablets. The pills called to him with an irresistible force. He saw his father's name on the Duane Reade bottle and a sticker that read: "Side effects may include . . ." Fuck it, Stone thought.

He dropped a pill into his hand and, heart stammering in his chest, crushed the pill beneath his heel. Stone dropped to his knees, pinched a nostril, and snorted the powder off his father's parquet floor.

Oh, the torment is over, Stone thought, a glowing warmth radiating through his whole being—massage on an atomic level. The pain dripped off him like the wax of a guttering candle, a most profound dissolution of self. Freed of his body, he was weightless, sleepy, and he floated to his father's bed. Stone did not hesitate to lie down where his father had died; his mind was calm, soft as putty. The ceiling was melting in beautiful transparent crystal stalactites, and Stone contemplated them, trying to understand their meaning. The edge had disappeared from everything; even the itching on his elbow and abdomen was magnificent, orgasmic, because he could finally scratch the itch he had had for years, an itch he hadn't even known was bothering him. He fell deeper and deeper into the bed, his senses emptying out, and as his eyes slipped closed, something or someone lay on top of him, holding him in a weightless, tight embrace as it pressed its mouth against Stone's lips and sucked the breath out of him.

When Stone awoke, his left cheek and shoulder were sticky with fresh vomit. Nauseated and full of fever, Stone shivered. He realized he was lying in his father's bed, the spot where he had died, and he dry-heaved over the side. He had to get out of there, but his limbs were numb and heavy. It hurt to breathe, his lungs packed with fluid, a terrible thick phlegm in his throat. What an atrocious awakening, to find himself alone in his father's deathbed. He still clutched the pill bottle in his hand and debated whether to snort some more to take away the horrible hangover, but he was too weak to open the child-proof bottle.

The sheets smelled sour and Stone itched all over and he just wanted to leave this place and never return. His father's cancer was metastasizing within his own body now, and he knew if he didn't climb out of the bed in three, two, one, he would die there. He was overwhelmed with fatigue, but he managed to find his feet, the room whirling around him. Stone made his way to the bathroom faucet, stuck his mouth under, and drank until his whole body was cold.

He climbed into the Thunderbird, rolled down the windows, and slowly, slowly made his way back to Pinky's.

Pinky was standing outside his apartment on the sidewalk, smoking and talking shit with the homeboys from the Walt Whitman Houses, who were in their usual places, playing cee-lo on the sidewalk, sweaty piles of dollar bills clutched in their hands.

"What the fuck happened to you last night?" Pinky said, trotting over to Stone, who was having trouble parallel parking the car. "You just up and disappeared."

Stone wanted to go inside and lie down and die a little, ease the oppression of his headache, but Pinky reached through the window, popped the lock, and climbed inside. Stone asked him what he was doing.

"I need your wheels."

"I am really, really sick," Stone said.

"Don't come crying to me, pal. That's what you get when you drink too much." He chucked Stone on the shoulder. "At least you got laid last night, right?"

Now, in the bright light of afternoon, a piercing headache thumping in his skull—the ultimate reality check—Stone wasn't even certain Zohar had followed him out of the bar last night.

"Where the fuck were you?" Pinky said. "You smell like shit."

"It's a long story," Stone said.

"Well, I don't have time for a long story, and I've got stuff to do." Pinky hung his head out the window and spat. "You know, you'll never get into this spot. Not in a boat like this."

"Where am I supposed to park?"

"Slide over, let me drive."

"This is my father's car," Stone said.

"You are fucked up. You're in no condition to drive anyway. Just take a look at you." Pinky saw the rearview mirror was gone and shook his head in disgust. "Slide over, shitbird."

They switched places and Stone noticed with a creeping sense of disquiet that the hood of his father's car was broadly dented, as if a large sack of potatoes had been dropped onto it. He was certain the exterior body of the Thunderbird had been absolutely pristine for the entirety of his father's ownership. As far back as Stone could remember, the Judge had taken great pains to keep his car in immaculate condition.

First the mirror and now this, Stone thought, a tidal wave of nausea gathering strength in his belly. His head pounded.

"Look at that," Stone said.

"What?" Pinky said.

"The goddamn dent," Stone said. "On the hood."

"Where?" Pinky said. "I don't see no dent."

It bothered Stone more than it should have. The car was nearly twenty years old; it was bound to take its lumps driving the potholed streets of Brooklyn, but his father had managed to avoid any such damage. Stone could not imagine how it even got there.

"It's right there," Stone insisted.

"I don't see it," Pinky said. "Just chill the fuck out."

"You must be blind, if you can't see it," Stone said, noting the contours of the impression, shaped, he thought, like one of the Great Lakes or an amoeba. "Forget it. Nobody's driving, then. Let's go inside. My head's killing and I'm going to puke."

Pinky slammed his hands onto the steering wheel. "I'm driving and that's it. There's nothing there." He jumped out of the car and slammed the door, the sound cannonading through Stone's head like a nuclear blast. "Look," Pinky said, running his palm over the glossy sheen of the Thunderbird's hood. "Nothing. Nada. No fucking dent."

Pinky climbed back in the car and pulled a baggie of weed out of his pants pocket. He packed a bowl and handed it to Stone. "Listen," Pinky said. "You need to fucking chill. This will make you feel better. I guarantee it."

Stone put the pipe to his lips thinking, it's there, it's still there.

Pinky screeched onto Myrtle Avenue and floored the gas. They passed Fort Greene Park and the dreary brick towers of the Whitman Houses, stopping short for red lights. They turned left at Flatbush Avenue and Pinky gunned the engine through downtown Brooklyn. Stone slumped in the passenger seat, tried to spark the lighter, and failed. "Do I have to do everything?" Pinky said, lighting the bowl for Stone.

Stone drew in the smoke and held it, feeling afraid. What if this headache was a tumor? What if it got worse and worse, until his head split open from the pain? Where was the bottle? He wanted to pop one of those pills, to get back to the warm floaty place he had been. The insides of his eyelids itched, one of his kidneys itched, and some place in the center of his brain itched, but he couldn't find a way to scratch them. He must have nodded off because when he next looked out the window they were driving along streets Stone had never seen before, and he had no idea how they had arrived there. Skinny, stunted trees stood naked before brownstones crumbling from age and neglect. A clutch of old Puerto Rican men sat on milk crates, flipping cards onto the sidewalk.

Pinky pulled the car over on a crooked one-way street where cars sat double-parked and a hydrant leaked water into the trash-littered gutter. "Back in a minute." Pinky slammed the Thunderbird's monstrous door. He crossed the tilted slate sidewalk and walked up the steps of a brownstone stripped of its facade. The walls were gray and rutted, with rusted ribs of iron showing through. He disappeared through a battered green door.

The dent was still there on the hood, the car as lurid as his impoverished surroundings. Stone fought the urge to close his eyes in the hopes it would just disappear. But out of the corner of his vision, he caught a group of pigeons rising from the roof of a building across the street. They formed a pattern against the sky, undecipherable, shifting and turning and finally breaking up into smaller groups and landing on an adjacent rooftop. It was fascinating how they moved, together and then apart, as if some sort of higher magnetism controlled their movements. How wonderful it would feel to be part of something like a flock of pigeons, to move with such grace and ease, to just know the correct thing to do.

Pinky returned to the car and they stopped at several more places, each stop more bleak and depressing than the last. Stone slipped deeper and deeper into himself. He imagined the pigeons were following, and each time the Thunderbird came to a stop, he tried to count and catalogue them, his mind doing anything to avoid the indentation on the hood. The birds all looked alike to Stone, but he was sure they were always the same ones. Were they following him, or was he following them?

Pinky drove with one hand on the steering wheel and the other, a tightly curled fist, holding a cigarette, which he smoked with intensity and portent, his brow furrowed in deep concentration as he inhaled the blue-gray smoke. They passed one of R. R. Nation's storefront Brotherhood Ministries, a sign emblazoned with the words, TRUST NATION. HE WILL LEAD YOU!

A long black car that looked as if it had just rolled off the lot pulled up at the curb in front of the Brotherhood Ministry and two smartly dressed black men stepped out—they were tall and broad-shouldered, sturdy like former college football players. Stone told Pinky to slow down, and Pinky pulled over to the side of the road and asked Stone if he was going to throw up. From a distance, the two men looked to be moving in slow motion, as if grooving to their own private sound tracks. One of the men opened the passenger door and out stepped the Reverend Randall Roebling Nation, immaculate in a blue pin-stripe suit, his hair gleaming in the afternoon light. Stone regarded Nation, watched him walk with the arrogance of a complete fraud who has managed to fool the world.

"Jesusfuckingchrist. Stop scratching yourself," Pinky said. "You okay?"

"He's alive," Stone said. He hadn't even been aware he was scratching at itches all over his torso and arms. "And my father is not."

"Let's get out of here. We've got one more stop."

This was just too much for Stone to handle, and he told Pinky he wanted to go home now, right now. Something was haunting him, everything was haunting him, and he just wanted to drift away into a dreamless sleep and wake up free of his past.

"You know, I think my father would still be alive today if it weren't for Nation."

"Fuck Nation," Pinky said, starting up the Thunderbird. "Let's get out of here."

"Take me back now," Stone said.

"We've got one more stop, and I'll take you back."

A few minutes later, Pinky parked the car on a side street. Stone sank down in the seat and closed his eyes, hoping sleep would take him.

"Come on," Pinky said. "You're coming with me."

"I'll wait here."

"No, you won't."

They walked a few blocks in silence, Stone feeling winded, emptied out. He had no idea where they were, but the simple act of walking shook him somewhat from his lethargy. A breeze blew past, a hint of ocean salt in the air.

"Where are we going?" he asked.

"Here," Pinky said.

They stood before an old Art Deco movie marquee, its chrome oxidized and stripping in places, a three-story tower rising from the top. The burned-out remnants of the word PALATIAL were faintly visible. At one time it had been arranged vertically in neon bulbs, but the bulbs had all been smashed. The title of a long forgotten movie from the late seventies clung beneath the words ELC ME TO T E ALAT AL.

Layer upon layer of movie posters covered over with handbills, advertisements, and announcements had been peeled away from the wall at a corner, revealing burnished chrome beneath the phonebook-thick agglomeration of glue and paper. The windows had long been smashed and the booth behind the bronze cage was filled with assorted detritus, including a haphazard pile of plush velvet chairs, their torn seats the result of age and vandalism. The door, by contrast, was new and was the type one might find on a suburban home, with its raised moldings, mail slot, and knocker. Pinky knocked twice on the door, and it opened after a moment.

He shook hands with an unshaven man who must have weighed three hundred and fifty pounds; his close-cropped skull was shaped like a warhead and his tiny eyes looked cruel. What was Stone doing here? This creature was absurd. What was this beast supposed to be, an idiot, a prophet, a warning? His eyes were so small, like pencil dots on a blank sheet of paper, and Stone stared into them, trying to decipher what, if anything, was behind them.

"He's here to play?" the man asked Pinky, with a lumbering Russian accent.

"No. He's with me."

The lobby was stripped and bare, and a clutch of middle-aged women in gaudy housedresses pressed forward toward the candy counter. A sign read: OASIS BINGO—CARDS, DAUBERS, CHIPS, WAITERS, CUSHIONS, ETC. alongside a list of prices. The whole scene before Stone's eyes was grotesque, and he had the urge to run, if only his body would agree.

"What is this?" Stone said.

"I'm here to make sure no one cheats."

"And why am I here?"

"You're here because you're here," Pinky said, allowing no room for response. He threw an arm around Stone's shoulder as they passed through a curtain into an auditorium. An oppressive wall of cigarette smoke burned Stone's eyes.

"B-12," a gruff voice said into a microphone, echoing through the hall. "B-12 vitamins. Take 'em every day." A false ceiling hung dangerously low; banks of fluorescent tubes lit the room with a greenish glow. Stone was shocked to see that the original seats had been plucked from the sloping floor of this vast theater, and folding card table after card table had been set up to accommodate what must have been at least four hundred people.

"N-41," the caller said. "Forty-one. A year that will live in infamy." He coughed rudely into the microphone.

Dozens of heads bobbed up and down, in sync. They sat waiting for the caller to pull another number, their necks bent like supplicants, heads dropped like Christians at prayer.

"I-30," the voice on the stage called. "That's a thirty."

Stone followed Pinky as he wound through the rows of tables. He walked with more of a swagger than usual. The players were mostly women, white and Hispanic and something else. They looked like grown-up parochial school dropouts. Many of the women were old enough to be grandmothers, and some wore nets in their hair, cheap dye jobs burning against the greenish light. In the taut silence of the room between calls, Stone realized these people had prematurely gone to their graves; a walking death that was more impulse than desire, their lives flaming out beneath the low fluorescent sky.

"N-43."

THE BOOK OF STONE

Stone caught up with Pinky. "What's going on?"

"Just stand right there for a minute," Pinky said, throwing his arm around him again, flashing what he thought was a charming smile. "Don't move. Just stand there."

"I don't feel so good," Stone said. The ceiling pressed down on him, his senses overwhelmed by the humming babble of voices. "What is this?" His mouth was so dry the words barely came out.

"I am their worst nightmare." Stone smelled a strong musky odor emanating from Pinky's body. "Half the players are addicted to the fuckin' game—welfare cases, unemployed, and losers—it's gambling for the lower classes. A quick fix."

"O-61. Maris, sixty-one in sixty-one," the caller said.

"Like going to the racetrack," Pinky continued. "Except there's no bookies and no ponies. But it's serious shit. They cheat, they're out." Pinky shot a sharp glance at a woman who sat before a half-dozen cards, a plastic troll at the head of her table. "On average, I would say they drop over fifty bucks a pop in here."

The entire scene was incomprehensible to Stone, and he managed to say, "That still doesn't explain why I'm here."

"O-75," the caller said.

"Bingo! Oh my God. Bingo." A woman moved with a speed and dexterity that belied her bulky form. A collective groan rose from the room as the woman rushed to the front to verify her card. A woman in a HEAVENLY MOTHER OF GOD T-shirt ripped up her cards, threw the pieces in the air, and muttered, "Shit on a stick." A woman wept quietly before a spread of cards. A man in a heavy ski jacket and hat called out "I ga a goo one."

There was some invisible creature under Stone's skin, tormenting him, and he wanted to peel his skin back and find that little bastard. Terminate, with extreme prejudice. His heart beat deep within his body, a slow, distant banging of a drum.

"All right, all right," the caller said. "Let's play blackout bingo. Winner gets the big payout. Mark your cards. Be careful now."

The crowd buzzed in anticipation, raucous chatter bouncing off the chrome and ebony walls.

"Okay, boys and girls. Eyes down."

There was instant silence.

The next game began with an increased intensity. Muttered prayers and curses floated through the air, a collective desperation voiced by the bingo players. Pinky moved with martial precision among the tables, his pale body stretched out like a piece of gum pulled from a child's mouth.

"G-33. Thirty-three rpm."

A woman with crossed fingers scanned the array of cards before her and slammed her hand onto the table.

"B-5. Still alive."

The room spun like a carousel, a phantasmagoria of grotesque faces melting in and out of focus, slowly at first, then faster as the caller barked out letter-number combinations with a mystical inscrutability as if the correct combination would solve some eternal riddle. Rows of lights glittered above the tables, so pretty, like precious gems, and Stone wanted to go to them, hold them in his hands, press his lips to them, but could not, suspended as he was in a sticky, weblike darkness.

HE LAY ON the cool floor of the bingo hall. Pinky's face came back into focus, as if through a rippling sheet of water. Stone's head pounded in a new way. He must have passed out and hit his useless skull on the floor. The caller matter-of-factly said, "B-8. Don't be late."

"What the fuck," Pinky said. "You okay?" He signaled to somebody behind him in the far distance—an ambulance? A hearse?

A small crowd had gathered around Stone. A woman leaned in and asked if he wanted a glass of water. This would be a perfect time for somebody to shout, "Is there a doctor in the house?" But a doctor was not likely to be among this crowd.

"I'm dying," Stone said.

"Get the fuck out of here," Pinky said, pulling Stone to his feet. His legs were rubber bands, his tongue swollen like a dried-out sponge. As his eyes came back into focus he saw the overhang of a balcony beyond Pinky's profile, pushing closer like the prow of a great ship. In the darkness, he thought he saw the outline of figures moving about behind the brass railing. He saw a glimmer of light, as if someone's glasses had caught a snatch of light in their lenses.

"I'm taking you home," Pinky said.

"I-17. Sexy and seventeen," the caller said, and the bingo game continued.

4 Though Stone had told him he was fine and didn't need to see a doctor, Pinky dropped him off at the walk-in clinic on Atlantic Avenue. He said he had things to do and would pick Stone up in a couple of hours. Stone sat in embarrassed silence in the passenger seat of his father's car the entire drive over, hoping Pinky would just take him back to his room and another round of the glorious morphine. But Pinky would have none of it.

The waiting room was crowded. Stone was prepared to leave when a seat opened up in the corner, its stained cushion welcoming his exhausted body. Stone sat and quickly drifted off into a fitful sleep. Sometime later, a dreadlocked nurse in pink scrubs woke Stone with a clammy hand on his cheek and asked him to join her in the examination room.

She left him alone in the bare room and told him to undress and slip into a disposable gown. He waited nearly fifteen minutes until the nurse returned and took Stone's pulse, blood pressure, and temperature. He felt as if he were being processed rather than being treated. She pressed the cool disc of a stethoscope to his chest and back and asked Stone a few rote questions, ending with: Are you a smoker? She wasn't even looking at him when she asked the questions, not the slightest show of investment in his answers. Stone had only this one life; the least the nurse could do was pretend to care, he thought. Wearing just a thin paper gown, he knew he must have looked frail and disposable, of no consequence. The nurse left and, again, Stone was alone beneath the fluorescent lights of the examination room. He could hear a child crying in the waiting room and was about to get dressed and leave this misery behind when there was a soft knock on the door. It was the doctor asking to enter.

The doctor introduced herself as Dr. Xiao, and Stone was immediately comforted by her presence, her soft, compassionate eyes. "Your temperature is just a touch above normal, but your blood pressure is very low," Dr. Xiao said. "I'm not surprised you blacked out. Are you taking any prescription medications?"

"No," Stone said.

"Illicit drugs?"

When his father had taken the morphine, it had not been illicit. Stone answered, "No."

"Did you eat breakfast this morning?"

"I don't remember."

"Perhaps hypoglycemia?" Dr. Xiao took out a pen and wrote something down. "Is this common for you? To lose consciousness?"

"I don't think so."

She asked him if his thyroid levels had ever been tested, or if there was a history of diabetes or hypotension in his family. "Sometimes we inherit things from our parents that we would rather not receive. Genetics can be a bit of a dice game. Wouldn't it be great if we inherited only our parents' strengths?" She smiled. "I'd like to do some blood work, a basic metabolic panel to rule out any underlying issues."

The doctor was small, just under five feet, with an almost childlike build; her hair was pulled back in a tight ponytail. Her black eyes reflected a surprising warmth. There was something trustworthy about her, and Stone wanted to tell her everything.

"My father just died."

"I'm so sorry to hear that," Dr. Xiao said, and she really did seem to be sorry. "It can be very challenging to deal with the loss of a loved one."

She allowed a moment and when Stone responded with silence, his mind stuck on the all-purpose term *loved one*, she continued.

"My father died when I was eleven, when we first moved here from Guangzhou. It was very difficult, so many mixed emotions. I was full of regret and anger and confusion. He wasn't supposed to die so soon."

Stone nodded his head. She understood his loss.

"Were you close with your father?"

It was almost too painful for Stone to answer, but he managed to say, "Not really."

"I apologize for asking. But I understand," Dr. Xiao said. "Parent-child relationships can be complex."

She peeled back Stone's eyelid and flashed a small penlight into his iris. His pupil constricted, a dull ache flooding back through his retina. His head pounded.

"Did you love your father?" Stone asked.

Dr. Xiao smiled and said, "Yes. Yes, I loved my father."

Perched on the edge of the doctor's table, Stone examined the glossy anatomical chart pinned on the wall across from him, the gaudy horror show of human anatomy. He saw a man's round head flayed on one side, exposing incessant multiplying networks of blue veins rising from the thick cords of the neck to delicate tributaries in the face and skull. Stone took in the pink fibrous muscles and tendons, a rich garnet cord twisting up through the neck into the jaw. His eyes drifted down to the digestive system and the variegated shades of brick, rose, and scarlet; the nut-brown liver; the warm pink of the smooth stomach, tight as the skin of a newborn; the intestines coiled like sleeping nudes; flaming valves and tubes Stone could not name but could not turn from; and the layered walls of the stomach in cross section, piled high like the silty deposits of an archaeological dig. Amazingly, every color of the spectrum was contained within the human body; a wondrous palette of shades and tints that made it hard to question the existence of God.

"Mr. Stone," Dr. Xiao said, "I was asking you to give me one word to describe how you feel."

He apologized for blanking out on her and said, "Melancholia, malaise, desolation, disconsolation. I feel alone and completely lost. I don't know where I belong anymore."

"Any thoughts of suicide?"

Stone said nothing. He had never *really* thought of killing himself so much as he had thought of being dead, flying to a better place.

"Mr. Stone? Any thoughts of suicide?"

"No. Not seriously."

"It is normal to feel sadness and loss after the death of a loved one. Do not beat yourself up over your feelings. Grieving is part of the natural cycle of life, and pain is the other side of pleasure. Now, if you'd like, I can prescribe you something to help you get over the hump, a five-day course of diazepam. It's an anxiolytic that will help take the edge off while you deal with the immediacy of your loss. But I am not a fan of pharmacological treatment for grief, because I believe we need to face our loss and sort things out, rather than throwing a cozy blanket over it. Escapism is not healthy."

"What do you suggest I do?"

"Speak to somebody; a counselor, a therapist, even a good friend can be helpful."

"But I like speaking to you," Stone said. "I feel safe here."

"Well, thank you," Dr. Xiao said. "I can arrange for you to have a psychiatric consultation with my colleague. He's an excellent therapist and can provide you with some techniques to more effectively deal with your loss."

"I've been to therapists before," Stone said. "They don't help. I don't know, but if I can just stay here and talk to you . . ."

Dr. Xiao smiled. "I am glad you feel comfortable speaking with me, but I'm a general practitioner, and a mental health professional will be more equipped to help you."

Stone did not respond, the flickering fluorescent lights lending his skin a dull greenish hue. He just wanted to talk to Dr. Xiao, to keep her in the room with him as long as he could. "I had a breakdown. Junior year of college. I expected to do so well, ace my exams, write essays in my sleep and still finish at the top of my class, but things didn't work out that way. Just before Thanksgiving, I couldn't sleep, I couldn't eat. My mind was racing, thoughts upon thoughts upon thoughts, just piling up like an inbox that remained forever full. But those thoughts were all tangled up; they didn't make any sense to me. Sometimes I burned myself. My girlfriend wanted me to see a therapist, but I was afraid she was just looking for an excuse to break up with me, so we got in a fight in her dorm room and I called her some terrible things and she left me. Suddenly I realized I was in the middle of nowhere, in the dead center of Connecticut with winter creeping in, and I had nothing, nothing at all."

Dr. Xiao had been listening intently, and she lifted the sleeve of his gown above where he'd been scratching and pointed at the scars on his forearm and bicep. "Is that when you did this?"

"Yes," Stone said. "Some."

"Did you try to kill yourself?"

"Honestly, I don't know. He had such high expectations for me, and I was pulling in Bs and Cs, which to him were as bad as Fs. I went into this sort of fugue state and ended up on the roof of the Fayerweather gymnasium. I think he wanted me to jump, he kept telling me to jump, but I wouldn't and that just made him more angry. I don't even know how I got up on the roof."

"Who is *he*?"

"My father," Stone said.

"He was there with you? At school?"

"No," Stone said. "Of course not. But he was always there in my mind, criticizing, judging, telling me I was a failure. I was constantly in disgrace. Do you know how badly I wanted to please him? It's just, for some reason, I couldn't do it. Like every step I had to climb to reach him was two or three times higher than the last. I just didn't have the strength, so I defied him at every opportunity."

"And then what happened?" Dr. Xiao asked. "After the roof."

"I ended up in the psych ward in Hartford Hospital."

"And how did your father react to that?"

"He was embarrassed. For himself. He said, 'What will people think of me? You've ruined my good name.' His good name! That's what he was concerned about. Not me, but his name. My grandfather was a famous gangster and my father did everything in his power to make a name for himself separate from his father; I think my breakdown made him feel all the work he had done to build his life up from the ground was for nothing."

"But it's your life, not his."

"To be honest, it was never much of a life," Stone said.

"I'm sure that's not true." Dr. Xiao looked so sympathetic, the way her brow creased when she spoke. Stone just wanted to stay with her and hold on until his desolation passed.

"He sent me to Israel, to live on some crazy settlement in the West Bank where his old friend was a community leader and rabbi. At first, I was just so happy to get away, to leave Connecticut and school behind, to leave my humiliation behind and start fresh in a new country. But things didn't work out in a hurry. I didn't believe in the strict ideology that land was more important than human lives, that God had granted all the land of Israel to the Jews and nothing to the Palestinians. I wasn't even allowed to use the word *Palestinians* around my father's friend without him correcting me and saying the idea of a Palestinian people was just a cynical concoction cooked up by revolutionaries and murderers to delegitimize the Jewish State of Israel."

"So what happened?"

"I left," Stone said.

"And your father wasn't happy?"

"Not at first, but I told him that I was going to learn Hebrew and travel the country and learn about Israel in my own way, and I convinced him. Surprisingly that was good enough for him. Until . . ." Even after all this time Stone could not form the words, could not say out loud what had happened after he left the safety of Giv'at Barzel's red roofs and barbed-wire fences behind. Stone fell silent but feared Dr. Xiao would leave him, so he pressed on as best he could. "Anyway, it was bad, and my father was very upset and never forgave me and I haven't been back to Israel since." Stone's heart revved at the memory.

Dr. Xiao considered his words in silence, a kindly expression on her face. But then, as if abruptly aware she had a backlog of patients in the waiting room, she said, "Thank you so much for sharing your feelings with me, Matthew." She wrote something out on a slip of paper and handed it to him. "Here's a script for alprazolam. This may help you until you find your feet, but I'm not giving you a refill. Antidepressants tend to mask pain rather than heal it."

"That's it?" Stone said.

"Dr. Zeilich will be with you in just a few minutes. He is an excellent therapist. He can help you."

"Don't go," Stone said.

"I'm sorry, I have other patients to attend to."

"Please," Stone said, "just stay with me a bit longer."

Dr. Xiao's sympathetic expression reformed into a professional mask. "Please tell Dr. Zeilich about your grief, your feelings of inadequacy. He's properly trained to help you. It sounds like you've got a lot of work to do, but try to remember that you have the power to heal yourself."

For a moment, Stone thought she had said "you have the power to *kill* yourself," but it was simply an acoustic blip that made the two words sound similar.

"The nurse will be along in just a moment to take your blood," Dr. Xiao said.

She shook his hand firmly, professionally, adding, "Best of luck, Matthew. I know it doesn't feel like it now, but things will get better."

As soon as Dr. Xiao left, Stone slipped into his clothes and out of the examination room. He wasn't going to stick around for some pointless blood work, to share his misery with a complete stranger. Pinky had not yet returned in the Thunderbird, and Stone was in no condition to walk. Trembling, he leaned against a utility pole, trying to gather himself.

It was a sunny day and the warm air was pleasant—not too hot, not too cold—and life went on before his eyes, cars racing past along Atlantic Avenue, horns honking, shoppers going in and out of the colorful shops across the street: Fertile Crescent, Dar-Us-Salam Books, Treasure Islam, Zawadi Gift Shop.

It was then Stone realized that stapled to the pole on which he was leaning was a cardstock poster announcing an upcoming rally along Atlantic Avenue. There was a crude outline of the shape of Israel, filled in entirely with the colors of the Palestinian flag. It read: RALLY

FOR PALESTINE! The date for the rally was the anniversary of the Court Street Riot. There was a list of Arab dignitaries from the West Bank and Gaza and other parts of the Arab world who would be attending. Stone knew some of their names. He tore up the flier when he noticed the master of ceremonies was to be Randall Roebling Nation.

This time, Stone had no difficulty popping open the bottle of morphine pills; he swallowed two dry, hoping Pinky would arrive soon.

Someone was approaching at a quick clip down the sidewalk, a giant, dressed in the style of the ultra-Orthodox—dark rumpled suit, black hat, and a standard white shirt. He was walking with purpose, a slight hitch in his step, and Stone's stomach clenched. The man must have been six foot three or four, and before Stone realized it, the stranger was upon him. He did not smile; in fact, his bearded face showed no expression.

"Rav Seligman wants to see you."

"Pardon me?" Stone said, far more politely than he intended. He was reminded of the ultra-Orthodox man who had torn his suit at the funeral, and he considered spitting in the man's face.

"Rav Seligman wants to see you." The man turned to walk away, expecting Stone to follow, and, when he did not, stopped and repeated himself for a third time as if he were programmed to say only that one thing.

Stone had only just spoken with Seligman on the phone from Israel, and now he was here? It was understandable that Seligman could not make it on time for the funeral, which was held the day after his father had died, but why was he here now? There was no shiva, no memorial service, no reason Seligman could possibly need to speak with him again. He followed the giant down the block, overtaken by curiosity. What else might Seligman do to try to make him feel guilty and remind him of his shortcomings? Was he obligated to do something more than say the Kaddish? They turned right onto a side street where a black SUV waited, idling. Seligman's face appeared behind the windshield. He plucked a toothpick from his mouth, smiled, and beckoned Stone to get in.

He hesitated for a moment, expecting Pinky would arrive in the

Thunderbird looking for him, but then he realized it was just Pinky and Stone didn't give a fuck. He climbed into the back seat. Seligman looked as he always had, with his gray trimmed beard, knitted kippa on his head, aviator glasses obscuring his eyes. His face was bright and alive. He had not aged a day since Stone had last seen him. It was true that Stone hated Seligman: hated his fire-and-brimstone radicalism, hated his us-versus-them outlook, hated his strength. But he also realized there was something in Seligman that reminded him so much of his father he was drawn toward him: a second chance, in miniature, to make good.

"Matthew," Seligman said, turning and placing his warm hand on Stone's, "I know this is a difficult time."

"How did you know where to find me?"

"When I saw you at the bingo hall today," Seligman said, his sunglasses catching a spear of sunlight, "I saw a lost, sick young man in no position to refuse any help. I just want to make sure you are all right."

The morphine still had not fully taken hold, but Stone was slipping through the rabbit hole. Had he said he had seen him at the bingo hall? Why would Seligman be playing bingo? And why did Seligman give a damn about what happened to Stone? Seligman was not a warm and caring man. Seligman was a monster. Seligman was the one who had told him not to consort with Arabs when he had stayed with him at Giv'at Barzel. Seligman was the charismatic orator who pounded his clenched fist on the podium, spraying saliva as he shouted to the fired-up crowds about "Ishmael in Eretz Yisrael." He was frightening, he was dangerous. Yet here Seligman was in the flesh, warm, kind, alive. Seeing Seligman face to face, Stone had an intense urge to flee. He had turned tail and run last time they'd been together, but the thought of his father's avatar seeing him as a coward made him sick to his stomach.

"I've been better," Stone said.

"You don't look good," Seligman said. "That worries me. Is there anything going on I can help you with?"

Stone offered no response. Seligman was not a sympathetic man.

Seligman wore a hurt expression on his face. "Kid, I have known

you since before you were born. Your father and I go way back. You
know that. He was one of the smartest and best men I have ever
known. We grew up together, studied together. For goodness' sake,
you're his only son. I'm talking about *rachmones*."

"What do you mean?"

"Compassion, Matthew. I know it is not easy for you to be alone
now. And I know you and your father did not always see eye to eye."

"He's gone," Stone said.

"I know," Seligman said, squeezing Stone's hand. His father had not
taken his hand in his own in years, and Stone was nearly overcome by
the intimacy of this small gesture. He started to say something, then
remembered the giant sat less than two feet from him.

"Don't mind him. He's just my golem. Moshe," Seligman said. He
nudged Moshe in the ribs. "Drive us around the block."

The side and back windows had been blacked out. The frigid air-
conditioning blowing against Stone's bare arms made him shiver.

"I was a disappointment," Stone said. "I always thought there would
be enough time to make good with him."

"*Der mentsh trakht un Got lakht.*"

Stone returned a puzzled look, and Seligman said, "Man plans and
God laughs."

"I don't believe in God," Stone said.

The car turned a corner. A group of schoolchildren crossed the
street, brightly colored knapsacks clinging to their backs.

"You must believe in something."

Stone's mind was already getting gummy and slow and he just
wanted to lie down and rest.

"I believe in the power of books," he said at last. "Books are the best
way to engage with humanity without actually engaging with humans.
The world is full of uncertainty. Books have all the answers."

"I know your father loved his books."

"And now they are mine," Stone said, an ecstatic rush overtaking
him. "I need to get back to them now."

"Are you afraid something will happen to them?"

"They'll start speaking without me," Stone said.

"Who will?"

"The books!" Stone replied. "With them I can know everything, knowledge is limitless, it fills the emptiness inside—"

"Matthew," Seligman said, squeezing Stone's wrist, "it's not healthy for you to be alone now."

"Imagine spending an evening with Churchill, T. E. Lawrence, Freud. They are all waiting for me." Seligman's face was melting and beneath that face was another face, full of evil intentions, and beneath that face was another face, calm as a night breeze, and the faces kept peeling back until Stone saw his father's face alive in Seligman's.

"Listen, it is the penitential month of Elul. A new year is upon us. It's almost Rosh Hashanah. Come pray with me. You shouldn't be alone. Come with me. You'll sit, you'll listen. You'll be with Jews instead of sitting like a hermit with your books. Your father would want you to be with family. And every Jew is family. Think about it?"

If every Jew was family, Stone thought, then there must be another father for him somewhere, perhaps many fathers. And as he regarded Seligman up close for the first time in years, he saw the Judge in Seligman's air of confidence, steadiness, self-assuredness. The raw timbre of their voices so much alike. There was even something about the way Seligman smelled that reminded Stone of his father, though he did not smell of cigarettes but carried some raw, masculine scent Stone could not place. He wanted to trust this person, he wanted to have a second chance, he wanted to believe it was he who was broken the last time he had seen Seligman, not the other way around. In fact, Stone's mind *had* been broken, and running away from Seligman had solved nothing.

"Matthew, must I remind you, it is your obligation to say the Mourner's Kaddish for eleven months after the death of your father. You said you believed you were a disappointment to your father? Let's put an end to that now and start fresh with a new year."

His father's face was gone and Seligman had returned, that repulsive toothpick in the corner of his mouth. "You are a one-trick pony, aren't you?"

"Matthew, I assure you I have only the most honorable intentions."

"I don't feel good. Please drive me to my friend's apartment."

"Relax, Matthew. You're not in your right head. I mean no offense whatsoever. You are part of a beautiful tradition, a beautiful history. The Mourner's Kaddish has provided comfort for grieving Jews for thousands upon thousands of years. I just can't understand why you wouldn't grab that lifeline."

5 When the morphine hit this time, it struck hard, and Stone found himself pinned to the bare mattress, straining for breath, staring at the ceiling, his vision doubled. He drifted in and out of consciousness, and when he tried to call Pinky, his throat was so swollen a beastly sound not resembling any language he knew tumbled from his dried-out mouth. His hallucinations were worse this time around as well. His mother's face appeared from a great distance, as if he were lying half drowned at the bottom of a swimming pool and looking up through a vast stretch of rippling water. She blurred into a dreamy soft focus and called to him, "Matthew, Matthew, do you hear me?" Of course he heard her; she was part of his imagination. He saw Pinky's face appear, lengthened as if through a warped fun-house mirror, telling someone there was no fucking way he was calling 911.

He heard his mother's voice again: "Take him to the hospital, you have to take him to the hospital."

"Have you heard of the Rockefeller drug laws?"

Everybody these days was listening to "The Rockafeller Skank." Everywhere he went, he heard that song—it had even been playing quietly on the radio in the limousine on the way to his father's funeral. Yes, Stone thought, the funk soul brother. And now he was dancing, dancing upside down on the ceiling, spinning a gorgeous treble clef, arms around its tapered waist. Pinky and his mother stood way below him, staring up at him with their arms spread wide as if waiting to catch him. But he wasn't going to fall, he was never going to fall; he could fly, he could fly if he wanted to!

He is six years old and his mother has taken him to the Brooklyn Botanic Garden to stroll through the greenery. They walk through the Rock Garden, the Children's Garden, the flaming purple Bluebell Wood, and through the entire cross section of the Native Flora Garden, where they stop along a ledge of limestone. Everything is fever bright and vivid as an oil painting. He hears Pinky's voice underneath everything, solemnly intoning the word *Draconian*, rolling it around on his tongue as if he's never said the word aloud before: "They're fucking Draconian."

"Here is the bladdernut tree, and there the butternut and the angelica tree," his mother tells him.

Matthew grips his mother's hand, feeling some import in her words but not understanding the meaning. "If you can name it, you own it. It becomes part of your life, part of your world forever. Nobody can take that knowledge away from you. If you don't have a name for something, how do you think about it, talk about it?"

Somehow Pinky's voice is still there, but Matthew hasn't even met him yet, and he's saying, "First offense possession. Class I felony," and Matthew has no idea what that means so he points out into the middle distance instead.

"What's that?"

"Slippery elm."

"Yuck."

In the Herb Garden she identifies *Conium maculatum*, which is poison. "Stay away from hemlock."

She shows him lavender, rosemary, mint, and thyme and explains their various healing qualities.

"Time?"

"*Thymus vulgaris*. It means 'courage' in Greek."

"Courage." Matthew rolls the word around his mouth like a cat's purr. "It smells good."

On their way home, Matthew points to a tall, leafy tree, its graceful leaves palmlike, almost tropical, swaying languidly in the spring breeze.

"What's that?"

"That's an ailanthus tree."

"Why would they call it that?"

"It means 'tree of heaven.' I read about it as a little girl. *A Tree Grows in Brooklyn*."

"Can I climb it?"

"No."

"Why not?" He stamps his feet, raising his voice in bitter objection. "Please, please. I want to climb the tree of heaven."

Now Pinky's voice is back, saying, "He'll fucking go to jail—do not pass go."

But Matthew can't figure out why he would possibly go to jail for climbing the tree of heaven. Maybe it's like the tree of knowledge of good and evil, but even Adam and Eve didn't go to jail; they were just sent out of the garden, and Matthew has just left the garden with his mother. The bark is smooth and she has to boost Matthew up to the first branch so he can climb to the yawning Y of the next branch. The leaves are smooth and tear-shaped, tapering out in the end to a fine point. He can see the tops of cars passing by. His mother looks small, girlish, standing below, her face tight with worry. The canopy is fuller above him and he wants so badly to climb where the leaves are thickest; beyond is heaven after all. I can fly, he thinks. All the way to heaven.

"Don't go any farther," his mother calls.

"One more branch."

"No. Come down right now."

Matthew moves to climb higher up the tree when his foot slips against the smooth bark and he tumbles to the ground below, hitting his head on the recoil.

"Oh my God. Are you all right?" his mother screams. She places her hands under his head and kisses him on the forehead.

"I'm fine," Matthew says, more embarrassed than hurt. He's taken worse in the schoolyard. He is a big boy, after all, and he has climbed the tree of heaven.

"Are you sure? Do you need to go to the hospital?"

"I wanna go home."

"You know I love you and wouldn't want anything bad to happen to you."

"Yeah, I know."

"Okay. Let's don't tell your father about this. It will be our little secret. Deal?" And she extends her trembling hand to shake.

Matthew knows it is a mistake to shake her hand, to betray his father, but he reaches out and takes her hand in his. "Deal."

STONE'S HEAD THUMPED and the air smelled of vomit. Somebody was in the room with him, but his eyes, still unfocused, couldn't make out the figure sitting in a chair at the end of his mattress.

"Matthew, I was so worried about you."

That voice, that voice was so familiar yet so alien at the same time. It was the same voice he had just heard in his dream, the same voice that had comforted him and nurtured him as a small child before it had disappeared from his life. He ached all over and his clothing stuck to his body. Stone reached behind his mattress for the pill bottle but his blind hand found nothing except street grit tracked onto the floor.

"If you're looking for the pills, you're not going to find them," the voice said. "I flushed them down the toilet. They are all gone."

Stone was unsure whether he was still in the grips of delirium. How could his mother possibly be here, now, after almost fourteen years? How could she even find him? And why would she come now after staying away through crisis after crisis in which he had no one to turn to? He sat up on the mattress, the room rotating around him. Was this really her, and not a figment of his imagination? Was this the woman who brought him into the world, the woman who ran away? He didn't even know what to call her after all this time: Mom? Abi? Bitch? Coward?

"The pills are gone, you're not getting any more."

He looked at his mother's face and saw no warmth, nothing—it was too late for that. She had missed too much of his life. Her face had hardened with the years. But though her skin was tanned and worn, she was still pretty. It was still the same face he had known as a child.

"What are you doing here?"

"You need help," she said. "You look terrible."

"But what are you doing here? How did you know where to find me?"

"Matthew, I'm here. That's what's important," Abi said. "You need a mother right now. Someone to take care of you."

Stone regarded her for a moment, unsure how to respond. This was not motherly love, this was remorse speaking, and Stone had no intention of helping to alleviate her guilt. She was dressed in black and muted grays in the Banana Republic style, with its timeless lines, its clean cut eschewing fads and trends. She looked like the consummate New Yorker—urbane, cynical, confident—and it struck Stone that perhaps she had never even left New York but had been living across the river all this time, painting her pictures while he struggled to keep himself together.

"I wish it was you who died instead of him."

"I don't blame you for hating me," she said, staring down into her lap. "But I'm here now, and I want to help you. I just want you to know you are not alone." His mother raised her eyes, but they were black pools, showing nothing. "Will you forgive me?"

This was the most power Stone had held in years: the power to destroy his mother was hanging on those four meager words. He noticed she had stray gray strands in her shoulder-length hair that had once been as black as sticky summer tar. "I just want you to understand I always loved you, and I hurt every day I didn't see you. I'm your mother, Matthew, and you are my only son. How do you think it feels?"

There was a bucket of vomit beside the mattress, and Stone leaned over and retched into it. He knew there were disgusting strings of saliva hanging from his chin, but he didn't care. "So you're some kind of martyr now. I'm not going to feel sorry for you."

"I don't want you to. I just want to explain. Maybe we can find a way to start all over again."

"Why now?"

"You know what kind of man he was."

"So you're here to dance on his grave. Is that it?"

"He was a very willful man, very powerful. He had strong ideas about how the world was supposed to be, and I crossed him."

"So now you come crawling back to me."

"It was the hardest thing I ever had to do. Leaving you."

"Then why did you do it?"

Stone would not dare admit out loud that for years he had expected her to walk through the door and hold him in her arms. He had been safe with her, comforted, and then without any explanation, she was gone. She had disappeared from Stone's home, his life, but not from life, the life out there. He read about her periodically in the Arts section of the *Times*, touted as one of the most important American figurative painters of the second half of the twentieth century. She had last appeared in the paper three years earlier, when the National Gallery in Washington had purchased her work for its permanent collection.

"I was afraid of you becoming like him."

Stone almost laughed, but he wasn't capable. "A Jewish mother who doesn't want her son to become a lawyer, a judge?"

"There's so much you don't understand about your father. And for that, I am so thankful. I would have taken you with me. I tried once. Do you remember the time when you were twelve and we went down to Florida and you met Papa Julius?"

"You just wanted the painting, to add it to your rogues' gallery." Stone had gone to see her painting of Papa Julius years later on a break from college, at Abigail Schnitzer's first showing at the Whitney, entitled *American Portraits at the End of a Gun*, which included his grandfather, Julius Stone; John Hinckley Jr.; Bobby Seale; Bernhard Goetz; and the "Son of Sam" killer, David Berkowitz.

"You're nothing but an opportunist, and now you expect to swoop in and take on the mantle of mother of the year."

"I don't know how he found us, but he did and he brought us home. He hadn't spoken to Julius in years. I don't know how he figured out we were going to see him. But he knew. Matthew, he said he'd kill me if I tried to run away with you again."

"And you believed him?"

A vein trembled in her neck. Her voice wavered, no longer the confident, flat tone.

"The year I left, I sent you a birthday card, a Chagall painting of a mother and child. I'm sure you never got it, because a couple of weeks after I sent it, I was out in San Francisco staying with friends from graduate school, when one of your father's associates, some Midwood lowlife, showed up at the apartment where I was staying and said if I ever tried to contact you again, he would shoot me in the back of the head and throw me in the bay. He pressed the gun to my skull. I still feel it. And he meant it, Matthew. I had never been so scared in my life—not for me, but for you—because I was beyond helping you. I had to leave you on your own with him and you would have to fend for yourself."

"So you are some sort of tragic hero. Is that the way you imagine it?"

"That's not what I'm saying."

"Do you know what it was like growing up, learning about your mother through the newspaper and through her paintings? Every time your paintings turned up in a gallery I went. I wanted to see if there was a sense of sadness in your paintings, something that showed me you cared, that you had lost something precious, something to explain the unexplainable. You ran out on me and your career took off, and now you want me to forgive you. Did you remarry? Have kids? Run out on them too?"

"Matthew, enough. You're being cruel."

"You know what? Get out! Do you know how many times I pictured a reunion with you? I expected it to be the happiest day of my life, but you know what? I feel worse. Seeing you just makes me wish I was never born."

"Don't say that."

"You're in no position to tell me what to say. I want you to leave."

She sat still, at the end of the mattress, her eyes unblinking as she looked at Stone. "Oh, Matthew, I'm terrified to death for you."

"Good," Stone said. "Now you know what it was like for me all those years, not knowing where you were. When I managed to find out about a show, I'd call the gallery but no one had an address for you, not even for your own son. I guess you didn't want to be found."

She stood up and said, "I did your laundry. You might want to shower and put on some fresh clothing."

After she left, Stone emptied his wallet in search of the Xanax prescription from Dr. Xiao but couldn't find it. He looked all around his room, in his bed, and in the kitchen garbage but could not find the prescription. Had his mother plucked it out of his wallet and flushed it down the toilet? He needed something, but he had nothing he thought could calm him down, so he took a shower.

Beneath the burning-hot water he reconstructed his memory of the only time he'd met Papa Julius. After a horrible fight with the Judge, his mother had packed a suitcase and flown to Florida with Matthew. He remembered thinking she was taking him to Disney World and the Judge would meet them there. Instead, they arrived at his grandfather's humid apartment, thick with the smell of illness, where he lived alone overlooking a verdant golf course. His mother shook his grandfather's hand, and Matthew noticed she was trembling as she said, "Nice to meet you, Mr. Stone. It's an honor."

"Don't charm me, Abi. You got me."

Matthew was surprised to discover his grandfather was so frail and so small. His thick hair had gone white, his bare feet were purple, and he wore a pair of striped pajamas with the sleeves rolled up. A blurred tattoo of a pair of dice crept out of the sleeve and onto his forearm. At first Matthew was afraid, seeing this little man walk toward him, cognac glass in hand.

"How ya doin', kiddo?" Papa Julius said, and splashed the drink in his face. But it was a trick glass, something found at a joke shop, and Papa Julius was laughing as the golden liquid splashed around beneath its clear concave top. "You gotta be quick," Papa Julius said, shaking Matthew's hand. "Hey kid, nice to meet you. I'm your grandpa."

He thought his grandfather looked kind, like someone he'd throw a baseball around with all afternoon.

"Okay Matty, go watch TV in the guest room. I'm going to paint your grandfather." Stone recalled the disappointment he felt, being sent away so soon after arriving. He just wanted to be near his grand-father, to watch him move, to hear him speak. He sounded like someone out of a movie with that thick Brooklyn accent, like a Bugs Bunny wiseguy. Matthew pretended to go to sleep as he'd been told but instead stayed up listening to his mother and Papa Julius talk, her voice soft and respectful, his good-natured and full of laughter. He listened to the low murmur of their voices until he fell asleep.

Matthew awoke late at night to the sound of Papa Julius coughing in his bedroom, phlegmy coughs rising from somewhere deep inside his small frame—the sounds of the dying. Matthew was afraid something was the matter, but he stayed in his bed until the coughing stopped and then fell back to sleep. He never saw his grandfather again, after that visit. But he did see the painting years later at the Whitney; Papa Julius sat back on a tattered blue couch, arms spread wide on the high back, his wrinkled face worn from a lifetime of violence, his pajama shirt open at the neck. He looked sly, streetwise, as if he were calcu-lating his next move. There was pathos, humanity, even humor in the portrait as he stared down Death, his final adversary. His mother had captured something so elemental in Julius that Matthew had stood before the painting of his grandfather feeling his entire history had been spread across that canvas.

The shower was not the least bit soothing, exhaustion rippling throughout Stone's entire body. His hands and feet tingled and, no matter how much he scrubbed, his skin still itched all over. He found Pinky in his room, popping security tags off a rack of dresses with a flat-head screwdriver. "Why did you let her in?"

Pinky looked up from his work and said, "She's your mother."

"Not anymore. She hasn't been my mother in a long, long time."

"Oh, Jesusfuckingchrist, get over it, you crybaby."

Stone wanted to lunge at Pinky and throttle him right there on his bedroom floor, but he knew he was too weak right now to do any significant damage. "How did she know where to find me?"

"I figured you told her," Pinky said, lighting a cigarette and offering one to Stone. "And you were sick as shit. Three days."

"She was here for three days?"

"She was afraid you were going to die. But you rode it out. Now move on. And stay off the fucking opiates. You want to wake up dead?"

It dawned on Stone that Pinky was not his friend at all, but rather his enemy, and he asked him, "Who told you to bring me to the bingo hall?"

"Say what?"

"You heard me. Who told you to bring me to the bingo hall?"

"You are fucking paranoid, you know that?" Pinky's face showed no recognition he knew what Stone was talking about, and Stone worried he had imagined the whole conversation with Seligman, that his scrambled mind had met with him under the influence of morphine and not as he remembered, in Seligman's SUV near Atlantic Avenue. But he had seen him; he knew he had seen him.

"Does the name Zalman Seligman mean anything to you?"

"Is that supposed to be a name? Because it doesn't sound like a name to me."

"You know who he is," Stone said. "You are a terrible liar."

"And you are the worst roommate I've ever had. Now, you can either shut up or get the fuck out of my place. I'm letting you stay here out of the goodness of my heart, and you are nothing but a pain in my ass."

Stone went back to his room, locked the door, and draped himself in his father's robe. Surrounded by his father's books, he thought, the flesh dies, but the property lives on. That is our legacy. But this inheritance was not silent like an armchair or sideboard; these books continued to speak, all Stone had to do was listen. He pulled a book out of the pile. A yellowed, torn envelope with Israeli postage, addressed to Walter J. Stone, had been folded as a bookmark. The return address was from Abba Eban at the Ministry of Foreign Affairs. The envelope was empty.

Stone found a package of his father's cigarettes, opened the flat cardboard pack, and placed a Nat Sherman between his lips. The smoke curled in the air and danced before him, spinning up into the light and dissipating. He picked up a copy of *The Power Elite*, written by one of the Judge's professors at Columbia. It was inscribed in faded blue ink: "To Walter, Prestige is the shadow of money and power. Best of luck."

The cigarette failed to calm his racing heart—he was still feverish, his nerves vibrating. The whispering got louder, sharper with each book he opened, and, like a lens coming into focus, Stone was viewing his father in a way he never had in life. He picked up *Othello* and turned to the pages his father had used to humiliate him all those years ago. He read: "Reputation, reputation, reputation! O, I have lost / my reputation! I have lost the immortal part of / myself, and what remains is bestial."

His father was speaking to him through his books, and with each word Stone began to understand the enormity of his betrayal. He had been instrumental in destroying his father's carefully constructed reputation. He was guilty, there was no doubt. Proof of Stone's disgrace lay before him and condemned him. Stone determined to make good on his sins. He would read all his father's books, piece him back together like a child's jigsaw puzzle, and solve the mystery of the man he could never please.

6 Stone read for three days straight, not leaving his room to eat or shower. Reading his father's books galvanized some triumphal life force within Stone, made him feel a small temporary victory over the ever-lurking Angel of Death. He pissed in the vomit bucket and dumped it out his window when it was full. He slept in twenty-minute snatches, just long enough to jumpstart his brain before returning to the books. Change a couple letters in *Stone*, he thought, you had *alone*; change another, you had *atone*; split that word, you had *at one*. When he was with the books, he was at one with them—alone, but not alone. His father's handwritten marginal notes made it easy to focus his attention, the Judge's script curling out with the same confident tone he had used when he spoke: "This is hypocrisy," triple underlined; "Check your facts," written in red; "Smilansky agrees," appended with a furious exclamation point. His father, with his emphatic jottings, exercised more influence over Stone now than he had in life, his voice as clear as a bright spring day. Something was under the robe with him as he read, massaging his skin, soothing his muscles, the whispers like oxygen breathed into his lungs. Once or twice in the middle of the night, the street outside silent, it dawned on Stone that he might be losing his reason. He couldn't go forever without sleeping, but an inner urgency drove him to read these books as quickly as possible. He didn't need to eat; he devoured the words, and they filled him. He rationed water from a gallon jug and smoked cigarettes and refused to answer the door when

Pinky knocked. Pinky slid periodic scrawled notes under the locked door telling him to stop feeling sorry for himself, he just needed to get laid, his mother had called twice and wanted to speak with him, and some giant, bearded man in a black suit and hat had been looking for him each of the last three mornings. Stone found a store-bought birthday card from his mother among the notes and lit it on fire, together with the notes, watching with fascination as they burned to nothing.

A leather-bound book by Henry Ward Beecher was of particular interest to Stone, considering he had studied at the school the preacher had founded near the end of his life. A quotation had been underlined by the Judge in reference to the Sharps repeater rifles abolitionists had shipped to Kansas in crates labeled BIBLES: "There is more moral power in one of these than in one hundred Bibles."

Stone had spent six years at Beecher Academy in downtown Brooklyn, but he hardly recalled a single thing he had learned. The school was housed in an old Tudor Gothic structure, its brownstone facade covered in creeping ivy, the school's maroon-and-white flag hanging limply on its pole beside a dispirited-looking Stars and Stripes. Beecher Academy had been established after the Civil War by Henry Ward Beecher as an institution of higher learning "founded upon the principles of abolitionism, liberalism, and faith," but clearly the school's mission had changed by the time Matthew arrived. Beecher Academy had been on the verge of going broke throughout the sixties and seventies, as enrollment dropped and drugs found their way into the classrooms. Students graduating with inflated grades and poor skills became known as Beecher bums, fit only to work in the service industry or, at best, to join the white-collar assembly line of corporate America. Infusions of private money, particularly from the Jews of Brooklyn Heights, turned Beecher around during the eighties, and by the end of the decade, it was one of the top-rated independent schools in the tristate area, boasting a 99 percent graduation rate and college acceptances at the top schools across the country. After Stone's mother left, the Judge had chosen Beecher because of its proximity to the courthouse and its graduates' high acceptance rate at Ivy League schools. Matthew had refused to go to an Ivy League school, but now, thinking back, he had no idea why.

There was one day at Beecher Academy that stood out from all the others, a day that would define his father, and Matthew's broken relationship with him, forever. It was a Friday afternoon in early September of Matthew's sophomore year. He had been dozing through math class when he heard sirens in the streets, filling the air, layer upon layer, in a rising pitch.

Matthew would soon learn that Menachem Wuensch, an Orthodox Jew driving a truck for Court Street Medical Supplies, had run over and killed a seven-year-old Arab boy as he sped down Atlantic Avenue. Wuensch, afraid to get out of his truck in the heart of Brooklyn's Arab shopping district, rolled down his window, saw the boy's broken body, and drove off. Within minutes, the store shutters all along Atlantic clanged shut and dozens of Arabs charged toward the medical supply shop shouting, "Kill Jews!" They threw rocks and bottles, smashed windows, pulled the teaching skeleton into the street, and burned it in effigy.

Court Street was burning. A fire engine blocked the entrance to Joralemon Street, where Beecher Academy was on lockdown, and a police officer called out instructions through a megaphone. "Please lock your doors and stay inside until order has been restored. Please stay away from windows, and do not open your door for anybody." There were rumors Molotov cocktails were flying in front of Borough Hall.

The riot became a media sensation, another link in the narrative of Brooklyn's racial strife. Only this time, the spin was new: African Americans were not at the boiling center. The oldest conflict in the world, as old as Isaac and Ishmael, was playing out on Brooklyn's mean streets, and the media descended hungrily.

A boy had been run over on Atlantic Avenue, and in the ensuing riot one Arab man had been killed, almost a dozen injured.

A twenty-two-year-old yeshiva student named Isaac Brilliant, who worked as a part-time stock boy at the medical supply shop, was charged with aggravated assault and the murder of Nasser Al-Bassam, a sixty-three-year-old Palestinian-born shopkeeper who died of his injuries.

The case went before the Supreme Court of the State of New York; Walter J. Stone presiding.

The flamboyant Reverend Randall Roebling Nation, a preacher who claimed to have been ordained at the age of eight, took up the fight in his daily soapbox orations: "The elucidation of the struggle is coming to a head; the judges will be judged and the people will have justice, freedom, and liberty at last!"

Matthew knew Nation, with his tailored suits and gold jewelry, was full of wind, politicking simply to get his face in the papers. Every day in front of the courthouse, he took aim at the Judge, shouting, "I beseech you all to listen to R. R. Nation, as Nation speaks God's truth. Judge Stone is a criminal, a crook, and a thief, and if he is not punished in this life, God will punish him in the next."

Even as Brooklyn's Arab community protested Walter Stone's selection, picketing outside the Supreme Court building, the Judge said nothing. A spokesman stated, "The Judge's record speaks for itself."

Matthew heard nothing from his father, who had receded into his study with his law books for days on end, leaving only to dump his full ashtray into the toilet. By the time the case went to trial, Matthew had developed constant canker sores in his mouth; he found it difficult to speak, his mouth a piece of tenderized meat. Some days he didn't even want to leave his room. He gargled salt water, apple cider vinegar, peroxide; nothing helped.

One evening, his mouth on fire, sucking on ice cubes to numb the pain, Matthew knocked on his father's study door. "I want to go to the emergency room," Matthew said through the closed door.

"Fine," his father said after a moment.

Matthew remained at the door, his fist poised to knock again.

"I said fine."

How wretched, how awful Matthew felt knowing he was just a repulsive, inconsequential insect in the pitiless eyes of his father. That night, Matthew burned himself for the first time. He realized, as he stood, match in hand, in his bathroom, that out of all things in the entire universe, he truly had control only over his own body. He could cause pain whenever he wanted and remove it just as easily. What a release!

MURDER INC. KIN TO RULE was headlined the day before the trial, and the story was picked up by the national media. The trial had all the makings of a Movie of the Week, said a *Los Angeles Times* columnist, who joked that Marlon Brando as Colonel Kurtz from *Apocalypse Now* should be cast to play Judge Walter Stone. Matthew was amazed by the shallowness of some of the coverage, at the reporters playing casting director as if this trial were first and foremost a commodity to be gobbled up by Hollywood.

The Judge broke his silence the day before the trial was to begin. Appearing on the front steps of the Supreme Court, wearing his gray three-piece suit and half-moon glasses, he read from a prepared statement: "I am addressing the spurious canard that appeared in this morning's paper in relation to my father. What my father may or may not have done before I was born holds no bearing on today's proceedings, and I expect to hear nothing more on this matter."

The jury was comprised of seven women and five men, three of whom were African American, four Hispanic, four white, and one Korean American. There was one Jew on the jury: Emile Alcalai, a teacher from Sheepshead Bay.

Brilliant, flanked by his lawyer and the court bailiff, wore a black suit, a white shirt, and a black silken yarmulke on his head. He smiled from behind his beard and nodded his head confidently at the court assembly, as if he knew all along he would soon be free.

When friends and family members attesting to the character of Al-Bassam were cross-examined by Brilliant's lawyer, the courtroom buzzed. "Is it not true Mr. Al-Bassam, a fervent Muslim, has three times made the hajj, the pilgrimage to Mecca—"

"The question is not relevant," the prosecutor interjected.

Judge Stone flatly said, "Answer the question."

Later, Brilliant's lawyer said, "Mr. Al-Bassam left the Samarian town of Tulkarm in June of 1971. Local records show he had his daughter killed two years earlier in what is known as an honor killing—"

"Objection. The question is inflammatory and improper," the prosecutor said.

"The question is allowed," Judge Stone answered.

When Brilliant took the stand, he was unable to fully explain how the bloodstains on his shirt had come by self-defense, but when grilled by the prosecution he claimed he was attacked by a vicious Nasser Al-Bassam, whom he identified in a photograph as the man he had tried to stop from throwing a garbage can through a plate-glass window. Brilliant maintained that Al-Bassam had turned his fury on him.

"Considering the victim's chronic epilepsy," the prosecuting attorney replied, directing his comment toward the jury, "where convulsing seizures strike in moments of exertion and stress, it is unlikely, almost impossible to believe, that Mr. Al-Bassam, a very careful man who was in fact so impaired by his condition that he did not drive, was capable of posing a threat toward Mr. Brilliant. In addition, witnesses at the scene testified Mr. Al-Bassam was turned away from Mr. Brilliant when he received the deadly blow to the back of his head."

Judge Stone commenced his charge to the jury after lunch. Quoting Gibbon, the Judge said, "'In every deed of mischief he had a heart to resolve, a head to contrive, and a hand to execute.' Here we are absent the heart and the head, so I ask you, is there an act of mischief, a crime?" He spoke at length into the early evening, explaining the nuances and minutia of the law until the jury retired to deliberate. The jury reached a decision shortly before midnight. The press was confident Brilliant would be found guilty of murder. But instead he was found guilty of the lesser charge of aggravated assault and not guilty of murder. The headlines screamed the next morning: NOT SO BRILLIANT VERDICT.

Now, Stone puzzled over the words his father had underlined in Beecher's book: "There is more moral power in one of these than in one hundred Bibles." Stone was captivated by the quotation, the violence of it, the self-assurance of it, and he flipped through the pages to see if his father had marked anything else; he had not. The book was an old hardcover with crisp yellowed pages, bound in soft leather. He pressed his nose to the cover and breathed in deeply, the smell rich and luxurious and soothing. Something told him to open the book again, and he spread the pages wide before him on the floor, cracking the spine. It was a terrible sound, like a tiny bone breaking. He had destroyed something beautiful and it sickened him. Henry Ward Beecher smiled an inscrutable half smile from a black-and-white photograph on the book's frontispiece. How could a simple photograph terrify? There was something haunting about those old daguerreotypes—the eyes especially—as if the subjects had already crossed over to the other side, even as their pictures were being taken. A surge of panic rose in Stone as he regarded the naked spine of the book. The cover lay limp on the floor like wings, grounded forever. The glue had dried out and cracked, and he brushed aside the amber bits of residue with his finger when he noticed something had fallen out of the binding and onto the floor. It looked like a small blank business card, but when Stone picked it up he realized it was a little envelope—something was inside. He pinched the envelope open and held it upside down, and a bank card embossed with Chase Manhattan Bank's symbol clattered to the floor. The account number was printed across the laminate front of the card, above the name Walter Stone and the raised words THE ERETZ FUND. Underneath was the expiration date. The card would not expire for another four years. The card was practically brand-new, showing no damage or wear.

That magnetic force was close enough now to touch him, but when Stone turned around there was nothing, just a sort of abstract whisper guiding him, directing him toward a book about one of the former prime ministers of Israel. The book opened to a page on which a quotation was underlined in his father's hand: "A man who goes forth to take the life of another man whom he does not know must believe one thing only—that by his act he will change the course of history." Then, as if by instinct, he sifted through the pile, discarding the heavy biography of Moses Montefiore and Émile Zola's J'accuse, his hand reaching for a book by his father's friend Rabbi Avraham Grunhut. Stone flipped from page to page until he found this single sentence circled again and again and again, the ink on the page whirling like the eye of a tornado around the frightening words: "Nothing is more righteous than revenge administered at the right time and place."

The card burned in Stone's hand, heavy as a piece of iron. He knew this bank card was the vehicle for that revenge.

Was he crazy? He closed his eyes against the words his father had highlighted in these books. The room closed in on him, the walls pressing in. His father had brought all his intellectual power to bear to ensure Isaac Brilliant would get away with murder. Why would he risk his entire career, his reputation, so a Jewish man would not be found guilty of murdering an Arab man? And Demjanjuk, the accused prison guard from the Treblinka death camp—his father had been instrumental in sentencing him to death, only to have the judgment overturned by the Israeli Supreme Court. And who else had there been over the years? There had to be others, there had to be.

Stone had always assumed his father was a man of law and order, operating in good faith from the bench, acting as a moral and honest broker. But now, tearing off his father's robe, Stone was beset by doubts. The card had been planted in the book for Stone to find, for him to complete his father's work. But it was not right. He knew whatever it was he was tasked to do with that card involved terrible violence. Stone's stomach lurched, but he had nothing inside himself to throw up. He began shouting at the books, railing at them, tossing them about the room. Why did he ever take those books, when he might have left them at his father's apartment and been free of him forever? He had not slept in three days, had not left his room in six, and his head was a storm of confusion. Was he losing his mind? Was his exhausted brain making connections that did not exist, or had he reached some higher level of understanding? He knew he couldn't stay in this room forever, and, casting around for an excuse to leave the fetid bedroom and his father's books behind, Stone remembered he had an appointment the next day (or was it today, or yesterday?) with his father's lawyer to discuss the Judge's will. He stretched a trembling hand for the nearest book, something by Horace, and opened it to the middle pages, hoping to find something benign, meaningless. He read: "Wisdom is not wisdom when it is derived from books alone."

"Who are you to say when wisdom is wisdom and when wisdom is not wisdom? You've been dead over two thousand years." Stone laughed and laughed until his sides ached and he tumbled onto his mattress and into a dead sleep.

He slept for sixteen dreamless hours and awoke the following morning, cleansed of whatever madness had overtaken him the night before, with the bank card still clutched in his grip. He had found a bank card, that was all; nothing about that discovery constituted an obligation or marching orders of any kind. Dozens of books still lay tossed about the room; he gathered up the scattered books and stacked them back on top of the piles. The sun shone in through his windows, and Stone desired to be out in the fresh air. He found the lawyer's card in his wallet and discovered his appointment was for that day—in two and a half hours. The homeboys from the Whitman Houses laughed on the pavement outside his window. The fact that joyous laughter still bloomed made him feel unaccountably hopeful. Stone decided he would walk the mile or so to Brooklyn Heights. He slipped the card into his pocket, ate some dry cereal while standing over the sink, and drank three glasses of water. He was prepared to handle whatever came his way. His mother had left a long handwritten note for him taped to the back of the front door, but he disregarded it and locked the door behind him.

ZOHAR WAS WAITING in the street for Stone. His suit was rumpled, tie knotted loosely at his neck, face unshaven—he looked as bad as Stone imagined he himself looked after his marathon tangle with the Judge's books. "Good morning, Matthew," Zohar said, approaching, a crushed Styrofoam cup in his hand.

Stone wanted to be irritated by Zohar's intrusion on his privacy at a time like this, but now that he had seen what was in his father's books, he was also curious to know what Zohar had to say. Who was his father after all, and what did he expect of Stone? His father's legacy would become his own, in the same manner the Judge had been obliged to carry his own father's bad name around with him like a yellow star pinned to his chest. Stone knew whatever Zohar was up to concerned his own future and that his prospects depended on the past and how it was framed. This was an opportunity to gain perspective, to understand how the critics and haters saw Walter Stone. He needed to know what Zohar was up to if he was going to fight back and defend his father's name, his own life. Stone said a curt good morning and turned onto Myrtle Avenue. Zohar, at his heels, burned-coffee breath in his face, said, "Going somewhere, Matthew?"

"You certainly are observant."

Zohar stepped in front of Stone and blocked his way with his body, arms crossed. "Maybe you can tell me why Zalman Seligman's man, Moshe Reisen, has called on you three mornings in a row."

"I have no idea what you are talking about."

"But you do know Zalman Seligman."

Stone continued to walk. Let Zohar beg.

"I know you know Zalman Seligman. You're not going to deny that, are you?"

"If you know the answer, why are you asking me?"

"Do you know who Zalman Seligman really is? He is not some kindly old rabbi living out his golden years in Miami Beach. He is a violent criminal, hiding behind his faith, who has been arrested more than a dozen times in the past twenty years in relation to violent incidents throughout the West Bank."

Stone couldn't help but roll his eyes at Zohar's intensity.

"Maybe this laundry list will put things in perspective for you. Seligman is alleged to have assaulted a Palestinian mother of two while her children watched; he has been arrested for overturning shopkeepers' carts in the Hebron casbah; he has been cited for firing his pistol in front of a mosque on numerous occasions; he has been fined for trespassing, harassment, arson, vandalism of property. He was arrested for shooting a Palestinian man's donkey, for which he spent fifteen days in prison. The list goes on and on: harassment, intimidation, violence . . . Rabbi Seligman will stop at nothing to advance the cause of a Greater Israel."

"That's quite a resumé," Stone said, "but it means nothing to me. Sounds like you know Zalman Seligman a lot better than I do."

"Does the name Avraham Grunhut mean anything to you? Another rabbi—also connected to your father and the Eretz Fund, the foundation Seligman and your father co-founded. He was a controversial religious leader until he was assassinated."

"Assassinated?" Stone said, amused at how a subtle shift in language could so alter meaning. "That's sort of gilding the lily, isn't it? I'd say he was murdered. He wasn't exactly a head of state or Nobel laureate."

"He was close friends with your father."

"What exactly are you suggesting?"

The words his father had circled in Rabbi Grunhut's book certainly gave credence to whatever Zohar was implying. But there was a disconnect, a misreading of intention. The Judge and Grunhut had been friends and partners, but that had all ended when the rabbi was killed.

Stone picked up his pace, his languid blood circulating throughout his body and awakening some desire deep within him to fight, to punch back hard.

"Matthew, just hear me out."

"I'm not my father's keeper, and you're nothing but a parasite. Why don't you go home and get some sleep? You smell like shit."

Zohar laughed. "So Grunhut was 'murdered' by whom? The common belief is that he was killed by a Palestinian terrorist—a bullet in the back of the head. Yes, they arrested a Palestinian, put him on trial, and convicted him, but he wasn't the killer; he wasn't even involved. He had gotten himself in trouble elsewhere, so the killing was pinned to him to avoid reprisals and to close the book."

"You sound like a crazed conspiracy theorist."

A bus roared past, blowing a huge cloud of exhaust in their faces.

"You know, Matthew, I hated my old man," Zohar said. "He used to hit me with a belt when I was a kid. If I struck out in baseball, if I came in second, if I got a B in school, out came the belt. Strict immigrant father trying to make it in America through his son. Nothing was ever good enough for him. I always let him down. I prayed for him to die, prayed for it as I lay in bed at night. What did I know? Then one day he was gone—but I'm never rid of him. He's always there, an indelible print I can never wash off."

"Are you trying to suggest I hated my father? Are you trying to make some sort of false connection with me, one disgruntled son to another? I'm sorry you hated your father, and I'm sorry for you that you can't get over him, but that's not me. You've got it all wrong. You don't know me, and you don't know my father."

Zohar pressed on, undeterred. "I know about him. I know his life, the milestones, the ins and outs, the facts of his life, his accomplishments and failures. I know he was a tenacious bulldog. At the age of twenty-two, he prosecuted organized crime figures as the state's youngest assistant district attorney—notably street gangs in Hell's Kitchen. He doggedly nailed down prosecutions after the theft of priceless jewels from the Museum of Natural History. Wouldn't Dr. Freud have a field day with that knowledge?"

In the sky above the park, to their left, a red kite flew against the pure blue sky, flashing back and forth like a streak of blood.

"I know your father received a Bronze Medal for Meritorious Service after serving as a judge advocate general in the Twenty-Fifth Infantry Division in Vietnam from 1966 to 1968. By all accounts, he sounds like a good man. Doesn't he?"

"Am I supposed to be impressed?" Stone said. "Are you going to tell me about his kindergarten crayon drawings next? The past is past."

"Matthew, you are smart enough to know the past is never past, especially when it comes to Israel and the Palestinians. I want you to help me know him, the flesh-and-blood man he really was. I want you to help me complete the picture before something terrible happens. I know Walter Joseph Stone, but I know him academically, the way you know Whitman—intimate yet distant."

"Whitman?" Stone stammered. Now Zohar had hit the mark, finding that tender spot behind Stone's heart that made it hard to breathe, his failure writ large for everyone to see. He'd heard enough from Zohar.

"I know you were halfway through your graduate thesis on the universal spiritualism of Walt Whitman's work before you took a leave of absence from your studies to tend to your father. I know it was to be called 'Perennial with the Earth' and that you'll never go back and finish it, will you? I know you took a leave of absence as an undergraduate five years earlier after suffering a psychotic break in which you spent a month in a mental health facility."

"Enough," Stone said, covering his ears. "That's enough."

But Zohar continued, keeping pace with Stone. "I know of your predilection for self-mutilation, burning in particular. I know your father sent you to Israel when you came out of the psych ward, and I know you spent time with Zalman Seligman at Giv'at Barzel. But most importantly, I know all about your relationship with a Palestinian girl named Fairuza Freij and I know what happened to her after you left."

This was too much for Stone to handle, her name in his ears after all this time. A hot knife of shame plunged into his lungs. Gasping for air, he ran down Myrtle Avenue, past the toppled trash bins, past the black albino rapping on the corner, past the fried-chicken joint, and, howling some barely articulated curse, he crossed busy Flatbush Avenue against the light, not caring if he was struck down by a speeding car.

7 Try as he might, Stone could not outrun Fairuza forever. Memory was an impossible, inscrutable thing. He marveled at how moments of intense pleasure disappeared into nothing as if they were just figments of a distorted imagination, and other, painful moments—traumatic tearful scenes—came to life without any warning, darkening his entire day, just like that. He had always been vulnerable to the influence of his memories; his moods shifted like the ticktock of the metronome that sat atop his childhood piano. He had done a good job of forgetting Fairuza, washing her from his brain. That was the power of shame, and he was so ashamed of what he had done to her, every time her image appeared before him, or a snatch of conversation ticker-taped through his brain, he found a way to push her down under the dark waters of his subconscious. When the memories came, they were as raw as if they'd happened yesterday, and he hated himself.

He'd met Fairuza Freij one night at a teahouse off of Nahalat Shiv'a in Jerusalem. He had fled Giv'at Barzel a few days prior and was staying at a nearby youth hostel on King George Street. So far from home, far from everything he knew, he had nothing to grasp on to; it was as if he could just drift off into the vastness of space and disappear. She was sitting with a group of students, noisy Israelis, from Hebrew University. He had noticed them as they smoked and laughed in an atmosphere of heightened youthful drama, waving their arms and touching each other for punctuation. Fairuza sat at the edge of the circle, absorbed in a water-damaged copy of *Light in August*. He didn't know she was an Arab. She was dark and pretty like so many Israelis, that exotic history and geography compressed into a seemingly impossible genetic mix so startling in comparison to the pale, doughy American Jews with whom he had grown up.

He gathered the courage to sit down next to her, and she smelled ever so slightly of citrus. She read on, a smile playing at the corner of her lips. A vein pulsed visibly in her neck, and he wanted to bury his face in her dark, fragrant hair.

"Would you like to borrow this?" she said in English, smiling.

Matthew's face flushed with embarrassment, but he had wanted her to notice him and now she was talking to him. He said, "No thanks. I've read it."

"Me too," she said, closing the book and extending a hand. Her fingers were so long. "I'm Fairuza."

They spoke at length about Faulkner's misanthropy and black humor, then eased into discussing their favorite novels, Matthew citing *The Castle*; Fairuza *The Alexandria Quartet*. Matthew found that, as their conversation shifted from books to more personal subjects—she had always hated her nose; he wondered why he was predictably surprised by the awkward sound of his recorded voice—he was able to escape the darkness of his mind, the persistent focus on his internal deficiencies that had caused him to flee Giv'at Barzel. He felt liberated in those moments to speak his thoughts freely, to discard his image of himself as hopelessly flawed, and to invent himself anew.

After some time, during which their bodies had inched closer and closer to each other so that he could feel her leisurely movements syncing with his, Fairuza said, "I'm tired of sitting. Would you like to go for a walk?"

They headed down Jaffa Street and through Jaffa Gate and along the dark, narrow streets of the walled Old City. He hadn't been to the Old City since he was a child; his father had taken him there, providing his own personal archaeological tour, spinning facts and figures about this king and that church and whatever else Matthew had been too young to understand at the age of seven. Now, the city was magic, the moon so low in the sky they could practically climb a ladder and sit up there, in the comfort of a scooped-out crater, looking down at all the silly people on earth.

"I like coming here at night," she said.

"Isn't it dangerous?" Matthew said. The streets were crooked and ill lit. They looked to be especially treacherous at night.

"At night, I have the city to myself, without all the shouting and tourists and ugliness of all the people who claim this city as their own." She spoke beautifully, with just a hint of an accent. Maybe *this* was Matthew's reward for surviving the psych ward. "I can be me. Just a person, enjoying a beautiful night in the history of the world."

They found themselves on a rooftop facing the golden Dome of the Rock. On the quiet evening air, a shepherd's bell clanged mournfully in one of the valleys outside the city walls. His fingers breezed the small of her back, and she said, "You're not like most Americans. Thoughtful, respectful, humble. You don't brag about accomplishments you had nothing to do with, as if you personally invented liberty and freedom."

"Ouch," he said, laughing. "Are Americans that bad?"

She laughed too.

"Well, you aren't like most Israelis," he said. "At least you'll talk to me."

Fairuza was silent, clearly unsure what to say next. Matthew, still warm with the heat of laughter, realized he had said something wrong, but wasn't sure what. She lowered her voice, looked him square in the eye, and said, "Matthew, you should know, I'm not Israeli. I'm from Beit Jala." He wasn't sure what that meant, and she added, "I'm Arab, a Christian."

And now Matthew realized why *Light in August* had spoken to her strongly enough that she was rereading it. In the same way Faulkner's biracial character Joe Christmas was neither black nor white but guilty of being both, Fairuza was guilty of being neither Jewish nor Muslim, but somehow suffering the slings of each side of this age-old conflict.

"That doesn't bother me," Matthew said. "You're a beautiful, intelligent, and kind woman. That's all that matters to me."

Later, on their way back to Jaffa Gate through the narrow streets of the shuttered souk, they saw an Israeli border guard posted at the bottom of David Street checking an Arab man's ID card. Matthew was so used to seeing similar scenes outside grocery stores, and while queuing up for buses, that he thought nothing of it, but Fairuza was crying. He asked her what was the matter.

"They're as bad as the settlers at Gilo, with their checkpoints outside my village. They destroy everything. They take what's not theirs and make us feel like we do not belong."

"Don't let that spoil tonight," Matthew said.

"He's just going home. He's only going home to his family," she said.

"Please don't say anything," Matthew said, afraid of this incident tipping the delicate balance they had found between them.

"I hate them. I wish they were dead. I wish they were all dead," she said, wiping tears from her cheek.

"You don't mean that," Matthew said, shocked by her abrupt turn to violence. Rabbi Seligman had warned about the Arabs' innate violent tendencies, and Matthew had been revolted by his words. "They have families of their own. You don't mean that."

"I do," she said. "I hate this world, I hate this country, I hate this time. But I love this city. I love it. I feel like hugging the entire city, kissing the stone streets beneath my feet."

Her face was so sad and so beautiful that Matthew took her in his arms. He held her for the first time and her body relaxed into his. "But good things can happen in this world too," he said. "One day there will be peace."

After a moment she said, "Sometimes, I wish I were a giant who could carry Jerusalem away."

"Where to?" Matthew said.

"Somewhere far away where nobody can have it. Maybe the moon."

That was when Matthew realized he loved her. That simple whimsical response was enough to flood his heart with warmth and overcome any doubts he might have had about loving an Arab woman.

It sickened Stone to think about that period of his life, because he knew it was gone and it was never coming back. The six months he and Fairuza had spent together—exploring each other's bodies in bed in her tiny dorm room on Mount Scopus, sitting in the cafés in the German Colony discussing art and literature, attending lectures at the university, wandering the length of the country on weekends—had been the only time he had been happy since he was a small child. Her family had welcomed him and treated him with kindness. A glowing bubble had descended to protect the two of them from earthly concerns. After that first night, she had never again wished harm to anyone.

Matthew kept in touch with his father via obligatory weekly phone calls back to Brooklyn, lying about his progress in learning Hebrew and never once revealing his relationship with Fairuza. When his father spoke in Hebrew to test his son's proficiency, Matthew claimed the connection on his end was bad and blamed Bezeq's shitty pay phones for his lack of comprehension. Sometimes he even scripted simple, transliterated Hebrew phrases he could toss out at his father, just to put his mind at ease. But mostly Matthew wanted to share his feelings about Fairuza; how they understood each other, how he felt safe when he was with her, how because of her he had finally grown into the best version of himself. He hadn't felt this good in years; his mind was clear, his body free of the usual hypochondriacal aches and pains. He was in love and it felt both liberating and binding, freeing him from his troubled past while joining his life with another smart, caring, sensitive soul. He knew his father would think his relationship was wrong, an abomination even, but Matthew teased around the edges, once even telling his father a city only truly became your own when you loved someone in it. The city was Jerusalem, but the Judge never asked who the woman might be. His father was dead to love anyway. Matthew was certain that after Abi had run away, his father had given up on the entire notion of love, focusing instead on his career and his work for Israel.

The Judge informed Matthew he was coming to visit, and Matthew, swept up in a sudden wash of optimism, decided it was time to tell him about Fairuza. It wasn't that he expected his father's blessing; he simply believed the Judge had the right to know about his girlfriend before he met her. He certainly didn't plan on hiding Fairuza from his father when he came to see him. His father just needed to meet Fairuza to know she was a good thing in Matthew's life.

"What kind of name is Fairuza?" the Judge said over the telephone, the day before he was to arrive.

"It's a name," Matthew said.

"I know it's a name. What kind?" He heard the disapproval in his father's voice. Then there was silence on the line and Matthew feared his father had hung up on him.

"Matthew, I am coming to get you. I am bringing you home."

"What?"

"Tell me you are joking. This is some stupid adolescent joke."

"I don't know what you mean."

"You never miss a single opportunity. You *davka* decide to screw a Muslim girl in a country bursting with beautiful Jewish women. What is the matter with you? I'm coming to get you."

"Why?" Matthew said. "I love her. I don't give a shit what you say." Matthew was astounded by his own words, as if his convictions were solidified by the simple act of vocalizing them. "She's not Muslim. She's Christian," he added.

"You are unbelievable," the Judge said. "You are doing this just to spite me, to humiliate me. Matthew, I swear to God, in all my life in which I have worked harder than any man, you are my only failure. What are you going to do, marry her? Have babies with Amalek?"

It was the first time he recalled hearing that word.

"I don't know."

"I'm coming to get you. You'd better kiss her good-bye now because tomorrow you're flying back to New York with me."

Matthew was supposed to meet Fairuza at a coffee shop on Azza Street, but she hadn't arrived yet. She'd said she was looking forward to meeting his father and wanted to buy a present to give him. He had told her not to bother. "Please don't spend your money. My father

wants for nothing." The truth was too painful to speak out loud. He
had never told Fairuza that his father would be likely to object vio-
lently to their relationship when he discovered it. He had lied instead,
concocted stories about his tolerant, accepting father and how much
he would love her. It was a mistake, he now knew, but he had hoped
somehow to find a way to make the truth of his imagination align with
the truth of his father's hardheaded reality. He realized now he was
terrified of introducing Fairuza to his father.

When Fairuza arrived, over twenty minutes late, her face was thin
and drawn; worry filled her eyes. Her expression said everything: bad
news. She sat across from him, looking sorry and sad. Matthew had
drunk three cups of muddy Turkish coffee as he waited, his nerves
pulled taut, like bowstrings ready to go off. As he sat, staring into the
rich sediment at the bottom of his coffee cup, he realized the Judge
had gotten into his head.

"There was a bombing near Sheikh Jarrah," Fairuza said. "The bus
had to detour."

Matthew was nakedly aware of her Arabic pronunciation, the way
she articulated *bombing*, emphasizing the second *b*. That first night,
she had wished the Israeli border guard dead. She had wished them all
dead. Did she mean Jews? Israelis? She couldn't possibly love him and
want him dead at the same time.

"We have to talk," she said.

"I know," Matthew said. He wasn't sure what he was going to say;
even as the words gathered in his mind, he knew he could have gone
just as easily in the other direction.

Let's run away together.

It's over.

But she spoke first, saying, "I'm late."

"I know," Matthew said. "Nearly half an hour." He still didn't know
what he was going to say, *he loves me, he loves me not*, but he saw in
Fairuza's stricken face someone he had not seen before, imagining the
lens through which his father would view her.

"I missed my period," she said. "I missed it."

"Are you sure?"

"Yes, I'm sure. I never miss it, and we haven't exactly been careful."

For a moment Matthew envisioned a future in which he had a half-Arab child and how his father would cut him off forever. But his father could not destroy him, not when he was safe in Fairuza's arms. He could build a new life of his own, without judgment, without expectations. He would have a new family, his own family. But it would not be easy. Even if Matthew decided to stay, he would have to become an Israeli citizen and fight in their army and where would that leave Fairuza and the child? He was too young for all these complications. This was not supposed to happen. He threw his arms around Fairuza and they held each other. Somewhere deep inside her belly a tiny rice grain of a human being was making its way toward existence. It was so small, so insignificant, but it was everything, and he just wanted it to go away.

"We have to get rid of it," Matthew said.

"Matthew," Fairuza said, shaking her head, her brown eyes uncomprehending. "I love you. And you know, anyway, I can't get rid of it."

"I love you too," Matthew said. But he knew fear always overpowered love and he was afraid, even as he repeated the words a second time, he would bend to his father's will and receive nothing in return.

8 Breathless from his run, Stone walked the last stretch toward the law offices of Holland, Rowe and McKim, the bright sun burning above. He had never imagined when his father presided at the courthouse across the way, all-powerful and impregnable, that one day he would return to hear the reading of his will.

The lawyer rose from his desk, hand extended, a confident smile on his face. He was about fifty years old and wore his hair slicked hard against his scalp, like a helmet.

"Matthew, Charles Taylor Holland." His eyes were a pale, silvery blue behind round, rimless glasses. He shook Stone's hand, blue-blooded vigor pulsing in his touch. "Have a seat."

Stone sat in one of the two stuffed leather and mahogany chairs across from Holland's desk and wiped his brow.

"My condolences," Holland said, leaning forward in his chair. "I was fortunate to have gotten to know Walter well during his time on the bench. He was a good friend and a fair judge." He spoke in a flat, dry tone free of any accent or affectation. "Now, since you are the only beneficiary to your father's last will and testament, we can begin. Bear in mind, it may take a few months for the will to clear probate. However, what we are going to read today, assuming no unexpected bumps in the road, is his legal will."

He slid some documents across his spotless desk and Stone picked them up and flipped absently through the pages.

"Most of this page is standard boilerplate stuff—name, domicile, etcetera, revoking all previous wills and codicils. We have debts, expenses, taxes. You needn't worry about that. As the executor, I'll see to it his debts and funeral expenses are taken care of. These expenses will be subtracted from the estate."

He spoke clinically and matter-of-factly, as if he were discussing a car warranty or baseball trade, and not the remnants of a man's life.

"After your father liquidated his home on Ocean Parkway, he lived a pretty austere life in a rented two-bedroom apartment in Midwood. As a result, his personal effects are few. They devolve to you, Matthew Stone, his only heir." Holland pointed to a few single-spaced columns near the bottom of the page. "This means you get whatever was in his apartment at the time of his decease. This includes ownership of his 1980 Ford Thunderbird."

Holland did not look up at Stone as he spoke.

"There is also a property on Henry Street in Brooklyn Heights that your father co-owned with Zalman Seligman."

"Wait a second," Stone said. "If my father was co-owner of the property, wouldn't that make me co-owner with Seligman?"

"Yes. You are co-owner with Seligman," Holland said. "I suggest you speak with Zalman Seligman about any concerns you may have. It's between the two of you now."

Holland tapped his desk, anxious to move on.

Seligman's SUV had been parked on Henry Street, around the corner from Dr. Xiao and the walk-in clinic on Atlantic. He hadn't flown back to see if Stone was all right and to offer him guidance within the framework of traditional Judaism; he had come to attend to the property, to assert control over a valuable asset. But what could he possibly want in a property so far from his life in Israel? Stone was about to ask another question about the Henry Street property, but Holland had already moved on.

"And now your father's foundation that he chaired: the Eretz Fund, with assets exceeding forty-five million dollars," Holland said, rolling a pencil between his fingers as he puzzled over the text.

"Forty-five million dollars!" Stone said. "Holy shit." The bank card embossed with the words THE ERETZ FUND pulsed against his thigh.

"It's not all liquid, Matthew. This includes property holdings, annuities, and other appreciated assets. This is a 501(c)(3) not-for-profit organization, registered with the Internal Revenue Service. The bulk of the monies are restricted funds, designated for existing projects. What this means is the Eretz Fund raises and distributes funds to programs it supports, and it enjoys the tax benefits that come along with being registered as a 501(c)(3). Are you following?" Holland asked.

Stone nodded his head.

"It also says in the event of the chair's decease, the beneficiary becomes president of the foundation. That means you."

"Me?" Stone said. Why would his father put that much faith in him, especially entrusting him rather than his friend, Rabbi Seligman? Anxiety whirled in Stone's stomach. This was more responsibility than he had ever imagined. The Judge expected Stone to become him, to act on his behalf, carrying out his wishes from beyond the grave.

"All foundations are required to file 990 tax forms with the IRS. This is how we keep track of the money and how it is allocated." Holland scanned a page with his pale eyes. "There's Project Natan, which supports the absorption of new Russian immigrants to Israel; there's Etz Haim, a group responsible for planting trees throughout Israel; the Trumpeldor House Museum; Ghetto Fighters' House Holocaust Museum; Worldwide Friends of Yad Vashem; American Friends of Hebrew University in Jerusalem; American Friends of Bar-Ilan University; there's a grant supporting American Jewish students studying a year in Israel; the American Friends of the Crown of Solomon, which has something to do with purchasing properties in Jerusalem."

Stone imagined the properties to be in Abu Dis and Ras al-Amud. The naive protesters at his father's funeral did not understand: he was not stealing land, he was buying it.

"Does it say where in Jerusalem?"

"It doesn't specify. But, Matthew, there is a slight hitch. Your father was the chair of the Eretz Fund. However, there seems to be an issue with the account I have here. I made some inquiries following your father's death and it appears the bulk of the Eretz Fund's Bank of New York account has been transferred to another account at another bank. Only a token sum remains, a few hundred thousand dollars."

"So where is the money?" Stone said.

"Your guess is as good as mine. Just know I am looking into it," Holland said, cleaning his glasses with a handkerchief. "You didn't happen to find any paperwork for another account, did you?"

Stone had the card for Chase Manhattan Bank in his pocket. The lawyer, it seemed, knew nothing of its existence. "No," Stone said, his entire body penetrated by a soothing light and warmth. His father had hidden something for him to find and he had found it. "When did the money disappear?"

Holland flipped through some papers on his desk but could not find what he was looking for. "I believe it was sometime in March."

That was when Stone had been called back to Brooklyn to tend to his father. After Stone came home, his father had never left the apartment without him, so he must have moved the money just prior to his arrival.

"The account was never closed. Money is still being fed into the account by automatic deposit, so that's why there were no red flags. Don't worry, Matthew, we will figure this out. I have contacted the Bank of New York and my understanding is the bulk of the assets have been transferred into another financial institution. They are looking into it, and I'll be sure to let you know as soon as I hear back."

Now things were starting to fit together. His father's apartment had been ransacked by someone looking for the card Stone had found in the binding of the Henry Ward Beecher book. There was nothing coincidental or random about the break-in, or about the estate dealer who had been so quick to offer up cash. Seligman had to be behind both the estate dealer and the break-in. Seligman needed the money. The Judge had indeed been talking about the property on Henry Street with his final breaths, warning him that Seligman would be after the money, but he had also been signaling for Stone to look inside the book by Henry Ward Beecher—*Everything is in the books*. Both were connected to the bank account.

Holland turned back a page and cleared his throat. "There is also the Bensonhurst Community Initiative," he said. "This initiative is an enterprise under the umbrella of the Eretz Fund, which oversees a number of small community-based projects, both local and abroad, including the Bensonhurst Initiative. The money is used to support after-school programs, sports teams, neighborhood watch, and various local projects."

Strange. His father had never lived in Bensonhurst, never so much as mentioned it. It wasn't even a Jewish neighborhood. His entire life had been about Israel and the Jewish people, not a working-class Brooklyn neighborhood.

"Where does the money come from?" he asked.

"A charitable bingo operation called Oasis Bingo. The money is granted annually to those community groups. Any of the remaining monies are unrestricted in use."

When Stone had visited the bingo hall, it was packed. It must have been raking it in. "What does that mean? Unrestricted monies."

"It means the trustees of the Eretz Fund can use the remaining money in any way they see fit."

"Is that legal?"

Holland looked over the top of his glasses and said, "If it wasn't legal do you think I would consider for one moment discussing this with you?"

"And who controls that money?" Stone said, his head swirling.

"Why, you do, in theory," Holland said. "The proceeds from bingo feed into the larger fund, the one from which the bulk has been transferred. The money can only be withdrawn by the chair, who was your father, and is now you. Zalman Seligman, as vice president and co-founder of the fund, I believe, is also a trustee and is attached to the account."

"Seligman and my father were the only people who had the power to withdraw and transfer money?" Stone said. "And now it's me and Seligman?"

"Yes, for the remaining . . ." Holland plucked a statement out of a pile of papers and read, "One hundred and twenty-three thousand dollars, and seventy-seven cents. Those funds, taking into account regularly scheduled withdrawals, would have come from the bingo hall in the last five months."

"So the Eretz Fund has been operating on its own since March?"

Holland smiled. "Listen, the power structure is somewhat complicated. Your father co-founded the Eretz Fund with both the late Avraham Grunhut and Zalman Seligman. Your father and Grunhut, who resided primarily in America, were co-presidents, with Seligman, residing in Israel, acting as vice president. That's how it went until the decease of Avraham Grunhut. After Grunhut's death, your father was the sole chair of the fund."

"And Seligman expected to become co-president?" Stone asked.

"A power-sharing troika such as this is bound to have difficulties, especially with three very driven and influential men with strong ideas as to how things should be."

"So Seligman is entitled to access the money now?"

"As a co-founder, he was one of only three people who had access to the account. But he is not, and has never been, president of the fund and, as such, could not have transferred the money without the approval of the president, your father."

Stone closed his eyes. In the absence of his father, he was now bound to Seligman for better or for worse.

"Of course, as vice president, Seligman does have access to the greatly diminished sum of money in the Bank of New York account."

Something was going on just beneath Stone's awareness. Everything that had happened since his father's death was in some way connected to a larger story. Zohar, Seligman, even Pinky, who had called him after the discovery of the break-in and dragged him half conscious to the bingo hall, were fragments of a puzzle of which Stone was only now becoming aware.

"Finally, the issue of the trust agreement," Holland said, flipping back a page.

Stone was already gripped with fatigue; his first day out in the world in nearly a week and a cruel gauntlet of rude bombshells had been dropped directly onto his head. He wanted to crawl back into bed and sleep forever.

"Wait," Stone said, "can I have a glass of water?"

Holland nodded, picked up his phone, and called to a secretary in one of the outer offices. "Okay?" Holland said. "Ready?"

Stone still didn't have the glass of water, but he was assured it was on its way.

"This is an agreement between the creator, your father, and yourself, the beneficiary. It is a standard, revocable trust agreement with one special proviso. It says here, 'the creator bequeaths a one-thousand-dollar monthly allowance to the beneficiary until the beneficiary achieves something measurable: completion of a law degree, medical degree, PhD; attainment of a full-time tenure-track lecturer position at a private or public university, excluding community college and trade school; publication of a full-length book with a reputed university or trade publisher; invention or trademarking of a product not commercial in its usage that benefits mankind; making aliyah and dwelling in Israel eight months out of each year for no fewer than three years; marriage to a woman whose lineage, through to her grandparents, is Jewish. The rest of the assets will be paid in a lump sum to the beneficiary upon meeting one or more of the preceding provisions.'"

The proviso was a repudiation of Stone's entire life. Embedded within a single paragraph was his father's disapproval not only of his mediocre academic performance but of his personal failings as well. The abhorrent sentence about marrying a woman whose lineage was Jewish through to her grandparents was something worthy of the Third Reich. Even in death, his father demanded influence over his choice of whom to love and marry. In that moment, Stone wished he had *davka* stayed in Jerusalem with Fairuza and never returned home, simply to spite his father.

"Am I supposed to feel some sort of gratitude for this?" Stone asked.

"There's more," Holland said. "'Failure to achieve any of these provisions within five years after the decease of the creator voids the trust agreement between the creator and beneficiary. All remaining assets and fiduciary concerns will be transferred into the accounts of the Eretz Fund.' That would be the Bank of New York account."

The Judge's strong hands closed around Stone's throat, his beloved school ring ice-cold against his skin. "Why is he doing this to me?" He pounded his hand on the lawyer's desk. "He's just trying to hold power over me for as long as he can."

"This is not such an unusual way to devise a residuary estate," Holland said.

"It's like I can never escape him," Stone said.

"You can walk away, Matthew. It's written into the foundation's bylaws that the foundation would default to making grants in perpetuity to the organizations we've already discussed."

"You know, I was alone with him when he died," Stone said. "I stood over him, almost in triumph, staring into his sunken face, his eyes emptied out. His domination of me had finally ended. He had instilled fear in me for so long that I was certain, now that he was gone, all the guilt feelings would fall away and I would be free. But he expects me to live my life in his image or I become nothing; is that it?"

"I don't think he expects anything anymore," Holland said. "Your father is deceased."

9 Stone was beholden to no one, living or dead. His life was his own. He was determined to destroy the bank card before his resolve had a chance to wilt. Seligman would never touch the money without him, and the thought of wounding Seligman filled Stone's belly with warmth. Standing over a storm drain outside the lawyer's office, the card held between two fingers, Stone was prepared to let it drop into the rushing darkness beneath Montague Street. But then he was characteristically overtaken with doubt and he returned to himself, thinking, why give up something that gives you power? Stone hated his father, and he hated Seligman, but the simple force of that hatred did nothing to soothe Stone's pain. He was privy to a valuable secret, and though he knew his father desired to possess him, to control his actions, Stone knew he could use the card to harm Seligman and his machinations. He tucked the card back into his wallet and made his way over to the Henry Street address he'd written on a scrap of paper at the lawyer's office.

Stone wasn't surprised to see Seligman's black SUV parked in the street in front of a three-story brownstone not far from Atlantic Avenue. The brownstone was a rich chocolate color, like many of its neighbors, but it had seen better days. The upper-floor windows were boarded up; the masonry was cracked; the facade was spattered and streaked with filthy bird lime; cooing pigeons roosted under a storm-damaged stone cornice, despite the sharp-tipped spikes intended to keep them away. The tiny front garden was littered with refuse: trash, sodden newspapers, warped wooden doors; young ailanthus trees sprouting haphazardly, giving credence to the pejorative "ghetto palm." In pristine condition, the brownstone would have been worth millions. But the place was a mess, and as Stone approached he just wanted to cry. Wasn't there anything beautiful left in the world? Brooklyn Heights had always been his favorite neighborhood in Brooklyn—with its Federal-style row houses predating the Civil War, old-money brownstones, historic churches, the promenade offering a breathtaking view of the Statue of Liberty and Lower Manhattan—and this was the property he co-owned with Zalman Seligman. He sat at the bottom of the stoop, head in hands, muttering, "This world is nothing but shit."

Some time later, he heard voices behind him; he turned to see the front door of the brownstone had swung open. Seligman said something to Moshe in Hebrew, and Moshe answered in kind, before they saw Stone slumped against the wrought-iron railing at the bottom of the steps.

"Matthew!" Seligman said. "What a pleasant surprise."

Stone stood up too quickly and found himself light-headed as Seligman greeted him with a warm hand on the shoulder. "So nice to see you. Are you feeling better?"

It was strange; Stone had wanted to lash out at Seligman, say something cruel, but now, seeing the paternal concern in his face, he wanted to collapse into his arms. But no, he wouldn't. Seligman had to tell him what he wanted, what he needed from Stone. Moshe positioned himself before the SUV, arms crossed, an empty expression behind his wild beard.

"I just came back from my father's lawyer. He read me the will."

Seligman's eyes said nothing behind his blacked-out aviator glasses, but he withdrew the toothpick from his mouth and regarded it thoughtfully before tossing it into the garden. "I'm sure you are well taken care of," Seligman said. "Your father loved you very much."

"Yeah," Stone said, gesturing to the brownstone. "This place is a shithole."

Seligman laughed. "Not the word I would use, but, certainly, the place needs some fixing up."

"So why don't you fix it?" Stone said.

"Your father and I purchased the brownstone for a song back in the seventies when Brooklyn was a war zone. We rented it out for years, and for a while Walter had an office on the third floor, away from the bustle of the courthouse. But as you can see, the place is starting to crumble. The foundations need to be reinforced, the roof leaks. I'm afraid it may be condemned by the city for destruction if we don't make the repairs soon."

"And you don't have the money to do it?" Stone said, waiting for the ask.

"Old houses can be expensive to fix. And the city inspectors always want their piece."

"Then why not just walk away? You live in Israel anyway. What good is this place to you?"

Seligman ran a large hand over his trimmed silver beard. "You don't know? I was certain your father would have told you about this. It was so important to him."

Stone didn't know what he didn't know. "Tell me and we'll see," he said.

"Oh, you would know if he told you."

Stone started to shake. It had been so awful watching his father's spirit simply disappear; he was alive, and then he wasn't. He had tried to convey something important in his ruined voice, barely a whisper, about Seligman and the property on Henry Street, but Stone couldn't understand him, could not decipher what he'd been trying to say. Since his father's death, Stone's entire path forward felt like a high wire strung above a vast and dangerous expanse, with no net waiting underneath to catch him. Was Seligman a safety net, or something else altogether?

"I don't know what he wants. But I know he wants something from me."

"Matthew, a son's obligation to his father never ends," Seligman said. "I know as well as anyone that Walter could be a sonofabitch. I knew him nearly fifty years. But I know one thing for sure, and that is he loved you more than anything."

"He told you that?"

"All the time."

Stone did not know if Seligman was telling the truth, but it felt good, regardless, to hear his father loved him. Perhaps his father had been unable to say it to Stone because of his relationship with his own father, Julius, but to Seligman, his close friend, he may have said things he had been afraid to tell his only son face to face.

"Your father's wish was to repair the house on Henry Street and turn it into a museum dedicated to American Jewish lawmakers, from Judah P. Benjamin to Louis Brandeis to Felix Frankfurter, Benjamin Cardozo, Irving Lehman, Brooklyn's own Ruth Bader Ginsburg. Sort of a hall of fame of great Jewish minds. Just imagine," Seligman said, spreading his arms wide, "the Walter Stone Museum of American Jewish Jurisprudence."

"That's what he wanted? Why didn't he just tell me?"

"Well," Seligman said, reaching into his chest pocket and producing a fresh toothpick. He jammed it between his teeth. "The monies accrued for this project come from a somewhat bizarre, but absolutely legal source. You've been to the bingo hall," Seligman paused, adjusted the toothpick. "The lawyer may have mentioned an arm of the Eretz Fund called the Bensonhurst Community Initiative? There is money allocated for specific projects in Bensonhurst itself, and then there is the rest of the money, which can be used as we see fit."

"You're talking about a slush fund?"

"Well, let's just say the Heights are a long way from Bensonhurst."

Stone looked hard into Seligman's face trying to determine what he was up to, what he really wanted. His father had been disgraced, and now Seligman wanted to erect a museum in his honor. This museum was just a cynical whitewash of the Judge's tarnished name, a harmless attempt to memorialize his father—even if it did mean obscuring some inconvenient facts. Stone thought for a long moment about the unfortunate location of his father's would-be museum; it was just a few hundred yards away from where Menachem Wuensch had run down that Arab boy on Atlantic Avenue, the event that triggered the Court Street Riot and the Judge's subsequent demise from the bench.

Seligman had to be lying. His father would most certainly want any sort of memorial as far away from Court Street as possible.

"A museum? Really?"

"Yes," Seligman said. "Your father wanted to be remembered as part of this pantheon of great Jewish lawmakers."

"And what about the Court Street Riot? I'm sure you're planning a special exhibit dedicated to that clusterfuck."

Seligman laughed, as if Stone were a small child who needed the most basic things explained to him. "Matthew, you're familiar with the existence of presidential libraries, whose goal is to promote under- standing of said presidency and to help cement that president's legacy. Of course the Richard Nixon Library mentions Watergate, but you have to understand, it is the trustees of the library who curate and shape how such information is presented. Do you really think the Kennedy Library highlights Jack's philandering, or the Gerald Ford Library chooses to show him as a bumbling fool? Of course not. These libraries are, and your father's museum will be, about taking control of the narrative, changing any lingering negative perceptions to posi- tive ones. Your father was a brilliant and important adjudicator. His museum will focus primarily on his many triumphs."

Stone had to admit there was a certain logic to this argument. The Judge's reputation had meant everything to him. But Stone couldn't figure out why his father would have moved the money.

"And of course," Seligman continued, "your father always meant to take care of you."

"What do you mean?" Stone said.

"The museum won't occupy the entire building, just the lower floors. The third floor, when renovated, will be a great place for you to live."

"I can do what I want with my half of the property," Stone said. "I might not agree to the idea of a museum."

"I'm surprised to hear that," Seligman said. "I imagined you would have been excited, not only by the prospect of honoring your father's name but also by the thought of living in Brooklyn Heights. Where exactly are you living now?"

"Isn't that money supposed to be used for the benefit of Benson-hurst and the surrounding area?"

"That's what your father was afraid of. That rebellious spirit of yours." Seligman laughed, but it was not a natural, easy laugh. "How much do you think a few Ping-Pong tables and park benches cost? There's money left over. We are not required by law to use all the money for the stated purpose. Whatever is left over at the end of each fiscal year can be redesignated. This museum was your father's wish."

"Then why wasn't it written into his will?"

"Your father may have had a king-sized ego, but he was no narcissist," Seligman said. "Let's just say, over the years, through many private conversations between me and your father, this idea evolved."

"And what do you need from me?" Stone replied.

"I want to tell you a story," Seligman said.

"About my father?"

"About a father and a son. But you'll make your own connections, I'm sure. Have you heard of Eliezer Ben-Yehuda?"

"Of course," Stone said.

"Well, there was another sonofabitch, depending, of course, on your point of view," Seligman said. "Hebrew would not be a living language in Eretz Yisrael today if it wasn't for him and his determination. But Ben-Yehuda was not much of a father, unless of course you consider his great dictionary a child, and his flesh-and-blood son a petri dish in a lab."

Seligman paused and ran his fingers over his trimmed silver beard. "You think you had it bad? You think your father was hard on you? Think about the son of the great lexicographer, Ben-Zion Ben-Yehuda, the first Zionist baby, the first child in modern history to grow up speaking only Hebrew. Can you imagine what that was like? Can you imagine speaking a language only your mother and father could understand? Remember, Hebrew had not been spoken outside the synagogue in nearly two thousand years. So Ben-Yehuda, driven by his passion to renew the language after all those centuries lost in the Diaspora, took extreme care, to the point of mania, so his son would hear, and consequently speak, only the Hebrew language. He would not let his son hear foreign languages, so where could he go? Nobody was speaking Hebrew then. He wouldn't even let his son listen to the sound of chirping birds, or the barking of dogs, or the crow of a rooster, since they, too, communicated with foreign languages. Well, it wasn't Hebrew; that was the point. One day, when Ben-Zion was still a small child, about four or five years old, his father was away and his mother, frustrated by her crying child who still would not speak, slipped into her native Russian and began to sing lullabies to the boy. Can you guess what happened?"

Stone thought of his father walking through the front door as the man and woman from the district attorney's office concluded their interview. "Ben-Yehuda came home."

"That's right. Ben-Yehuda came home early, and heard his wife, who had broken her pact to speak only Hebrew, speaking Russian to their son. Well, the shock of Ben-Yehuda's anger had several effects; one was that the boy, as if woken from a daze, spoke at last, his lips unclamped, free to speak the words that had been forced upon him; and second, well, let's just say it's not a coincidence he made his name as an adult as Ittamar Ben-Avi and not Ben-Yehuda."

"That's a terrible story," Stone said.

"Matthew, it's a beautiful story. Hebrew exists today because of that man. His son lived, he had a life, and he died, like the rest of us. His son may have been collateral damage, but Hebrew remains a living language. Now, your father did not want that to happen with you, so rather than force a life on you, he may have been more distant than he otherwise would have. Of course he wanted you to follow in his foot-steps, to be his spiritual heir, but he knew the dangers and he didn't want to dictate to you, because he knew that would ultimately push you further away. I know for a fact that he always thought you would come around eventually. Only he died too soon."

Stone thought about his father finally, finally reaching out to him when it was too late, his words lost beneath the death rattle. If only he had spoken sooner, if only.

"All right," Stone said, "tell me what my father would want."

Seligman smiled and readjusted his toothpick. "Walter controlled the Eretz Fund's account. The Bensonhurst Community Initiative fed into the same account, allowing us to apply the unused funds to support the renewal of Jewish communities in Judea and Samaria. He was here in New York, I was in Israel. It made sense. He was president, I was vice president. We were fundamentally equal partners. I've always had the passcode to access the funds and I have never had a problem."

"So why do you need me?" Stone asked, noting how Seligman had pivoted from the museum to grabbing land in the West Bank.

"Did the lawyer say anything about the money being moved?"

"No," Stone lied.

Seligman chewed on the end of his toothpick, considering his next move. Some silent impulse told Stone that his father, for whatever reason, did not want Seligman to access the money.

"You know the Bank of New York account is passcode-protected, of course, because of the large sums of money involved. You'll be needing this if you plan to continue his work." Seligman removed a piece of paper from his inside jacket pocket and unfolded it. "3548671 is the passcode to access the account. We created a new passcode after Rabbi Grunhut, may his memory be a blessing, was murdered. It was just me and your father. The passcode has never changed since. Altering the passcode would have required the approval of both me and your father." Seligman smiled and handed Stone the paper. There was the Bank of New York logo at the top of the heavy bond paper. The numbers swam before his eyes. Stone had found the Chase Manhattan Bank card in the binding of the book, but he had seen no reference to a passcode.

"Thirty-five for the year of my birth and your father's birth. Forty-eight for the establishment of the State of Israel. Sixty-seven to honor the great victory of the Six-Day War and the return at last to the biblical heartland of Judea and Samaria. And one, for the one true God."

Seligman stared hard at Stone, and Stone remembered there was a fanatic behind those aviator glasses. "You can use that passcode yourself and see that most of the money is gone."

"Where do you think it went?" Stone said.

"I wish I knew," Seligman said. "Did you find anything among your father's belongings about another bank, another account?"

So, Seligman was behind the break-in and the visit by the estate dealer. Both attempts at learning where the money had been moved had been laughably amateurish.

"No," Stone said. "I didn't find anything."

An awkward silence followed before Stone was able to say, "What do you really want?"

Seligman, taken aback, responded, "I want you to be happy."

"What is that supposed to mean?"

"I want you to stop beating yourself up over your father and get on with your life."

That sounded reasonable, but Stone didn't know what Seligman actually meant.

"Tomorrow is Rosh Hashanah, a new year, a chance for a new beginning. Forget about the bank account for now. We'll figure it out together. Why don't you come with me to shul? The gates of repentance are open wide. This is your chance to square things with your father and with God."

"I should have known," Stone said, wanting to be back in his room, surrounded by his father's books, reading, understanding where he came from and where he needed to go. The books would guide him, not some cruel abstract God who had shown up in a blazing desert two thousand years ago and had never been heard from since.

Seligman laughed. "Matthew, don't be so shocked. I'm a rabbi. You're not upset when a doctor takes your blood pressure, are you? So, I mentioned God. That's what I do. If there is no God, then how do we explain all the diverse marvels of the world? Look, I'm trying to help you out here."

"My father was always judging," Stone said. "And nothing is going to change that. It's too late now."

"Listen, there's only one true judge, and when you buried your father and the prayer *Baruch Dayan ha'emet* was recited, you were blessing the one true judge. Who was that?"

"I don't recall blessing anyone."

"Play along with me, Matthew, you're not an idiot. It's God, and he's the only one who judges. Think about that while the Book of

Judgment is open. The new year is upon us, and Yom Kippur after that. Join me at Beit Avraham on Ocean Parkway. If it's not for you, no harm done."

Then Seligman did something that surprised Stone—he embraced him, held him in his strong arms, massaging warm soothing circles at Stone's back. Feeling Seligman's solid body pressed against his, the masculine scent of Seligman's aftershave filling Stone's nose, he realized he did not remember his father ever hugging him, and he began to cry. He cried until his sinuses hurt, until his vision was blurred with tears, Seligman rocking him back and forth in his arms, humming an upbeat, wordless tune.

"It's all right, *bubee*," he said. "You've suffered a terrible loss."

"I'm worthless," Stone said, embarrassed that he hadn't even known the new account had a passcode, afraid he didn't know whether Seligman was a friend or enemy.

Seligman handed Stone a crumpled tissue from his pocket and said, "Don't be silly. You are worth more than you can possibly know."

10 Stone heard his mother laughing through the apartment's steel door. How could she laugh after what she had done to him? He pressed his ear to the door and listened for a moment. "You think it will look good?" he heard Pinky say.

"I think it will look true," his mother said. "But I'm warning you, true and good are often quite different."

Stone opened the door—it had not been locked—and stood in the entryway, regarding the disaster before him. A charcoal drawing of Pinky, sketched onto a long stretch of butcher paper, was taped to the exposed brick wall, a filterless Kool hanging from his mouth. His mother's easel and canvas were set up before it. Then Stone saw something incomprehensible, which knocked the breath out of him like a punch in the gut. His father's robe was spread on the floor beneath the canvas, spattered with drops and splotches of paint. Stone's legs went loose beneath him, as if they would buckle and give, but he managed to steady himself against the door.

"There he is," Pinky said. "The man himself."

"Hello Matthew," his mother said. Her voice was flat, flinty. Her hair was tied in a loose ponytail, her eyes black pools. She wore an old pair of jeans and a faded T. Rex T-shirt.

"Looks like she's gotten younger, while we've gotten older," Pinky said.

"Abigail Schnitzer," Stone said. "The artist at work."

"I was just waiting for you to get back, and Michael asked me to paint him," his mother said. She made some gesture with her hands that might have meant something to him if he had been in contact with her all these years, but now it only underscored how little he knew her.

"Another painting to add to your collection?"

She stood up, wiped her hands on her jeans, and said, "That's not fair."

He said nothing.

"You wouldn't come to the phone. I was worried."

"You can't come back here now and tell me you're worried about me after all this time."

"You've got to admit, you've been pretty fucked up," Pinky said.

"Michael, would you mind leaving us alone for a moment?"

"I'm out," Pinky said, beelining for the front door. "*Hasta*."

Stone had no intention of being alone with his mother. "You got paint on my father's robe."

His mother didn't seem to understand what he meant, and then, realizing what she had done, said, "Oh my God. I asked Michael for an extra sheet so I wouldn't drip paint on his floor."

"And his floor is more important than my father's robe. Look," Stone said, pointing to the corner of the living room, "there's mouse shit on his beloved floor and, over there, that's a dead roach."

"I didn't know." Her face looked old, a sour canvas left to molder. Stone wanted to see that face break into a thousand pieces. "It's acrylic paint," she said. "I'm sure I can wash most of it out."

"That was my father's robe."

"I didn't do it on purpose," his mother said. "But look at you, with his books and his robe, you've made a shrine out of his life. You think he's Mr. Clean, shiny head and all, because he was a judge."

"I don't want to hear it," Stone said, a tight ball of belligerence gathering in his belly. "You have no right to tell me what you think about my father. You forfeited that right a long time ago."

He went to his room, closed the door, and locked it. Seeing his father's books piled around him, Stone took a deep breath, the musty smell of the old pages soothing him. This was where he belonged. Everything he needed to know about the world was contained in this room.

He slipped the bank card from his wallet, held it before him and regarded it from various angles, the afternoon light glancing off the card's glossy laminate. It was a simple bank card, with the Judge's name and THE ERETZ FUND embossed beneath a string of random numerals that formed the account number. His father's legacy depended on what Stone did with this card, but he still could not determine what his father actually wanted. He did know if he satisfied his father's wishes now, he could finally be at peace. Stone repeated Seligman's passcode to himself to be sure he had it right, hoping his father had not changed it. He dialed the phone number for Chase Manhattan Bank.

The automated system asked him to punch in the account number and then, after a long pause in which the phone's earpiece was filled with easy-listening music meant to soothe, but that instead jangled Stone's nerves, a customer service representative came on the line.

"Good afternoon, Mr. Stone. My name is Julia. How can I help you today?"

Stone held the receiver to his ear, speechless, his quavering stomach twisting in terror. The bright-voiced woman at the other end of the line was speaking to his father, not to him. She had no idea she was addressing a dead man.

"Mr. Stone?"

Stone did everything he could to harness his voice in response, and managed to offer up a humble, "Yes."

"How can I help you today?"

"The balance," he said. "I'd like to know the balance."

"All right," Julia said. "I'll just have to ask you a few simple security questions."

Stone paced about the room, the receiver wedged between his shoulder and his ear. These questions would likely be basic, but Stone was not familiar with the intimate details of his father's life.

"What is the name of your paternal grandfather?"

Relieved he had been asked a question to which he knew the answer,

Stone very nearly shouted *Julius* into the mouthpiece but caught himself in time to realize he was answering for his father. He collected himself and named his great-grandfather: "Friedrich."

"Okay," Julia said. "What was the name of your favorite elementary school teacher?"

It was no secret the Judge had skipped two grades of elementary school on his way to graduating from high school at fifteen. He'd once joked he'd learned more from reading the dictionary than he had in the classroom with those nose pickers at PS 177. Stone had just unpacked his father's childhood dictionary a few days earlier, an illustrated *New Handy Webster Dictionary*. It was a battered blue hardcover with cracked and yellowed pages and a broken spine. Many of the pages were loose and out of alphabetical order. It was clear his father had loved this book.

"Webster," Stone said, "Noah Webster."

"Mr. Webster," Julia said. "Great. Last question."

Stone felt a magnificent burning in his belly as he realized how close he was to discovering whether or not the passcode was correct. His father's books were stacked in piles everywhere.

"What was the name of the first girl you kissed?"

Stone went blank, the depths of his mind silent, empty. Nothing. He could think of nothing at all and stammered, "Pardon me. Can you repeat the question?"

Julia did so, but still no name presented itself. His pulse raced and he grabbed for a pile of books, seeking anything to trigger his memory— a word, a name, a place, some sort of mnemonic clue that might dislodge a trivial fact buried deep in his subconscious. Stone plucked a thick biography entitled *Aeschylus: Father of Tragedy* off one of the piles and flipped through the pages: nothing. He scanned the pages of *The Divine Comedy* and *Doctor Faustus*, his heart thudding in his ears, but nothing came to mind. The laughter of the homeboys on the sidewalk outside his window mocked his pitiable efforts. He would never guess the right name, never access his father's account, never unravel the mystery of Walter Stone.

"Mr. Stone, are you still there?"

He told Julia, in his most imperious tone, yes he was still here and he'd be with her in a moment, someone was calling on his private line and to please hold.

"All right, Mr. Stone."

The mountain of books stacked before him was enormous, impossible, and he stared at the spines trying to decipher their meanings. The books oppressed him, tormented him. He knew all the answers were in the books, but where? His ears filled with an unbearable white noise, the static of the universe humming incoherently. The disquiet penetrating his body must have taken over, as he found himself inexplicably on the floor surrounded by hundreds of books, toppled from their majestic piles. He did not know how he'd ended up on his back beneath an avalanche of books.

The telephone was just a few feet away and he heard Julia calling out, "Mr. Stone, Mr. Stone, are you there? I'm going to hang up now."

He got to his knees and snatched the receiver. "I'm here," he said.

"Mr. Stone, if you can't answer the security question, I'm afraid—"

"I can," he said, and then noticed, fanned out before him, two translations of *Madame Bovary* and a leather-bound hardcover in the original French. The answer was clear to him now, his ears screaming her name. His mind was lucid and he was certain the first girl his father had kissed was named Emma, like Emma Bovary.

"Thank you, Mr. Stone," Julia said, her taut voice relaxing.

Stone's entire body was coated in sweat; he allowed himself to exhale fully for the first time since he had dialed the bank's phone number.

"All right," Julia said, "I'll just need the passcode and we can get the balance for you right away."

Stone's mouth was dry, his tongue like sandpaper, as he voiced the passcode Seligman had given him.

"I'm sorry, Mr. Stone, can you repeat that?"

"3548671," Stone said, but he knew it was pointless to continue. The passcode had changed. Seligman did not have the passcode. The Judge had deliberately cut him out.

"Um, that's not the correct passcode," Julia said. "Are you certain that's what you have?"

Stone apologized and said he must have written the number down elsewhere and would call back when he found it. He hung up the phone, his face burning with humiliation.

His mother was at the door. "I have the robe. I got most of the paint out. Please open up."

He had forgotten she was still in the apartment, but the sound of her pleading voice stirred in him some untapped power he had yet to exploit. He did not respond. She was out there, waiting for him. Let her wait.

"Matthew, please."

He opened the door, hand extended to receive the robe, but his mother edged her way into the room and stood before him, the robe hidden behind her back as in a child's schoolyard game. "Just give me a chance," she said. "I want to talk to you. I don't blame you for being upset with me. Just put the books down for a few minutes, okay?"

He was certain the passcode was somewhere in the books. Everything was in the books.

"I like reading," he said, wanting her to leave him alone. "That's more than I can say about you."

"Matthew, try and be civil. Just give me a chance to make good. Let's have it out right here, right now. I want to get this over with so we can move on. Now, are we going to get along or not?"

"I don't even know why you're here. We haven't seen each other in years."

"Yes," Abi said, "but I'm here now."

"I can't understand how you found me."

"A mother knows these things," Abi said.

"That sounds like bullshit to me. How did you know where to find me?"

"Matthew, come on."

"Tell me," he said. "Because it doesn't make any sense for you to just show up here. Tell me how you knew to find me here."

"Please. I'm here now. For you."

"He's gone," Stone said. "And I get you."

Was there something triumphal glittering in those dark eyes? The Judge was dead, and she was back. He had never imagined a moment such as this could be possible.

"Give me the robe," Stone said.

"Then you'll talk to me?"

She trembled with worry, her face showing a vulnerability he did not recall.

He stared at her in amazement for a moment and then uttered a quiet "Yes." She was close enough to reach out and touch. It was almost impossible to believe after all this time. She had been a good three or four inches taller than him when she left; now it was the other way around. For the first time, Stone was able to observe Abi objectively, not as a mother but as a woman. Her lips were full and pink and her thin neck was long and slender. Looking at her now, he tried to imagine how she and his father could ever have had a life together: Abi, a Barnard-educated, dark-haired beauty, and Walter, a larger-than-life compassion-less judge, thirteen years her senior. There must have been something between them at some point, but in Stone's mind they just didn't match.

She had been cut out of all his childhood photographs; they could teach him nothing about the relationship except that it had ended in bitterness and hatred. Stone knew he hated her now only because he had loved her once.

"Why did you marry him?" Stone asked, genuinely curious. He took the robe in his arms.

His voice was solicitous and Abi offered a small smile, her shoulders relaxing. "I was so young," she said. "I was just twenty-two years old, and he was so charismatic, so driven, so fully realized as a person that I thought he would show me a whole new world I'd never seen before, an adult world, a world where things mattered. I was too young to know he never wanted a friend in me; he just wanted someone to make a home with, and I was never going to be that woman. I thought I was entering history, but he never let me in. And you know what? I thank God I was never a part of that sick cult of violence and lies. I didn't have the stomach for it."

She narrowed her sharp eyes. They were black and glossy as licorice candy. "Matthew, after you were born, he and I lived separate lives. He was rarely home anyway, you know that. And still, I didn't mind because I had you, and I would take you everywhere with me. We'd go to the big library at Grand Army Plaza for story time, we'd visit the Botanic Garden and you were so curious, asking questions about everything. I remember riding to Prospect Park with you on the back of my bike, one of those old foldable one-speeds, and taking you to ride the carousel. You loved it, Matty; you would have ridden around and around all day long, and sometimes I had to bribe you to get off that horse."

"I did love it," Stone said. He hadn't been called Matty in years. "I did." He didn't want to feel anything for his mother, believing he was somehow being disloyal to himself just by hearing her out. He owed her nothing but contempt. But her voice, his mother's voice, was the same voice that had soothed him as a child. He didn't remember her voice so much as he felt it, playing on that most human part of his heart. I won't cry in front of you, he thought.

"Where did you go?" Stone said. "When you left."

"Where didn't I go?" His mother had relaxed, and now sat down cross-legged on Stone's mattress. She made space beside her, but Stone remained standing. "Sometimes I feel like the original Wandering Jewess. I was out West, in San Francisco, painted indigents in the Mission District; went to Seattle; Portland; Kansas City, if you can believe that; taught at the University of Chicago; I went up and down the East Coast as well; Washington; Philadelphia; Portland, Maine. It was lonely a lot of the time. Matthew, you might not believe this, but I hurt every day that I was not with you."

There was something disingenuous in her statement, and it enraged him like a hard slap to the face. She had been gone over half his life. She chose to leave. She left him behind and never looked back, until now. No matter how hard his mother tried to make up for all those lost years, it was too late; the damage had been done. "You were lonely? You hurt every day? What about me?"

"This isn't a zero-sum thing, there are no winners here. I know you were hurt, I know how much you struggled. Trust me, I would have done something if I could have."

"I had a breakdown. In college. It was bad," he said. "I didn't want to get out of bed, I couldn't think a straight thought. I didn't want to live. And you weren't there." He draped his father's robe over his shoulders and carefully selected his words. "Sometimes I'm afraid it's going to happen again."

"Matthew, I want to help you. It's not too late for us to start over."

"I spent a month in a psych ward. I would rather die than go back there again."

His mother was still for a long time, so long that Stone picked up a book from one of the piles and began to read the front matter. "I know," she said. "I knew."

"You what?"

"I—" She paused, measuring her words. "Every few months, for years, I would speak with your father's secretary, Marcia. She would call me when your father was out of the country or immersed in a trial, and she would tell me things about you. Not much; it was only scraps, but it was better than nothing. She stayed on working for him after he left the bench, keeping his appointments in order, taking phone calls. She called me when she learned you were in the hospital and I knew I had to see you. She told me not to go, she told me she would lose her job, she told me the Judge would know she had called me. But I didn't listen: I went anyway. I remember flying to Bradley International Airport, so desperate to see you, wanting so badly to help you get better."

"That's bullshit," Stone said. "You never came to see me."

"I did. Trust me, I did."

"You're lying because you know he's not here to call you out on your lies."

"She had worked for your father for almost twenty years. When he left the court in disgrace, she left with him. After she called me, he fired her. Did you ever hear Marcia's name mentioned again?"

"That doesn't prove anything."

"Matthew, why do you think Marcia, your father's secretary, making thirty thousand dollars a year, gave you such generous birthday presents? Didn't you ever question why? I remember them all: the Rawlings baseball glove, tickets to see the Who at Giants Stadium, a ten-speed bicycle."

"It was you?"

"Of course it was me," his mother said.

Now Stone sat down beside her on the mattress, his head a swirl of confusion, his heartbeat thumping in his inner ear. She was telling the truth. This changed everything, and nothing.

"When I got to the hospital, I ran into your father in the lobby and he gave me a look of such cruelty I thought he was going to hurt me. The way he clenched those giant fists of his I knew I'd better not get too close. His face was red, almost feverish, when he said, 'You can't be here, Abi. You're not wanted.' I told him I was there to see you, I didn't care what he said, and then he blamed me for your breakdown, blamed me for all your problems and said you had never recovered from my leaving. He said it was my fault and told me to go to hell, and I, like a coward, went back to the airport and never reached out to you again. Until now."

Stone knew she spoke the truth, but it didn't matter; she had been the coward who left, she had been vanquished, she had left him alone with the Judge.

"And you just gave up?"

"Matthew," his mother said, "I want you to come with me back to California. It's beautiful there. You can live with me, go back to school. I teach at UC Berkeley. I'm sure I can make a few calls and transfer your credits over. The semester's just begun."

"What are you talking about?" Stone said. "I don't even know you anymore. I live here, in Brooklyn."

"You've got bars on your bedroom window like a prison, for God's sake. That's not a healthy way to live. There's so much despair. Just look outside your window. Everywhere you turn there is filth, graffiti, anger. Do you want to be part of this world?" As if to punctuate her words, one of the homeboys out front shouted, "Motherfuckin' bullshit!" at one of his dice-playing friends.

"Come with me. Finish your degree. Do yourself the honor of completing what you started."

"Who needs another useless master's thesis? I'm staying in Brooklyn. My father and Zalman Seligman have a property on Henry Street in Brooklyn Heights, and I think I'm going to live there."

His mother stiffened at the mention of Seligman, and touched Stone on the shoulder. "You need to stay away from Seligman. Trust me, Matthew, he will only cause you pain."

"You're being paranoid," Stone said, feeling his stomach drop. "And I don't like it."

"Please, promise me you'll stay away from Seligman."

"You're the last person who ought to be giving me advice. I've made it this far without you."

"You have *struggled* this far without me. I'm here to help you."

"You need to leave," Stone said. "I have to get back to my reading." He stood up from the mattress and opened his bedroom door.

"Look," his mother said, following him. "I don't want to argue with you. I just want you to give me another chance. Tomorrow is Rosh Hashanah. I know you don't believe in all that, but I'm going up to Uncle Mark's in White Plains and I want you to come with me. We can stay for a few days, get to know each other again. You should be with your family. It's a new year; let's make this a new beginning, okay?"

Stone knew he had no family. His uncle was only forty-five minutes away in Westchester County, and he, too, had vanished from his life when his mother had left.

"Please, Matthew, please," she said. There was something in the way she pleaded with him that made Stone want this moment to last forever. She was the child now, his love something worth bargaining for. She threw her arms around him and held him in a tight hug. Feeling how fragile her body was, how insubstantial, Stone knew she would never be able to give him the strength and support he needed.

11

After his mother left, Stone found a bottle of vodka under the kitchen sink. He brought it back to his room, without a glass, and settled in for an evening of reading. Exhausted by the conversation with his mother, Stone did not have the stomach for his father's heavy biographies, philosophical treatises, or other dense nonfiction books. In the mood for a novel, he searched the piles until he found the Judge's copy of *Light in August*. It was bound in Moroccan leather, with gilded lettering on the cover and gold gilt on the edges of the pages. Stone opened the book, and it was clear by how it resisted that his father had never so much as looked inside. Was he rebelling even now, reading the same book Fairuza had been reading when he met her? He did not know. But the choice made sense to him, so he read. The book was unmarred, unread; it was time for him to leave his own mark. He took a mouthful of vodka straight from the bottle as he read, underlining along the way. Maybe, someday, someone would read his notations and understand where his mind had been when he read the book. He wanted to hate his mother, but he couldn't help but pity her. He was afraid if she came around again, he would throw himself into her arms and never let go. He could not let himself love her again.

Darkness had fallen and Pinky was home, booming his bass beat out in the living room. Stone had polished off nearly three-quarters of the bottle and was in no mood to be distracted from his reading. But Pinky was out there, that motherfucker. He had invited Abi into the house, and stirred up all sorts of complications in Stone's mind. Stone sat in the dark, jaws clenched, his chest heaving, simply wishing she had left him alone. Things would have been so much easier if she had never shown up. Stone was thirsty, and he padded down the hall to the kitchen sink. Pinky danced shirtless in the middle of the living room, eyes closed, a blissful look on his face.

Stone found the volume dial and turned it all the way down.

"What the fuck?" Pinky said.

"Why did you let her in?"

"My apartment. I do what I want. I'm having a party tonight, and if you don't like that, you can leave."

Stone's temples pounded. He wished he had something to throw up.

"I just want to be alone."

"Then be my guest," Pinky said. "But you'd better do it somewhere else."

"It's Rosh Hashanah, dammit," Stone said.

"Good for Rosh Hashanah."

Stone dressed himself, grabbed the car keys and a small pile of books, and headed out the door. He knew he looked like shit sitting in the driver's seat of the Thunderbird, the entire world bent and refracted by the cheap vodka, as if he were inside of a fishbowl. When he went to examine himself in the rearview mirror, he remembered he had thrown it out the window. He stumbled out of the car and regarded his gaunt face in the side-view mirror. His eyes were bloodshot, his tongue a pale whitish hue. Stone leaned against the cool glossy hull of the Thunderbird, looking up into the dark sky. There were stars up there somewhere, but he saw nothing but the electric glow of the city reflected back at him. He lay back on the hood of the car, and there was the dent in the hood. It was a real, tangible hollow in the steel, not a creation of his broken mind. Pinky was an idiot who couldn't tell a penguin from a pigeon. They were all just fucking birds to him. How could he have missed this? Stone eased his body into the concave dip formed in the steel hood. The depression was shallow but broad, deep enough to collect pooled rainwater in the scooped-out curve of its shores. It wasn't awful to look at, but it bothered him that something like this could happen to his father's car so soon after he had taken possession of it as his own.

Stone must have drifted off, because he was suddenly aware he had been sprayed by a passing insecticide truck tasked to eradicate West Nile Virus in the city. He didn't know if the poison he had breathed in was Scourge, Anvil, or Malathion, but his throat burned, and he threw up into the street. A pair of miscreant kids applauded his performance from a nearby apartment window.

He drove seven or eight blocks before he realized if he didn't lie down now, he was going to pass out. The night was horrible; he was woken by hacking poisonous coughs every time he managed to drift off.

IT WAS MORNING, the day was well underway, and Stone had no idea where he was. One of the books he had used as a pillow as he tried to sleep stretched across the front seats of the Thunderbird was one of his father's prayer books. It was thick and had been comfortable beneath Stone's head, making it a fair pillow for a rough night. He picked it up as a German shepherd urinated on a hydrant beside the car, and he read the book's title. It was called *Days of Awe: A High Holidays Prayer Book*. Stone had had no intention of joining Seligman at synagogue, but his mother had commanded him to stay away from Seligman. That made him want to disobey her wishes, simply out of childish spite.

There was no going back to Pinky's place right now. The apartment would be a war zone of empty bottles and pizza boxes and strewn bodies. He started the car and drove toward Ocean Parkway and Avenue X.

The synagogue was a large, redbrick, square building, several stories high, adorned with golden-hued Hebrew and English letters: CONGREGATION BEIT AVRAHAM, FOUNDED 1920. The building was set back from Ocean Parkway, separated from it by a small service road on which cars were parked and children played. Small groups of men and their wives gathered in the warm sunshine. Stone faltered across the street. Most of the men were dressed in black. Some were dressed in white. He wound his way through them as he would a bed of tombstones, careful not to touch any of the gathered crowd as he passed.

He was not surprised to see Seligman, wearing his ever-present aviator glasses, holding court before a group of younger men who wore knitted kippas on their heads, the young men eagerly listening to his words. Stone walked toward him, feeling the full weight of his hangover pressing down on his head.

Seligman saw Stone approaching, smiled, and waved him over as if he had been expecting him. "You're just in time, *bubee*."

Why was his belly flushed with warmth every time Seligman called him that? It was familiar, friendly, intimate, and he wanted to hear it again.

The sun was so bright that Stone, his eyes narrowed to slits, saw a halo-like glow emanating from Seligman. His gold wedding band caught a flash of sun.

"Glad you made it," Seligman added, pulling Stone into an embrace. Once again Stone was aware of Seligman's awesome power, as if he could crush him if he so desired. He smelled like fresh laundry and the vital beginnings of perspiration. "Since it's a holy day, I assume you walked." He smiled. "I'm just kidding. I know you drove your father's trusty old warhorse."

Stone was silent, his mouth coated in a thick pasty film.

"You know, many consider Rosh Hashanah to be the anniversary of the creation of the world. Not just that, but a chance to start over . . ."

The idea of starting over, being born anew, was very appealing to Stone at that moment.

"*L'shanah tovah tikatevu*, Rabbi Seligman." A young yeshiva student pumped Seligman's hand and turned to Stone.

"This is Matthew Stone," Seligman said.

"The Judge's son?" the student said, wide-eyed. "What a terrible loss. I'm honored to meet you," he said, shaking Stone's hand. "Be inscribed in the Book of Life for a good year."

"Same to you," Stone said. The student walked away and was

immediately replaced by three other yeshiva students wishing Seligman well. Two were very thin and one was very fat. All of them wore knitted kippas and were dressed in identical black suits with white shirts. Stone looked down at his wrinkled pants and was glad that at least he wasn't wearing jeans.

"*Shanah tovah*," the first one said to Seligman. "Welcome back to galut."

"Next year in Jerusalem," another student said, laughing. "Or *Gan Eden*."

The third student added, "*Baruch Hashem*," and they all laughed again.

There was something familiar about these faces; perhaps he had seen them at his father's funeral. Then another thought occurred to him, that perhaps one or more of them had broken into his father's apartment in search of the bank details. Seligman needed the money and these boys surely would do his bidding. What was he doing here? He stepped outside of the circle, feeling faint, a chemical taste in his mouth, but Seligman's firm hand squeezed Stone's shoulder.

"Stay with me."

Seligman whispered something into the ear of one of the students, a final word at the end of an embrace.

"No problem," the boy said as he removed his suit jacket and handed it to Seligman.

The student said "*Shanah tovah*" again and bounded off to meet his friends.

"Put it on, Matthew," Seligman said. "It's a perfect fit."

Stone tried to refuse, but Seligman would have none of it. He slipped into the jacket, wishing he had planned better. But he was here now, and, strangely comforted by Seligman, he allowed him to guide him toward the stairs leading into the synagogue. "We'll talk more later," Seligman whispered in Stone's ear. "The service is starting."

The sanctuary was larger than Stone had expected it to be, with a balcony on three sides where the women sat. The ceiling was very high, scooped out like the dome of the sky. Light shone in from small windows and filtered down onto the front rows with a distilled radiance that Stone understood to be appropriate for a holy place. This was no place to be hungover. Seligman led Stone down the center aisle to a reserved seat near the front, just to the right of the bima and the ark, both of which were covered with a pure white fabric. Hundreds of voices buzzed in Stone's ears all at once. Something in his mind wanted to tease apart each of the separate speakers' words and file them into their proper places, but he found himself feeling nauseated, and he focused on his breathing to tune out the disarrayed sounds.

"Here's your machzor," Seligman said, handing Stone a thick prayer book. "There is an English translation on the left."

"Am I supposed to be wearing . . . ?" Stone indicated Seligman's prayer shawl. Most of the men around them wore long flowing prayer shawls over their shoulders.

"Are you married?"

"No."

"Then, no." Seligman chucked him softly on the shoulder as if to say, "One day."

The rabbi appeared before them, followed by the cantor, both dressed in white. The cantor began to sing in Hebrew and the congregation rose, Stone a second behind the crowd, his hangover slowing him.

"Just follow along," Seligman said, pointing to the place in the prayer book. The Hebrew lettering on the right side of the page looked like the blackened bones of the dead.

He thought of the pigeons lightly singing beneath the eaves of the apartment's roof and thought, their prayers have as much strength as these. Seligman sang along in a firm voice, his Adam's apple jumping in his throat. What did he see that Stone was missing? He was an intelligent, educated man, but he believed so fervently in the legend of God. The prayer ended, and Stone was about to sit back down when the congregation began singing again. This went on for more than twenty minutes, the congregants alternately standing, sitting, standing again. He just wanted to sit in a comfortable chair, and close his eyes, and wake with a clear head. Stone swayed with exhaustion, and as he did so he noticed the men of the congregation also swayed back and forth in their prayers.

Seligman, too, swayed seductively, eyes closed, his lips speaking the ages-old prayers. Powerful Seligman, a supplicant, burning with an obsessive flame, all his intelligence and knowledge turned inward, all his energy directed toward an absent God. This was more alien to Stone than anything he had encountered in all his years at school. His mind had been trained in the art of reason, conquering the unknowable, Stone's cynicism penetrating any lie. He knew God was a construct, created by man to explain the manifold mysteries of the universe, a character out of an ancient book read into existence by sheer repetition.

Seligman leaned in close to Stone and whispered, "You may want to join in." He pointed to the page in the prayer book. "You are in mourning, aren't you?" The whispering in his ear was such an intimate gesture, he could not ignore Seligman's words.

The Kaddish, the age-old prayer of sanctification, lay on the page in its strangely rhythmic transliteration. Seligman had told him it was his duty to say Kaddish for his father and he had been resistant, but now, with his father's friend standing next to him, it would be rude to ignore his wish. Perhaps it was Stone's blinding headache or his exhaustion, but the italicized words were frayed at the edges—blurry, impossible to read, like an ancient tablet rubbed out by the sands of time.

"I can't," Stone said.

The voices rose again in song. This time the reverberation hummed off the walls and domed ceiling, running up and down his spine like a chill.

"*Avinu Malkeinu.*" Seligman pointed to the left side of the page.

"Our Father, our King," Stone read, recognizing the tune. He read the words and saw the contradictions of an accepting father, a loving father and a stern, unforgiving father. He thought of the Judge and his cruel, unblinking blue eyes as he lay on his deathbed. Why hadn't his father told him what he expected?

Seligman continued to sing along. His voice robust and full, he leaned close, singing the simple chorus, his mouth articulating, insisting Stone join in. Stone sang out tentatively, as the prayer came to an end, "Our Father, our King, hear our voices!"

A moment later, the worshippers stood again—this time, though, buzzing in expectation as the Torah scroll was taken down from the ark. For the first time, Stone noticed the flickering red eternal light burning above the ark, winking at him like an ever-seeing eye. The rabbi made his rounds, up and down the aisles with the Torah hefted high onto his shoulders. Men reached out with their prayer books, kissed them, and touched them to the passing Torah. The Torah reached Stone, and Seligman touched his prayer shawl to it.

"This is the Torah portion," Seligman said. "Follow the story in English," he added, sounding to Stone like an old teacher easing his student into work. Several men were called up to the bima to join in with the reading. The first man's voice was high and nasal, and his Hebrew sharp and jagged, in contrast to the flowing voice of the cantor.

Stone read ahead—of the birth of Isaac to the aged Sarah and Abraham and of the exile of his half brother Ishmael. The story fascinated him as he read on about God calling out to Abraham, demanding he sacrifice his son. And the fanatic Abraham, who had circumcised himself at the age of ninety-nine, unquestioningly accepting God's request, taking his beloved son to the land of Moriah to sacrifice him. As Stone read, he imagined young Isaac bound on the altar, and the humiliation and fear and worthlessness he must have experienced in the deepest part of his being when he asked his father, "Where is the lamb?" And Abraham lied; he told his son God would provide a lamb just as he unsheathed a knife and pressed the blade to his son's throat. Then the angel of the Lord called out of heaven to Abraham, "Lay not thy hand upon the boy . . . for now I know thou art a God-fearing man."

Stone imagined Isaac's permanent anxiety, distrust, and guilt, his feelings of failure and disgrace before his awesome father, bound on the altar beneath the devastating blade. Stone finally understood why the Jews, descended from the patriarch Isaac, were such a neurotic people. They were born from this frightening act of faith, a psychological wrecking ball echoing through the millennia.

Seligman cleared his throat and coughed, and Stone saw dust motes descending on the shafts of sunlight. A sorrowful moan escaped from the center of the sanctuary. A dark-bearded man, prayer shawl casually draped over his head, raised a twisted ram's horn in the air, his hand halfway up the shining shaft, as he blew three notes followed quickly by shorter staccato blasts. There was something primal and timeless in these cries, and Stone's blood stirred, his heartbeat quickened. He wanted to cry out, he wanted to run, he wanted to close his eyes and drink in every sound. The blast of the shofar was both beautiful and horrifying.

"Got your attention," Seligman whispered. Stone nodded his head in assent. "It's your wake-up call," Seligman added as the last long note sounded, filling the sanctuary with its mournful cry.

The Torah was returned to the ark, and the rabbi stepped up to the bima to give his sermon. His voice sounded so different in English than it had in Hebrew; Stone had to look twice to make sure it was the same person speaking. The rabbi's accent had a strong local flavor.

"Last Rosh Hashanah, I spoke about the murder of Moshe and Devorah Blickstein and their infant Rifka, former congregants who were gunned down as they drove from their home in Giv'at Barzel toward Jerusalem to celebrate the new year. Their first yahrzeit passed this week—and was marked in Israel by stone throwing, a stabbing, and an attempted suicide bombing perpetrated by their 'neighbors,' strangers in the land of Israel, descendents of the Canaanites who cry 'occupation' while plotting to push the Jews into the sea. I said last year we would not stand silent on the graves of fellow Jews. I said we were on the threshold of redemption and the new Kingdom of Israel. And we have not stood silent. The reclamation of the land of Judea, Samaria, and Jerusalem has continued. Fourteen new communities have been established. The outpost community of Rifkia, commanding the hilltop above the spot where the Blicksteins were killed, is a living testament and an affirmation we will not stand silent when Jewish blood is shed."

The rabbi's words were typical of the oratory red meat tossed out
to the right wing who believed God had bequeathed the entire land
of Israel to the Jews. This was the sort of speech Stone had loathed as
a child when his father had taken him to see fist-pounding lectures in
synagogue basements with absurd titles like "Ishmael in Eretz Yisrael"
and "Enemies in Our Midst." But Stone had known Moe Blickstein,
had gone to elementary school with him. He remembered hearing
years later that Blickstein was moving to Israel, seeing his picture in
a local paper. What did anyone care whether Moe Blickstein, whose
ill-timed jokes made him a laughing stock in the schoolyard, moved
to Israel? Now he was dead. Now he was a martyr and Stone saw the
worshippers wiping tears from their cloudy eyes.

"Looking back through the prism of time," Rabbi Heimlich continued, "we see that Jews have always been abundant upon the land.
God promised the land to Abraham and to his descendents, and
promised they would be as plentiful as the stars in heaven. It was
the Almighty who chose, from all the nations, the Jews as his chosen
people—and in return for observing his laws and statutes as given at
Mount Sinai, we were given Eretz Yisrael, decreed Eretz Yisrael as
our home in perpetuity. Today we stand on the threshold of redemption as Hellenists and socialists and every other kind of abomination,
including the sons of Ishmael, sit in the seat of government in Jerusalem negotiating so-called peace accords, engaging in a so-called
process to return the land to our sworn historical enemy. They come
under many names: the Amorites, the Canaanites, the Hittites, the
Jebusites, the Philistines, and, now, the Palestinians, though it is a
known fact the so-called Palestinian people is a fiction created in the
second half of this century by politicians, revolutionaries, and murderers. The sages said, 'Great is peace, for God's name is peace.' But
what kind of peace is contingent upon the wholesale destruction of
the land of Israel? We will not stand silent upon the graves of Jews
murdered for living on their land. The so-called government sitting
in the Knesset in Jerusalem is bankrupt, foggy-headed, and a danger
to the future of Israel. The prime minister says peace is at hand as
terrorists blow up our children in the streets. The prime minister says

there will be a Palestinian state while their children learn hatred in their schools and their clerics preach hate from the loudspeakers of their mosques. The prime minister turns a deaf ear to the murderous mantra, 'With blood and spirit we shall redeem you, Palestine.' Their fantasy maps of a future state cover all the land of Israel, from Metulla to Eilat. This peace is Chamberlain's 'peace in our time.' This is not peace. This is suicide."

Stone had once believed peace was at hand and his time with Fairuza was the dawn of a new era of happiness and pleasure. They had shopped together in the open markets of West Bank towns, had hiked through the rough hills, barren as a distant moonscape, had made out in the darkness behind the gnarled branches of olive trees; they had even talked about taking a trip to visit Beirut and Damascus. Anything was possible. Even the haunting call of the muezzin was beautiful to Stone, something quaint and historic and entirely harmless. But then the suicide bombings came one after the other, killing and maiming innocent civilians on buses, in the market, at discotheques. With each sickening tally of casualties, Stone believed it was just a small minority set on scuttling the peace process. He had been wrong.

"It seems in the face of this bitter reality to be so simple, logical— our universal right to defend ourselves against our enemy who has sworn our destruction. It is written in Deuteronomy, 'When you go forth against your enemies—confront them as enemies. Just as they show you no mercy, you show them no mercy.' Strangely, through the looking glass of modern Israel, we are considered zealots, villains, bent on bloodshed and destruction, though our ethical foundations are built upon the word of God and his commandments. We agree: to kill innocent people is evil, though sometimes we must kill to protect our land. Our enemies kill innocent people in the name and service of some dark god. It is written in Isaiah, 'Woe unto them that call evil good, and good evil.' We will not stand silent upon the graves of Jews as the secular government of Jerusalem fans the flames of our ene-mies' hatred, showing eagerness and weakness, willing to make peace at any cost the way a schoolchild bribes a bully with his milk money. As we all know, too painfully, he always comes back for more. We must speak out. We must act. We are on the threshold of redemption. The Temple of Israel is poised in the heavens, waiting to descend. The Kingdom of Israel lies before us, this Rosh Hashanah, as we mark the first yahrzeit of the martyred Blickstein family."

Blickstein and his family had been martyred because they believed in something, and they had died on soil rich with history and meaning and import. Stone knew for certain now if he had taken that final step into the void and jumped off Pinky's roof, he would not have been celebrated or honored in any way; he would have died for nothing. Sometimes the pain of going on was too much to bear, but the thought of lying for eternity in a potter's field, anonymous on Hart Island with all the other refuse—the city's stillborns, criminals, and John Does— made Stone realize his father, the Creator, was right to insist in his will that Stone, the Beneficiary, must achieve something measurable before he was free to close his eyes forever.

Rabbi Heimlich went on, "As Jews, we must continue steadfastly to honor God's commandments and covenants. Every Rosh Hashanah, as self-reflection, penitence, teshuvah fill our very souls, we read of the story of the Binding of Isaac, the *Akeda*, a story which tells of our father, Abraham, and his willingness to sacrifice his beloved son, Isaac. It was Abraham's act of faith, over five thousand years ago, that bound the Jewish people forever to God and God to the Jewish people. The Lord said, 'Because thou hast not withheld thy son, thine only son, in blessing I will bless thee.' Today, in a reversal of that act of faith, the secular government is sacrificing Jewish children upon the altar of peace, and in return for that sacrifice, giving away land God granted us to bloody-handed murderers. There are nabobs and naysayers who claim we do not want peace—that we want to live behind our fences and walls in a perpetual never-ending garrison state. That could not be farther from the truth. We want peace. It is the Arab who does not want peace. So we must stand strong in the face of our enemies. It is our duty and obligation to history to fight those who seek our destruction. We have a blood tie to the land and cannot give up one grain of sand, one blade of grass, as we stand on the threshold of redemption. The secular government seeks instant redemption in the eyes of the world, like an unpopular child giving away its toys in return for friendship. But this sort of capitulation will ultimately bring tragedy and death not seen since the darkest days of Auschwitz and Majdanek and Treblinka. Instant peace is an illusion, a mirage shimmering on the desert sands. True peace and true redemption will come only with teshuvah—penitence—a return to God and his commandments. Rosh Hashanah is a day of judgment, and God will look back on our deeds of the past year, at those who have misbehaved and those who have lived by his commandments. And he will decide who will be inscribed in the Book of Life for another year and who will be burned into the Book of Death. A year ago, it was the secular government who condemned the young Blickstein family, righteous Jews just twenty-six years old, living on our God-given land, to the Book of Death. We must live by our swords even as we pray for peace. It is our duty to do all we can to ensure Jews can live in peace and safety in Eretz Yisrael and continue to populate the land and flourish as we have since the days of the Patriarchs. This is the time of year to ask God for forgiveness, to atone for sins of the past, and to look toward a bright shining future in which all Jews will live in peace in the Kingdom of Israel."

The rabbi's booming sermon ended and the congregants slipped quickly into another prayer. Seligman looked at Stone and smiled. Repeating the liturgy had been a challenge for Stone, the words sticking in his throat, but the sermon hit Stone like a hammer. It wasn't so much that he believed the content of Rabbi Heimlich's sermon, but Stone had long suspected being dead got you farther in life than being alive. Moe Blickstein had died because he had lived on disputed land in a violent part of the world, invisible ley lines pulsing a mystic energy beneath his feet. Blickstein's death was tied to a long litany of historic tragedy reaching back thousands of years; he had become part of the continuum, part of the long Jewish narrative of heroism in the face of tragedy.

The sanctuary was quiet, the congregants lost in silent meditation. The streaming shafts of light were too bright for Stone and he closed his eyes. The murdered Moe Blickstein appeared before him—his bearded face broken, shattered by gunmen's bullets, his skin grayish-green, his eyes a cold silver. His jaw was thick, his cracked lips purple. He was trying to speak out but was unable. "What is it?" Stone asked as a pale grave worm slithered from Moe Blickstein's nostril. "What's in your mouth?" Moe Blickstein coughed and vomited out dirt and dust and sand and said, "The land of Israel." Stone heard a man fart several rows back, breaking the stillness of the sanctuary. A cold rivulet of sweat dripped down his arm. So that was what martyrdom looked like? There was nothing beautiful or romantic in his death—death is always ugly no matter how it is dressed up. Stone wanted to ask Blickstein if it was worth it to trade his one life for admiration, but he had disappeared. To his right, Seligman prayed, eyes closed, oblivious. Stone wanted to reach out, touch him, feel the warmth of another person, clear his mind of the awful vision. He closed his eyes again, but this time the darkness was golden, suffused with sunlight.

Seligman leaned close to Stone and whispered, "Pay attention to this one. It's an ancient poem by Rabbi Amnon of Mainz. This is the big prayer. It's magnificent."

The congregation took up a plaintive singsong and Stone followed along in his machzor.

The words immediately frightened Stone, speaking directly to him as no other words had before—apocalyptic, cruel, and violent. The eerie chanting and rhythm sounded like a judgment upon him alone. Stone's father appeared radiant before him, wearing an immaculate white robe. He sat high above, his shining gavel held aloft in the air. His hard eyes were implacable, unforgiving, chastising his son for not following his commandments. And from his heavenly bench, he pronounced with terrifying clarity:

How many shall pass away and how many shall be born,
Who shall live and who shall die,
Who shall reach the end of his days and who shall not,
Who shall perish by water and who by fire,
Who by sword and who by wild beast,
Who by famine and who by thirst,

Who by earthquake and who by plague,
Who by strangulation and who by stoning,
Who shall have rest and who shall wander,
Who shall be at peace and who shall be pursued,
Who shall be at rest and who shall be tormented,
Who shall be exalted and who shall be humbled,
Who shall become rich and who shall suffer penury,
But repentance, prayer, and righteousness avert the severe decree.

As Stone stared at the machzor before him, he realized he was guilty and would have to pay. He knew it the same way certain animals could tell bad weather was approaching; not precisely a sixth sense, but a sharpening of an existing sense, the way a falling barometric pressure plays on one's sinuses, on one's bones.

Seligman leaned close and spoke softly into Stone's ear. "Are you all right?"

"I've made so many mistakes."

"We all have," Seligman said. "That is the beauty of a new beginning. The *Unetanah Tokef* can be quite powerful." Acid crept up Stone's raw, swollen throat as if a hand were reaching up and out of his belly. He sat down in a chilled sweat and remained sitting through the reprise of *Avinu Malkeinu* and the Mourner's Kaddish.

The blast of the shofar roused Stone, and the room was alive with shifting bodies and the voice of a man calling out the order of the shofar blasts: "*Tekiah, teruah-shevarim, tekiah . . .*"

Afterward, out in the street, in the sunshine, strangers, people he had never seen before, wished Stone well, wished him "*Shanah tovah*," and their eyes were kind and sincere and made him realize he was being accepted because he was a Jew and he was not alone.

He sat on a low brick wall, neck bent, head between his knees, marveling how his father, even now, had the power to pass judgment on him. He was haunted by the service. Even in death the Judge was invincible; freed from his corporeal body, he had the power to paralyze Stone, suffocate him, destroy him. The world was uncertain in so many ways, but Stone knew his father, his very own creator who still whispered in his blood, transmitting his dismay from beyond, would remain a part of him forever. Stone had turned away from his father to explore the world on his own and had failed again and again. He had ignored the ruthless call of his blood for too long, and it had cost him his health, his vitality, and his desire to live. Now it was time to answer that call.

Seligman greeted the congregants lined up to get a word with him. The nature of his celebrity eluded Stone as he watched the tributes and praise unfold before his eyes.

"Rav Seligman, we're so honored. Thank you for blessing us with your presence."

"You are a great and wise man."

"It is such a pleasure to have an esteemed prophet in our midst on this most special of special days."

They would kiss his cheek or shake his hand. He conferred privately with each one, whispering intimate wisdom into their ears.

"Matthew," Seligman said, approaching after a few minutes, "are you all right?"

"Headache," Stone said to the pavement below. He was parched with thirst and just wanted to crawl into a hole somewhere.

Seligman sat on the wall beside Stone. "It's an intense service. It can be difficult to face. Reflective. A time to look back on our lives and make changes." He paused and then said, "Like a New Year's resolution."

"I don't know," Stone said, raising his head. "I don't feel well."

Seligman smiled broadly. "And whose fault is that? Did God tell you to go drinking all night long? You smell like a Bowery bum. You've got a hangover for the ages," he added, ruffling Stone's hair with his rough hand. "That's what people do in the secular world, a world with no sense of proper values. Do you want to live like the goyim, drinking and rutting like a beast? I understand you've lost your father, but you are not alone in the world. We can help you."

Stone said nothing, doubting every thought he had ever held.

"There are means built right into your own culture to help you release the pressure stored up inside. Why do you think the Jews have survived so long?" Seligman paused as a fire engine raced down Ocean Parkway. "Your father was very proud of you. It wasn't easy for Walter, Matthew. You were his only son. He loved you, you have to know that."

Stone wanted to believe him but he could not erase his certainty that his father hated him.

"You can trust me, Matthew. Your father and I were as close as brothers. He spoke about you all the time. He had such hopes."

"And I disappointed him."

Seligman stood up, straightened his suit, and said, "No, no, not at all. Come on. Let's go to lunch. We're going to be late."

Stone begged off and said he needed a shower and a nap.

"Come to lunch, kid, you can sleep when you're dead. You'll wash your face in the sink. The walk will do you good."

Seligman handed Stone a breath mint, and he looked at it doubtfully.

"Maimonides says it is a mitzvah to celebrate and eat together."

"I'm not hungry."

"Eat, don't eat. But come to lunch and be among your people, your family. You'll see that you never have to be alone in the world."

12

Seligman hummed under his breath as he and Stone strode west on Ocean Parkway beneath a bright September sun. He took long, vigorous strides that forced Stone to push himself to keep up. Stone had been a cloistered hermit for much of the past week, and he sensed himself awakening, his blood racing through his veins, cycling out the poisons of the night before and replacing them with the fresh rush of oxygen.

The prayers had, much to Stone's surprise, worked their mysterious rhythms and eternal cadences into his mind so that he felt chastised, not just by his father but by the entire history of the Jewish people. He'd known, as he stood in communal congress with hundreds of others in the sanctuary, buffeted by thousands of years of tradition, that this moment provided a genuine chance to start over, to construct a new beginning, to square things at last with his father. Seligman could be the vehicle to take him where he needed to go.

"You said my father wanted the museum built in his honor," Stone said, catching up to Seligman, "but I'm a little bit confused. You mentioned Judea and Samaria and how the money would be used to build those communities."

Seligman slowed, a soft smile coming to his face. "That is one of the key dictates of the Eretz Fund."

"Assuming I'm able to track down the money, and I agree to using a portion of it to build the museum, I don't think I can support West Bank settlements."

Seligman laughed. "These are your father's wishes. It's the mission of the fund. This isn't some à la carte restaurant where you pick and choose which wishes you honor and which you won't. That's not the way this works."

"But West Bank settlements are illegal. The settlers are stealing land that doesn't belong to them."

Seligman laughed again, but he was not impressed. "Look at the inflammatory language you're using, Matthew: *settlers, illegal, stealing*. You're using the words every Jew hater wants you to use to delegitimize our God-given right to Judea and Samaria . . ."

Stone tried to interject, but Seligman waved a hand close enough to Stone's face that he was afraid Seligman might clap his palm over his mouth so he could be heard.

". . . which were biblical provinces in the Kingdom of Israel. Jews had lived peacefully in Hebron, side by side with their Arab neighbors, for hundreds upon hundreds of years until they were massacred by Arab rioters in 1929. Synagogues were ransacked, women and children murdered, and that was the end of the Jewish community in Hebron, until, that is, your father and I helped facilitate the renewal in the years after the Six-Day War. I'll bet you didn't know that."

Stone was silent. He did not know Jews had ever lived peaceably with their Arab neighbors. He had assumed there had always been open hostility.

"I know as an aspiring liberal academic you believe you are questioning everything, but you are just spewing out lies perpetrated by the media and the academy. The truth is entirely different. Israel is a tiny country, roughly the size of New Jersey, the fifth smallest state in the union. Do you know how much it costs to buy an apartment in Tel Aviv, or Yerushalayim, or any of the major population centers in Israel? Let me tell you, the price is prohibitive. Most of the Jews who live in Judea and Samaria are ordinary working people who just want a better life for themselves and their families. They're not a bunch of gun-toting Wild West outlaws. They're people."

They walked along in silence, Stone absorbing Seligman's words. He imagined what would happen if he tried to rent an apartment in Manhattan or the Bronx and was told it was illegal for Jews to live there. The whole idea was absurd, impossible. The more Stone thought about it, the more he realized it was indeed strange that of all places in the world, the biblical heartland of the Jewish people should be *Judenrein*, free of Jews.

"What do you think happened to the account?" Stone asked. "Don't you think it's weird all that money just disappeared?" Stone wanted to know Seligman's thinking behind this, how he would explain his father transferring the money and leaving him in the cold.

"Matthew, I know it might not seem fair to ask you to jump into the middle of all this while you're still in mourning, but there are very important projects depending upon this money, projects your father signed off on long ago. The sooner we have access to those funds, the better."

"But why do you think my father moved the money? So I couldn't touch it?"

"No," Seligman said, "of course not. He never once doubted you would succeed him."

Seligman slowed to a stop and placed his hand on Stone's shoulder. "I believe your father thought his life might have been in danger."

"What do you mean?" Stone said.

"I don't want to upset you," Seligman said, starting off down the sidewalk again.

"Tell me," Stone said, catching up. "Tell me."

"Listen, Matthew," Seligman said, "you know your father was never the same after he resigned from the bench. He withdrew into his books, mistrustful, even afraid of the world outside. He believed the Arab dog who killed our friend Rabbi Grunhut, may the memory of the righteous be a blessing, could have just as easily killed him. Maybe he thought letting go would somehow protect him against the assassin's bullets, turn them elsewhere."

"But my father was already dying."

"Your father was ill, but he was never going to die of cancer. He believed he was going to live to a hundred and twenty."

That was why he had never told Stone his wishes, why he looked almost surprised when he realized his life was draining away and there was nothing his giant intellect and iron determination could do to reverse the inescapable fact of death.

"Listen," Seligman said, "if you find out anything about the account, please tell me as soon as you do. Some of these slated projects are very controversial, and a lot of people aren't happy about Jews developing their own holy city. Whoever controls that account could be at risk. I want to help you, Matthew. I want to make sure you're safe from harm."

The Rosh Hashanah meal was already underway when Seligman and Stone arrived at a white brick house just off one of the lettered avenues bisecting Ocean Parkway. They entered to much fanfare, a surprising mood of levity.

"Finally, Zalman arrives!" a bearded man at the head of the long luncheon table called out. "We were placing bets about who would arrive first—you, or the Messiah."

"You know," Seligman said, "the Messiah will only come when Jerusalem is a Jewish city again."

"Meanwhile, we eat," the man said, laughing.

The Judge, not a mystic by any stretch of the imagination, had held feelings similar to those of Seligman. His father's friend, former mayor of Jerusalem Teddy Kollek, had written in one of his books, to the Judge's enthusiastic underscored approval: "Take Saudi Arabia. They have Mecca, Medina to build their capital there. . . . The Jordanians had Jerusalem, but they built a capital in Amman, not Jerusalem."

Seligman was not his father, but now that Stone had been immersed in his father's books, sifting through the words he had read, panning for gold, he realized Seligman echoed a frightening number of his father's thoughts and beliefs. Somehow, he imagined he could please his father through Seligman. Even the nagging distrust he held toward Seligman reminded him so much of the way he had reacted to his father that he decided going forward he would hear out Seligman before reflexively rejecting him.

A ceiling fan rattled above the long dining room table. The table was covered with an off-white lace cloth, wine-stained here and there with pinkish glyphs and splotches. A wooden hutch stood to one side of the table, piled high with plates, saucers, and teacups. A honey cake sprinkled with confectioner's sugar and several other desserts languished in the sunlight and the light breeze of the dining room's only window. About fifteen people of all ages sat around the long table, eating chicken and brisket, noodle kugel and cucumber salad, tzimmes and candied yams—the sort of standard holiday fare Stone had not seen in years. A glazed round challah sat at each end of the table beside small pots of honey and fans of sliced apple.

"Take a seat. Eat! Eat," an older woman seated next to the bearded man said.

"I want to introduce you all to Matthew Stone," Seligman said. "He's family."

"Is this Walter's kid?" the man said, chewing a mouthful of brisket.

Stone smiled and nodded, his entire body warming. He had always known words could be seductive, but rarely had the power of language so plainly played on his emotions. Perhaps he had been primed by the intensity of the service, or his days of solitude, or his state of mourning and loss, but he was aware now he was under the sway of something he had not known he desired.

"Truth?" the man said, sizing up Stone.

Seligman nodded. "Matthew is quite the scholar himself."

"You don't say. Walter's son," the man said. "Then it will be a sweet year."

A pale-skinned girl across the table with straight black shoulder-length hair smiled at him. She was thin with a very straight posture, high cheekbones, and a crooked nose pierced with a sliver of diamond. A first glance, she was nothing special, but the way she looked at Stone with those deep black eyes made him reconsider. He had never thought much about religious girls, but there was something different about her that he could not quite pin down. Three yeshiva students wearing matching white shirts and knitted kippas nodded their heads. The older woman who had beckoned Stone to eat reached out her arms and raised her eyes to the heavens. She muttered a prayer. It was as if he were given an instant line of credit solely because he was Walter Stone's son.

"Matthew, I'm only going to say it once—so pay attention," Seligman said, gesturing to the bearded man. "This is, uh . . ." and he paused in jest, finger extended, pretending he had forgotten the host's name.

"David Grunhut," the man said, laughing. "You'd better keep an eye on your uncle. He knows more than he lets on."

And now the word *uncle*. Stone knew in his rational mind his feelings were being manipulated by language, but the flood of endorphins washing over him made him want more.

Seligman laughed and extended his hand, moving it counterclockwise around the table as he spoke. Stone didn't care to know anyone's name except for that girl across the table.

"Esther," and the older woman smiled again. "Yossi, Dov, Natan, Meir, Malka, Dasi." Seligman stopped again. There was an empty high chair next to the pale-skinned girl named Dasi.

"Where's Arieh?" Seligman said.

"Napping," Yossi said. "I'm ready to crash, too."

Dasi's eyes focused on Stone, as if she were looking for something in particular in his face. She had the kind of dark eyes that made Stone feel like he was the only person in the room and they both shared some secret. He wanted to know what that secret was. But this was not the time or place, so he forced himself to look away, following Seligman's introductions.

"This is Dr. Cohen," Seligman said, gesturing to the thin elderly man sitting beside Stone at the foot of the table. "Matthew, you know who you are. I'm Zalman Seligman."

"The revered Rabbi Seligman. Huzzah!" David Grunhut called out, laughing again. "But, seriously, we are honored to have you here in Brooklyn this Rosh Hashanah. I know you've traveled far to share this simcha with us."

"And so have you, David!"

"Lakewood is not that far," David said, "assuming there is no traffic."

"*Baruch Hashem!*" someone called out from the near side of the table.

After Seligman finished the introductions, he went to wash his hands in the kitchen. Stone sat and served himself some brisket and challah. He had never particularly liked Jewish soul food; he thought it was heavy and too full of garlic. He had barely eaten in a week though, so he forced himself to eat some of the brisket.

He and Seligman had arrived in the middle of an intense exchange, and David Grunhut picked up his broken strand of conversation. "Nachmanides says, 'Do not abandon the land to any other nation.'"

"That is correct," someone to Stone's right said, "and that is exactly what Rabbi Heimlich was saying in today's sermon. That we have been commanded not to surrender a single inch of Jewish land. To do so would be—"

"Catastrophic," the elderly Dr. Cohen interrupted. "I was a young man in Germany and, bit by bit, Germany grew: the Sudetenland, the Anschluss. It's true the German thunder rolled slowly at first, as Heinrich Heine warned. But he also said you will know the German thunder has hit its mark when you hear a crash like nothing has ever crashed in the history of the world." He paused for a moment and took a sip of wine. His white hair was combed back beneath a blue-and-white knitted kippa, his frigid eyes pale as fresh rainwater. "We were warned. The world was warned. Heine wrote his prophetic essay on Germany in 1834, a full one hundred years before the Nazi war machine rolled. Germany's intentions were no secret."

Stone had often thought Jews were too quick to play the Nazi card and that the true horrors of the Holocaust were lost with these simple comparisons. But having read so many of his father's books, studying his marginal notes, he saw more similarities between the so-called peace process and Neville Chamberlain's appeasement than he ever imagined. After each suicide bombing perpetrated by the Palestinians, the peace process went on unabated, as if innocent lives had not been taken in cold blood. Not long ago, he had thought the peace process to be pure good for all parties involved, but now he was not so sure. What was peace worth if ordinary citizens could be blown up in the streets?

"Irving," Seligman said, drying his hands on his pants as he sat back down, "we endured. We are living in the land of Israel while Hitler burns in Gehenna."

"Piss on Hitler," Dov said. An arrogant, angry expression remained after he had spoken. Dasi twisted her red-painted lips and took a large gulp of wine. She wasn't like the rest of them. There was something unusual in the way she carried herself, a sort of bemused detachment Stone could not figure out how to decipher. She was of their world but, at the same time, she was not of their world.

"Listen," Dr. Cohen said.

"We understand," a voice said from the other end of the table.

"No, you don't understand," Dr. Cohen said, pounding his fist on the table. "It's happening again. Amalek is gathering strength."

Though this talk appeared to be half mad to Stone, he envied their conviction, the sense there was something in the world to care about and to fight for. For as long as he remembered, he had been so focused on his own internal neuroses and dramas he had never put forth the effort to care about anything outside of his own personal solar system. He had willfully detached himself from history, while these people around the table plunged headlong into the conflict.

Though the brisket was overcooked and almost cold, he scarfed down his plate of dried-out meat with an almost animal ferocity.

"You're all familiar with the Amalekites," Dr. Cohen said, "that ancient tribe who tried to destroy us at the Exodus. You all know Amalek reappears every generation to bring us low, to fight us, to destroy us. Nazi Germany was the ideological bastard child of Amalek, so were the Tsarists, the Spaniards, the Romans, the list goes on—"

"We're ready to defend ourselves," Dov said. There was something about his sneering tone that Stone did not like. He was an insecure poseur, parroting the right words, the correct ideology, from the safety and comfort of his seat at the luncheon table. His jaw was firm as he recited, "From Dan to Beersheva, from Gilead to the sea, there is not one spot of our land that was not redeemed by blood."

"Yes, yes," Dr. Cohen said. "And even in poverty, a Jew is a prince, and you were created the son of a king—"

"But Jewish blood—" Dov interrupted.

"Crowned with David's crown," Dr. Cohen continued. "You say the words, but do you mean them? You're just a child. How can you possibly know?"

Esther broke in, "I've seen Amalek, Doctor. We've all seen Amalek. He killed my husband. This family is on a first-name basis with Amalek."

The wine went right to Stone's head. It was sickeningly sweet, like a child's glass of bug juice. His temples hummed, and he downed a second glass. This was the worst wine in the entire world, but he was determined to drink as much as possible to ease the perpetual discomfort of being. At least the hangover was gone now, but he was well on his way to building another. The glazed challah on his plate was tasty but filled with raisins, and the thought of eating soggy raisins was about as appealing as eating an eyeball. Stone tried to pick them out with his fork, wrapping them in his napkin.

"I really like your suit jacket," a female voice said.

Stone had forgotten he was wearing the jacket he had borrowed from one of Seligman's acolytes. It was a size too big for him, but for a moment he thought she was complimenting him, until Dasi broke out laughing. It wasn't a pretty laugh, but it was confident and full of certainty.

"Where did you get that?"

"It's all the rage in Ivanetz," Stone said. "Shtetl-wear for all seasons."

"Ha!" Dasi said, leaning forward, elbows on the table. "Really?" She wore a silver necklace with a greenish-blue Roman glass pendant. It looked like a drop of seawater, resting against her chest. "What do the women wear?"

"It depends where," Stone said. He had meant to suggest the synagogue versus the street and not the boudoir, but he knew from Dasi's reaction that she thought he had meant it that way.

"That's not what I meant," Stone said. "I mean if you think I meant what I think you thought I meant."

She offered up a "who me?" gesture with her long silver-ringed fingers.

Now the baby was crying in another room, and David said, "Somebody check on Arieh. He's crying."

"I know he's crying," Malka said, throwing her napkin onto the table and pushing back her chair.

"Ask him what he's crying about," David suggested.

"He's hungry," Seligman said, through a thick mouthful of something.

"Then feed him, Malka," David said.

"I'm going, okay?" Malka said. She was short with thick shoulders and was several months pregnant. A look of irritation appeared on her face as her blue floor-length skirt caught on her chair.

"Ask a man to know what a baby wants," Dasi said. "I'll bet he pooped himself."

"Hadassah, not at the table," Esther said, scolding Dasi.

"Not back from Israel two weeks and your head is already in the toilet," David said, smiling but stern.

Dr. Cohen cleared his throat. "We were talking about 1933 and the historical parallels—"

"He pooped!" Malka said, bursting back into the room, baby in her arms, her hair tied back with an elastic.

"Thank you for the announcement," David said. "I've lost my appetite."

Dasi was already cooing at her baby nephew and pulling silly faces to make him laugh.

It was strange to think that a couple of years earlier, under different circumstances, he might not have been attracted to Dasi. She would have been too pale, too familiar, too close to what his father would have wanted for him. But now, adrift, afraid, and desperate for connection, he looked at Dasi and realized that, yes, she was the type of girl his father would have wanted for him, so why shouldn't he want her for himself?

"Look, Irving, we're closer to redemption now than we are to a repeat of 1933," David said.

"The difference between then and now," Seligman added, "is we've got the hammer. We've got the bomb. He who has the bomb has the land."

Yossi spoke now. "And he who has the land—all of it—gets Moshiach and the Heavenly Kingdom."

Stone finished a third cup of wine, feeling flushed and happy, and leaned forward. The buzz in his head told him to speak, and he said the first thing that came to his mind. "Then we might as well nuke the Arabs now and get it over with."

"What?" Dr. Cohen said, his blue eyes hard and cold.

Seligman interjected, apologizing on Stone's behalf. "Irving, you have to understand that Matthew went to a fancy private school in Connecticut. He was just being ironic."

"Irony is nothing more than half-educated, childish sarcasm," Dr. Cohen said, turning away.

Seligman leaned close to Stone and said, "Maybe slow down with your drinking, all right?"

Stone had not meant to call attention to himself. He hadn't even meant to speak, but the words had come out anyway. Dasi leaned across the table and said, "That was funny. I'm a huge fan of mutual assured destruction."

"Welcome to my life," Stone said.

They were both silent for a moment. "I'm sorry about your dad," she said, her voice soft. It was full of tenderness and warmth. "It must be hard."

"It is," Stone said, realizing he was having a good time, laughing and drinking as if he were not in mourning. But he instinctively knew he was doing something wrong, and that his father would disapprove.

Dasi looked on, a tiny crease forming between her eyes, waiting for him to respond. Her red rose of a mouth was just a little slack, wet and warm, and all he could offer was a barely articulated, "Where's the bathroom?"

"Down the hall," she said.

The harsh bathroom light was as sharp as an interrogation lamp, so he flicked off the vanity light and turned on the ceiling fan. The tiny guest bathroom smelled of scented soaps and air freshener. A single dim bulb lent the scene a squalid, smoldering glow. Stone could hear David's raised voice in the dining room as he continued

to debate the humorless Dr. Cohen, against the backdrop of silverware clinking against plates. He knew his father would approve of
Dasi. The funny thing was, she didn't even look Jewish, whatever
that was supposed to mean, with that white skin, hibernal, almost icy
in contrast to her fiery lips and glossy black hair. But, fueled by the
sweet wine, he wanted her; he wanted her so bad he could think of
nothing else. He was the worst person in the world for thinking this.
He deserved to die alone. He was in mourning but couldn't mourn
the way he was supposed to mourn. His father would be disgusted
with him for thinking of Dasi as an object of his need, his desire, at a
time like this. Why would she ever want him anyway? He was a mess,
with purple wine crust at his lips and a borrowed suit jacket. Who was
he fooling? He was a joke. His father would be embarrassed for him,
humiliated for him.

He opened the medicine cabinet. It was full to bursting with
pill canisters and half-crushed tubes. He found Esther's heart pills,
a long-expired antibiotic, an unlabeled canister filled with black-
striped yellow capsules, buzzing like bumblebees, "Take me! Take
me!" Yes, this would take him somewhere better, away from doubt
and fear and self-hatred. He tapped a handful of the mystery capsules
into his shaking hand in the bleak sterility of the bathroom, his left
hand both leaden and light at once. He counted out eighteen pills,
for good luck, and was about to pop them when there was a knock
on the door.

"Are you all right in there?" It was Dasi.

The pills jumped in his palm. "A minute," Stone called.

He considered dumping them all down his throat but he was too
much of a coward, especially with Dasi on the other side of the door.
He lifted the toilet seat, threw the pills in, and flushed. Then, standing
at the sink, he turned on the faucet and ran some cool water over his
skin, splashing some on his hair as well. He wiped his lips and rinsed
his mouth out with a smear of toothpaste.

"Open the door."

"Hold on," he said, thinking this had to be a sign of some sort.
This was the lifeboat he needed so badly, and a Jewish lifeboat at that.

He'd show his father he could do it, make him happy with a woman he would approve of. He capped the pill bottle and threw it back into its approximate place before shutting the cabinet. His face stared back from the mirror, crooked, exhausted, but handsome. He smiled a rakish smile and opened the bathroom door.

Dasi stood in the half-dark of the hallway, wearing a fitted black skirt. In heels, she was nearly as tall as Stone's five foot eight. She had narrow hips and narrow shoulders, but she did not look the least bit fragile. One of her incisors sat twisted sideways between a row of straight white teeth. Up close she was as beautiful as she had been from across the table, but her nose—it was bent as if it had been broken. It didn't make her any less beautiful; right then and there he wanted to exchange salt for salt, fluid for fluid, him for her.

"What's the matter?" she asked, leaning close.

"Too much wine," Stone said.

"Beware the Manischewitz hangover. It can last for forty days."

Stone tried to smile, but he was deep into one of his maudlin moods now. "You know, everything's hilarious, and then you just get sad."

"I shouldn't have mentioned your father."

"No," Stone said, "it's not that."

"Dasi, what are you two doing back there? It's time for dessert," David called from the dining room.

"Coming, all right?" She turned to Stone, squinting. She had a tiny freckle under her right eye and he was seized with a shock of delight as if he had been the first to ever notice it. "You'll eat some dessert?"

"I should go," Stone said.

"It's cinnamon babka. My favorite thing in the whole world."

"Really?" Stone asked. "In the whole world?"

"You have to taste it."

"Did you make it?" Stone said.

"I bought it," she said, laughing. "But the line up at Schick's was out the door."

"In that case, I'll have some."

"You'd better," she said, and then, switching to a comical Old World bubbie's accent, "We must to fatten you up."

"Hey," Stone said. "Thank you. Thanks for checking on me. I really appreciate it."

"I'm sure you'll pay back the favor sometime." She smiled broadly and led him back to the dining room.

Dr. Cohen was still going on about the fate of the Jews, a piece of honey cake crumbling between his thumb and forefinger.

"If you look at the level of anti-Semitism today compared to then, you will see precious little has changed. Wake up, Jews!"

Arieh started crying again in the bedroom, harsh and high-pitched like a siren.

"At least someone is listening to Dr. Cohen," Dasi said.

"God in heaven, see what he wants," David said. "Feed the boy, he must be hungry."

Stone sat back in his seat beside Seligman; Dasi settled in across the table. "Are you all right?" Seligman asked quietly.

Across the table Dov frowned and whispered something to the other student.

"Just too much wine."

"Well, watch yourself. You were gone a long time."

"Maybe you've made a *shidduch*, Zalman," David said, broadly.

"That would please his father," Seligman said.

Stone's face burned with embarrassment and he looked across the table at Dasi who smiled calmly back at him.

Dov leaned forward, an elbow on the table, and craned his neck toward Dasi. "That's right Das, we all know how much you like to please other people."

Without even looking his way, she said, "That's enough, Dov."

"Now, Walter Stone," David Grunhut said. "There's a Jew who did all he could to hasten redemption and hold back the flood tide you speak of, Irving."

"I knew the man," Dr. Cohen said, in a sepulchral voice.

Stone's attention was split now by the spat between Dasi and Dov and the talk about his father. Who was Dov to Dasi and what did he mean about her liking to please other people?

"I'll say when it's enough," Dov said.

"You know what, I think I need to use the bathroom," Dasi said, standing up and pushing her chair in, her dark eyes staring for a hard moment at Dov.

Stone wanted to go after her, but he was drunk, and nothing good could come of pursuing her now. No matter how well they began, matters of the heart always, always crashed in tears of ruin and regret. He stared at her empty seat for a moment, conjuring her back into being, but his memory could not put her features properly back into place. The conversation about his father continued.

"The Judge worked tirelessly, raising capital for the Eretz Fund, building communities throughout Israel, Kiryat Arba, Gush Etzion. You've been to Silwan, you've been to Har Homa. Where were they ten years ago? One day all of Israel will be Jewish."

"And what then?" Dr. Cohen said. "We are sitting ducks waiting to be gassed."

"We must carry on," Seligman said. "If it is written: catastrophe, then catastrophe. But it will bring the Jews closer to redemption."

"Dasi believes in redemption, doesn't she?" Dov said.

"Be nice," Yossi said. "Remember, *hotzaat shem ra.*"

Stone's dislike for Dov tingled in his extremities, and he clenched his hands, testing them. It would feel so good to bury a drunken fist in his arrogant face. He knew Dasi in some intimate way that made Stone burn with jealousy. But his curiosity to learn about his father overwhelmed his desire to coldcock Dov right there at the table. He had to keep it together, so he drank a fourth glass of wine.

"And what of Walter's initiative to construct a new neighborhood in south Jerusalem?"

"Near Wallajeh village? That's just a dream," Dr. Cohen said.

"Nearly two thousand dunams of land have been purchased from the Arab squatters."

"He's right," a voice down the table intervened. "The neighborhood will be able to absorb nearly fifty thousand Jewish residents, connecting Yerushalayim in an unbroken chain to Gush Etzion."

"What's going to happen with the Eretz Fund now that Walter, bless his name, is gone?" a voice asked from the far end of the table.

"Yeah," Yossi chimed. "Are you going to take over, Matthew?"

Dov snorted at Yossi's question.

"I am the de facto chair now," Stone said, aiming his words directly at Dov.

"He's still in mourning," David Grunhut said. "Leave him alone."

Stone had not expected to be invited into this exchange. He was hardly conversant on the subject matter, and he was now quite drunk.

"What is that supposed to mean?" Dov said.

"It means, I know where the money is."

He hadn't meant to speak those words aloud, but the desire to show up Dov overcame him. He felt Seligman's brutal hand at his collar, and he snapped his mouth shut. *Showing off like an insecure schoolboy*, his father would have said. *Pathetic*.

"Okay, it's getting late," Seligman said, squeezing the scruff of Stone's neck. "We still need to *bentsch*."

"Hold on, Zalman," a man in his fifties, whom Stone had heard but not seen, said as he tilted back in his chair. He turned his face to Stone and addressed him directly. "I knew the Judge well." The man wore his rust-colored beard close-cropped and had tiny black eyes set far back in their sockets.

"Eli, listen," Seligman said. "Not now. It's getting late." Seligman seemed afraid Stone would speak again, but Stone just wanted to sit and listen to what these people had to say about his father.

"Just a story," Eli said, "about a great intellect, lawmaker, and Jew who straddled the secular and Jewish worlds with the ease of a statesman."

"It's all right," Stone said. "I'd like to hear about my father."

Seligman leaned close to Stone and whispered, "You're drunk."

"Hear, hear," David said, clinking his glass with a dessert fork.

"Well, all right then," Eli said.

Dasi reentered the dining room but did not take her seat as before; rather she stood against the wall, listening in silence.

"Now, you all know," Eli said, leaning forward in his chair, his delicate fingers tapping softly on the table, "there are many myths surrounding Walter Stone—some are true and some not."

Eager anticipation flashed through Stone's innards, that particular feeling of having to pee, when just a moment earlier he hadn't.

"I was a young yeshiva student in 1968—a million years ago—after the great victory in the Six-Day War. I remember the excitement at the time, returning for the first time to the land of our forefathers: Hebron, Beit Lechem, Shechem, the Kotel. Praying in those places was intoxicating, like being in the center of a whirlwind."

"*Baruch Hashem*," several voices interjected.

"Anyway, Pesach, 1968, Rav Grunhut, may his memory be blessed, rented the Park Hotel in downtown Hebron for us to celebrate the Passover. Surrounded by thousands of Arabs, mind you, we were there, on our land, at long last. The Israeli government wasn't happy with the idea of Jews moving into the heart of Judea and Samaria. They wanted us out. But the army did nothing as we moved in. The living conditions were terrible. Our first step to redemption consisted of sleeping in sleeping bags on the concrete floor, and cooking with old army gas stoves that stank of kerosene. We had nothing and the government wanted us to leave. But Rav Grunhut said we were staying until the Messiah came. So, one day, a couple of trucks arrive. A man steps out of one with a big, fat Perfecto between his teeth—he's tall and rugged and bald and embraces Rav Grunhut. He was so handsome, fit like a marine, and at the time, before I knew who he was, I remember thinking he looked cut out of pure Jerusalem stone. It was Walter. Just arrived from a tour of duty in Vietnam, it turns out."

Dasi regarded Stone, tilting her head just so as she sized him up. He knew he looked nothing like his father. Stone was struck with the realization that Rav Grunhut, the Judge's murdered friend, was Dasi's uncle. How could it be that he had never heard of her before, never met her? Had he really been that estranged from his father? He knew the answer was yes, and that after years of stubbornness and self-denial, he was ready to step into the eye of the storm, if that's what it took to be close to Dasi.

"Walter and Rav Grunhut visit for hours. There are rumors the government is going to throw us out by force, and we're thinking Walter's an emissary from Jerusalem, negotiating some kind of deal to withdraw. But Walter was a true rainmaker, bent on getting things done. Next thing you know, we are unloading the trucks with the Rav's belongings, everything he has in the world. There are beds, proper stoves and refrigerators for us. We're staying. Later, they go for a walk, both he and Rav Grunhut carrying Uzis at the ready. Remember, Jews had been massacred there thirty, forty years earlier, before being evacuated. Myself and a couple of other students join them as they move through the dusty cinder-block streets. Walter knows some Arabic and he is translating what the Arabs shout as we pass. Nasty stuff. Kill the Jews, Zionist dogs, monkeys, pigs. The whole menagerie. We arrive outside the city on the jagged rocky slopes, overlooking Hebron. And the Judge and the Rav walk ahead and kneel and touch the earth. I'd swear I saw tears in the Judge's eyes. Two years later, the city of Kiryat Arba is established right on the very spot where they knelt. Rows and rows of Jewish houses springing out of the land, with watchtowers rising to ensure a massacre will never happen again. Today, Kiryat Arba thrives and Jews still live in Hebron."

But there *was* another massacre, Stone recalled, just four years ago, this time perpetrated by a Brooklyn-born Jewish doctor gunning down dozens of Palestinians at prayer. Though it would have been reductive to say it never could have happened if his father had not visited that day in 1968, he heard his father shout from the pages of his books. He had read the words just that very week, underlined in bright red ink: "There will be a day when Jews will take revenge on the Arabs," and, scratched in the margins, the single word: "Soon."

"They were quite a team, Walter and my brother," David said. "You could always count on the Judge to get things done. He was the pragmatist. Isn't that right, Irving?"

"Yes, that's right," Dr. Cohen said, wiping his thin lips with a napkin.

Dasi's eyes were fixed on Stone as if she were looking for Walter in his meager frame, but it was pointless, like looking for a bit actor in the gold reflection of an Oscar statue.

"Now, I can tell you that is true, because I was there," Eli continued, "but there are other stories that are apocryphal that I would be willing to bet are true as well. I came to know Walter, and he was capable of the most amazing things."

"I beg you Eli, it's nearly three o'clock," Seligman said. "Perhaps you can save the tribute for another time. I'd like to take a nap before going back to shul."

"Go on," Dasi said, "I want to hear more about the heroic Walter Stone."

"I'll keep it short, Zalman."

What was Seligman afraid of? Did he think that Stone was not aware that the settlement Eli claimed his father was instrumental in founding was a hotbed of fanatics, radicals, and murderers?

"Give us the *Reader's Digest* version, *al regel achat*," David said.

"Okay," Eli said, straightening his kippa. "Moshe Dayan was minister of defense at the time and ran Judea and Samaria with an iron fist; he was not happy. But he was in the hospital, practically paralyzed with broken ribs. Walter pays a visit to him. Walter's about thirty-five years old, charismatic, an important face of civility for the movement. You'll excuse me, David, but a lot of people thought your brother, may Hashem avenge his blood, was a bit extreme for their taste and wouldn't touch him with a barge pole. Walter, he spoke perfect Hebrew like a poet, like a philosopher. He was at home in the halls of power and he got what he wanted. He went to see the Old Man at his home in the Negev. He visited every member of the Israeli cabinet at their homes, pleading his case. Not long after, the cabinet voted to allow us to stay in Hebron. The first permanent community reestablished in Judea and Samaria, the first step toward redeeming the land of Israel. And do you know why Walter was able to have the ear of the Israeli cabinet? Given the opportunity to change hearts and minds, and push the vote through—"

"All right," Seligman said, standing up and stretching his back. "We don't need the whole megillah. Let's *bentsch*."

"Awww!" Dasi said. "Why? Tell us!"

"I'd better defer to the Rav," Eli said, picking up a napkin and wiping the corners of his mouth.

"Another time. It is getting late."

The table slipped quickly into prayer, Seligman beside Stone, singing in his robust off-key tenor, but Stone could not stop thinking about the why of the thing. How could his father, a thirty-five-year-old American judge, have the ear of David Ben-Gurion, Moshe Dayan, all the cabinet members? How could he possibly have become so connected to these men of power?

For now, it didn't matter. Stone was overwhelmed by a burning pride for his father and his accomplishments. This was a man who had made a difference. It was clear these people loved the Judge in a way Stone had never loved his father, or been loved by him.

13 Stone didn't remember getting back to Pinky's or peeling off his clothes, but he awoke early the next morning completely naked, with a hangover of biblical proportions throbbing in his skull. Job may have suffered the way he did now, but Stone had never been a righteous man. He vaguely recalled Seligman taking a glass of wine out of his hand and pouring it down the kitchen sink, and Dasi calling a taxi to take him home. He had dreamt about her that morning as he floated in and out of sleep, and in his dream he had kissed her and more. Sometimes it was difficult to tell the difference between truth and reality. She had been his whore, taking him in her mouth, swallowing everything. But had he so much as shaken her hand at Esther Grunhut's? He could not remember. Stone imagined trying to kiss Dasi with his purple, wine-crusted lips, and was terrified he had humiliated himself before her.

Lying on the bare mattress, surrounded by piles of books, Stone knew he was slacking on some vital responsibility. The books themselves needed him to justify their existence. A pigeon cooing at his window shamed him to get out of bed. He couldn't stand the thought of being seen by anyone or anything in this condition and he took a quick shower, managed to shave without cutting himself, and drank three glasses of water. He padded back into the bedroom, threw his father's robe over his bare shoulders, and sat down before a stack of books. Stone rarely knew exactly which book he was going to read when he settled in. He was never lonely when he was with the books, because he was not in fact alone. The whispering, just beneath his comprehension, would become louder, more definite as his hand breezed upon certain books. Stone picked up a copy of Walter Benjamin's *Illuminations*, and nothing; he placed it back in the pile. He found a book by Benjamin Disraeli, nothing. The same went for a massive tome on the Crusades, *Un Coeur Simple* by Flaubert, *The Principles of Psychology* by William James, *My Life* by Marc Chagall, *Germinal* by Émile Zola, and the writings of Abraham Isaac Kook.

He found a copy of Ze'ev Jabotinsky's novel *Samson* at the bottom of a pile and managed to slip it out without knocking over the entire stack. It was a musty old hardcover, with crinkly, water-damaged pages. Stone settled in to read but the translation was archaic, tin-eared, laughable. After a few minutes, he decided he could not read any farther. He was about to toss the book aside when he was gripped by pang of guilt, so he flipped ahead to see if the Judge had written anything in the margins. The pages were clean. There were no underlined sentences, no marginal notes, no asterisks, no exclamation points, nothing highlighted at all. Stone flipped to the front of the book where he saw that it was signed, but not to his father, who would have been only five years old at the time. The inscription read:

To Julius,
The Movement appreciates
your support and friendship.
Hazak V'Ematz
Ze'ev Jabotinsky
August 1, 1940, Brooklyn

Why did his father still have this book? He must have taken it with him when he moved uptown to Columbia at the age of fifteen, and kept it, despite his estrangement from Julius, because it had been signed by Jabotinsky himself. But this was more than just a tossed-off signature. Julius was more than just a simple gangster; he was a power broker at the highest levels. Jabotinsky had called Julius a friend and said the movement appreciated his support.

This was 1940, and the movement would have been the Irgun, a
Jewish paramilitary organization operating within Palestine before
the establishment of the State of Israel. Jabotinsky was the supreme
commander from 1937 until his death in 1940, three days after he
signed the book to Julius. The Irgun believed force was the only way
to liberate the homeland from the British; after restraining themselves during the early months of the Arab Revolt, the Irgun began
to retaliate in kind after Jews were attacked by Arabs. Under Jabotinsky's leadership, the Irgun undertook acts of terror against both the
British and the Arabs, striking back hard against their enemies. But
what could Julius have done to help?

Somebody or something was under the robe with Stone again, that
invisible occult force seizing his shoulders, gripping him. He knew
he was wide awake, sober and alert, yet he felt this weight upon his
back and, as he stood up, it was as if he were carrying around a heavy
burden. He was either broken in some profound way, he thought, or
he was privy to some truth beyond his understanding; his grandfather
had been a gangster, not a terrorist. Sometimes he dreaded that this
being, this presence, this whatever it was that whispered behind his back
whenever he sat down to read had come to replace him, to erase the old
Matthew Stone and supplant him. With a quavering hand he flipped
through the pages of *Samson* one more time, looking for something—
some code, some message—to explain what he was supposed to do.
But he found nothing except stilted prose and musty paper. Julius was
a killer, what difference was it to Stone who he had killed?

The Judge had marked some books with a severe ferocity, going
as far as rewriting phrases that displeased him. His marginal notes
snaked down both sides of many pages, his spidery script screaming
above the typeset text. Stone discovered, as he read, that his father had
been tracking the pattern of victimization that brought tragedy and
ruin to the Jews throughout their tortured history, and he realized his
father was prescribing solutions, posthumously, to tragic events that
had already occurred: a savior out of step and out of time.

His father had found a way to avert the Exile; the last stand at
Masada would never have occurred; Bar Kokhba's rebellion would

have succeeded; the Spanish Inquisition, Chmielnitzky, the pogroms beyond the Pale, the Holocaust especially, occurring as it did right in the middle of modern twentieth-century Europe—all could have been avoided. The Jews might have been minorities, but they were large minorities with untapped potential, unharnessed power spent waiting for the Messiah to save them.

The Judge reserved unusual scorn for the early Zionists who tried to compromise with the Arabs and with the British. In a book in which the essayist Ahad Ha'am had written that nineteenth-century Palestine was not empty but was populated with indigenous Arabs, the Judge had written in red: "We Were the Victims." Beside a passage about Chaim Weizmann and his philosophy of *Havlaga*, or restraint, against the British, the Judge had written one word: "Lapdog."

The buzzer rang, and Stone waited for Pinky to answer. It rang again, a long persistent whine vibrating in Stone's ears. Stone would not have answered the door, as there was nobody he wished to see, but he was unnerved on this sunny morning by the vague phantoms swirling about his father's books. I am losing my mind, Stone thought. I am a prisoner to these books.

Abi was at the door, a concerned look on her face. "Can I come in?"

Stone let her inside without a word of greeting.

"I feel terrible, Matty," Abi said. "I should have insisted you come with me, rather than leaving you here alone. It's just, I didn't want to push too hard; I was afraid of driving you away, but when I got on the Metro-North train, I imagined you alone here with all these books, and I thought, no, you shouldn't be alone. I should've turned around and come right back, but I didn't, and I'm here now, and I hope you forgive me."

Abi held a plastic bag of leftovers in her arms and she handed it to Stone. "You have to eat something. You look terrible."

For a moment, Stone was prepared to give in and thank Abi for the food—he was hungry after all—but he was reminded of the painting of Pinky across the room, incomplete, repulsive. She had violated the closest thing he had to private space, and she had used his father's robe as a drop sheet. He wanted things to be okay with her, but he couldn't find a way to allow himself to forgive her for everything she had done.

"You can't just show up here and expect me to welcome you," Stone said, dropping the leftovers to the floor.

Abi sighed and said, "I've tried calling. I've left messages for you. What more can I do?"

"You can leave me alone," Stone said.

"You don't mean that," Abi said. "Please tell me you don't mean that."

"Can't you just understand I don't need you anymore? I survived without you."

"Oh, Matty," Abi said, "I can tell you I'm sorry a million times, and I understand that won't make up for me being absent all those years, but I'm here now and I'm offering myself to you as a mother, and as a friend."

He did not want her to leave, but he did not want to accept her either. It was empowering to see his mother wiping away tears from her eyes, and he wanted more of that feeling. He wished only to stay in this intoxicating middle ground, where he had the whip hand and she groveled for his absolution. It would be near impossible to maintain this tenuous balance for long. "You look like shit yourself," Stone said.

"I'm worried about you, Matthew," Abi said, brushing her fingers through her hair. There was a lot more gray visible in her hair today. "I didn't sleep. I can't sleep. Look at you in that robe, like some sort of mad medieval monk, and those books, those goddamn books. What is going on with you?"

"Maybe whatever it is you are trying to do with me, make good on all those years of disappointment, I'm trying to do with him."

"That's what I was afraid of, but he's not worth it. And he's dead. You can't change that," Abi said. "You follow your father down that rabbit hole and you will come out the other side a completely different person."

"That might be exactly what I need," Stone said. "At my age, he was already working for the DA's office, and what am I doing? Your knee-jerk hatred for him is just—"

"All right, all right," Abi said. "I won't speak about your father anymore. I promise. Not a word. I just worry, that's all."

"Why do you hate him so much? He's gone. You won. How can you expect me to forgive you, when you won't forgive him?"

"I think I've said enough. I'm sorry." She paused, and looked at her tiny wristwatch. "Now, it is a beautiful, sunny day outside. Why don't you put on some clothes and come with me? We'll take a field trip, like old times?"

Stone balanced the possibilities of taking pity on her and going out or staying in his room with the books and going mad. Every time he looked in the mirror now, he saw the face of Julius. His own existence may have been predicated by him, but he wasn't him; he was nothing like him. But that face, the stiff wire-brush hair. How could his father not have hated him, a constant reminder of a legacy he worked so hard to leave behind?

"It smells terrible in here. Come on, what do you say?"

THE WARM BRIGHT air and the brisk walk refreshed Stone, and his hangover all but disappeared. Abi was a fast walker and he had to work to keep up, but feeling his heart pumping, his lungs filling and unfilling, he was glad to have left his room. He recalled now his mother's spirit of adventure, how one minute they could be buying ice cream on the corner by their house and the next collecting sea glass in Far Rockaway, how they had bought fresh flounder on City Island in the Bronx and carried it all the way back home on the subway packed in ice. And of course, they had once flown to Florida to see his grandfather, but that had been their last adventure, and soon she was gone from his life.

The lonely, tomblike halls of the Brooklyn Museum echoed with the sound of Abi's footsteps mismatched with the slow, reluctant steps of Stone, several feet behind.

"I'm glad you decided to put down your books for a few minutes."

"No friend is as loyal as a book," Stone said.

"Who said that?" Abi asked.

"I did," Stone lied.

They stopped before a papyrus rendering of Nefertiti, her right arm raised before her. "What do you think?" Abi said. "Do you think she's beautiful?"

Her neck was long, with dark skin and night-black hair, an enduring icon of feminine beauty and power. But she was nothing compared to Dasi, with her pale skin, her bright red lips around his cock.

"Not my type," Stone said. "She looks as if she's been run over with a steamroller."

"Well, the ancients hadn't figured out the third dimension yet," Abi laughed.

A group of public school children entered the hall, led by their harried teacher, a pole-thin, middle-aged black woman with a shaved head. The children may have been third or fourth graders, their faces turned in every direction, their feet poised to follow their impulses.

"Children!" the teacher shouted, in a voice that sounded like God, echoing in the hall. "Can we all say *pharaoh*?"

"Pharaoh," they responded.

"Let's get out of here," Abi said.

They climbed up two flights of stairs, passing a couple on the way down, and Abi's voice was lost in the echo chamber of the stairwell. They found themselves in the cool air of a sculpture gallery, half-nude bodies frozen in time, unashamed.

"There won't be any schoolkids up here," Abi said. "Doesn't mesh with the public school curriculum."

Stone, breathless from the climb, leaned on a bronze Rodin.

"Nefertiti's not your type," Abi said. "I get it, you don't like older women. She must be more than three thousand years old anyway. So, what is your type?"

This was not the kind of conversation he would have liked to have with his mother, but Abi was no longer his mother; she had forfeited that title and he wanted to shock her, scandalize her. "Are you trying to find out who I'm fucking?"

"No, not really," Abi said. "But since you bring it up, is there anyone special in your life?"

He said nothing, refusing to give Abi the opportunity to advise him, mother him, guide him. She had not earned that right. There was no shortcut.

"Come on," she said. "Don't hold back. I know there's someone. A mother can tell these things."

Was she that deluded by her own narcissism, or was she simply trying to make a cheap connection with him?

"There's nobody," Stone said.

"You're too handsome for there to be nobody in your life. You have to see all the beautiful women in the Bay Area. They are everywhere. You wouldn't be alone for long, trust me. You know what they say about California girls. I could introduce you to some of my graduate students."

"What are you, their pimp?"

"Matty, come on, enjoy your life while you're young. Before you're tied down by family and responsibilities."

They passed into the next gallery—European paintings and sculptures. Lifeless faces peered down from the walls, their gilt frames contrasting with their ashen skin.

"That didn't stop you from doing what you wanted." He shivered in the frigid gallery.

Abi touched him on the arm and said, "You're not being fair. Mea culpa, okay? Can't the past just be the past?"

"It's too late for that."

"I only want the best for you."

Abi was silent, her eyes moist. At last she said, with a broken voice, "I've never stopped loving you. Please give me a chance to make it up to you. Come back to California with me."

She was begging again, and Stone's entire body warmed with the power he wielded. "There is someone. I met someone." He thought of Dasi from the luncheon the day before, and how she had looked at him with a strange sort of desire, those dark eyes promising. This was his chance to make good on all those failed relationships, this was his chance to show his mother he didn't need her.

"Who?" Abi said. "Who is she?"

"A woman," Stone said, walking away.

"What's her name?"

Abi was still at his back and Stone picked up his pace.

"Matty, don't play games with me. At least tell me how you met her?"

He stopped and she caught up with him. She offered a small, hopeful smile.

"Rabbi Seligman," Stone said. "He invited me to a Rosh Hashanah luncheon, and she was there."

"Seligman? No, no, no. You must stay away from him. What did I tell you about Seligman?"

"I don't know what you told me and I don't care." That was why he didn't want to tell his mother anything. Her meddling and empty counsel. "This is my life, and it's not your place to tell me who I can like and who I have to hate. You don't know me. We are strangers."

"Matthew, nothing good could come of this. You have to understand, Seligman and anything connected with him is toxic. Trust me, you don't want this."

Stone's heart thudded in his ears. He felt the urge to strike his mother, tell her he was never leaving Brooklyn and that she should go back to California and die there if it was such a paradise. But instead, he gathered himself and said, "I need to be alone."

He found a bench before a large painting of Niagara Falls, the green-black water churning, luminescent, falling away, tumbling in swirling waves into a ghostly, rising mist.

Stone had been at this crossroads before, when his father had come to Jerusalem and refused to accept Fairuza.

Despite the fact she had just told him she had missed her period, Matthew left her in the café, preferring to face his father on his own. He kissed her on the lips, smelled her hair, and said he would be back in an hour. She pulled a book out of her bag—it might have been something by Turgenev or Lermontov—and said "good luck" and "hurry back" and, maybe, "I love you." That was the last he ever saw of her.

His father was staying in his usual suite at the King David Hotel, his home away from home. Stone remembered riding up the elevator feeling, not nervous, but elated, that he was finally going to stand up to his father and convince him he was right and that his father was narrow-minded, old-fashioned, and wrong.

The door was open, and Matthew let himself in. The Judge sat on a cushioned chair in the middle of the well-appointed salon, tossing a painted ceramic pomegranate from hand to hand. His half-moon glasses were up on his forehead. He wore a bemused smile on his face and said, "*Baruch habah*. Don't sit down. We won't be staying long."

Matthew only wanted to appeal to reason, to let his father know he was happy and that there was nothing to worry about, when his father said, "Where's the whore?"

His father might as well have slapped him in the face.

"She's not a whore," Matthew said. "You don't know her."

The Judge tilted back his head as if he were searching for some specific information in his mind. "According to Islam, Allah forbids any relationship between a man and a woman outside of marriage. In fact, a woman cannot even look at a member of the opposite sex—she must lower her gaze. Now, you have had sexual relations with this . . . individual?"

Matthew tried to interrupt, "It's my life—" But his father raised his voice and spoke over Matthew's feeble words. "According to Islam, premarital sex is a sin and an abomination and those who commit such an offense will be flogged, lashed with a hundred stripes across the back."

The Judge was silent again, and Matthew's knees went weak beneath him. "But she's not Muslim, she's a Christian."

The Judge dropped the pomegranate to the floor, and it shattered. "Matthew, do you think that makes a good goddamn difference? Scratch an Arab, you find the beast. All Arabs, no matter what they claim to believe, are descended from Ishmael, and Ishmael and all his children are wicked. Now, you can go back to her if you plan to turn your back on me and your entire heritage, but you have to understand there is no coming back from this."

"But I love her," Matthew said.

The Judge laughed. "Love is nothing but weakness and want."

"She is not wicked. You don't know her. She's a good person and she makes me happy."

"So you think she makes you happy? You've made your decision?" the Judge said. "Fine. But first you need to receive your punishment. Come here."

The Judge rolled up his sleeves, showing his powerful forearms, and unbuckled his belt. There was a matching ottoman before the chair, and his father gestured for him to lie across it. "I would take my shirt off if I were you," the Judge said, snapping his leather belt in the air. "One hundred lashes. Think about it, Matthew. Is she worth it?"

"She's worth a million," Matthew said.

"Listen to you," the Judge said. "You sound like a child, a pathetic little virgin."

"You don't know what you are talking about. Your own wife ran away from you."

The Judge did not react, did not so much as blink an eye.

Matthew thought of Fairuza sitting alone in the café anticipating his return, a new life stirring in her belly, and he wanted to run to her, take her hand and never come back. But he knew, after losing his mother, he couldn't afford to lose his father as well.

"You don't understand. She loves me and I love her."

"This creature may 'love' you today," the Judge said, making derisive air quotes with his huge fingers. "But what about tomorrow, or the day after? Are you prepared to risk your entire future for the childish abstraction of love?"

"Yes," Matthew said. "I love her more than I ever loved you."

The Judge laughed his most contemptuous laugh. "Just let me clarify the timeline of this wonderful affair."

Matthew tried to interrupt but the Judge cut him off.

"Please indulge me for a moment, and then you are free to leave and you need never suffer my advice again."

"There's nothing to say," Matthew said. "I love her and I want to be with her."

"Just a few weeks out of the psych ward, your mind was still feeble, delicate. You were confused. You left the safety of Giv'at Barzel in tears, on the verge of spiraling out of control once again. And you hitched a ride to Jerusalem, lied to me, and said you would enroll at the Hebrew University and learn Hebrew. Am I right?"

"I was not spiraling," Matthew said.

"Zalman tells me otherwise. You were on the very razor blade of another psychotic break."

"He's wrong. I was emotional. That's something you don't understand."

"Matthew, let me say it clearly. This affair of yours has nothing to do with love. She is an easy lay and a security blanket during a difficult time. She will not last forever, but I will. Blood is eternal."

"No," Matthew said. "You're wrong."

"There are other women, Matthew."

"I don't want other women," Matthew said.

"You will meet another woman, a Jewish woman, someone who will bring out the best in you."

"Fuck you," Matthew said. "I'm leaving."

"You realize, of course, if you disobey me now, you will have no father and no mother. You will be an orphan."

These were precisely the words Matthew did not want to hear. He would have liked to believe his father couldn't possibly mean that, but he knew the Judge meant every word.

"Then you won't have a son anymore. You'll never see me again."

"I'd rather have no son than a collaborator who turns his back on his people. Now," the Judge said, "are you ready to submit yourself for punishment?"

"You can't hurt me anymore."

"Matthew, what you don't understand, what you've never understood, is that it's you who is hurting you. It's always been that way."

"And if I just walk out this door?"

"Then I'll know you are both a traitor and a coward."

"Fine," Matthew spat as he pulled his shirt over his head and approached the ottoman. "I'm ready."

He lay across the ottoman, trembling, imagining Fairuza at the café, pregnant with their shared future, waiting for his return.

What would she say when she saw his back, shredded from the lash? Would she see him as weak, cowardly, for submitting to his father's punishment?

"I'm already an orphan anyway," Matthew said.

The Judge whacked Matthew across the back with the strap of his thick leather belt, sending white-hot lightning bolts of pain throughout his entire body. Matthew could not see, his field of vision blurred from the force of the blow.

"Matthew, this is not love you're talking about, but a sickness. You are not well."

"I am," Matthew managed to say. "I know that I love her."

Matthew heard the whistle of the leather belt cutting through the air a second time, and he knew his father would not let up until he submitted to his will.

Again, snow-blind with pain, the tender skin of his back afire, Matthew cried out, "I love her."

The Judge swung the belt through the air, preparing for a third strike. Matthew flinched at the sound of it. "Now stop acting like an adolescent and put your shirt back on," the Judge said. "Our plane is leaving in two hours."

"No," Matthew said. "I'll take my punishment."

"Matthew, listen carefully, because I want you to understand that I am deadly serious when I tell you if I strike you again, there will be no more chances. I will not stop until the prescribed punishment is complete."

"And what if I just leave? Just get up and walk out. I don't care if you think I'm a coward."

"Try it, Matthew. Do you really think I would ever let that happen? You're not walking out of here unless you are coming with me to the airport."

Matthew could have remained where he was, but he knew he would not survive another ninety-eight strokes. He lay across the ottoman, his back pins and needles of fire, weighing capitulation against Fairuza and her love. But now he wasn't certain he was in his right mind. He remembered at that moment how she had cried that night in the Old

City and wished the young border guard dead. That border guard was somebody's son, and he couldn't have been more than twenty-two or twenty-three years old. He was only doing his job, defending his country, defending Jews, defending Matthew. And when the suicide bombings hit, he didn't recall Fairuza ever shedding a single tear. She had mouthed the right condemnations, raised her voice in indignation, but never did she show the emotion she showed that first night at the bottom of David Street. Perhaps Fairuza was just a figment of his need, a replaceable part he could find anywhere. He was young and knew so little of the workings of the world. He could start over again in New York with a clean slate.

"All right," Matthew said. "I'm just going to say good-bye."

"A man never knows how to say good-bye," the Judge said. "This is for the best."

"But she's waiting for me," Matthew said. His father would humiliate him to the end for daring to stand up to him. Matthew's meager words stood no chance against his father's actions.

"And we've been waiting for the Messiah for thousands of years. She will survive."

Though Matthew submitted to his father's wishes, he hated his father for months afterward, years even. He had never been so impotent as he had been, lying half naked across the footrest in his father's suite at the King David Hotel, the Judge's leather belt snapping in the dry air, cracking cruelly against his skin. They did not speak on the entire flight home nor did they speak again for months. Matthew thought of reaching out to Fairuza countless times, calling her, writing long letters of explanation, but he was afraid of what she would say to him—tell him he was weak, a coward, pathetic. In time, he taught himself to forget about her, as if she had been a creation of his fevered imagination back when his mind was broken. He didn't meet another woman, just empty release in one-night bursts every so often, but now that he had met Dasi he realized that his father might have been correct all along.

She was the woman he had been waiting for. Fairuza had been an act of rebellion, a stupid youthful misadventure, something to be erased and forgotten. Though he didn't know it at the time, his father had saved him from a life of apostasy and disgrace. He owed his father a debt of gratitude and he wanted to find a way now to thank him.

THE PAINTING'S ELEMENTAL power echoed the upset and turmoil boiling in his stomach. He could hear the water, too, deafening as it crashed over the lip of the falls, a constant, never-ending roar that filled the entire room. Stone tried to imagine riding over the edge, crashing to the bottom and surviving. It would be like witnessing the big bang or the Ice Age firsthand. Survive that, and anything was possible.

The Judge had saved him from the catastrophic mistake of Fairuza, but Stone realized now with a sudden, bracing comprehension that he himself was a father, and far, far worse than his own father had ever been toward him. Fairuza appeared before him, a plaintive expression on her face, a shrouded child in her arms. Was it a boy, a girl? He had thought many times about what might have become of her after that missed period, but he had always pushed it out of his mind, hoping nature had taken care of itself. Now he knew for certain the child had lived, and that he had been instrumental in creating his own needy ball of resentment and hate.

"That's Mignot," Abi said. "Niagara. From the American side."

"It's incredible," Stone said, not taking his eyes off the painting. He was drowning the memory of Fairuza in there, holding her and the child under, holding them, letting go.

"It's one of my favorite paintings," Abi said. "Look how he has infused life into every square inch of the painting, every brushstroke."

"It looks like a photograph," Stone said. It was so real. He might have been standing at the brink of the falls, watching Fairuza and the child slip away under the foaming knots of dark water.

"Mind if I sit?"

Stone shook his head.

"It's more than just that. He's telling us something about ourselves that can't be said in words. It's something you feel."

"Yes," Stone said.

"This is the power of the act of creation," Abi said.

Where Abi saw creation, Stone saw destruction.

"That's why I paint. I create something that tells the truth that can't be told in any other way. It's frightening," Abi said.

"You're frightened by a lot, aren't you?"

"What do you mean?"

"Seligman, my love life. You know, it's not your business."

"But, Matty, I care about you. And I don't want you to get hurt."

"If you want to have me back in your life in any way, you will never tell me what to do again. This is the right thing for me in so many ways. Don't make me choose."

Abi was silent for a moment, then she put a soft hand on Stone's shoulder and said, "I won't. I promise."

14 Stone had always coveted his father's 3,500-page *Webster's New International Dictionary*, second edition, published in 1948 in Springfield, Massachusetts. It was as thick and heavy as a blacksmith's anvil, but it was a beautiful leather-bound book with marbled endpapers and full-color plates of the official flags of the United States, the great seals of the states and territories, flags of the nations of the world, and house flags of various steamship lines. The Judge kept it on a walnut book stand in his study, and Matthew, as a child, would flip through the pages, believing the key to all knowledge was contained inside. If a word was not in the dictionary, it could not exist, and he believed this magical book gave him power. In second grade, Pinky had called Matthew a moron in front of some fifth graders, and Matthew looked up the word when his father was busy on a phone call; like a wizard making a frog disappear, he crossed it out. He couldn't be a moron, he thought, if there was no such thing.

He now realized, his love of language and books might have come from this very dictionary, as he had spent countless hours poring over words and their meanings. But he had forgotten he had this habit of striking out words, a photo negative to the manner in which his father marked his own books. As a child, Matthew the Destroyer killed the words *dolt, idiot, Jew, moron, retard, faggot, weakling,* and dozens of others. The words still existed, he understood, but somehow he believed he had sapped them of their power to hurt. If his father ever found the defaced pages, he never said a thing. Just having the book spread out before him that morning on his bare mattress brought back a flood of memories, and he recalled the time he crossed the word *mother* out of the dictionary. He was thirteen years old, and well beyond the age when he believed his childish vandalism could make a difference, but there it was, x-ed out in furious black ink.

His mother was back now and he tried to read the dictionary's definition beneath his scribbles, but he could make out only the partial, "that which has produced or nurtured anything." He found a pen and finished the job he had started all those years ago.

He thought about Dasi and the words *love, lust, desire, need,* and was about to read off the definitions to see if he could sort out his feelings for this woman he had only just met, when the buzzer rang. It couldn't be his mother. She had promised to give him some breathing space, saying she was just a phone call away, but she was so full of wants that Stone was afraid she had already broken her promise. The buzzer rang and rang for five uninterrupted minutes as Stone lay on his mattress, pillow over his head to muffle the sound. Then the buzzing stopped and someone was banging on the apartment door. Stone charged down the hall in just his boxer shorts. He opened up to find Moshe hulking in the doorframe. He was dressed in a black suit with a white shirt and a broad-brimmed hat cocked on his cinder-block head. "Get dressed," Moshe said, peering into the apartment, his eyes as dull and stupid as a cow's. "It's late."

"Late for what?" Stone said.

"Get dressed. It's late."

"Don't you know how to say anything else?" Stone said.

Moshe thought for a moment and then said, "Rav Seligman sent me."

He was just an oversized errand boy with a limited vocabulary. Of course Seligman wanted to see him. Stone realized this was his chance to find out more about Dasi. He rushed to his room and threw on some clothes.

"Where is Rabbi Seligman?" Stone said, locking the door behind him.

"Follow me."

They crossed Myrtle Avenue, dodged a bus, and continued past the tangled vacant lot where the rusted hull of an old car sat on blocks, overrun by weeds and vines and whip-thin ghetto palms. A small sign on the fence warned of rat poison with a grotesque skull and cross-bones. Another, perched above a crumbling brick wall, read: LISTEN TO R. R. NATION.

They descended the slope toward the BQE in silence, Moshe several paces ahead of Stone.

"Hey, where are we going?" Stone asked, but Moshe did not respond.

Moshe walked fast, but with an awkward hitch in his step. One of the heels of his scuffed leather shoes was two or three inches higher than the other. Moshe crossed during a break in traffic and did not wait for Stone, who was held back by a row of cars driving abreast, one of them blasting its deafening horn. For a moment he thought of turning back, but Moshe was eyeballing him from the other side of the street, so he gave up the idea and crossed when traffic broke.

They arrived minutes later at a decrepit brick warehouse across the street from the Catbird Seat. It looked unassuming and nondescript in the daylight. This was the place Zohar had been asking about: the Crown of Solomon Talmudical Academy. What a wreck of a place, Stone thought, and to call it an academy of all things. Stone glanced around to ensure Zohar wasn't following him now, but he was nowhere to be seen. Moshe climbed the concrete steps and rang a small buzzer. A face appeared at the caged window set high on the iron door and then the door opened. "You're late."

"What are we doing here?" Stone asked.

Moshe pointed with his thumb at Stone. "You're a Jew. Say Kaddish."

"You had to trick me into this?"

"Not a trick," Moshe said. "You'll see Seligman after."

Stone stepped inside, remembering vaguely that Seligman had asked him to come say Kaddish here and, in his drunken state after the Rosh Hashanah luncheon, he might have agreed to do so. Now he would know what was going on inside the warehouse, but he would never tell Zohar. He was disappointed to find they stood in a bare, high-ceilinged room with concrete floors and exposed light bulbs burning at the ends of naked wires. Stone followed Moshe up a dusty flight of stairs, past a religious seminary on the second floor where ultra-Orthodox men in black swayed over their prayer books, to the third floor, and along a narrow hallway to a small room where a red eternal lamp burned above the ark and the bima.

There were fewer than twenty men at prayer, and the room smelled close and stale. A few young men turned their heads when Stone entered. He recognized the three students from the luncheon at Esther Grunhut's, but only Dasi's cousin Yossi acknowledged Stone with a wink. Why would anybody want to pray in such a makeshift, unspectacular place? Moshe handed Stone a prayer book and pointed to a corresponding page in his own.

He wished the sanctuary were illuminated with the warm magisterial glow of Beit Avraham, that numinous God-light sifting down through the high windows of the temple, that sanctifying quality he had always associated with what was considered to be a holy place. Stone thought he recognized the yeshiva student who had lent him his jacket whispering to the man next to him, who in turn whispered something to the one behind him. A young man with a wide prayer shawl thrown over his shoulders ascended the low bima and began to read from the Torah.

Stone followed along in silence, observing the congregants in their prayers, and wished he could feel the warmth and intimacy these worshippers experienced, something to grasp on to in the darkness. But he was bored, and began to conjure Dasi in his mind. There was something about her that made him feel everything would be all right if he could just possess her, make her his own. He wanted to climb inside her, wear her, look out on the world through her eyes.

Moshe leaned over toward Stone. His breath was otherworldly, like burned coffee and gum rot. Streams of sweat ran down his face. "The Kaddish," he said, turning the pages of Stone's book.

Now that he was faced with the Aramaic words before him, laid out like tiny prehistoric fossils on the page, he realized that his refusal to say the prayer was a pointless and childish rebellion. How narcissistic had Stone been in his mourning, how selfish that he could refuse completing such a simple task? His reason for refusing to say Kaddish for his own father was nothing but a petty, juvenile act of defiance. He had failed to honor his father during his lifetime, and he had come to understand too late that his father had been distant to him not because he didn't love him or care about him but because so many other people depended on him and his vision and strength. Stone could have joined him on his mission, but he had chosen not to out of ignorance or arrogance or the simple fear that he would be subsumed by his father, a homunculus clinging to a giant.

And though he could not understand them, Stone read the words easily—a distant memory instantly recalled. He read the words in lockstep with the voices of the worshippers and knew there was no God. But he understood the prayer wasn't for God, it wasn't even for his father; it was for him and his own comfort, declaring himself as a member of a community. The simple recitation of this prayer would place him upon the shoulders of countless generations of Jewish men before him who had mourned for their fathers. Though his mourning and pain felt unique in the history of the world, Stone understood now he was one of many.

When the service ended, Stone searched his memory for a time when he had felt this peaceful inside, his stomach a calm sea after a terrible tempest. He had awakened at last, placating those self-denying doubts that had tormented him for so long. Yossi approached him and offered a warm handshake, as did several other yeshiva boys. One of them asked Stone if he would be returning tomorrow to join their minyan, and he said yes.

Moshe appeared and told Stone he would take him to see Seligman. The black SUV with the tinted windows was parked around the corner by the Brooklyn Navy Yard, and Moshe lifted off his broad-brimmed hat and placed it on the passenger seat so that Stone would have to sit in the back. It was a short drive to Schochner's Glatt Kosher Diner, a converted mobile home anchored on blocks beneath the hum of the BQE in the Williamsburg neighborhood. It was hard to believe anyone would ever want to dine at such a place. The sounds of Yiddish and English mingled in the greasy air. Four broad-backed men in matching suits sat hunched on low stools at the counter, eating. They gesticulated and held court, clinking their silverware against chipped plates and dishes, mouths full of food. Moshe stood silent sentry at the door, his fringed *tzitzes* hanging sloppily from his shirt.

Stone took a seat at a faded Formica table across from Seligman, who was absorbed in a newspaper. He looked up and smiled warmly.

"Glad you could make it," Seligman said, plucking a toothpick from his mouth.

"I'm not sure I had much of a choice," Stone responded.

Seligman looked concerned and said, "He didn't strong-arm you, did he? Moshe's harmless."

"Let's just say he's got a very heavy buzzer finger."

"Well, Moshe's Moshe. What can I say? You're here."

Stone wanted to ask Seligman about Dasi, but he thought it would be indecorous to say something so soon, particularly since he had made a fool of himself at lunch the other day. Seligman wasn't going to give a glowing recommendation to a drunk, so Stone shifted the conversation in a more advantageous direction. "You'll be happy to know I said the Mourner's Kaddish for my father this morning."

"I'm very proud of you, Matthew. You are a good son." Seligman smiled, and through his tinted aviator glasses, Stone saw his eyes were full of kindness. "My apologies for eating without you. My blood sugar gets low and I don't think straight. Why don't you order something? My treat."

"I'm not hungry," Stone said.

"You've got to eat something. Especially with a fast day coming up. You fast on Yom Kippur, not before," Seligman joked. "If you do, all bets are off."

"What do you mean?" Stone asked.

"The Book of Judgment is open now, and it is sealed on Yom Kippur."

Stone puzzled over the mackled letters of the grimy cardstock menu, stripped of its jaundiced lamination. "Are you trying to scare me into ordering some of this awful food?"

Seligman let out a roaring laugh. "Of course not. What I'm saying is this is a chance for you to clean your spiritual house. Start again with a clean slate."

"I said Kaddish today," Stone said. "Doesn't that bring me some level of forgiveness?"

"It's a good start. But one is not instantly a righteous man for doing what is expected of him," Seligman said. "You need to learn to forgive yourself as well. Matthew, we are all deeply flawed. That's what makes us human. We are all sinners. Yom Kippur, the Day of Atonement, is a day of healing and forgiveness, and it is available for anybody willing to receive it. Who wouldn't want to receive healing and forgiveness?"

"You know I don't believe in God."

"But you do believe in metaphor, and God is a powerful metaphor if that's the way you want to see it. There are three ways of sinning. There is sinning against God, violating his ritual laws. There is sinning against somebody else, another person, acting in a hurtful manner. Most importantly, there is sinning against yourself, bringing harm to yourself."

How much did Seligman know? Certainly he had seen him at the luncheon as he drank glass after glass of terrible kosher wine. He had drunk so much he had blacked out. But with all of his years of wisdom, did Seligman know of his suicidal ideation? Did he know about the pills, about the burning? Did he know that his father's books spoke to him and that he would do anything they suggested in order to satisfy his father?

"Order something, Matthew. I'm sorry there's no alcohol on this menu, but I'm sure you can do without for a little while."

Stone was being lightly admonished by Seligman and his only response was to order kasha varnishkas.

Seligman lowered his voice, and Stone had to lean in to clearly hear what he had to say. "Now, Matthew, you mentioned at the luncheon the other day that you know where the money is."

Stone froze. He had no recollection of saying anything about the money. Perhaps in his drunken state he had let slip in a moment of boastful pride that he was in charge of the funds. It was possible; he was trying to impress Dasi. But now he worried about what else he might have said.

"Did I?" Stone said.

"Don't be coy, Matthew, my time is very valuable."

Stone waited to answer him, trying to read the expression on Seligman's face, which was tight with anticipation. "I don't recall," Stone said. Seligman's eyes narrowed behind his aviator glasses. He knew Stone was lying and Stone wasn't certain if he was better off if Seligman knew or did not know where the money was.

"Okay, I know where the money is."

Seligman exhaled and smiled warmly. "Attaboy, Matthew."

"The account is passcode-protected and I couldn't access the account."

"Did you try the passcode I shared with you? It was the only code we ever had."

Stone told him that he had indeed tried the code and even went as far as repeating the numbers to Seligman.

Seligman breathed out a long breath and took a sip of his tea. "That's too bad. I know how much you would like to move into the apartment on Henry Street. It is such a beautiful property. The perfect place for a young man to start out again on his own. I would hate to see the building condemned by the city. Your father dreamed about that museum for years."

Stone was certain there was never going to be a museum. He had read enough of his father's books, knew enough about his obsession with his reputation and legacy to understand that honoring Brandeis, Cardozo, and Frankfurter would only underscore how flawed Walter Stone was as a judge. The public would never accept that this museum was anything more than a crass publicity stunt to elevate the disgraced Judge to the same level as those great men and women. How could there be a Walter Stone Museum of American Jewish Jurisprudence without mentioning his father, Julius Stone the murderer, without mentioning Demjanjuk, without mentioning the Court Street Riot? The scrutiny alone would be enough to smear his father's name anew. Stone had found an article about his father's resignation tucked into one of the Judge's books, torn from a Columbia alumni magazine, in which his former colleague, New York State Supreme Court justice Leonard Samuel, said: "Walter was embarrassed, humiliated. He was never the same again." His father had scratched a red checkmark of agreement in the margin. It was strangely surprising to find his father was indeed a human being, not an impervious demigod but a human being prone to the same pain and doubt as anybody else.

"There is not going to be a museum, is there?"

"Of course there will be, Matthew. But we need the money to make this happen."

"Why did my father move the money without telling you?"

Seligman let out a long sigh. "To be perfectly honest with you, I have no idea for certain. You know as well as I do your father was a complex man. I believe he may have done this as a way for you to prove your worth, to show that you really have what it takes to step into his shoes."

"What are you talking about?"

"He wanted to keep control of the Eretz Fund in the family. Who would be more fit to forge his legacy than his own flesh and blood? He is providing you the chance to accomplish everything he did not."

Stone sank back in his seat stricken by the certainty that Seligman was correct. The books, the notes, the underlinings; *everything is in the books.* The passcode was, without a doubt, in the books, and Stone was uniquely positioned to find it. This was a purposeful challenge his father had set for him, a chance to prove once and for all he was worthy of Walter Stone. Seligman had been sent here to guide him in his father's stead, to shepherd him through this challenging time, and to stifle his most cowardly impulses.

"I've been reading his books," Stone said. "I've learned so much about him in such a short time."

"Are you absolutely sure you have not come across any significant numbers among your father's belongings?"

"I'm certain," Stone said. "But I feel as if he is speaking directly to me through those pages. If there is a passcode hidden somewhere in the books, I know I am meant to find it."

"Your father would be so proud of you," Seligman said. "I am proud of you. You're just a young man, still at the beginning of your journey through life. Sometimes it is difficult to live in the shadow of greatness, and now that he has gone to the other world I believe you will finally be able to come into your own as the man you can be."

Stone looked Seligman squarely in the eyes and said, "Trust me. If I find the numbers, you will be the first person to know. I know how important this was to my father."

A grim-faced waiter dropped a plate of kasha onto the table in front of Stone.

Seligman was proud of him, his father was proud of him. It might be true there were no second acts in American lives, but Stone knew that everything up until now had been preamble, a tortured opening to the greatness that would be his life.

"I wanted to ask you about Dasi." Stone imagined Dasi across the table from him in place of Seligman. He ached for her red lips, her long pale neck, and he imagined his father blessing them with his approval. Life was only now beginning.

Seligman smiled. "She's a lovely, vivacious girl—and smart. You know, she's just moved back to do her master's at Columbia. You and Dasi had a lot to talk about."

"I didn't say anything . . . strange? At lunch the other day?"

"I don't know," Seligman said. "Why do you ask? Do you like her?"

Stone just wanted to know whether she was available, or even open to spending time with someone like him who wasn't immersed in the depths of Judaism and its endless rituals and restrictions. But the answer had to be yes, it had to be. "She's sharp, irreverent," Seligman said. "You'd like her."

"Is she married?"

Seligman laughed a full belly laugh again and said, "Her parents would love someone to take her off their hands. She drives them crazy."

"There was something about her that made me feel I could be the person I always wanted to be."

"Like right now you feel like you're only half a person?"

"Not really," Stone said. Most of the time he was barely a person at all.

Seligman held his cellular phone out to Stone. "Call her."

"I can make my own date," Stone said.

"Then do it. Now is as good a time as any," Seligman said.

"Why are you so interested in taking care of my love life?" Stone asked.

"A good woman can do a lot to heal a damaged spirit."

"But, did I say or do anything stupid the other day after I drank all that wine?"

"Call her and find out yourself." He began dialing. "She's staying with her aunt, whom you know, so—hello, Esther? Zalman. Where's the *vildechaya*?" He paused and raised his eyebrows. "Put her on."

15

Stone took a taxi to Beit Avraham on Ocean Parkway, saw the red Thunderbird was still parked in the street where he left it on Rosh Hashanah, and walked the rest of the way to Esther Grunhut's house. He was on the cusp of something important, though he couldn't say what. He wanted to have somebody in his life who would fill the space around him, someone who would understand him and not judge him.

Esther Grunhut opened the door as if she had been standing behind it waiting for him to arrive.

"Matthew, I'm so glad you could come," she said. "Hadassah will be ready in a moment."

The house had been transformed since the day of the luncheon. Without the conversation and laughter, the silence was unsettling. Esther wore the permanent countenance of the widow, the face of someone too familiar with death and the hurt left behind. Stone saw death in everything these days. This was the late Rabbi Avraham Grunhut's house after all, and he had been close friends with Stone's father before he was assassinated. Stone was certain he would have been more curious the day of the luncheon if he had not been seated across from Dasi, if he hadn't drunk so much. But now, waiting for her, he thought of his father and Grunhut. Had he and Grunhut talked late into the night at the small kitchen table, reminiscing about Hebron and Kiryat Arba, planning the establishment of other Jewish communities in the West Bank?

Dasi appeared a moment later, her painted lips an impossible red. "Hi," she said. "Are you feeling better?"

She wore a freshly scrubbed citrus scent, suggesting she had just stepped out of the shower. A snatch of late afternoon light fell across her face, highlighting the stark whiteness of her skin. Her black hair was pulled back into a tight ponytail, emphasizing her bangs cut straight across her forehead.

"I've never felt better."

"Seriously, how are you feeling?" Her voice was higher than he remembered. She looked at him with those dark eyes of hers, thick with black eyeliner. He had cleaned himself up since they had met at the Rosh Hashanah luncheon. He had shaved and showered and was wearing all his own clothing: a clean shirt his mother had washed and a pair of pressed pants. Most important, he wasn't hungover. He promised himself he would not drink with Dasi.

"That could take all night."

"That's okay. You can talk to me."

"Thanks," Stone said.

"I know you're going through things."

She asked if Stone was ready and he said he was. Dasi called out to her aunt Esther, "Be back later."

"Not too late, huh?" Esther called back. "And take the mobile in case I need to reach you."

In the car, Dasi asked Stone if he remembered what they had spoken about the other night.

"We talked about a lot of things," Stone said. He wasn't sure what she was getting at; he barely remembered anything.

"*Tashlich*?" she said.

"Remind me again, what's *tashlich*?" He did not recollect ever having heard such a word in his life.

"You said it sounded fun. Ring any bells now?"

As he drove, Stone had this uneasy feeling that he was living an entirely different life from the one he was aware of, a parallel, shadow life. When he drank, took pills, smoked weed, another person appeared who looked just like him, acted in his name, and stole away with his memories—a most profound abnegation of self. He admitted at last that he did not remember. *How fucked up was I?* Stone wanted to ask, but didn't dare.

"It's my favorite Jewish custom. You were drunk and you said you had to come back for your car anyway and you asked if I wanted to see you, and I suggested *tashlich*. It's fun, really, and it's supposed to be done after services on Rosh Hashanah, but I wanted to do this with you."

"Of course I remember," Stone said.

"No, you don't."

"Well, refresh me then."

"I will," she said.

The sun was setting as they arrived at the Fulton Ferry Landing, just in time to see a wedding party, dressed stiffly in full regalia, mock-smile and pose at the photographer's insistent commands, barked with all the decorum of a middle school gym teacher. They looked anxious and miserable. "And they can't figure out why I'm not married," Dasi said.

"Tempting though, isn't it?" Stone joked.

"Very."

"Aren't you supposed to have three children by now, halfway to a first set of twins?"

"Yep," Dasi said. "I'm an old maid at twenty-four. And I wouldn't have it any other way."

They leaned against the low metal barrier on which the lines of a Walt Whitman poem were cut out along the entire length. "And you that shall cross from shore to shore years hence, are more to me, and more in my meditations, than you might suppose."

"It's like he anticipated this moment and is speaking directly to us," Stone said.

"Maybe he did," she said.

"So, what happens next?" he said.

She leaned out as far as she could over the railing and said, "Look." Stone stared past the hulking mass of a dormant warehouse, past the Brooklyn Bridge, toward the southwest and the setting sun. The brackish smell of the East River stabbed at his nose as he leaned out, his thighs pressed against the cool steel.

"See her?" Dasi asked. In the distance, crowned with the pink-and-orange nimbus of the setting sun, the Statue of Liberty stood, proud arm raised in the air.

"Beautiful," Stone said. He had forgotten the surprising sensation of recognizing beauty in the world.

"Look how strong she is, standing sentry at the mouth of the harbor," Dasi said. "This is my favorite spot in the city. It's so tied up in poetry: Emma Lazarus, Whitman, Hart Crane and his bridge."

"You read Hart Crane?" Stone said.

"Do you think I only read Torah and Talmud?" Dasi said.

"No," Stone said. But he wasn't sure what to make of her. "I love Crane." He recalled how Hart Crane had drowned himself at sea and how his body had never been found. His poems remained, so that he still lived in books.

"I read a lot, I'll have you know."

"Me too," Stone said.

A dipping cormorant wheeled across the sky, offering the illusion of strumming across the bridge's thick cables. The sun was sinking in the distance over New Jersey, and the bursting palette of colors bled and faded in an instant, leaving the city across the river cold, hard, and steely. The Twin Towers rose above the jumbled chaos of Lower Manhattan like the two tablets of the original Law—austere, forbidding, and awesome—the many lights in their narrow casements burning against the coming darkness.

"You studied Crane in graduate school?" Dasi asked.

"Yes, but my thesis was supposed to be about Walt Whitman."

"Supposed to be?" she said.

"I didn't finish . . ." Stone trailed off. "My father."

A tugboat passing by blew its horn, and Stone was aware of the sound of waves lapping beneath them.

"I'm sorry."

"Don't be sorry. It wasn't meant to be," Stone said. "Hey, tell me about Columbia. Are you taking a class with Mr. Palestine himself, Winston Haloumi?"

"May he die and be well," Dasi said. "First day of classes he was out on the steps of Low Library again, spreading his hateful propaganda. You should have heard the crowd cheer when he said the Israeli occupation is being funded by money from the United States and how Columbia must divest its money from Israel the way it did from South Africa in the 1980s. It was disgusting."

"My father called him an A-list celebrity terrorist."

"It's true. He's shouting, 'No to apartheid. No to Israeli occupation!' as he stands on the stairs of the Low Library beneath the statue of Athena, goddess of wisdom, crying academic freedom, as if that is the highest virtue, ignoring the fact that just last year he was filmed throwing rocks with a bunch of teenagers in the Security Zone in Lebanon. That's terrorism! He promotes violence and hatred against Jews, and Columbia is a private institution and he's using his position as a shield." Dasi paused and shook her head. "I thought I was getting away from all that, coming back to New York. I'm so tired of politics."

"Then why are you studying politics?"

"That's me. Full of contradictions. Who knows? Maybe I'll join the State Department one day."

"Show me what this *tashlich* is all about."

"Of course," Dasi said. "You'll see that Judaism isn't all about synagogue and restrictions."

She turned away as she dug into her bag on the ground beside her, the buttons of her spine pressed against the light material of her dress. A moment later she produced a large Ziploc bag full of old scraps of bread.

"Time to cast away your sins," she said. "Throw them all away."

"Seriously?"

"This will make you feel better. I promise. Let the river carry your guilt and vices of the past year away."

He tried to joke, "Were your sins so bad you have to drown them in *that*?" But Dasi held her focus.

"For ordinary sins," Dasi said, holding the challah out to Stone. Her almond-shaped face looked so earnest he just wanted to pull her close by her ponytail and kiss her hard on the neck, hard enough that it hurt, so she knew she belonged to him. This was a new sensation for Stone, so accustomed to treating women with tenderness. Some overwhelming force was at play, and Stone knew he had better follow those impulses or remain alone forever.

She gestured for him to tear off a piece.

"I think I'll need something stronger than that," Stone said. When it came to sins, he didn't even know where to begin.

"Take a piece," Dasi said, and he tore off a corner of the glazed loaf.

"What is a regular sin?"

"Small stuff, like letting a door slam in someone's face, cutting off a car in traffic, not phoning someone back."

"Leaving the toilet seat up?" Stone asked.

"That's two pieces, at least," she said.

She had moved closer to him, and Stone allowed her to enter his space.

"Now hold the challah in the air."

"Do we have to say a prayer?"

"You can, but I just fire away." She drew back her arm and threw the challah out into the river. Stone did the same.

She had such a look of concentration on her face that Stone concluded Dasi was dredging up every transgression she could recall and tossing them into the East River. Seeing her body in motion was exhilarating, thrilling in his most private places. He watched Dasi and the swift motion of her arm, followed by a slight breathy gasp, and he could no longer consider his sins.

"Done," Dasi said at last. A thin film of perspiration shone on her forehead; she wiped it away with the back of her hand.

"You must have been really bad this year," Stone said. "That was fun, but I don't feel absolved."

"We're not done," she said, reaching into her bag and producing two fossilized pieces of bread. "Rye bread."

"I suppose I'm expected to say something wry," Stone said.

"You could do that, but bad puns are the worst sin of all and can't ever be cast away. It's a personality flaw."

"Got it," Stone said. She reached for Stone's hand, pried back his fingers, and placed the bread into his palm. Her fingers were long and

slender and radiated a profound energy. It was the first time his skin
had touched hers, and it was like an affirmation of Stone's entire life.
This could be something real, he thought. Just the way she touched
him, so intimately, convinced him Dasi wanted him as much as he
wanted her. This was no hallucination, it was as real and concrete as
all the pain he had suffered over the past months and years. Her body
spoke to his on a level beneath words, that irresistible magnetic power
that drew lovers together.

She held the bread in the air; Stone did the same.

"This is for the sin of *lashon harah*—the sin of gossip, slander,
speaking badly of others."

Why now? Stone thought. Couldn't they stay right here in this
moment, just a little longer? He had no doubt in his mind he had
committed *lashon harah* against his father in every way imaginable.
Stone tore off a piece of bread and threw it into the river. He had
slandered his father through both words and deeds—his way of life
was slanderous to his father's name. He threw another piece of bread
into the river. He had slandered his father before his community, by
refusing to say Kaddish, to honor his name the way sons had done
for their fathers for thousands of years. It was a sin of stubbornness,
arrogance, and youthful determination, suggesting he was somehow
bigger than history, family, wrenched from the continuum of blood
ties reaching back through the years to the original flame of life. But
Stone was facing up to his sins now, and with every piece of bread that
sank under the diamond-black water, a small piece of the old Stone
drowned as well; he reveled in the dualistic joy of both killing himself and going on. He threw the last scrap of bread far out into the
river, and was aware of the lights running along the taut cables of the
Brooklyn Bridge, hanging in the sky like a low-lying constellation.

Stone had not been aware of Dasi as he tossed the bread, but she
was watching him now with a worried look on her face. His heart
thumped hard in his chest.

"Are you all right?" she said.

"I think so," Stone said. "That was more intense than I thought."

"Do you want to stop?"

"No, no," Stone said. "I'm okay."

A smudge of moon appeared like a thumbprint on the screen of the sky, and disappeared just as quickly behind a bank of drifting clouds. Dasi held a piece of honey cake in one hand and a piece of whole wheat bread in the other. "What's next?" she said. "Sins of the heart or gluttony?"

"Gluttony sounds Christian to me," Stone said.

"Well obviously you've never seen me eat," Dasi said, laughing. She put down the bread and tore off a piece of cake.

"If you were such a glutton, would you throw away a piece of cake?"

"Good point," Dasi said.

"You know, I think I've had enough, if it's all right with you. Are you hungry?"

"Always."

"Then let's eat."

They found a restaurant on Smith Street and sat by a picture window with a view of the street. Dasi ordered a plate of pasta with tomato sauce and no meat, and a glass of red wine.

"Vegetarian?" Stone questioned. Everyone he knew at Wesleyan was a vegetarian, or a vegan, or macrobiotic, or something else altogether.

"Are you kidding?" Dasi said, gnashing her teeth. "Kosher."

"But you'll eat in a nonkosher restaurant."

"I'm kosher," Dasi said, "not crazy."

The wine arrived and they clinked glasses and drank. This wine was so much better than the cough syrup sweetness of the Manischewitz that Stone considered ordering a bottle for the table. He wanted to ask her so many things, but before he had a chance to speak, she said, "I'm trying to figure out what your thing is."

"My thing?"

"Yeah," she said. "You know when you meet a new person and they are just so great, it's hard to imagine what their flaws can possibly be? But of course we all have flaws, none of us are perfect. It can take a while to figure out, but I'm a blunt Israeli and an inquisitive New Yorker. I like to just jump ahead, get things out of the way so I know what to expect." She took a sip of wine, and Stone did the same. "So, what's your thing?"

He could not tell her misery was his thing, that he had been unhappy for so long he didn't know what it felt like to experience sustained joy. "I like to read," he said. "All the time."

"That's not a thing! It needs to be a personality thing, or a vice, or something that you wish you could change about yourself."

"Like a red flag?"

"More like a coming attractions advertisement."

He couldn't tell her about the pills, or the nights he had zoned out so high on marijuana he was floating in space. He couldn't tell her about burning himself, or his half-assed suicide attempts, and he couldn't tell her about his mother, how sometimes he wished she was dead. He couldn't tell her about the disappointment he had been to his father or about his failed studies, and he could never ever mention the heart wreck of his past relationships, so he threw the question back at her. "What would you change about yourself if you could?"

"You're not playing fair," she said.

"Who says I'm playing?"

Dasi paused for a moment as the food arrived, considering her words. "Okay. My room is messy. It would shock you how disgusting it is. Clothing all over the floor. Piles everywhere. You can get lost in there."

"Tell me something of substance," Stone said, emboldened by the wine, "if you want me to know you."

Dasi spun a bale of spaghetti onto her fork. "I'm good at breaking hearts," she said.

"Is that a warning or a threat?"

"You asked, I told."

The image of her grinding someone's heart under the high heel of her shoe ignited a flame within him, and he wanted to know more. It was dangerous getting involved with her, and that threat of heartsickness and emotional destruction just made her all the more alluring. Her wineglass was stained with the blood-red prints of her lips and, with the pretense of asking if she wanted more wine, he reached out and touched the lip marks on the glass with his fingertips.

"Tell me more," Stone said, pressing his knee against hers beneath the table.

"You don't want to hear this."

"I do," he said. "Tell me how many hearts you broke."

"Just one," Dasi said, her eyes downcast. "But many, many times."

"Tell me who," Stone asked.

"Not now," she said.

"Come on," he nudged.

"Okay. I've known him since I was four or five," Dasi said at last. "Like forever. Sometimes it feels even longer."

"You hurt him?" Stone asked.

"Yes," she almost whispered.

"How did you hurt him?"

"I don't want to talk about it."

"Just tell me," Stone pressed. The vicarious thrill of her damaging another man was too much to resist.

"Not now."

"That's not fair. Just tell me."

Dasi took a long sip of wine, placed the glass carefully on the table, and said, "I saw your father on his last trip to Israel." She bit her lower lip, as if she had been thinking about mentioning his father for a while and now wished she hadn't.

Stone wasn't sure he'd heard her right, his scalp shrinking against his skull, a tightness and itching around the temples, pulling irresistibly at his skin like a thousand minuscule hooks. Was this the sensation of aging all at once? Of dying? His father, his creator, his master, had known Dasi but never once mentioned her name. The Judge really must have hated him, hoarding the best and most beautiful woman Stone had ever known, but why?

"On Tu B'shvat," Dasi said. "Before he got sick."

Stone had been wasting his time researching his worthless Whitman paper in the Olin Library when he could have been with Dasi, if only his father had bothered to introduce the two of them.

"You knew him?" Stone said. He had to look away, afraid Dasi would read his face and make out the shock in his features.

"Of course. He was good friends with my uncle, may his memory be blessed, and my father, and, of course, Zalman. I'd see him two or three times a year."

"He never mentioned you."

"Oh," Dasi laughed, "I'm just a kid to him, his best friend's niece. I would still be a kid in his eyes no matter what. But he was always polite, unflappable, confident. He was doing such important things for Israel. He was amazing, his tireless energy, his commitment, but he always took the time to sit and talk with me. We talked a lot about graduate school and how I wanted to study international relations. I had been thinking about going to Hebrew University, and he suggested Columbia. And I guess he convinced me. He was like a mentor to me; I was so honored to have known him. Of course, I was just a minor character in his life. But he was very important to me. He always will be."

She offered a small smile, and Stone remained silent. He had always suspected if he only applied himself, laid off the drugs, paid careful attention, he was capable of knowing everything, the way his father had known everything. But, paradoxically, Stone knew attempting to know everything would only lead him to the conclusion that he knew nothing at all.

"Tell me about my father," Stone said. "Tell me anything." She was a living conduit to the mystery of his father, and she sat right before him sipping her second glass of wine, her face flushed in the candlelight.

"He spoke about you a lot."

"He did?"

"Yeah," she said, smiling, her teeth bright. "Of course. 'My son Matthew won a medal for his swim team; my son Matthew wrote a poem and was sent a glowing rejection letter from *The Paris Review*; my son Matthew is studying Aramaic; my son Matthew won a scholarship to Columbia.' He spoke about you all the time. Even as a teenager, I knew one day we would meet and I would fall for you."

A confluence of joy and hatred washed over Stone like ice-cold water dumped onto his head, breathlessly bracing in its pure unexpectedness. His father had lied to Dasi, speaking of his own accomplishments as his son's. It was the Judge who had won a medal for his swim team as a senior at Brooklyn Tech, with a hairline fracture in his tibia yet. The Judge had received a two-page rejection letter from George Plimpton himself requesting more of his poems. The Judge had studied Aramaic and mastered it in two years. And Stone hadn't even applied to Columbia. His budding relationship with Dasi was predicated on a heap of lies. She had fallen for his father and his accomplishments. She could never have loved Stone for himself. But why had his father done this? Was this a gift from the other world? Right now, as Stone finished his second glass of wine, it didn't matter. Who was he to argue with his father's reasoning when Dasi sat before him and his father lay dead in the ground? This was the greatest gift his father had ever given him. At that moment, beneath the dim light of the restaurant, Dasi's warm knee touching his beneath the table, her breath quickened from the telling of tales, Stone didn't care.

"I want to kiss you," Stone said.

"You will," Dasi said, leaning forward, teasing. "When it's right."

"And when is that?" Stone asked.

"You'll see."

Stone was about to reach for her hand when her aunt's cellular phone rang. He was tempted to tell her not to answer it, but she was already rooting through her bag in search of it, saying, "What does that yenta want now?"

She flipped open the phone and managed a bright hello, but her features quickly clouded, transformed into an expression of concern. "Okay, just tell me where," she said. Then, looking up at Stone: "Do you know where Brooklyn Hospital is?"

He nodded his head in assent. She hung up, her pale face gaunt in the glimmering candlelight.

"That was my cousin," she said, shaking almost imperceptibly. "Remember Dov from Rosh Hashanah? Something terrible has happened."

Dov had been the surly yeshiva student whom Stone had instantly disliked. Stone called for the check, threw down some cash, and followed Dasi out of the restaurant.

Dasi was silent the whole way over, and Stone watched her pick nervously at her nails, out of the corner of his eye. He wanted to find a comforting sentiment, something wise to say, but nobody had been able to comfort him in his grief, nobody had yet found the right combination of words to soothe him, so he offered nothing, knowing it would be futile. But Dov? Why would she care about him, of all people?

THE HOSPITAL ELEVATOR opened at a crossroads of identical gleaming hallways, near a swarming nurses' station. Dasi received directions to Dov's room from a nurse. They found Dasi's cousin Yossi and a friend arguing outside of Dov's room. They both wore baseball caps and had *tzitzes* hanging from their shirts. The friend had a soft doughy paunch and wore a thin beard that barely covered his cheeks.

"This is fucked-up shit," the friend said.

"Be cool," Yossi said. "We'll take care of it."

"Who's going to call his mother?" the friend said.

"Aren't you?"

"I thought you were!"

Dasi called out to her cousin and the two stopped arguing.

"Hey Das. So glad you're here," Yossi said. "Better say a *mishebe'rach*."

"What happened?" she said, eyes glassy. "Is he going to be okay?"

"Some black guy sprayed him with lighter fluid and set him on fire," the doughy friend said, stepping close to Dasi.

"What?" Dasi said. "Why would someone do that?"

"It's pretty ugly," he said. "You don't want to go in there."

She ignored him and turned to Yossi. "What happened? Why did this happen? That doesn't make any sense."

Stone had disappeared. All of her energy was directed outward, away from him, and he felt foolishly bereft.

"We'll find who did this," Yossi said.

"And we'll deal with him," the doughy friend said. "In the meantime, all you can do is pray for a *refuah shlema*."

"Why don't you call his mother in Israel?" Dasi said. "And tell her what happened."

Dasi went into the room and Stone followed, leaving Yossi and his friend arguing in the hall. It was a semi-private room, and the curtains on the far side, where a muted television played, were drawn. Five yeshiva boys stood in silence around Dov's bed. Two wore Yankees caps; the others wore knitted kippas. They were all dressed in slacks and nondescript button-up shirts with fringed *tzitzes* hanging out. It wasn't until Dasi and Stone approached the bed that the group realized they were behind them.

"He's out," one of them said in a half whisper.

"How long?" Dasi asked.

"Since we got here."

"How bad is it?"

"Doctors don't think the burns are that serious, but he got knocked on the head pretty good."

Dov lay still on his back, tubes strung between his supine body and the humming machines. His face and neck and hands were loosely bandaged. Dasi leaned forward over the bed and Stone sensed the warmth of her presence dissipate; she had been standing that close.

She whispered, "Dov. Dov, it's me, Dasi."

"He can't hear you," one of the yeshiva boys said. "They've drugged him up."

"It's me, Dasi. Dov?"

She leaned close and whispered something Stone could not hear. The gesture was so intimate that Stone wanted to tear the tubes from Dov's body and pull the plug on the humming machines. This was his night with Dasi, and Dov had spoiled it. Nobody told Dov to go and get himself hurt. That was his own doing. Dasi sang something quietly in his ear, a soft, lilting Hebrew tune Stone did not recognize. It dawned on Stone that it was Dov she had been talking about at dinner—they were the ones with a history. Whatever it was that constituted Stone's ego throbbed in agony, his countless nerve endings afire with envy.

"Somebody do something," someone said behind Stone.

"What do you want me to do? Petition Hashem directly?" someone else responded.

"It wouldn't hurt."

Yossi came back in the room. "Avi, there's a cop outside who wants to talk to anyone who was there."

"Aw, shit," Avi said.

They all ignored Stone, as if he were not even present, but he understood it to be part of the selfish tunnel vision of grief. How could Dov engender such feelings when Stone knew nobody would mourn his own passing?

"Dov was just coming back from the *beis*," one of the students said.

"Then what happened?"

"Ask Avi."

"Avi's a schmuck for letting this happen."

"That's enough," Dasi said. "Arguing isn't going to help Dov now."

"I can't believe it," one of the kippa-wearers said. "Three years in the IDF and nothing, not a scratch. Come to New York—and this." Stone noticed his face was sharp and arrogant and ratlike. "This is what happens when Jews are in galut. This is exactly what happens."

"Bad things happen everywhere," Dasi said. "This has nothing to do with America."

"Yes," the rat-face said, "but in Israel, it is credit toward redemption. Here it's pfff, nothing, a Hollywood movie to eat and throw away."

"Dov will be all right," another said.

"We have to liquidate the Diaspora before the Diaspora liquidates us," the rat-face continued. "Whenever a Jew is violated, it is an assault on all of us. We must fight back."

"Who knows? Maybe this happened for a reason," one of them said. It was the first time he had spoken. He was the shortest of the group and wore his hair cropped in a military buzz cut. He spoke with a Hebrew accent. "*Heshbon nefesh*—accounting of the soul."

"What?" the rat-face said.

"Maybe he was not so good this year."

"I should punch you in the face," the rat-face said. "Who invited you here anyway?"

"You know why I'm here," the Israeli said. "You couldn't piss straight without me. Maybe he was not a good Jew."

"For that he has to die?" Yossi said, his voice cracking. "Dov makes a few mistakes. He's human. For that he has to die?"

"He's not going to die," Dasi said. "Nobody dies while the Book of Judgment is open."

Dasi bolted out of the hospital room. Stone followed. She had kicked off her heels and walked quickly with a shoe in each hand. Stone caught up to her at the elevator bank and touched her lightly on the wrist. Without her heels on, she looked so small, her shoulders hunched from crying, stockinged feet crossed one over the other. She was beautiful.

"Don't," she said. Her eyeliner had streaked, as black tears ran down her face. "I just . . ."

"Are you okay?"

"Not now, Matthew. Please."

The elevator arrived and they stepped in. A man strapped to a gurney was already inside, attended to by two members of the hospital staff. Dasi found a tissue in her bag and cleaned her face. The elevator doors opened and she stepped out. She slipped her shoes back on, her composure regained. Stone needed to find the right thing to say, to draw her back in, to make her understand that he cared about her and that he could be a good thing for her. "I'm sorry," Stone began.

"No, no. It's okay," Dasi said. "I just get embarrassed." She gestured to her smudged eyeliner. "Look at me with my stupid panda eyes. I'm sorry. I should have just had you drop me off."

"Then I would've had to come back to drive you home." He smiled what he thought was a warm smile.

"I would have found a way back by myself," she said, "but thanks." They walked out into the night and Dasi said, "In a way, I'm glad you're here with me."

"I know it can't be easy to see someone you care about suffer." He was careful with his words, measuring to see how Dasi would respond. How much did she care about Dov? And what did this mean for him?

"He's someone from my past, but somehow finds a way to stay in my present. Sometimes I think he's always going to be in my life, and now I feel terrible for wishing otherwise, seeing as he's in there now and who knows what's going to happen."

"He's going to be fine. This is a good hospital. He's getting the best care he can get," Stone said, not knowing the first thing about the hospital or the quality of care. "And I'm sure your visit helped."

"You think?"

"I'm certain."

He opened the Thunderbird's passenger door for Dasi and watched her slide into the plush front seat. Through the windshield, she looked exhausted, drained by the evening's events, a pensive expression on her pale face.

"You know what, Matthew?" Dasi said as he started the car. "You're kind. You are a kind person."

"Thank you," Stone said, "I think?"

"It's a compliment," Dasi said. "I don't think I would ever call Dov kind. He was, is, passionate, strong-willed, intense, dedicated, but I don't think I would ever choose to call him kind. There is not enough kindness in this world. What I'm saying is, I appreciate you, I appreciate your understanding. I know this has not been the most stellar first date, but I want you to know I learned something important about you tonight. You are everything your father ever said about you."

16

Dasi sat in the passenger seat, pulling on the ends of her hair and staring blank-eyed out the window, her thoughts somewhere far off. The serene confidence she had projected before seeing Dov in the hospital had melted away. Both she and Stone were in pain, and he wanted to show her they could help each other ease their hurt. But he couldn't scrub the image from his mind of Dasi softly singing into Dov's ear, her mouth so close to his face. He wanted that sort of intimate attention for himself, and he burned, his lungs billowing in his chest to gather ample breath, his neck hot with jealousy. He rolled down the window a crack to let in some fresh air. They stopped at a red light somewhere along Ocean Parkway and Dasi looked over at Stone, her jaw tight, pale skin luminous in the sweep of oncoming headlights. "Matthew, I'm so sorry about tonight. This wasn't what I had in mind."

"It's all right," Stone said. "We're together now. That's what's important."

It wasn't that late, and he didn't want the night to end on a down note, with Dasi lost inside her worries, so he said, "Do you want to go for a walk?"

"That would be nice," Dasi said. "I really do want to speak with you more. I have so many questions. But I'm such a mess."

"You're a human being," he said. "That is the human condition."

She laughed. "You think so? We're just neurotic masses of cells bouncing from one crisis to the next?"

"Pretty much."

"Yet we strive for perfection."

Dasi was silent for a moment. "For whatever reason, I feel like I know you, but I just met you. Does that make sense?"

"Of course," Stone said. Everything she thought she knew about him was a lie, but it didn't matter because she was here with him now. Dasi was the purest form of redemption, and Stone was prepared to say anything to make it happen. "I feel like I can tell you things."

"Me too," Dasi said. "You know, it's not easy being me." She slid closer to Stone. "There are so many expectations and I've done everything I can, but sometimes it's like it's never good enough."

It sounded like she was talking about his life, though he had done little to meet his father's expectations.

"I went to yeshiva, took care of the house, did two years in the army, served as a drill sergeant, a *mefakedet*, and shot better than the men. But yet, that's not enough. I want to continue my studies and not feel guilty if I don't want to get married on someone else's schedule. As a woman, I'm expected to be everything at once, a tough but delicate creature made of steel and silk, like some ideological Frankenstein."

They drove beneath an overpass. The wheels of a subway car clicked and clattered and faded into the distance. The smell of the salt air was stronger now as they approached the ocean, and Stone rolled his window all the way down.

"I understand expectations," Stone said, "and I understand disappointment."

"I know you do, but I'm bad news. I make people angry when I can't give them what they want."

"You're talking about Dov, right?"

Stone didn't want to imagine them together in the present, future, or past, but he knew if he was going to supplant Dov, he needed to learn what it was that had driven her away.

"Are you sure you want to hear this?"

"Of course," he said, turning onto Surf Avenue, where he quickly found a parking spot.

He flicked off the ignition and turned to Dasi.

She looked into his eyes with astonishment. "Okay," she said. "It's just hard sometimes."

They walked up a sand-strewn path toward the boardwalk, Dasi careful in her heels, until she decided it made more sense to take them off. Stone offered to carry her shoes and she let him. The heat rising off the insoles of her shoes provided Stone the awesome sense of her body heat against his skin, radiating its own sensual power.

"It was just always expected, me and Dov, though I don't remember anyone ever asking me. When we were kids, it was sort of cute, how he said he would marry me and give me everything I wanted. He was always around, whether we were in New York or Israel, and I think that made him believe we were meant to be. But I grew up and there were boys and crushes and all the ordinary feelings and confusions that come along with adolescence. I just couldn't give him what he wanted."

The bright lights of the Wonder Wheel were extinguished. Coney Island, ordinarily a glittering jewel box of amusement park rides and rigged games of chance, was shut for the season. It was a cool night with a soft breeze blowing off the ocean. The sky out over the Atlantic flickered with a handful of stars. A hulking 747 circled somewhere above the Rockaways, red lights blinking as it prepared for its descent to Kennedy Airport.

"What did he want?"

"I don't know. It doesn't feel fair talking about him like this while he's suffering in the hospital, but I can't live my life for him."

They reached the boardwalk, and the sand beneath their feet crackled. Dasi's voice was tight with worry, but determined.

"Dov would get jealous when I liked another boy, and he would bully them and harass them and tell them to stay away until I was afraid to tell him anything. But while I was in the army, something awful happened. I couldn't tell my parents about it, and I didn't want to tell my friends, so I went to him to see how he would react— maybe to punish him a little bit—but he was really good to me, understanding, caring even, and I guess I was so needy at the time I just gave in."

"What happened then?" Stone said. Her body slumped when she spoke, as if she were speaking of a great defeat.

"We dated on and off for almost four years after that, and he took that to mean we were going to be together, we were inevitable. Every few months, I would break up with him, tell him he wasn't what I wanted, but he refused to believe it was for real. In the end, through tears and arguments, I always came back to him. But it's over, it's been over for a while, and I don't know what I can do to make him understand we can never be together."

The boardwalk was quiet, the silence underscored by a Russian couple strolling past, speaking tenderly in that sonorous language of poets, despots, and madmen, their words floating on the air like fragile bubbles. Dasi was crying, softly at first, her face turned away. Then her face was aflame with emotion. "What if he dies, what if he dies in there? That's not how I want it to end."

Stone leaned in and pressed his lips to hers with the blindness of instinct. They were warm and wet with tears, and she accepted it for a second, two, and then her eyes flew open and she said, "No, no! Not now, not like this."

Before he had a chance to respond, Dasi took off running down the boardwalk with a dull cry of raw emotion, leaving Stone feeling gut-punched and vacant. His need and impatience had ruined everything. Though her slim frame did not look athletic to Stone, she raced down the boardwalk at an incredible speed, her thin arms pumping at her sides. He watched her for a moment, sick to his stomach, trying to comprehend what he had just done, and then, realizing he still held her shoes in his hand, took off after her in the direction of the Parachute Jump and the pier.

Stone was in no shape for running and still had a twisted knot in his calf muscle from the time he'd run from Zohar down Myrtle Avenue. His body was little more than a receptacle of pain and his lungs could barely take in enough air as he sprinted along the boardwalk. He saw Dasi turn onto the pier and he slowed, knowing there was nowhere she could go. It was surprising how many people were out fishing along the length of the pier. Some fishermen had tents and portable grills set up. Another blared the Yankees game in Spanish from a crackling radio. The air was cooler out over the water and the old wooden boards smelled of fish and seaweed. Dasi stopped at the end of the pier, the loneliest place in the world—a deep, boundless ocean between her and the next living human. She had collected herself, but he was afraid she might still be upset with him. He'd made a terrible miscalculation and wasn't sure she'd ever give him another chance. The waves crashed below, and that eternal sound of the sea rolling in and out made him feel sentimental for something he wasn't sure he had ever experienced.

"Dasi," he called.

She turned, offered an awkward smile, and said, "I've messed everything up, haven't I? This must be the worst first date in the history of the world."

"I can take you home now if you want," Stone said.

Dasi looked surprised and said, "You're not going to give me a chance to make it up to you?" She tied back her windblown hair with an elastic. "You know, your father always told me never to cry."

"Just because he never cried doesn't mean it's not all right for you."

"Thanks," she said. "But really, twice in one night is a little much, don't you think?"

They stood side by side, looking out over the dark water, a vast, complex world hidden beneath its depths. "Tell me what was special about my father."

"Whenever we spoke," she said, after a moment, "we always spoke in Hebrew. It was especially important for him to speak Hebrew in Israel. He considered it his responsibility to the language to ensure it thrived. We all spoke English perfectly, but he made it his mission to speak Hebrew no matter what. One of my first memories of him: I was a little girl and my mother was off somewhere with my brother, who was sick with the flu. Your father tucked me into bed, and I handed him a bedtime book to read to me. I wish I remember what it was now, but I know it was in English and it was one of my favorites; your father translated the story, on the spot, into Hebrew as if it were the most natural thing to do."

Stone recalled that his father had cultivated a pitch-perfect Israeli accent, and remembered his own shame at not comprehending a word his father said when they had checked out of the King David Hotel as Fairuza sat waiting in a coffee shop. If only he could have made his case in Hebrew, things might have turned out differently. He thought his father was speaking Hebrew to the hotel clerk, the cab driver, the airport security agents, and the flight attendants simply to punish him and make him feel small, but now he realized his father was sticking to his convictions, and that he would have done the same with anyone.

He was afraid Dasi would say something to him in Hebrew and he would be exposed as a unilingual fraud, so he said, "My father loved books as much as anyone I ever knew. I have all his books piled up in my room. I'm reading them now. I find it's the best way to feel close to him now that he's gone. In some ways, it feels like he's more alive now than he was before."

Stone didn't want to spend the evening speaking of the sick and the dead, but his father's presence loomed over their entire connection with each other and he wanted so badly to know why the Judge was so special for Dasi.

"Does reading his books help you cope with his loss?"

Stone exhaled a long, audible sigh. "He made notes in his books, mapped out plans, formed counterarguments in the margins, railed at stupidity, inserted his own thoughts, made connections between texts published across centuries. Reading for him was a full-contact sport, an intellectual jousting match between himself and all the great thinkers who came before."

"You're lucky you've got his books," Dasi said. "In that way, you'll always have him."

"But it's not easy. I can see so clearly what came before me, and I know I will never be able to fill his shoes."

"I think you're doing all right," Dasi said. And then, "Come here. It's getting cold."

Stone moved behind her and slid his arms around her waist, his groin pressed to her behind. He could smell the salt on her neck and something floral in her hair. It was soft against his cheek and he breathed in, feeling safe and content. Though he had not held a woman in ages, it felt completely natural to hold Dasi in his arms as she eased her body into his, breathing evenly.

"My father would be happy," Stone said. "I finally met a Jewish girl."

"Is that all I am? A Jewish girl?"

There was laughter in Dasi's voice.

"You're more than that," he said. "Much more." Stone couldn't help but think about his father and his deft guiding hand, how he had anticipated this moment for years much the way a chess master sees checkmate from the opening.

In the distance, a container ship slipped out toward open sea, its tremulous lights pulsing faintly at the point where water met the sky.

"Where do you think it's going?" Dasi said, after a long moment of silence.

"Somewhere far away," Stone said. "Maybe Nebraska."

Dasi laughed. "This is nice," she said. "It sort of feels like déjà vu, don't you think? As if we've been here before?"

"Like we've been watching that boat drift away forever?"

"Not like that. Just this feeling of familiarity. I can trust you. Tell me something you've never told anyone before."

Her chest expanded and fell with her breathing, her skin cool in the evening air. If he moved his hand just a little higher, he would feel the rhythmic drumming of her heartbeat, but he continued to hold her as they were, just the delicate materials of her dress separating her body from his. Perhaps it was the realization that the two of them occupied the same close space at the end of the pier, their bodies warming each other as the waves crashed beneath them, but Stone felt safe to open up about his loneliness. "For the longest time, I was like an orphan, all alone in the world. Even when I wasn't alone."

Dasi turned to look him in the face and said, "That's terrible. I didn't know you lost your mother as well."

"It's complicated," Stone said. "I did lose her, a long time ago. She went away, and now she's back and I don't know what to do."

"You're upset with her for leaving you."

"I was upset for years," Stone said. "I felt abandoned, betrayed, and then nothing at all."

"And now she's back, you want to punish her?"

"I just feel so confused. There's no room for her in my life anymore."

"It may feel that way, but you have to know that your life can never be right until you straighten things out with your mother. She is the root of everything. Please, Matthew, give her another chance. No matter what she did, she will always be your mother."

"But now that my father is gone," Stone said, shifting the subject, "I have him in a way I never had him when he was alive. It's different, but if I want to know precisely what he believes about Spinoza's *Ethics*, or the Trail of Tears, or the Nuremberg Trials, all I have to do is open his books and he's there."

"I guess that's kind of beautiful," she said, squeezing his hand. "A different sort of immortality. But you still need your mother. Everyone needs their mother."

He hadn't had her in his life through so many important milestones, and it was too late now. Any relationship he could piece together with his mother would be for her own benefit, to assuage her guilt for abandoning him.

"Matthew, I hope you understand you're not alone."

It made Stone uncomfortable to discuss the subject of his mother. He had not planned on talking about her. "Tell me more about my father. You said he was a mentor to you."

"He was," Dasi said. "If it wasn't for him, I would be living a completely different life."

Stone buried his face in her neck and felt the pulse of her words as much as he heard them. "He was the one who encouraged me as a young teenager not to forget about the secular world. I remember your father telling me he believed Shakespeare's sonnets are every bit as beautiful as King David's psalms, and that I didn't need to choose one or the other. It can be so easy to lose yourself in Torah and Talmud and all the laws and leave the rest of the world behind. So many of my friends became insulated, isolated, especially living out there in the hills of Judea and Samaria, and they lost all perspective on what was important. You can fight forever over who owns an olive tree, but one day you realize your whole life has been about a single tree, and I wasn't going to make that mistake. He helped me realize I wasn't a fragile flower, and that I could choose what I wanted to have in my life and what I didn't want to have in my life. You know, I could have received a service exemption from the army on religious grounds, and I remember speaking with your father about it. I was only eighteen, so young and so full of fire. My parents didn't want me to serve, but I thought it was hypocritical that we were living surrounded by Arabs, protected twenty-four hours a day by the IDF, and I wanted to do my part. A friend of mine was stabbed to death by an Arab in a nearby wadi when I was fourteen. I was never going to let that happen to me. I was prepared to die for what I believed in, so I went to the army."

Stone had never really believed in anything, but he was certain he believed in Dasi. "Did you ever have to shoot anyone?"

Dasi turned around, her dark eyes inscrutable. She did not answer the question, but instead said, "Tell me more. I want to know all about you."

Stone did not hesitate to answer. "I never thought I'd make it to my thirtieth birthday."

"That's sad," Dasi said.

"Until now," Stone replied.

"Really?" she said.

"I finally feel there is something meaningful to live for."

Dasi lowered her eyes and brushed her fingers softly across his face. "You can kiss me now."

"Are you sure?"

"Yes. I want to kiss you."

And as they kissed, they pushed their bodies into each other as if neither one of them could get close enough. Her breath was hot at his ear and she whispered, "You're so tender, so careful. I would never have expected that from Walter's son."

Stone did not answer. He knew his father, always vigorous and strong, was at the front of her mind. She was looking for the Judge in him. Dasi had been set up to fall in love with a lie, and now that she was with him, he didn't measure up to that fiction. He imagined the Judge's giant hands gripping her slim waist, bruising her skin, his mouth pressed to hers, a hint of danger in his kiss as if he would swallow her whole. She kissed almost mechanically, her tongue probing Stone's mouth with a rhythmic tedium. This was the most humiliating kind of disgrace, failing to match up to his father as a sexual being, and Stone was electrified with a surge of anger gathering in his extremities. He grabbed a handful of her hair and pulled back hard, kissing her with force, their teeth colliding, before they lost themselves.

Dasi leveraged her body against his as she gasped into his mouth, and he pulled her hair back again, exposing the length of her neck. He had always been so respectful to women, almost tentative with their bodies, afraid he might in some way harm them. Her eyes rolled back in her head, eyelids fluttering; he bit into the soft flesh of her neck, a vein pumping beneath her skin, and he drove his teeth in again.

"Don't stop," she said. "Don't stop."

"You want me to hurt you."

"Yes," she said.

"It may leave a mark," he said, kissing the raw skin on her neck.

"That's okay," she said. "I'll just wear my hair down."

Try as he might to clear his mind, to disappear into the moment in the darkness out there at the end of the pier, Stone could not get Dasi's words out of his brain: "You still need your mother. Everyone needs their mother." The more he tried to push them from his consciousness, the more he found his mother gathering strength in his mind's eye, until she was fully dimensional before him, her arms wrapped tightly around him, fingernails scoring his back, and it was not Dasi he was kissing, but his mother. He tried to wrest her away, hands at her neck so she would vanish and leave him be, and he squeezed at her windpipe, thumbs pressing in, choking her, so she gagged and retched, making the most horrible, inhuman sounds he had ever heard, and then he saw that his hands were at Dasi's neck, her face coloring beneath his grip.

Stone dropped his hands to his sides, horrified by what he had done as Dasi coughed and gasped for air. "I'm so sorry," he said. "I'm so, so sorry."

She straightened her dress and fixed her hair. Her lipstick was smudged around her lips as she looked him in the face and said, "Just be careful."

He didn't know how to respond to that, so he said, "I don't know how that happened. I guess I lost myself. Are you all right?"

"It's okay," she said. "Don't worry about it. I mean it. It's okay."

She offered him her hand and he took it as she said, "It's getting late. I need to get home."

17

First thing the next morning, Stone returned to the warehouse and said Kaddish with renewed fervor. The yeshiva boys he had seen at the hospital greeted him warmly. Though they had not spoken to him the night before, he had been elevated in their eyes solely based on his association with Dasi. Each one came over and shook his hand, asking how he was, and he, in turn, asked about Dov. He didn't care about Dov, of course, but he wanted to show his kindest face to the world so no one would see him coming if he had the chance to take Dov down.

He felt a strange, almost seismic release joining the others in unison as they uttered the words "*yehe shemeh rabba*"—Aramaic words believed to have power in obtaining forgiveness. He had returned that morning on his own, without coercion, and did what a father expected of a son; unclogged whatever was blocking that ragged thing called his soul and cleared the slate for the rest of his life. Stone knew, with absolute certainty, that the Judge heard his purifying words, and that Dasi was a gift in exchange for Stone's uttering of them.

The yeshiva boys asked if he wanted to stick around after the service, but he begged off, saying he had some reading to do. He was working his way through his father's twelve-volume *Jewish Encyclopedia* published by Funk and Wagnalls in 1901. He was particularly fascinated by the legend of Akiba, which he had found at the bottom of one of the pages dedicated to the Kaddish. His father had written Matthew's name in pencil in the margin of the enormous book and then erased it, leaving behind a heart-aching palimpsest that managed to both chide and comfort. Stone read, again and again, how Akiba met a spirit in the forest, gathering wood to be used as fuel for the fires of Gehenna. The spirit told Akiba he was burned daily in punishment for the way he behaved in life, and he would be released from his terrible tortures only if his son would recite the Kaddish. On learning that the man had neglected his son, Akiba sought him out and educated him so that one day he was able to stand before an assembly of Jews, recite the Kaddish, and free his father from the burning fires of Gehenna.

Though the book was almost a hundred years old, and the tale many hundreds more, Stone knew his father believed it was Stone's obligation to save him from all his sins here on earth. The ghost of Stone's name scratched in pencil into the margin of the book was a tacit admission of his paternal failings, the closest his father ever came to admitting he had neglected Stone, and Stone knew that Seligman was a messenger sent to lead him in the right direction.

Stone was still thinking about that legend as he stepped into the bright sunlight and started up the street. Those whispers he had been hearing just beneath his comprehension, layered underneath the English-language words as he read his father's books, he realized, were in Aramaic, that ancient desert language, the eternal holy tongue, lingua franca of all the millions who had already passed into the world to come. His father was beseeching him to read those books in the only language he could use now, guiding Stone to drink in all the knowledge required to keep going on the Judge's behalf, so he could live on through Stone's deeds. In doing so, Stone knew he himself would grow larger and larger, buoyed by the foundation laid by his father.

Near the corner, by the underpass, he heard a car door open in front of him, but did not look up until he sensed it blocking his way. Still in the throes of ecstasy at having joined his people in saying Kaddish for his father, he tried to slip past the car door but heard Zohar's familiar voice asking him to get in. That was enough to chill his blood and stop him where he stood. Zohar sat in the driver's seat, wearing a

pair of dark sunglasses to obscure his fanatic eyes. How the fuck could
he interrupt a moment of private communion like this?

"Get in," he repeated, starting his engine. The relaxed confidence
Zohar had carried on their previous meetings was gone. "Let's talk."

"I have nothing to say to you," Stone said.

"Do you want me to take you in on suspicion?"

"Suspicion of what? I haven't done anything," Stone said. "Maybe
you'd like to be cited for harassment. How does that sound?"

What could Zohar expect to get out of him? He was a son in
mourning seeking comfort and solace. Stone had started to believe
Zohar had forgotten about him and moved on, but he had been wrong.
He knew no secrets that could have any impact on Zohar. Even if he
did know something Zohar could use, he was not inclined to tell this
government-issued cocksucker anything.

"Matthew, let's not get confrontational here. I mean you no harm at
all. But I believe you know a lot more than you are saying."

"Well, that's one of the issues with belief. Sometimes no matter
how right it feels, it's still wrong." Stone stepped around the door and
Zohar jumped out after him, pressing a rough hand into his chest.

"I know you were at the hospital visiting Dov Wexler last night."

"Don't you have anything better to do?" Zohar's shit-eating face
was right in his, and Stone considered ramming his head into it. "Stop
following me."

Zohar lifted his glasses from his eyes and said, "If they come out of
the warehouse and see you with me, things can get very uncomfortable for you. You don't want that to happen, do you? Come on," he
said, gesturing to the car.

"Go fuck yourself," Stone said.

"Do you know what happened to Dov Wexler? I mean, what really
happened? Because I know the real reason he's lying up there in the
hospital. That kid is lucky to be alive. Somebody must be looking out
for him somewhere," Zohar said, gesturing to the sky with a sort of
ironic tilt of his chin.

Now this was information Stone could use. He climbed into
the car.

"We're not going far. We'll take a walk, talk. No pressure. If you're good, maybe I'll buy you an ice cream cone."

They turned onto Myrtle Avenue, and Stone asked, "What happened to Dov?"

"Why don't you tell me what you were doing in there, first?"

"That's not the way it works," Stone said. "Tell me about Dov."

"You really want to know what happened to Dov Wexler, tell me what you were doing in the warehouse this morning."

"I was saying Kaddish. Remember, my father died. I'm in mourning. Your turn."

"Is there any reason you chose a synagogue tucked away in an abandoned warehouse to say Kaddish for your father?"

"So now my choice of synagogue needs to be approved by the federal government?"

"Very clever. Now tell me, why there?"

"It's near where I live," Stone said.

"And that's not a coincidence, is it?" Zohar paused to bang on his horn as a pair of gray-haired black men stepped out of a barbershop and into the street. "Tell me what you saw in there. Weapons? Explosives? Anything suggesting an attack of some sort is imminent?"

"What the fuck are you talking about? It's a synagogue. That's it."

"Listen Matthew, and listen carefully. If you lie to me, I will make sure you are punished to the fullest extent of the law. Now tell me, did anybody whisper anything to you, say anything, mention any dates, places, anything? This is serious."

"I don't know anything, and that's all I'm going to say. Now are you going to tell me what happened to Dov?"

Zohar pulled his car into a parking spot adjacent to Vaux and Olmsted's Fort Greene Park.

"I'll tell you," Zohar said, turning off the ignition. "But first, tell me what the yeshiva boys told you."

"Nothing," Stone said.

"Not one word?" Zohar said. "Not even hello? Yet you were visiting their friend."

If Zohar had seen Stone at the hospital, then he knew he had come with Dasi, and there was no way he was going to mention her name to Zohar.

"The ER doctor said the remains of Dov's clothing stank of 2,3-dimethyl-2,3-dinitrobutane, which is consistent with a blast caused by C-4 explosives. Among other injuries, he's got a compound fracture in his left tibia, grade-three concussion, bilateral tympanic membrane rupture, various fragment injuries, and a case of road rash from hell. He almost blew himself to pieces playing with a fucking bomb, didn't he?"

Stone reeled in his seat, his head dizzy with confusion. If Dov was making a bomb and Zohar was telling the truth, what did Dasi know about this? She had known him her entire life. Could they possibly lie to her about the cause of his injuries? Stone doubted it. She was a lot closer to Dov than he cared to imagine. If what Zohar was saying was the least bit true, it meant Dasi was not who she said she was, and Dov was not a victim but a potential perpetrator. If what Zohar said was true, Dov was permanently damaged and would never be the person he was before the explosion.

"So, they didn't tell you," Zohar said. "You really don't know anything."

"I told you, I don't know anything."

Zohar climbed out of the car and beckoned Stone to follow him into the park. Stone had trouble gaining his balance, his legs weak. They climbed the three flights of wide granite stairs in silence, Stone, deadly curious, several steps behind Zohar. The whole of Manhattan Island lay spread out at their backs as they reached the Prison Ship Martyrs' Monument, a giant Doric column standing atop a crypt that held the anonymous remains of a fraction of the eleven thousand prisoners who died aboard British ships during the Revolutionary War. A cluster of pigeons scattered as Zohar sat, his back to the column. He gestured for Stone to join him on the ground beside him. "Don't worry. Nobody will bother us here."

Stone sat. Zohar dropped a thick manila envelope on the ground between the two of them.

"Are you familiar with the execution-style killing on Atlantic Avenue last week?"

"No," Stone said. He had been so immersed in his father's books he knew next to nothing about what was going on in the world. You could shut yourself up in your room for only so long; eventually the world would come and drag you out by the hair. "What exactly are you suggesting?"

"Just hear me out, and everything will make sense."

Stone asked Zohar if he had a cigarette and he shook one from a pack, handed it to Stone, and lit it. Stone took a long drag of the cigarette and, still breathless from the stairs, blew the smoke into Zohar's face. Though he was thriving at the moment, Stone knew he was only a hair's breadth away from spiraling back down into the darkness. He tried to steel himself against whatever was coming, imagining himself armored in his father's robe, a chorus of ancient whispers and wisdom in his ears. How would his father deal with a situation like this? Like iron, Stone knew, imperious, impervious, unflappable. But he wasn't like his father, no matter how many of his books he read. His stomach was already tumbling with anxiety.

"The murdered man was a wealthy businessman involved in buying properties in Jerusalem, Jaffa, and Nazareth."

"What about him?"

"Last month in Jersey City, someone murdered another wealthy Arab businessman, Salmeh Gheith, a real-estate developer. Execution style. Bullet in the back of the head." Zohar paused for effect, allowing the details to sink in. "I just got back from the Detroit field office. They're investigating a murder, another execution in Dearborn, another wealthy Arab involved in real estate. Do you see the connection?"

"Three murders in three different states," Stone said. "That's hardly compelling evidence of anything."

But Zohar continued, his voice rapid. "Three executions. Same entry point, same caliber bullet. Same MO across the board."

"I'm not following your logic." The thought of him being connected to any of these executions in even the most tangential way was so absurd, so outlandish, Stone thought for a moment Zohar believed he was somebody else, a different Matthew Stone altogether.

"The point is, we have the killer's car—a rental. Found it outside a motel. We searched the trunk and found blasting caps, detonators, and a hundred thousand dollars in cash. Why do you think he had that?"

Stone took another drag of his cigarette to cover his astonishment. "I don't know. Why?"

"Because something much bigger is going on."

"If something's going on," Stone said, "arrest them. That's my advice to you."

"It's not a crime until it happens. I'm not going to arrest them on a traffic violation. Why do you think the killer had detonators and blasting caps in the trunk of his car?" Zohar paused and looked Stone in the eyes.

"I don't know. Ask the killer."

Zohar shook his head as if Stone were a slow schoolchild. "I can't prove it, but I'm certain this ties back to Zalman Seligman. That crew of yeshiva boys, Dov too. Maybe even Dasi Grunhut."

"No," Stone said. "Not Dasi. She's not involved in anything, she's innocent."

"So you're inferring Seligman and the yeshiva boys are involved?"

"In what?" Stone said. "Don't twist my words."

"What did they tell you?"

"Nothing."

"And Seligman? What do you know?"

"I told you I don't know anything."

"But you are certain somehow that Dasi Grunhut is not involved in this."

"I'm certain," Stone said. "I don't even know what you're talking about."

"So she really has her hooks in you, doesn't she? Get a little sniff of what she's got under her dress and suddenly you're blind, deaf, and dumb. I don't blame you. She is very attractive. But seriously, Matthew, are you going to throw your whole life away for a taste of pussy?"

Stone wanted to lunge at Zohar, but held himself. She was the promise of happiness and nobody was going to take that away. "That's not how you talk about a woman," Stone said. "Especially Dasi."

Zohar raised his hands in an "I surrender" gesture and continued. "Listen, the killers are traveling back and forth, beneath the radar, because of their dual citizenship. Wexler is part of Seligman's crew. I'm not saying your friend Dasi is a killer, but maybe she's a courier carrying sensitive information they wouldn't feel safe sharing by telephone. She just arrived in New York a couple of weeks ago. Is that a coincidence? I don't know. Maybe she's aboveboard, maybe not. You are the right person to find out whether she is or isn't involved in a larger plot. If you want to vindicate your girlfriend, you'll do as I ask."

Stone jumped to his feet. "You know what, you are out of your fucking mind. I'm done."

The homeboys from the Walt Whitman Houses down below the trees were playing basketball and laughing, and Stone wanted to know that alien freedom of pure laughter and friendship.

Zohar did not follow, but called after him. "Someone killed Avraham Grunhut with a bullet in the back of his head. The wrong man was charged and put away. Who do you think killed Grunhut? That was your Dasi's dear uncle, remember."

Stone stopped, curious to learn where Zohar was going with this conversation. He knew it was cowardly to walk away, but it hurt too much to stay and listen. "Everybody knows who killed Grunhut," Stone said. "And he's behind bars."

"Your father and Avraham Grunhut co-founded the Eretz Fund with Zalman Seligman, Seligman running the Israeli operations, your father and Grunhut sharing control in New York. I believe someone affiliated with Seligman or your father killed Grunhut because of financial issues, control issues, issues of money and the joint account. Now, why do you think Seligman is courting you like a debutante? Because he wants to suck your dick? No, it's because of the bank account. Seligman needs money, and he thinks you, as the beneficiary to your father's will, have access to it now."

It was true Seligman wanted the money, but Zohar was wrong about his motivations. Seligman was Stone's father's representative here on earth, and he had been the one who had convinced Stone to say Kaddish, to free himself of the guilt and spiritual pain. But Stone hadn't finished doing his father's work yet, and the more he read, the more he understood that his father viewed violence as having moral legitimacy, as a viable means to achieving a Greater Israel, and now that he was gone Seligman needed Stone to help him access the money in order to fulfill his father's wishes.

Just a few weeks ago, the thought of bloodshed and killing would have sickened Stone, but as he had read, he had come to understand that killing was wrong only if one's goals were not achieved, and that his father's life would have been lived in vain if his wishes were not carried out. He stood before Zohar trembling with anger.

"Do you even know where the money is?" Zohar said, his mouth twisted into a half smile.

"I might."

"You know your father would never have trusted you with something like that."

"You don't know my father."

"It will surprise you what I know about your father." He reached into his wallet and removed a hundred-dollar bill. "I'll bet you I know Walter Stone better than you do. He's not who you think he is." Zohar held the bill out to Stone.

"Don't insult me with that."

"It's yours for the taking," Zohar said.

"Your arrogance is astounding. Keep your money."

To obliterate his father would be the same as wiping himself off the face of the earth. They were different links of the same chain; they had the same blood, and blood could never turn against itself without disastrous consequences. Stone had learned that the hard way.

"Listen, Matthew," Zohar said, switching to a more solicitous tone. "I apologize for the hard sell. I'll be honest with you: I need you. I need you to help me break the case before something catastrophic happens. Zalman Seligman has made six trips between Ben Gurion and Kennedy in the last six months—each trip lasting less than forty-eight hours. This is a man who doesn't speak freely. This is a tight-knit group of fanatics. I've got to disrupt them, find out what they're up to, and I need you to be my eyes and ears."

Zohar needed him. He was nothing without Stone. He was lost, and the fact that he was turning to Stone now only underscored the fact that he had value, value not measurable in dollars and cents. Stone could not help him, even if he desired. But he wanted Dov out of the picture, and Zohar had the means to make that happen.

"If I help you," Stone said, "you'll take care of Dov?"

"So, you do know what's going on?"

"Have Dov arrested. Put him in witness protection, deport him. I don't care. I want him gone."

"All right," Zohar said. "I'm sure I can do something. But you need to help me first. I want something tangible, concrete, not some bullshit story that sends me halfway around the world for nothing."

"Get rid of Dov."

"Tell me something I can use. I'm listening, but I don't hear anything."

"I want Dov gone before I say another word."

Zohar chuckled. "You're a real purebred, you know that?"

"What's that supposed to mean?"

"I didn't think you were like your father, or your grandfather."

"My grandfather?" Stone said, his innards filling with ice.

"Yeah," Zohar said. "You know how it works. The father of your father."

"One was a criminal, the other a judge. They barely even knew each other."

"I understand, Matthew, but sometimes the apple really doesn't fall far from the tree," Zohar said. "That's what worries me about you. Getting mixed up with these fanatics without the proper guidance from me. You rebelled against your family, and I'm afraid the loss of your father has been a terrible shock to you and might cause you to reevaluate your most fundamental values."

"What's wrong with that? Change is the only constant in life."

Zohar offered Stone another cigarette, and he took it. Zohar lit one for himself as well. Stone took a long deep drag, considering Zohar—his dark, olive skin, the circular birthmark on his cheek, the masculine smell of his cologne. We all want something, Stone thought.

Sometimes it was just as pleasurable to deny someone something as it was to grant them something. But he was curious to hear what Zohar had to say about the Judge. Stone, through the books, knew more about his father than Zohar could possibly know. He might have known that his father had withdrawn his alumni pledge from Columbia University when Winston Haloumi, the Palestinian firebrand and "public intellectual," had been hired to teach in the Department of English and Comparative Literature, but did Zohar know that his father had learned Spanish just to enjoy the pleasure of reading Cervantes's *Don Quixote* as it was intended? He had even written his own notes in Spanish, cross-referencing between the original and its many translations. Did he know his father had read Rilke's love poems so many times the pages had come loose? Did he know anything but lies and innuendo? His father was an educated and cultured man, with broad interests and a strong sense of justice. He was a Renaissance man in an age of know-nothing dilettantes, a deep thinker in an era of sound bites and simplification. Why was that so threatening to Zohar?

"Let me start at the beginning to put things in a clear context for you. Okay, Matthew?"

Stone took another drag of his cigarette and nodded his head. "Go ahead."

"Your grandfather, Julius Stone, arrived at Ellis Island with his mother and his three sisters in the fall of 1913, at the age of five. His first image of America, after three seasick days below the deck of the *Excelsior*, was of Lady Liberty holding aloft a shining sword. This is a story he liked to tell with a laugh—it's on record on his FBI files. He must never have forgotten that sword, carried that image of America in his mind all through his formative years, years filled with so much violence.

"His father, Friedrich, a Berlin tobacconist, contracted pneumonia on the ship and died in quarantine on Hoffman Island in Lower New York Bay. So Julius was the man of the family, even as a child.

"Julius, his mother, and his three older sisters moved to the slums of Brownsville, Brooklyn. He was a small kid, with hair thick and wiry like a shoeshine brush, who grew no taller than five foot five. Julius had to learn young how to defend himself. At the age of nine, he beat up a Pole from East New York who was trying to steal the scrap metal he had gathered from the Canarsie dumps. Later, caught stealing a necklace from a Pitkin Avenue jeweler, young Julius grabbed the startled jeweler by the throat and said, 'It's for my mother.' He was a funny kid."

Stone imagined his grandfather, with the same thick head of hair he had on his own head, his roguish smile charming the jeweler even as he robbed him. He was the same man Stone had met in Florida, with the joke shop cognac glass and the jaunty demeanor in spite of the fact he was dying. He looked nothing like the Judge, but Stone looked like a revised version of Julius, brought up on vitamin-fortified foods and proper health care.

Zohar continued, "Julius had been arrested more than half a dozen times for theft, assault, and burglary by the time he was thirteen and was sent to a reformatory upstate, where he spent the next two years.

"Prohibition went into effect during his time away, and after his release Julius got busy delivering illicit booze to speakeasies throughout Brooklyn. From Bedford Nest to Gustavo's to the Bossert Hotel in Brooklyn Heights, they called him 'Big Julie.' After making his rounds, he would head toward the waters of Brooklyn's south shore, or desolate Breezy Point in the Rockaways, sometimes going out as far as Montauk on his regular liquor runs. You know your grandfather was a killer, Matthew."

"That's what they say," Stone said.

That's why his father stayed away from Julius, studied law, and became a judge.

"Julius was only seventeen years old when he was said to have killed his first man, a Cuban who tried to take his cash without making his delivery. The Cuban was found on the shore of Jamaica Bay, strangled by a makeshift garrote fashioned from a piece of scrap metal. As you know, Matthew, strangulation became your grandfather's trademark.

"Julius didn't know it then, but he was already tied up with Murder Incorporated. He must have met with Arnold Rothstein around that time, because it wasn't long before he was running with his crew.

Bootlegging, murder, and execution were his marketable skills, and Julius put them on display throughout the rest of Prohibition and into the darkest days of the Depression, killing over a dozen enemies of the syndicate.

"And then suddenly, after a decade of murder and bloodshed during which he routinely carried ten thousand dollars in his pocket, Julius decided it was time to settle down, find a wife, start a regular life. So he married, moved to Ocean Parkway, opened a tavern on Kings Highway, and had two kids; Walter and Bunny. They joked at the Bureau that Bunny and her Downs was punishment enough for his crimes, but I don't think so."

Stone had vague childhood memories of meeting his aunt Bunny in a group home on Mermaid Avenue. She wore a frilly housedress and carried a feather duster with her, keeping herself busy dusting. Stone remembered being terrified of her ghoulish, smiling face and telling his father he didn't want to visit her again. She died not long after, and Matthew was haunted by her in dreams for months afterward.

"Anyway, Lepke and Gurrah and all the major players were in hiding and Dewey was chasing down anyone connected with Murder Incorporated, looking to indict. Yet, somehow, your grandfather just slipped away in complete silence. He must have hidden out in Florida while your father was growing up; sending money on the sly to pay for the house and the kids.

"But Julius took one more shot at the big money. Now, this story is more rumor than fact, but it's a nice bridge between his life of crime and his life in real estate, and it explains how he became so wealthy. The Sixth Avenue El was torn down in 1938, and the street was widened to become the Avenue of the Americas. Julius returned to his original staple that made him his first dollar: scrap metal. Julius took the profits from the Sixth Avenue El, which was rumored to have been sold to Japan for their war effort, and reinvented himself as a legitimate businessman selling real estate in Florida and the south, far from the eyes of his enemies.

"But your grandfather could not stay away from the action for long, and he began, like his friend Meyer Lansky, to contribute large portions of his profits to the Irgun, the militant wing of Jabotinsky's Revisionist movement, through the guise of the New Zionist Organization; a legitimate, structured outlet for his lifelong bloodlust. In the years preceding Israel's creation, Julius helped arm the Irgun, sending over two dozen shipments of weapons from New York to Tel Aviv. It was a long way from Pitkin Avenue, but Julius was sending the same message he sent to the Pole who tried to steal his scrap metal as a kid: don't fuck with a Jew."

That sounded a lot like Stone's own father, who idolized Jabotinsky and refused to show weakness, even when a touch of remorse might have made things easier on him. Stone had taken the path of least resistance, deracinating himself, denying his heritage during his years studying at Wesleyan. He had kept his head down, and nobody ever singled him out as being different from the rest.

"Julius signed your father up to join the Betar youth movement when he was thirteen. You know your father was skinny, bookish, and small for his age, but he was sent to train in the summers at paramilitary training camps in the Catskill Mountains, where he met the young Avraham Grunhut."

It was difficult for Stone to imagine his father ever being skinny, short, someone to be picked on. He pictured his father buried in books by Robert Louis Stevenson and Daniel Defoe and Mark Twain, reading over the same stories again and again as Julius shook his head at this professor of a son who saw more value in books than real life. By signing Walter up for Betar, Papa Julius was shaping his son, molding him in his own image—not as a violent gangster, but as someone who saw violence as expedient when it came to protecting the State of Israel. Even though Walter and Julius parted ways when the Judge was still young, Julius had found a way to influence his son for the rest of his life. The Judge had similarly tried to introduce Matthew to that world after his bar mitzvah, but the speech by the fiery Avraham Grunhut so disturbed Matthew that he told his father he never wanted to return.

"The rest is history," Zohar continued. "You know he grew to the height of six foot three, nearly a whole foot taller than his father, as if through sheer force of will. To further affirm their differences, Walter was completely bald by his early twenties, his head massive and majestic, like that of a marble statue found in a museum."

"And that's the end of the story?" Stone asked.

"That's the end of the beginning." Zohar smiled, and his eyes suggested he knew something more. He reached for the manila envelope sitting between them and dropped it into Stone's lap.

"This will explain the rest. Open it."

There was something portentous in Zohar's words, and Stone felt as if he had a bomb in his lap.

"Open it."

Stone's breath caught at the back of his throat, his mouth coated with bilious saliva.

"Open it. You can't be ignorant forever."

Stone knew his father was not like Julius, but he had been forced to resign the bench in disgrace, and his credibility had been impugned for his judgment during the Demjanjuk trial. That was on the public record. What else was there that Stone didn't know about? He was afraid of what he would find in the envelope, but he knew he needed to confront it in order to fight it.

Stone peeled back the worn tab and dumped the contents of the envelope out into his lap. Dozens of photographs lay spread across his lap and onto the concrete below him. Zohar cleared his throat and pointed his hairy-knuckled index finger.

"This is Miami, January 1972, again in the summer of 1974, and here, 1977."

Stone could not believe what he was seeing: his father and Julius together in each of the photographs. There was nothing to suggest they had been doctored in any way, and Stone just wanted to close his eyes and make them go away. His father had withheld his grandfather from him, lied about their relationship, and kept it alive in secret.

"Here in Brooklyn, Sheepshead Bay, 1975. The upstairs room at Gage and Tollner, 1974, 1973, 1976, again 1973—Christmas, this time. They go all the way back to the 1950s, when your father was in law school."

Zohar seemed to be taking great pleasure in revealing this to Stone. "Look. Here's Julius. You can see him clearly through the balcony window, days before he died. See how the Judge is holding him up? Do you see the warmth in that gesture?"

In the photograph, his father held his grandfather around his fragile waist, Julius's head resting on the Judge's chest in a snatched moment of intimate repose. This photograph changed everything, and Stone feared he was about to slip down a dark hole to be swallowed up forever. He wanted just to be embraced by his father's robe, to hear those mysterious whispers from the other world, and he, in turn, would demand an explanation. Stone's farce of a life had been a hallucination, a gruesome mistake in which he had been denied his birthright.

His mouth was so dry he could barely speak. "Why? How?"

"Do you think the FBI takes their eyes off a man like Julius Stone when he is living right out in the open, for all to see?"

"Why didn't you arrest him?"

"He was square with us," Zohar said. "He gave us names. Lots of them. But we still kept an eye on him. Old habits. You know what I mean?"

Julius had become a snitch, and had aligned himself with the law after all, bringing him closer to the Judge.

"Your father lied to you. He kept you from your grandfather so you would never know him. Maybe he thought he was protecting you, maybe something more sinister—I don't know. Whichever way you look at it, your father deceived you, right up until the end. Your father started the Eretz Fund with your grandfather's dirty money, and never let you in on it. Never shared the secret. Why do you think that was?"

Perhaps his father had been trying to shield him from his most base instincts, yet the Judge had run toward his own father, cultivated those violent impulses, leaving Stone alone to wither on the vine, a spiritual orphan with no direction.

"Fuck you," Stone said.

His father didn't deceive him, he left him with an impossible riddle to solve, a challenge set to determine the path for the rest of his life.

"Your father didn't trust you because he didn't trust Abi Stone, formerly Abi Schnitzer, the artist, Barnard girl, free spirit, because he didn't trust that her son, someone born of her, could be trusted. He didn't trust you were his."

"You're lying," Stone said. He had said Kaddish for his father, and had been instantly unburdened of guilt after uttering the words in that eternal language. There was no lying in the spiritual realm, no tricks of the light, just pure, transparent truth. "He was my father. I know it."

"He was. But he doubted for a long time. The American Association of Blood Banks shows in their records that three times, between 1974 and 1977, Walter Stone submitted the old serological blood tests to determine paternity—of course this was before DNA testing and was not one hundred percent accurate. Despite the fact that all three tests came back over ninety-three percent probability of his paternity, he must have had the devil of doubt whispering in his ear right until the end. What else can explain the Judge being such a prick to his only son?

"I believe these killings happening now are tied directly to your father and the Eretz Fund, and link all the way back to Julius Stone and his financial support for the bombing of the King David Hotel. All signs point to the conclusion that something much larger is going to happen soon."

Stone was still trying to make sense of everything he had just heard.

"I need your help," Zohar said, "to save lives. Hundreds, possibly."

"You think my father was a criminal and murderer? You want me to tear down my father's legacy as a lawmaker and a scholar."

"He destroyed his legacy all by himself with his indiscretions during the Court Street Riot trial. He showed his true colors there. Do you think he thought twice before having Grunhut killed? Or the others?"

"He didn't kill Grunhut," Stone said, a vice-crush of a headache squeezing at his brainpan. "They were friends."

"They were all friends—your father, Grunhut, and Seligman—but someone connected to either your father or Seligman had Grunhut killed."

"Why would they ever think to do that?"

"They each had plenty of motivation. Without Grunhut, your father was alone as president of the Eretz Fund—all that money, all that power. Without Grunhut, Seligman may have had reason to believe he would be elevated to co-president with your father. It never happened. Now, why do you think your father moved the money? Maybe he was afraid Seligman was going to kill him, too."

"This is absurd. Everything you have said has been a lie."

"Do these photos lie?" Zohar said, sliding them back into the envelope. "I understand it is hard to believe your father and grandfather were both violent, bloodthirsty men, capable of anything; Seligman as well. But you don't have to be that way. I know you're not like them. You can put an end to this cycle of violence."

"How?" Stone said, knowing now he could never again betray his father, even if it meant a thousand lives.

"Wear a wire."

"A fucking wire?"

"Zalman Seligman wants access to the money. Find out what he needs it for. And stay close to Dasi and her crew of yeshiva boys."

"Keep Dasi out of this. Do not mention her name ever again. Or else I'm done."

"All right, all right," Zohar said. "She's off-limits. I got it."

"And you have to get rid of Dov."

"Absolutely," Zohar said. "As soon as I wire you up, I'll make sure he disappears."

"Why do you think I can help you?"

"I'll be honest, Matthew. There are no other informant candidates, and you are practically on the inside, given entry not by ideology, which is assumed, but by birth. You'll be a hero. I promise," Zohar said, his voice catching, betraying emotion for the first time. "This is something really important. I'll find you tomorrow and have you fitted for a body recorder."

18

Something terrible was germinating in Stone's blood, his nerves vibrating, his pulse racing. He needed to calm himself down or risk spinning out of control. He'd stood at this precipice many times before and knew that once he crossed it, it would not be easy to find his way back. He went to the bathroom and stared hard at his face in the mirror, eyes red with exhaustion. Was Julius hiding behind that skin somewhere, was his father? If he looked deep enough into his own eyes, would he see them down there in the depths looking back at him?

The medicine cabinet was empty, aside from a few loose Band-Aids and Q-tips, deodorant, and rusted nail clippers. His brain throbbed like a nerve struck with a hammer, humming with the impossible realization that he was poised to effect change in a meaningful way, and it was up to him to choose which direction to go. His body prickled with anxiety, so he threw his father's robe on and paced back and forth in his room, considering what to do. The books called out to him, but the voices were so jumbled, he knew he would never be able to concentrate on a single sentence.

He called Dasi, but Esther answered and said Dasi was at school and would not be back until later. He thanked her, his chest tight with that frightening sense of solitude that made him feel as if he were the last person on earth, the empty space around him expanding infinitely. He wanted to tell her all about Zohar and his investigation, and for her to say she was not involved in any sort of ridiculous terror plot. Of course she would laugh it off, but some hint of doubt still lingered in Stone's mind, and he wanted Dasi to help him quash it forever. He held the phone in his hand, considering whether to call his mother. After some minutes, he grabbed the scrap of paper on which his mother had written her number off the fridge. He might be his father's son, but he was also his mother's son. He dialed the number with a sense of resignation and doom. The phone rang and she picked up on the second ring. "It's me," he said.

"Are you okay?" Abi said.

"Can you come over?"

"I'll be there in an hour," she said. "Sit tight."

Now that she was on her way to him, Stone wasn't sure he had made the right decision. He was not a little boy anymore and could never go back to a time before the damage was done, no matter how much he might have wanted to reset the relationship. But it was too late to phone her back—she had left right away to jump on the subway at Ninety-Sixth Street. He knew he wanted her to comfort him, help him make sense of the confusion around him, and in doing so he had surrendered to his longest-standing living adversary. She wanted his absolution and forgiveness, and he was prepared to give it if it still allowed him to honor his father and keep his legacy alive. He was afraid that his mother's hatred of the Judge was so deep he would be forced to choose, and he was certain, now that he had seen Zohar's photographs of his father and Julius, that the son always comes back to the father, no matter what their differences.

Pinky's door was closed, and Stone knocked, hoping he had some weed to spare. Pinky was in there, moving around in bare feet, a heavy bass beat thumping from within his headphones. Stone knew he wouldn't hear the knocking; it was a miracle he hadn't already blown out his eardrums, so he turned the knob and opened the door. Pinky's bedroom was even larger than Stone's, with the same high ceilings and tall windows. A stained futon lay on the floor, sunken in the middle from the dead weight of sleep. The floor was littered with newspapers, magazines, socks, dirty T-shirts, mugs, plates, coffee grounds, peanut shells, computer parts, nails and screws. There was not a single book in Pinky's room. Factory-wrapped boxes lay scattered everywhere. Pinky stood hunched in the corner, his muscled back to the door, mid-lift, stacking one box on top of another.

Stone flicked the light on and off to get Pinky's attention.

"Hey," Pinky said, flipping off his headphones. "I kinda thought you moved out."

"Keep dreaming," Stone said. This was the first time they had spoken since Stone had railed at him before Rosh Hashanah. Nothing had changed between the two of them since they had words, but Stone, in his loneliness, realizing it was a new year, decided to forgo starting up with Pinky again. He was another living human being, and that was something Stone required right now.

"Help me move this shit," Pinky said, confident of Stone's accord.

"How many VCRs do you need?"

"Use your fucking brain. You think I keep them all?"

Already Stone wished he was alone, but he wasn't going to leave until he got what he wanted. "Do you have anything to smoke?"

"Sure thing. Just help me move this shit."

Moving the boxes helped Stone clear his mind, and after a few minutes, he had worked up a sweat and the doubts haunting his mind had quieted down. Pinky packed a bowl and offered it to Stone. Stone put the glass pipe to his lips and took a long hit, holding the smoke in his lungs until he could hold it no longer.

Pinky looked on with a broad smile on his moronic face. "Good stuff, right?"

Pinky took a hit, closing his eyes as he drew in deeply. Stone had known Pinky most of his life, and though the death of his father had brought them together, he couldn't say he was glad to have been reunited with his old friend. Where would he have gone if Pinky had not called him at just the moment he discovered his father's apartment had been ransacked? He would have had no choice but to stay in the tomb of his father's apartment, and that was unthinkable. How convenient, Stone thought, that Pinky could divine his need so precisely and invite him to stay in his place while he found his feet—his place,

which, as chance would have it, happened to be so close to the synagogue at which Seligman wanted him to pray.

When Stone had first returned to Brooklyn, they had seen each
other only once for quick, awkward drinks and Stone hadn't planned
on calling Pinky again. It was obvious within the first minute of their
reunion that Pinky was the past, that Stone's connection to him was
sentimental at best, dangerous at worst, and he knew he could gain
nothing from this friendship. But Pinky knew where he was staying—
the Judge's number was in the book—so he called, and Stone had
answered.

He took another hit from the bowl, and was indeed calming down.
This was not paranoia, this was something else altogether, a ringing
clarity of sorts. He knew Pinky had moved into this firetrap just a few
weeks before he invited Stone to live with him, so it was not strange
he didn't have a roommate yet, but now Stone considered that the
invitation might have been a setup from the beginning, to draw him
into Seligman's world. Zohar might have been right about Seligman
and the Judge and Grunhut, but he was wrong if he thought Stone
would turn his back on them now. This was the path he should have
followed from the beginning.

"When did you move in here?" Stone asked.

"Start of August," Pinky said, taking the pipe back.

"Why here? Didn't think the ghetto was your thing."

"Cheap rent, lots of space, you know."

"How do you know Zalman Seligman?"

Pinky's face betrayed nothing. He finished his hit and said a smoky
"What?" His question was obscured by a long, hacking cough.

"Isn't he the one who had you move in here? Isn't he the one who
told you to bring me to the bingo hall?"

"I don't know what the fuck you are talking about," Pinky said,
finding a wrinkled shirt on the floor and pulling it over his head. "You
better watch yourself. You don't want to insult your benefactor."

The thought that Pinky considered himself Stone's benefactor,
the fact that he even *knew* the word *benefactor*, caused Stone to laugh
cruelly in Pinky's face. He had only one benefactor and that was his

father. "You are a terrible liar. How else would you have ever known about the Catbird Seat if you weren't doing work for them over at the warehouse?"

"You're fucking high," Pinky said, getting up in Stone's face.

"You knew my father's place was broken into. That's why you were so quick to come to my rescue. Admit it. You work for Seligman. Tell me, what goes on over there?"

Pinky drew back his fist as if he were seriously considering punching Stone, but then he dropped his hand to his side and said, "You know, I'm going out. Before I do something you might regret."

Stone laughed, fully aware that he was very valuable right now to both Zohar and Seligman, and said, "That's right, but you would regret it."

Pinky slammed the front door, leaving Stone alone in Pinky's room, surrounded by boxes, trash, and other assorted detritus. Stone's elation was short-lived, as he understood how insignificant he was beneath Pinky's fifteen-foot ceiling. It dawned on him that if everything he thought was correct, if Pinky had been hired to set him up conveniently close to the warehouse, if he had brought him to the bingo hall so Seligman could evaluate Stone's state of mind, that could mean that Dasi was part of Seligman's plan. Seligman had been the one who asked him to lunch, and he was the one who made the call to Dasi at Esther Grunhut's. She had been suspiciously quick to accept when he asked her out. The thought that Dasi was something other than she claimed caused him to crumple to the ground, overcome with panic. Did she really even know his father, or was that a setup too? Why had he never heard of her before? He lay on the floor for several minutes, and gradually found his breath again. "She is who she is," he repeated again and again. "Dasi is real."

He wanted to call her again, but she was still at school: the thought of her not being in his life was just too much to bear. Stone crawled toward the doorway, gripped by self-pity, and pulled himself up by the doorjamb. Pinky had a pile of papers haphazardly tossed about in an old milk crate balanced on a stack of boxes, and Stone sifted through them, looking for something to support his accusations. There were old phone bills from Pinky's previous address, water and electric bills, unpaid parking tickets, Chinese takeout menus, and then, somewhere near the middle of the pile, Stone found the lease to the apartment. It was an ordinary one-year agreement with the typical stipulations about care of the premises, pets, and repairs, but the lease agreement Pinky had signed for was not between himself and an ordinary landlord; it was between himself and the property owners the Crown of Solomon Talmudical Academy. Stone flipped to the last page of the contract in search of Seligman's signature as the lessor, but instead found, written in very neat script, the name Isaac Brilliant.

The Judge had saved Isaac Brilliant from a long prison sentence after the Court Street Riot trial, which had been the beginning of his unraveling and his public disgrace. And now Brilliant's face appeared before Stone as he had seen him in the courthouse all those years ago, and he realized why the man who had sought to buy his father's estate looked so familiar: it was Isaac Brilliant. Stone had met Brilliant face to face, and had not known who he was. Brilliant had added some bulk to his slim frame, but he was the same arrogant prick he had been during the trial. He had wanted the Judge's belongings because he believed the information about the new bank account was squirreled away somewhere within them.

It dawned on Stone that his entire world right now revolved around him as if he were a dazzling sun, each circling satellite—Seligman, Brilliant, Zohar, Pinky, perhaps even Dasi—needing something from him. He had never held so much power in his hands before and he was afraid he might slip and fall with no one to catch him. He wanted so badly for his mother to hurry up and help him make sense out of this mess. He stared at Pinky's face in his mother's unfinished painting propped up against the living room wall, and he knew that everything in the world was an illusion, that life was an illusion and so was death.

When his mother arrived a few minutes later, Stone threw himself into her arms with a tight embrace. She held him as he cried and shook, overcome by emotion. She smelled of a mild perfume he did not recognize, and stroked his hair and shushed him as if he were still a small child, but he did not mind. The warmth of her body against his offered the sense of comfort and relief he had been seeking for the longest time. They sat together on the couch, hand in hand, as Stone blew his nose into a tissue, his mother softly asking what was wrong. He didn't care anymore that he was giving her what she wanted, because he couldn't stand up on his own right now. It might have been a capitulation, but it was in line with the order of nature, and this was the season of forgiveness.

"Matthew, please tell me what is going on. You're scaring me," his mother said.

His vision obscured by layers of cloudy tears, he saw his mother as a fragmented being, fractured into a dozen pieces like a cubist painting she would have despised.

"I'm so confused," he said, in a voice so distressed he barely recognized it as his own.

"Is this about your father?" she said.

"I don't know," Stone answered. His voice hit a high, tremulous pitch. "I don't know anything anymore."

"You can tell me anything. I promise."

"Can I ask you anything? And will you promise to answer me honestly?"

"Of course," his mother said, but there was a subtle hesitation in her voice as if she were afraid of what he might ask. But this was Stone's chance to learn the truth as to why she tried to run away with him, to take him from his father.

All he could manage was, "Why?"

"Why what?" she said, her forehead creased with concern.

"He thought I wasn't his? Why would he think that?"

"What are you talking about?"

"The paternity tests. He refused to believe he was my father. Were you sleeping around?"

"Where did you ever hear such nonsense? Of course I wasn't."

"Then why the tests?"

"I don't know of any paternity tests. Where did you hear such a ridiculous thing?"

"So, it's not true?" Stone said.

"I don't see why it would be. It makes no sense. Would he have just walked away from you if you weren't his biological son? No, Matthew, he was grooming you from day one to be his little protégé. That's what scared me."

"That's why you tried to take me away from my father?"

"Oh, Matthew," she said, stroking his hair. "I was afraid for you. I was terrified. I know it sounds so foolish now, but I really thought I could save you from the life he had laid out for you."

"Maybe that was just what I needed," Stone said. "Some structure, guidance, direction."

"He was a dangerous fanatic."

"He had strong beliefs, important beliefs," Stone countered. "Isn't that better than having no beliefs? Look what happened to me with nothing to believe in, nothing to hold on to. I lost my mind and I wanted to die. The world meant nothing to me, because I meant nothing to the world."

"Let's not go there, please. I am sorry about all that," Abi said. "But we can't change the past now. The important thing is what we do about the future."

They were silent for a moment, and Stone relaxed into his mother's embrace, safe in her arms. He had no idea whether this sense of comfort was a figment of his unbearable need or a very old habit rekindled, and for the moment it didn't matter.

"The FBI has been following me," Stone said, realizing at once how absurd that sounded. "Some suit named Larry Zohar from the Joint Terrorism Task Force." His mother stiffened, the muscles of her thin arms becoming rigid. "I don't like him. He wants to destroy my father."

"But your father is dead."

"Yes, but reputation lives forever. And a son's obligation never ends."

"It does end, Matthew. You honor your parents by living your own life."

Stone gave a dubious shrug and Abi continued, "What does the FBI want from you?"

Stone told her Zohar wanted him to wear a wire and provide

information about what was going on inside the warehouse on the other side of the Brooklyn-Queens Expressway. "I've been saying Kaddish for my father over there in a small synagogue."

"But why you?"

"Zohar believes these people need something only my father had, and that I, as his only son, have access to that same information. He believes a terrorist attack is going to occur, and somehow my father has something to do with this. He is wasting his time with me."

The delicate machinery of his mother's body came alive as she straightened herself and cleared her throat. "Zalman Seligman is behind this, isn't he? Matthew, he is a very dangerous man. Please stay away from him."

"He's not who you think he is," Stone said. "He is trying to help me. He is helping me."

"He is as transparent as a glass window," his mother said, her voice rising. "If you believe he is trying to help you, it is only because it helps him, and as soon as you are no longer useful to him, he will throw you away like a piece of trash. He cares for only one thing, and that is his radical idea of a Greater Israel."

"That's not true. He was my father's good friend."

"People like Seligman and your father don't have friends, only interests."

"And what exactly is the difference? You're not friends with people in the art world because they can help you get ahead?"

"Matthew, don't sound so cynical. I can't stand to see you this way. There's nothing here for you. Why don't you just pack a bag and come back to California with me, start all over again? We can leave this afternoon. The FBI will forget about you, Seligman will go back to Israel, and you'll never hear from him again."

"You can't save me; you can't save anyone."

"What do you mean?"

"Remember the woman I told you about?" Stone said, thinking about Dasi and that deathly pale skin and those dark eyes of hers and whether she was telling the truth about her feelings for him. "I think it might be serious."

"This is the woman Zalman introduced you to?"

"What does that matter?"

"You cannot trust Zalman Seligman."

"Fine," Stone said. "I can trust Dasi. She is good and kind and beautiful and makes me feel life is worth living."

"Oh, Matthew," Abi said.

"I'm serious," Stone said.

"Trust me, another one will come along before you know it. Women are not going out of style anytime soon."

"I can talk to her," Stone said. "She knew my father, and we have this connection, this understanding. I think this could really be something important."

Abi said nothing and Stone's mind filled with doubts. Was Dasi everything he thought she was? Was Zohar telling the truth or was Seligman?

"Matthew, I want to help you. Please tell me what I can do."

"There is nothing you can do. I have to live my own life."

"I'm not stopping you from doing that, I promise. I'm just trying to stop you from making a terrible mistake." She released Stone from her arms and stood up. Her movement was so abrupt Stone nearly fell over, his skin prickling with disquiet and worry. She marched down the hallway toward his bedroom, and Stone called out, "Where are you going?"

"I am packing a bag for you and we are leaving this place together."

Stone sat frozen in place for a brief moment as he gathered his thoughts. He did not recall his mother being so overbearing, and he understood immediately why the Judge would want her out of his life. She was headstrong, self-righteous, and interfering. His father never would have accepted anyone questioning his authority as she did. The marijuana had only temporarily relaxed him, and it had barely done its job.

He rose from the couch and followed her down the long hallway. He halted in the doorway, watching as Abi shuffled through a pile of cheap paperbacks the Judge must have read when he was traveling.

"Put the books down," Stone said.

"So this is what you have been doing, reading this garbage. If you want to read books all day that's fine with me, go back to school and get a degree. But don't sit here and think you're learning anything of value."

"They're not yours," Stone said. "They're my inheritance from my father."

Abi's eyes smoldered. "Really?" She picked up a well-worn paperback and slapped it against her hand. "This is just junk, Matthew, worthless debris from a misguided life. It's all garbage."

"No it's not. I'm beginning to understand my father at last."

"There's nothing worth understanding. He may have been sophistication and veneer on the outside, but he was pathological, bloodthirsty, just like your grandfather Julius."

Stone knew there was some truth to her words, because he, too, as the days progressed with his father's books, felt the irresistible need to harm someone, to put his power on display.

He grabbed for the paperback in Abi's hand—"Give that back"— but she was quick and pulled it away. Stone's anger surged into his fists, his mind cluttered with a chorus of whispers issuing from the pages around him. Sometimes he knew the books were reading him, rather than the other way around, and he understood they were trying to take measure of what kind of man he was. The books were ordering him to strangle his mother, choke the life out of her, and as she waved the paperback before his face, taunting him with it, he lunged for her with a heat-blind rage. He nearly fell to the floor, and as he righted himself against a stack of books he shouted, "I will not, I will not, I will not."

She couldn't possibly know what he was being instructed to do to her, and Stone was terrified.

"What can you learn from this mystical mumbo jumbo? That the world is going to end on such and such a date or that two plus two is actually five? It's garbage, Matthew."

"Give me that book," Stone said, snatching it from her hand.

The book was called *Hidden Worlds: Gematria and Its Secrets*. He had not seen it before among the thousands of books, but suddenly it was the most important book in the world. He clutched it to his chest. "You'd just throw all this away?"

"In a second. It's time to move on. You have a whole life to live."

"This is my life."

"Matthew, if you must honor your father then do so, but do not mistake that honor for becoming your father."

"That's it!" Stone said. "You're afraid of me becoming like my father and rejecting you the way he did."

"No, Matthew," she said. "You're living blind right now and you're going to stumble into something you'll never be able to get out of."

"How do you know so much about what's going to happen to me?" Stone asked. "After all these years. You barely know me, and now you think you can predict my actions? With all that you have seen in your travels, wandering the country, painting portraits of the great unwashed, what do you know that I don't? Tell me."

Abi stepped forward and placed a soft hand on his. It had an immediate calming effect.

"You know what, maybe I don't know anything at all, maybe I'm just rolling all those years of worry into one moment, and I'm sorry if I'm coming on too strong. I love you. And I don't want to lose you again. Does that make sense to you?"

It had been so long since his mother had said she loved him that it took him a moment to make sense of her words. She was here in front of him, and all the time that had passed since she left collapsed in an instant, and he said, "I love you too."

Abi offered a tentative smile and took him in her arms. "I really do believe everything is going to be all right as long as you understand I will never stop loving you."

Though he had been seduced by words before, the explosive power contained in the most simple phrase, he knew it was true his mother loved him and that in her own way she wanted the best for him. She didn't understand him, but he couldn't blame her for that. Who really understood anybody after all?

19 It had rained overnight. A late summer storm had filled the gutters with refuse and waste: candy wrappers, newspapers, cigarette packs, used condoms lay dispirited on the sides of the road, waterlogged and pale. Giant fernlike things, their razor-sharp fronds fanning over the top of the barbed-wire fence surrounding a vacant lot, had sprung up overnight—a verdant jungle amid the blighted landscape. The sky was gray, a sharp hint of autumn on the cool air. Stone slipped out the back door of Pinky's apartment and took an alternate route to the synagogue, cutting several blocks closer to Bedford-Stuyvesant, in the hope of flanking Zohar and his stakeout—he just wanted to be left alone to discover for himself what was going on inside the warehouse. He was beholden to no man except his father, and Zohar's cocksure manner, his certainty that Stone would do as he said, made him feel queasy.

After his mother had left yesterday afternoon and he had calmed himself down with a couple of drinks, Stone had gone to the main branch of the Brooklyn Public Library to learn what he could about Zohar. He knew some of what Zohar said about his father was true—he had no doubt the photographs with Julius were real, and the Judge had, indeed, highlighted many passages in his books about the importance of Jewish force—but a terrorist attack connected somehow to his long-dead grandfather sounded like some paranoid's fantasy, surprising in its scope and grandiosity. Zohar had an agenda, and Stone needed to know why he took such a personal interest in Stone and in the goings-on at the warehouse.

In just a few minutes of searching, Stone learned that "Lightning" Zohar had been a Golden Gloves boxer and had compiled a 15–3 record before being forced to quit after a severe concussion. A photograph of him, muscular in satiny trunks and taped-up boxing gloves, captioned LIGHTNING STRIKES IN RED HOOK, featured a dark and handsome Zohar with bitter, brooding eyes. Even then, as a young man poised on the brink of his future, he looked profoundly unlikable.

Larry Zohar attended the John Jay College of Criminal Justice in Manhattan and completed a law degree at Fordham University School of Law. He went on to train at the FBI Academy at Quantico, Virginia, where he finished near the top of his class. Zohar had been a member of the Joint Terrorism Task Force in New York when the World Trade Center was bombed in 1993 by Muslim extremists. Stone found a local Jewish paper on microfiche dated several months after the bombing in which Zohar, a local boy, had been interviewed about the attack. And here, Stone saw Zohar's motivation come sharply into focus. Though Zohar agreed the attack was the work of Muslim extremists, he also believed extremist Jewish groups had been aware of the attack in advance and had planned parallel attacks meant to be obscured by the Muslim one, though he presented no proof of such plans, claiming he needed to protect his sources.

The whole idea was absurd, and the disbelieving interviewer rephrased the question in case he had misunderstood Zohar's assertions.

Q: ARE YOU SAYING JEWS WERE BEHIND
THE BOMBING OF THE TOWERS?
A: I'M SAYING WE CAN'T LOSE SIGHT OF THE FACT
THAT UNDERGROUND JEWISH TERRORIST ORGANIZATIONS
ARE OPERATING IN AMERICA.

Zohar was the worst kind of anti-Semite, a self-loathing Jew, ashamed of his heritage and his people. It was a sickness that Stone understood well, but Zohar was wrong about Stone.

Some more digging and Stone discovered the Anti-Defamation League had a file on Zohar and that Zohar had been relieved of his duties in New York City and sent to the FBI's field office in Salt Lake City.

Stone kept all of this information ready in his mind as he made his way to the synagogue, in case Zohar were to ambush him with his rat wire. Stone's counterpunch would certainly send Zohar reeling, and would show him Stone could not be manipulated by a few photographs and some colorful stories. Stone wondered if Zohar even had the power to get rid of Dov, or was just blowing smoke to make Stone comply with his wishes.

He arrived without incident, rang the bell, and was buzzed in after a moment.

The old iron stairway before him wound its way up to the synagogue; another dark staircase, lit only by a dim bare bulb, led down toward a basement. Moshe met him at the doorway and patted him down vigorously, as if he had a clue Stone wasn't on the level. He hadn't done this the last time, and Stone wondered, why now? Moshe's hands were rough as they ran up and down the inside of his thighs, under his armpits, and inside the rim of his belt. He had earned the trust of no one.

The service was already underway, but Stone had not missed the recitation of the Kaddish. He had difficulty concentrating, his mind split between his daily obligation to his father and Zohar's warnings. Could his father possibly be involved in the planning of a terrorist attack? One thing Stone knew for certain, terrorism took on different meanings depending on one's perspective. It might be that terrorism involved the use of violence in pursuit of political goals, but one man's terrorist was another man's freedom fighter. Both Yitzhak Shamir and Menachem Begin had widely been considered terrorists before the establishment of the State of Israel, yet each had gone on to become prime minister of the only democratic country in the Middle East. They both had blood on their hands, but they had fulfilled their aspirations of an independent Jewish state.

Stone regarded the yeshiva boys he had seen at the hospital as they

prayed; they looked like ordinary young men, not the wild-eyed terrorists of Zohar's imagination. A couple of them turned and smiled at
Stone in recognition, and he smiled back. When Stone had completed
chanting Kaddish and the service was over, the gathered worshipers
shook hands and bid each other farewell. A few of the students hung
around as if they had nowhere to go.

"I'm sorry for your loss." A thin, clean-shaven student, his skin
ghastly and fishlike, offered an awkward smile. "I lost my father too. A
few years back, when the so-called peace process began."

"That's terrible," Stone said.

"His car was sprayed with bullets on his way home from Jerusalem.
They got him on a bypass road five minutes from home. Fucking
Arabs."

"I'm sorry," Stone said, overwhelmed by the instant comity of
shared grief. He had been so focused on his own grief he had almost
forgotten how to sympathize with others. This was a person who
could understand his loss.

The student extended his hand to shake and said his name was Itzy.

"I'm Matthew," Stone said.

"I know."

Dasi's cousin Yossi approached Stone and took his hand in his. It
was small and clammy; Stone shook it and looked him in the eye.

"Rav Seligman asked me to stick around after the service," Stone
said.

Yossi's patchwork beard barely covered his thin face, and his big
blue eyes looked watery. He might have been Dasi's cousin, but he was
gifted with none of her beauty. When he spoke, his prominent Adam's
apple bobbed up and down like a child's bouncing ball.

"You spoke to the Rav?"

"Yes," Stone lied. "He asked me to fill in for Dov."

"All right then," Yossi said, "glad to have you on board."

Stone was awash with nervous anticipation as he descended to the
basement of the warehouse, Yossi leading the way, Itzy at his back.
He did not know precisely what to expect, but he was quite certain
Isaac Brilliant would be somewhere at the bottom of those stairs. The

wide stairs were grooved in the center, the unmistakable signature of countless footfalls, and Stone grasped the iron railing at his left to ensure he didn't misstep and tumble to the bottom. Yossi stopped at the foot of the stairs, waiting for Stone to catch up. The basement of the warehouse was as cold as a meat locker and, in the dim light, Stone saw before him a mirror reflecting the images of Yossi, Itzy, and himself. The images swam before Stone's eyes in the half-dark as if he and Yossi and Itzy were submerged in murky water.

"If you see the mirror, you're going the right way," Yossi said, turning his face in Stone's direction. "We've got three other false entrances that lead nowhere."

Stone followed Yossi into a fun-house maze of mirrors, turning right then left then right again, their progression marked by the sound of electronic chimes—the sort employed by shopkeepers to alert them that a customer has entered. Stone fell behind Yossi and nearly walked into a mirror, catching himself at the last instant. The face in the mirror looked nervous, uncertain about what he was getting himself into. Itzy was there behind him. "Don't worry, you'll get so used to it you'll be able to do it with your eyes closed."

"It's really confusing."

"Supposed to be," Itzy said, "so we don't get surprised. Eighteen turns in all."

As Stone emerged from the mirror labyrinth, and his eyes adjusted to the dim light, he realized he was standing in front of a shooting range with low cinder-block walls and targets shaped like human silhouettes hanging at the end of long alleys. The walls of the room were lined with a layer of cork for soundproofing, beige sandbags piled against the wall.

"This is where it all happens," Yossi said. "We've got a lot of work ahead of us. And not much time."

Time for what? Stone wanted to ask, but he heard rhythmic footsteps on the concrete floor getting closer and thought better of it. He saw a figure approaching, as if through a fine mist, its features constituting themselves as it drew nearer and its form took on dimension. The man was tall and slim; he had a sharp, arrogant face with a high forehead and angular cheekbones that looked like they had been hewn with an ax. He wore his black beard cropped short and a kippa on his head.

"Matthew, I'd like to speak with you." His green eyes sparkled. Isaac Brilliant did not introduce himself, but seemed to assume Stone knew who he was. This was the same man who had tried to purchase his father's books. Yes, this was the man; this was he. How foolish of Stone not to have realized it at the time. In his grief and confusion as his father lay dying in stubborn silence, he had failed to recognize Isaac Brilliant outside the context in which he had forever associated this man.

Even though he had anticipated Brilliant would be present, he was surprised to find himself standing face to face with the man who had permanently altered his father's life. Though Brilliant was indebted to Stone's father, there was no kindness in his face, and Stone was afraid.

"Follow me," Brilliant said. This was not a request, but an order.

Stone turned to the yeshiva boys to gauge their reactions, but they were already involved in their own idle chatter.

As he followed Brilliant through the long darkness of the basement, their feet on the concrete floor kicking up dust, it occurred to Stone he was alone with Brilliant. A freezing cold sweat broke out over Stone's body, and he trembled with an obscure fear that Brilliant was intent on harming him. Zohar had asked Stone to wear a wire. Was it strictly coincidence that Moshe had searched him so thoroughly? Was Brilliant aware that Zohar was on his trail?

"Where is Rabbi Seligman?" Stone asked. Brilliant did not answer. "I want to see Seligman."

They arrived at a small, prefabricated room, smelling of new drywall, tucked into the farthest corner of the warehouse. Brilliant opened a windowless door and flicked on a bank of blinding fluorescent lights. He closed the door behind them and locked it. In the unnatural light, Brilliant looked furious, overwound, seething just beneath a surface of civility with violence that promised to crush anyone who crossed him. He snapped on a small space heater to cut the chill. Whatever comfort Seligman provided with his steady, paternal demeanor, Brilliant projected the opposite.

The back wall was covered with topographical maps, surveyors' maps, satellite images—not the familiar political maps with borders and lines and recognizable names. Stone stared, transfixed by the maps, understanding now that his father, who had scribbled with particular zeal in one of Jabotinsky's books beneath the words "demand the whole land in order to put an end to all the misery and solve the whole problem," was present in the room, in spirit. The Judge's greatest desires lay before them, yet to be executed. Blue and green pushpins marked off various spots like a scattering of stars on the night sky.

"The blue is the land we've already acquired for Greater Israel," Brilliant said, taking note of Stone's studied stare. "The green is the land we have yet to acquire. Take a seat, Matthew," Brilliant said, gesturing to a wooden chair nearby.

Stone sat, and Brilliant loomed above. "I want you to understand something, so there is no mistake."

Stone wanted to tell him he would do whatever he could to help, but Brilliant's cold hand gripped his throat before he had a chance to speak. The sudden violence of the gesture shocked Stone as much as if a hand had reached out of a mirror and taken him by the neck. He hadn't even had the chance to offer an explanation, his blood credentials, stretching back to Papa Julius and Meyer Lansky bankrolling the Irgun. Brilliant's grip tightened, the thumb pressing close to the concave spot beneath Stone's Adam's apple, crushing his windpipe. Stone thought of Dasi and how she had wanted to be choked for the erotic thrill, of how, instead, he had envisioned his mother beneath his own hands, her eyes growing large as she breathed her last breath. But now, as he looked into Brilliant's hard, impassive eyes, he remembered these hands had killed before. Yes, he had been found not guilty by judge and jury, Stone's own father, in fact, but he had killed; of that, there was no doubt. The epileptic Arab, Nasser Al-Bassam, had been smashed in the head with a piece of brick, pummeled out of this world by the young Brilliant, his bare hands covered with the Arab's blood. Sweat pooled in Stone's armpits, dripping down his torso, all his organs juddering with a primal terror. Stone tried to speak, afraid he was going to black out, but Brilliant squeezed harder, setting off an ion explosion of panic, Stone's feet kicking out uncontrollably as he tried to gain purchase.

"Look at you, a Shabbos carp in a bathtub, trying to save your useless life with a few meager breaths." Brilliant laughed a humorless laugh. "I called you here for me to speak." He relaxed his grip, but kept his hand in place. He spoke slowly and firmly. "Now that you have seen what we are doing here, you can't ever speak about our business to anyone. What goes on here never leaves here. Nothing is ever said. Nothing."

Stone struggled to find his voice, but managed, "What could I possibly tell anyone?"

Brilliant slapped Stone hard on the side of the head.

"Don't be stupid."

"Rabbi Seligman wouldn't approve of this." Stone rubbed his head.

"I'm not the Rav. You still have to earn my trust, but I don't think you're capable. I know you were the Judge's greatest disappointment."

Brilliant's words hurt more than anything he could have done to physically injure Stone, and he knew now he would do anything to quiet those doubts forever. He would find the passcode and offer up the account as proof he was his father's son in every way, their lives entwined like the ineffable strands of their undying DNA.

"Rabbi Seligman will vouch for me."

"I'm in charge of this operation."

"What happened?"

"I am not the Rav's keeper," Brilliant responded.

"Is he all right?"

"The Rav is very capable. He knows what to do."

"Did something happen to Rabbi Seligman?" Stone asked, his voice rising in pitch.

Brilliant smiled for the first time, his hard eyes mollified, bottomless.

"Do you really think you deserve to know anything? You're not like your father at all. You're nothing to me, and you walk in here thinking you can be part of history."

"My grandfather," Stone said, "he knew Jabotinsky, gave him money, when my father was just a child. I need to be a part of whatever it is you are doing here. It's in my blood."

"I know all about your lineage." Brilliant's breathing was heavy. He leaned in close to Stone. "We need more people like your father, like Rav Grunhut, and like Dr. Goldstein, the saint who had seen enough Jewish bloodshed as a doctor in Kiryat Arba. But you are nothing but seminal runoff that hit the mark. You are weak and cowardly."

"I'm not weak. I am my father's son. I am here to help finish off what he started."

"Are you willing to kill?" Brilliant said, his words short, clipped, cold.

Stone was silent. Brilliant's words hung in the air and Stone wanted so badly to say yes, yes I will kill, yes I will destroy, I will do whatever it takes, but he knew his words would ring false and that he would expose himself as a fraud and a liar.

"If a Jew is in need, or the spilling of enemy blood helps the Jewish cause"—Brilliant's eyes flashed from their depths—"would you kill?"

"I," Stone hesitated, "I don't know."

"Just now," Brilliant said, "you would have let me kill you without even putting up a fight. I could have choked the life out of you and not suffered a scratch of retaliation. Why? Because you have deliberately run away from your history, your heritage, your future, and as a result your life means nothing, and it can mean nothing."

He was right. Stone did not have it in him to kill, even if it meant saving his own useless life.

"Tell me what it was like, when you killed Al-Bassam."

Brilliant smiled as if he had been waiting to discuss this very subject, with the son of the man who saved him.

"I was young, Matthew, younger than you are now. I don't believe I even thought about what I was doing. It was just a natural feeling, killing the Arab, and it happened so fast, as if it were my destiny, as if I were entering history for the first time. It was empowering, Matthew, liberating, and I came to the attention of the Judge, your father, may his memory be blessed. He saved me from a long prison sentence. He saved me because he knew Jews stick together and damn the rest of them. I am everything I am today because of him. I love him like a father."

"But I am his son," Stone said, pushing back. "I know him better than you can ever know him." His father still lived in those books, still spoke from those pages, still had so much to teach Stone.

"You know your father saved me. But you have no idea how far he went to save my life."

There was something in Brilliant's tone suggesting he was about to tell Stone something he expected would shock him. But Stone was learning quickly not to be surprised by anything he discovered about his father.

"They were calling for the death penalty up in Albany, political anti-Semitism at its best. But your father would not see Jewish blood cheapened: *ladam hu-matar*, the permitted blood, so cheap for so long. He had had enough."

"Saving you cost him his career," Stone said.

And here Brilliant laughed again. "His career on the bench, maybe, enforcing their laws. But the Judge never gave up on his beliefs."

Brilliant ran a hand through the graphite filings of his trimmed beard and paused, as if measuring his words. "Do you know the name Emile Alcalai?"

Stone nodded. He was one of the jurors.

"The state subpoenaed him and scared him with all sorts of threats—deportation, prison, who knows what they had in mind? Alcalai's mother, from Morocco, was not a naturalized US citizen. He was going to talk eventually."

It all came back to Stone in an instant. "He died in a hit-and-run, didn't he?"

"He did," Brilliant said. "That was when I realized I owed your father my life."

Everything he had learned about his father since his death pointed in this direction. The dent in the Thunderbird's hood said everything that needed to be said. It was a reminder, a warning. Be ruthless, his father's marginal notes had told him. Be ruthless, or become nothing.

"You're saying my father ran Alcalai over? Why take such a risk?"

"If you want to kill somebody in civil society without risk of prosecution," Brilliant said, "run down a bicyclist. You can always claim, in the event you are caught: 'I didn't see him.' But no one saw Walter. Out there in the Rockaways, nobody around—"

"But he destroyed his reputation fixing the jury for you," Stone shouted. "For you!"

"You don't get it, do you? This was never about me. Forget your father's reputation with the anti-Semites and secularists and yellow journalists. He is a giant among the Jewish people. A great powerful mind, a visionary. If he had wanted, he could have been prime minister, anything. Jabotinsky to Begin to Stone, just connect the dots."

"I never understood my father when he was alive," Stone said, "but I understand now the immensity of who he was. Please, let me do my part."

Brilliant laughed and bade Stone to rise from the chair. Stone was trembling, either from cold or from the fear he would be shut out, left to languish outside history, alone.

"There is nothing here for you," Brilliant said. "You do not belong."

"What happens now?"

"You're going to leave the building, and I am never going to see your face again. Do you understand?"

Stone felt as if he had been lit on fire, and he cried, "I can help you."

"Your weakness is transparent. You mean nothing to me."

"The money," Stone said. "I know where the money is. I can get it. Look, I have the bank card." He reached into his wallet and produced the card.

"You can barely tie your own shoes, shicker. I have no use for you." Seligman must have told Brilliant how drunk Stone had been at Rosh Hashanah. He had disqualified himself without even being aware. "And a bank card without a passcode is useless."

Brilliant led Stone through the darkness in silence, passing wooden crates stacked one on top of the other, Hebrew writing stamped on their sides. Stone was overcome with emotion, with the naked realization he had just missed his chance to join his father, to join his own destiny.

"Please," Stone said, "I'll do anything you ask."

Brilliant said, "You will not speak a word of what goes on in here to anyone. Or else, I will kill you, and I would be doing it with your father's blessing."

The bright morning sun mocked Stone as he stumbled out a service door into the daylight. Brilliant did not say another word and Stone continued to humiliate himself by begging, pleading to be given entrée into his world. He had to find Seligman now, this very minute, and straighten things out, but he had no way to reach him.

Stone took the long way back to Pinky's place, wandering down streets he had never seen, afraid to be alone with his father's books, which would ridicule him for his failure. What had happened to Seligman? Where was he, and why had he disappeared? Stone knew something had gone wrong, and that everything he had done to ingratiate himself with Seligman was for nothing.

When he arrived back at the apartment, the Thunderbird was out front, the dent screaming his father's misdeeds to the world. How could his father be so careless, leaving evidence of his crime out in the open for all to see? Stone jumped into the car and drove to the nearest body shop and asked the mechanic how much it would cost to fix the dent in the hood of the Thunderbird.

"Depends how bad the damage is."

The mechanic asked Stone what year the car was and Stone said 1980. The mechanic whistled and said, "Good luck finding a replacement hood for that. Let's see how bad it is."

Stone led him out to the car and pointed at the dent; the mechanic eyed it for a minute or two before saying, "I can fix it for five hundred dollars, if you've got your heart set on it, but there ain't nothing there."

"What do you mean?" Stone said.

"What I mean is this car looks pretty much as good as new."

The breath seized in Stone's throat. He managed to ask the mechanic to look under the hood.

The mechanic nodded his head and disappeared from view, and for a moment Stone feared he was losing his mind. "Okay," the mechanic said. "Looks like there was a pretty big knock on the hood of this tank, but somebody, a real craftsman, hammered it back into place from the inside. You'd never know it by looking at it from the outside."

"So there is a dent?" Stone said.

"There was one," the mechanic said, "but it's gone now."

Stone thanked the mechanic and offered to pay him, but he refused, clearing his nose lumberjack style onto the grease-stained pavement.

Stone climbed behind the wheel and saw the dent was still there. This was a sign just for him. He drove back home, warm in the momentary glow of the knowledge that his father was communicating with him in some profound and mysterious way. But his warm feelings did not last, and by the time he had parked the car up the street from Pinky's apartment he was frantic at the thought of Brilliant shutting him out of his father's plan. Without the passcode, he was useless. He needed someone to tell him he was all right, that he was going to make it.

As soon as he unlocked the door, Stone rushed to the phone and called Dasi at her aunt Esther's. If she loved him, she'd pick up, if Dasi loved him, she'd pick up the phone. The phone rang and rang, a ball of anxiety gathering in Stone's belly. If she loves me . . . Esther picked up after several rings and told Stone Dasi was at school. He was about to ask her if she knew how to get in touch with Rabbi Seligman, but she had already hung up the phone.

Stone held the receiver in his hand, wishing it was Dasi he held instead. He wanted to lose himself in her arms, kissing her red lips, tearing at that pale skin. She could save him, vouch for him, tell Brilliant that he truly was his father's son, that he was worthy. But he knew he could never speak a word to Dasi, that doing so would be to sign his own death warrant. Brilliant would think nothing of destroying the two of them; Stone knew that for certain.

Alone in the empty apartment, Stone returned to the books, to his father, to everything in the world that still mattered to him. He threw on his father's robe, determined to show Brilliant what a foolish mistake he had made casting him out. He would prove himself, he would prove himself once and for all. Wearing the robe, he felt his anxiety ease. Stone realized his cowardice was an illusion, and he would prove the immutable fact that he was in fact his father's successor.

That barely discernible presence appeared beneath the robe with Stone, the tangible sense of spirit animated, alive, guiding him, with its ancient words vibrating on a frequency just beneath his conscious hearing. He was surprised to find his father had several books by Winston Haloumi, the radical Columbia professor Stone had seen on the news just that spring on his father's TV, side by side with Arab teenagers throwing rocks at Israeli soldiers in the Security Zone in Lebanon. How smug Haloumi had been in the interview that followed, unwrapping the checked keffiyeh from his handsome, lined face and speaking in his Oxford-educated accent about Israel's "cancerous occupation." Stone had no idea how he had missed these books when he had packed them and unpacked them, and stacked them in this room. But here they were before him, and it was clear his father had read these books despite the fact that Haloumi was an articulate apologist for the worst, most violent behaviors of the Palestinians. Stone had seen the same books lined up on Fairuza's bookshelf all those years ago, beside Frantz Fanon's *Wretched of the Earth*, and had thought nothing of it at the time. He put the books aside to look at later. Stone couldn't stomach the thought of reading the Arab's words right now. Every so often he took a break from his reading, called Dasi, and left a message with Esther for Dasi to call him when she got the message. By the fourth time, Esther answered the phone with a simple: "I promise to let her know you called, Matthew."

He lay back on the floor surrounded by books, exhausted, staring at a water stain on the ceiling shaped like the state of Texas. Perhaps he had been wrong all along, believing his father had stashed the numbers to the bank account somewhere within these books. If his father had, wouldn't Stone have found the numbers by now? Even if he did find the numbers, would it even matter? Stone had so anticipated Seligman's wide smile, his kind, encouraging words when Stone discovered the numbers, as if Seligman were a direct pipeline to his father; Seligman's approval undoing years of animus between father and son in an instant. But Seligman was gone. Now, Stone realized providing the numbers to Brilliant would have its own palliative effect—he could earn his trust in an instant and prove he truly was the Judge's avatar, ready, prepared, and willing to complete his life's work in his name.

Stone must have fallen asleep staring at the water stain. When he awoke, it no longer resembled the state of Texas but rather a ragged Star of David. He found his hand stuck to the glossy cover of the cheap paperback on gematria his mother had mocked. His mind clear and still from sleep, he picked up *Hidden Worlds: Gematria and Its Secrets* and flipped through the pages, looking for some sort of numerical pattern. How had he failed to make a connection sooner? The book, filled with the Hebrew numerology of the Kabbalah, was full of numbers and patterns and ciphers that claimed to explain everything from the rise of Shabbetai Tzvi, the false Messiah, to the Balfour Declaration, to the lightning victory of the Six-Day War. Stone flipped through the pages of the book looking for anything his father had underlined, but he found nothing. His mother was right, this book was nonsense, carnival-midway gibberish dressed up as mysticism. It was easy to predict the past when it had already happened. Stone tossed the book aside and it landed awkwardly, the front page folded out like a broken wing of a bird. When he went to pick the book up, Stone discovered his father had written a single word in blue ink on the inside cover. He at once recognized his father's careful hand; the word *BINGO* almost levitated from the stark white of the page.

The Judge had written this for him to discover, a riddle to be solved, one final hurdle that would vindicate him in his father's eyes forever. He knew he had found what he was looking for, but what exactly had he found in the word *BINGO*? The robe sat heavily on his shoulders as he recalled how in gematria every letter had a numerical value, and by converting Hebrew letters into numbers and then adding the numbers together, the practitioner arrived at another number; through this system, the mystics believed, the secrets of the universe could be revealed. His father intended the word *BINGO* to be the key to the passcode, but in Hebrew, not in the English he wrote inside the cover of *Hidden Worlds*. Stone found a scratch pad of paper and wrote out the letters בינגו, each letter matching its numerical equivalent—2, 10, 50, 3, 6—and he was certain, even before he called the bank and answered their security questions, that he had deciphered his father's numbers and would soon stand before the Judge, bathed in his heavenly light.

20

It was dark when Pinky returned home, slamming the steel door behind him and triple-locking it. He rapped haplessly about diamonds and gats and big booty girls, his raised voice ridiculous, absurd, like that of a deaf man who has never heard his own voice. Stone slipped off his father's robe and padded down the hallway toward Pinky's room. He smelled Pinky's marijuana smoke, but had no desire to join in. Stone arrived at Pinky's open bedroom door full of furious agitation.

"What the fuck do you want?"

"You're working for Isaac Brilliant."

"I'm not working for no one," Pinky said. "I'm a free agent. I do whatever I want."

"Why did you want me to move in here?"

"I don't know what you're talking about."

"You drive that cube van for them, don't you? Pickups and deliveries and whatever else, right? That's why you were so ready to help me move in. They wanted to make sure I was close by."

Pinky's room was still scattered with cardboard boxes and wooden crates, and Stone's eye caught the stamp of familiar Hebrew lettering on the side of one of the crates. "What, are you stealing Torahs now?" Stone said.

"Fuck you talking about?"

"That crate, it's from Israel. Tell me you know what's in there?"

Pinky's face went pale and he simply muttered, "Shit."

"That's right," Stone said. He had seen similar crates in the base-ment of the warehouse. "You made a mistake, didn't you? This isn't some made-in-China crap you can peddle on Canal Street for twenty cents on the dollar. This is something else, isn't it?"

"Fuck," Pinky said, slamming his fist into the wall.

Stone bent down and cut the security tape from the crate, then found a rusted metal hammer and began to pry back the wooden boards. "Help me out here," Stone said. "Maybe if you're lucky, it's just kosher wine."

"Don't," Pinky said.

"Why not?" Stone said. "Are you afraid of what's inside?"

"I," Pinky stuttered, "I got to return it. Now."

Pinky's panicked reaction told Stone Pinky was aware of the danger in which he had placed himself. Brilliant would be looking for the crate and the thief. This could be Stone's chance to gain entry back into the warehouse. "Not until we find out what's inside."

When the crate was open, Stone hunched low to take a closer look at its contents. He pulled the heavy cardboard off the top and stared for a moment, as if trying to place a vaguely familiar face. The crate was filled with package after package of bath salts from the Dead Sea.

"Harmless enough," Stone said, but Pinky did not relax, his posture as stiff and rigid as a statue.

Stone reached his arm into the crate down to the armpit, his fingers pushing aside the packages until his hand hit upon something hard. "And what do you think this is?" Stone asked.

"Stop," Pinky said. "I'm in a lot of trouble."

"I can help you," Stone said, sensing opportunity, "if you tell me the truth."

Stone had not seen fear on Pinky's face since their school yard days, and he enjoyed the sense of wielding power over him. "Tell me the truth. Do you work for Isaac Brilliant and his yeshiva boys over there at the warehouse? Under the BQE?"

"Yes," Pinky said. "Yes."

"And you invited me to stay with you why?"

"I don't know," Pinky said. "All's I know is they wanted you to move in with me. I don't know anything else."

"Asshole," Stone said, and began pulling out packages of Dead Sea salt and tossing them across the floor.

"I'm sorry," Pinky said. "The money's good and nobody's getting hurt, right?"

"Sure," Stone said.

"So," Pinky said, pacing, "you can help me set things straight with the Rosh?"

"Who's the Rosh?"

"That's what he's called. It's Hebrew for head or something. That's what they call him."

This was Stone's way back into the warehouse, his chance to show the Rosh he was a true unsentimental warrior who could be trusted to do what needed to be done.

"Anything for a friend," Stone said. "Now help me clear this stuff out."

"Why?"

"I want to see what you really stole."

When they had emptied the crate of hundreds of packages of bath salts, Stone lifted a small steel drum cradled in the center of the crate like the precious cargo it was. He wedged open the drum with the claw of his hammer and found a white powdery material he ordinarily would have assumed was drugs; but, aware of what had happened to Dov and the training taking place at the warehouse, Stone knew this was high-grade explosives, property of the Israel Defense Forces.

Pinky dipped his finger in, prepared to take a snort, but Stone stopped him. "Do you really want to do that?"

The powder smelled acrid and bitter like ammonia.

"It's some kind of explosive," Pinky said. "What the fuck?"

"You know somebody's going to be looking for this," Stone said.

"No shit," Pinky screamed. He paced back and forth across the floor, his face crumpled with worry. "You have to help me," Pinky said. "Talk to the Rosh, tell him it was a mistake."

Stone almost laughed at the pathetic, childlike tone in his voice, the delicious reversal of roles.

"I will help you," Stone said. "But you've got to return it."

"What do I say? I'm in deep, deep shit."

Stone regarded Pinky for a moment, his pitiful pleading setting Stone alight with the irresistible draw of brute power. Stone knew enough now about the fanatic Brilliant, the murderer Brilliant, to know that nobody would help Pinky; nobody would forgive him, nobody would show him mercy. No one would pity him.

"Just say it was all a big mistake," Stone said. "Tell them you didn't mean to."

"You'll come with me, right?" Pinky said.

"Of course," Stone said. "I'll be right by your side."

They passed under the BQE, Pinky struggling to heft the crate in his outstretched arms. The air was cool, but Stone was sweating, overcome with determination and expectation. This was his chance to prove to Brilliant he was answering the merciless obligation of his predecessors and that he was worthy of his father and whatever plans were underway inside that warehouse. Pinky walked in silence with an even step, turning around periodically to make sure Stone was still behind him. They passed the Catbird Seat and turned right at the warehouse, descending a gradual sloping ramp, stopping before a small door facing the haunted Navy Yard. Black clouds hung low in the sky, obliterating Manhattan from view. A tug moaned rudely out on the river. Pinky tapped on the service door with the back of his hand, then pushed a buzzer high up on the doorpost.

After a moment, they heard the lock being unlatched from the inside, steel sliding against steel; a bearded face appeared at a small caged window.

"Who's there?" the voice said.

"It's me," Pinky responded. "Your guy."

The door slid open, just a crack at first and then wide enough to accommodate Pinky and the crate. Moshe, ripe from the effort of physical exertion, led them in stilted silence through another maze of mirrors into a small anteroom where Dasi's cousin Yossi sat with several other young men, hunched intensely around a small, brightly lit table and what looked like a set of blueprints. Yossi offered Stone a half smile; the others offered nothing, their faces blank. Pinky cradled the box in his arms, a thick wire of exertion forming in the center of his forehead. This was Stone's chance to prove he belonged. He so badly wanted the approval of these yeshiva boys, to become one of them, to become something at last.

"I just wanted to return this," Pinky said, placing the crate on the floor.

Isaac Brilliant stepped into the anteroom, Moshe at his back, and said, "Thank you for bringing him, Matthew."

Brilliant's attitude toward Stone had changed, as if Stone had just passed a major test of character. There was something in his eyes, a glimmer of encouragement, that struck Stone right in the heart.

"You've done a mitzvah, Matthew," he said. "Now go home and get some sleep."

"But—" Pinky said, "what about me?"

"Quiet, *gonif*," Brilliant said.

"It was a mistake," Pinky said. "I didn't mean nothing. Matty'll tell you. He swears on my behalf, it was all a big mix-up. He'll vouch for me. Right? Won't you?"

Pinky glanced at Stone, seeking his accord, but Stone was already overcome by an astonishing sensation of inner peace, a white-hot starburst set off by Brilliant's praise, beginning in his chest and radiating through every muscle and nerve until his body smoldered with a joyful sense of well-being, of tranquility, of righteousness. He had earned the right to command Brilliant's respect.

"Matty, do something," Pinky called. "Do something!"

Both his father and grandfather had killed men in service of their beliefs and they had grown stronger, more powerful, had thrived, lived meaningful lives, while Stone, the erstwhile weakling, so fragile of mind and body, had habitually considered taking his own life when he should have been sizing up anyone in his way in order to cut them down. That was his true birthright. He felt the need blooming inside him, blood red and pulsing behind his ribs, the need to kill. Pinky had offered himself up to Stone and it was Stone's obligation to follow the call of his blood. In his triumph it occurred to Stone to laugh and call out, "*Heshbon nefesh*—accounting of the soul," but instead he said, "I have nothing to say in his defense."

Moshe directed Stone toward the mirror maze and the exit. Stone glanced for a last time at his friend Michael Pinsky and felt nothing but disgust for this piece of human refuse who had lied to him in his time of need, pretended to be his friend simply to line his own pockets.

"Thank you again, Matthew," Brilliant said, approaching, his voice dropping, for Stone's ears only. "I hope you understand killing one's enemy is not murder but a commandment of God. See you in the morning for Kaddish." He kissed Stone softly on the cheek, his breath lightly caressing Stone's face.

"Matty, please, please," Pinky called.

Now, Brilliant returned his attention to Pinky and the yeshiva boys and raised his voice like a seasoned orator: a lesson for his charges. "When the wicked are in trouble, they are penitent. But when the trouble has ended, they always return to their evil ways. Because you have committed the same offense *twice*, you must believe it has become permissible. But it is a worse sin to steal from man than from God."

Pinky was on his knees now, crying, begging for leniency. "I'll admit I was stupid, but I'll make it up to you. I'll pay you back for what I took. Matty, help!"

As Moshe led Stone through the mirrors, he heard Brilliant say, "A dead man owes nothing to anyone."

That night, Stone slept as soundly as he had in years. His mind was quiet and clear, and he awoke refreshed in the morning, ready to return to the warehouse to say Kaddish. He was certain Pinky was dead. His conscience was clean, alight with the joy of completing a task that needed to be done. His grandfather, Julius, had killed his first man as an undersized seventeen-year-old trying to make his way in the world, and had set the pattern for the rest of his life in which he was both feared and respected. The Judge, too, had run down the wayward juror, Emile Alcalai, with his Thunderbird because he believed in the power of a greater good, and he had been lionized as a hero by many. Pinky was nothing but a smudge of shit on the bottom of his shoe, but Stone understood he had finally become the man he was intended to be.

He wanted so badly to call Dasi on the phone and tell her everything about his rebirth, but he understood he could never say a word. She would have to figure out for herself how he had become his own man. Ordinarily, he would've been upset Dasi hadn't called or left a message for him, but now, Stone felt completely secure that she belonged to him, and that he could have her whenever he wanted.

Stone arrived on time for the service, found a kippa, placed it on his head, and picked up a prayer book. A man he did not recognize appeared at his side, took Stone's hand in his, and shook it. Then he wordlessly shuffled down the aisle to return to his prayers.

Before Stone had a chance to gather himself, another man appeared at his ear. Stone recognized him from the night before as one of Yossi's friends. His pale skin showed acne scars and uneven patches of sparse black hair sprouting from his Adam's apple and cheeks.

"*Kol ha kavod,*" he whispered, squeezed Stone's elbow, and returned to his prayers.

Three or four more men congratulated Stone, patting him on the back or whispering with their gamey breath in his ear. "Your place is reserved in the world to come," Itzy said, offering Stone a knowing wink. They knew. They all knew Stone had done his part in ridding the world of Pinky. He was now one of them.

Stone followed in the prayer book as best he could and muttered the liturgy under his breath. The words meant nothing to him, but his voice, joined with the voices of the others, rose in confidence as he read. He stood to recite the Mourner's Kaddish, and a familiar whispering filled his head as it did when he read his father's books, both English and Aramaic struggling for supremacy. It was the voices of the dead calling to him. The Judge was there and so was Pinky and the voices of others gone from this world, their ancient words layered underneath those of the more recent dead who still retained the ability to communicate in the language of this world. He heard Pinky call out to him to remember him when he recited Kaddish. Even with his eyes closed, the room was filled with brightness, sharp, unbearable white. The Judge, his voice strong and clear, rose above that of Pinky. "You owe nothing to that *gonif* motherfucker."

Stone stirred as if woken from a dream and said aloud the name: "Walter Joseph Stone," his exclamation point at the end of the prayer.

Zohar caught up with Stone in a bright patch of sunlight just shy of the humid shadows of the BQE. "Missed you yesterday," he said.

Maybe it was Stone's new knowledge about Zohar's career reversals, his self-hatred, but he looked beaten down, defeated, and Stone noticed an almost imperceptible change in the way Zohar carried himself, his movements overly precise as if compensating for an overwhelming sense of fatigue. He and Zohar were two comets streaking through the sky in opposite directions, Stone ascendant, Zohar falling fast.

"Sorry to hear that," Stone said.

"I had an interesting chat with your friend Zalman Seligman instead."

He wasn't surprised to learn Zohar, in his desperation, had taken a swing at Seligman, but he knew the Rav was too invested and too smart to do anything but stonewall Zohar with silence and misdirection. Stone did not say a word, waiting for Zohar to explain. He had less reason than ever to speak with Zohar, considering the events of the previous evening. He had the purifying blood of righteousness on his hands. Anything he said to Zohar now would clearly implicate himself in the eyes of the law.

"When you didn't show, I moved on instead."

"Good for you," Stone said. "I hope it was gratifying."

"Oh, it was," Zohar said. "I'll have you know, Matthew, they're playing you for a fool."

"You promised me you'd get rid of Dov, and you haven't done a thing."

"You need to give me something first," Zohar said. "Quid pro quo."

"I won't wear a wire," Stone said. "You've picked the wrong guy for that."

"Then listen to me," Zohar said. "Maybe this will change your mind. Zalman Seligman hasn't been close with your father in years. Now that your father is gone, he wants complete control. He is the last person your father would wish you to associate with right now."

"You figured that out all by yourself?" Stone asked. "The same way you figured Jews were planning attacks meant to be obscured by the bombing of the Towers?"

"What are you talking about?"

"You're just trying to prove to the FBI boys' club you're no Jonathan Pollard. You're ashamed of who you are. You humiliated yourself and destroyed your name. Isn't that right, 'Lightning'?"

Zohar laughed, the way only a man accustomed to taking body blows could laugh. "Have you ever heard the saying 'No good work goes unpunished'? Going back to Hoover, the FBI has never been comfortable with its agents thinking too far out of the box. An agent is supposed to think by the book. I used my brain, and I got slapped for it."

"You were dead wrong and you were fired."

"It was a minor indiscretion," Zohar said, clenching his fists reflexively as if he were readying to punch something or someone. "And no, I wasn't fired, I wasn't even censured. I was transferred to headquarters in Washington. Then to Salt Lake City, of all places."

"You deserved it."

"I'm a good agent, Matthew. I was the one who solved the case of the Mormon church bombings. It was a clan of polygamists who had broken away from the church and were striking out at the elders. I solved it and I was rewarded for my efforts. I need to be at the center of the storm, so they moved me back to New York."

"What do you want from me? You expect me to be an informant?"

"Semantics, Matthew. I say hero. Just appeal to your sense of reason."

"What, that Jews are terrorists bent on destroying the very fabric of our civil society?"

"Jews are not exempt simply because they are Jews."

"Wrong answer," Stone said. "Next you're going to claim Manhattan housewives are involved in the blood libel?"

"Matthew, you're being ridiculous, and you know it. What's gotten into you?"

"I'm not going to wear a wire. I have nothing to offer you."

Zohar paused and smiled a crooked half smile. "Perhaps you'd like to discuss this more formally over at Federal Plaza."

"On what grounds, Agent Zohar? If you're intent on throwing a temper tantrum because I won't do your bidding, you're going to find yourself in a world of trouble," Stone said.

"Obviously I'm wasting my time with you," Zohar said, lighting a cigarette.

"That's right," Stone said. "And you're wasting my time too."

21

Barely a block toward home, Stone heard the shuffling of heavy footsteps rushing behind him. He turned his head to see what the commotion was, heard the sound of labored breathing at his ear, felt a rag pressing at his mouth, and . . . that was the last thing he was aware of before disappearing into darkness.

Then, through a channel of whirling colors cycling from black to searing white, he was yanked back into consciousness, a coarse hand slapping at his cheek, smelling salts at his nose. Stone had no idea how long he had been out. He lay sprawled in the back of an SUV, head resting on a bulky suitcase, windows blacked out, a small dome light glowing on the ceiling like a gibbous moon.

"Matthew, it's Uncle Zal. Are you with me?"

Zal, Stone realized for the first time in relation to Seligman, was the Hebrew acronym for *zichrona livracha*, of blessed memory, and was commonly written alongside the names of the dead. Stone had no idea where he was or whether he was still among the living, but he heard seabirds squawking somewhere in the sky above, their cries resembling the cruel laughter of children. His feet were fastened down with something heavy and, as his eyes focused, Seligman's concerned face floated into Stone's vision, toothpick jammed into the corner of his mouth.

"Where are we?" Stone said, his tongue slack.

"Marine Park," Seligman said. "A beautiful salt marsh of more than five hundred acres, right here in Brooklyn."

Moshe laughed from the front seat as if Seligman had told a hilarious joke.

"What are we doing here?" Stone asked, his voice sounding foreign to his own ears.

"Don't worry about that, Matthew, I just want to ask you a few questions."

Stone tried to sit up, but Seligman pushed him back down with a stiff pair of extended fingers. "Relax," Seligman said, kneeling over Stone, his head just touching the interior's roof. "You're not going anywhere right now, so make yourself comfortable."

It was impossible to be comfortable with pins and needles simmering at his feet, Stone's circulation compromised by the bindings. His neck ached from the awkward angle of his head resting on the suitcase. He wanted to get up and prove to Seligman he was still the master of his own destiny, but he couldn't with Seligman's heavy hand pressing down on his chest.

"Don't make this any more difficult than necessary," Seligman said, shifting the toothpick from one side of his mouth to the other. "Now, is there anything you'd like to tell me?"

"I don't know," Stone said, frantic. "What do you want me to tell you?"

"You know what I'm talking about."

"I don't," Stone shouted, his throat hoarse with panic. "I don't know what you're talking about. I don't. I don't. I swear."

Seligman regarded Stone for a long moment and Stone could hear the rush of blood in his ears, the furious pumping of his heart.

"All right then," Seligman said. "We know you've been speaking with the FBI man called Zohar."

Moshe laughed again, this time at the mention of the name Zohar. Stone knew what he was laughing at this time. Nothing focused the mind like fear. *The Zohar* or *Book of Splendor* was a seminal mystical commentary of the Torah, and the Judge had several heavy prewar editions in his collection. Considering Agent Zohar's decidedly secular view of the world, his name was wildly unsuitable.

"Anything now, Matthew? Last chance to come clean."

"I didn't tell him anything," Stone said.

"You think siccing the FBI on me is going to derail our plan? Do you really think it's that easy? Tell me the truth, Matthew," Seligman said, "and choose your words carefully. It wouldn't take much for you to disappear at the bottom of this salt marsh. You're walking on a narrow bridge right now. You don't want to slip."

A burst of panic tore through Stone's body, a primitive terror awakened at the sudden prospect of imminent death. Now Stone understood why his ankles were weighted, and he was seized by the desire to tell everything. "Zohar really believes I hate my father, and that I will do anything to destroy him. But he's wrong—I am as much bound to my father as he was to his father. To go against him would be to go against the natural order of things. I'll never do it, never. Zohar wanted me to act as an informant, to tell him what is going on inside the warehouse, but I refused."

Seligman smiled. "And you told him you were simply visiting a house of study and prayer?"

"Yes. I said I was saying Kaddish for my father and for him to leave me alone with my grief." Stone's words, barely more than a gasp, robbed of the power of a complete inhalation, came out as weak as a breath squeezed out through a drinking straw.

"That's the right answer," Seligman said. "He thinks you are weak. He believes he can turn you against your father by throwing around words like honor and bravery."

"He's wrong," Stone said. He was through the worst of it. He'd said the right thing and he'd spoken the truth. "I owe Zohar nothing. I am, now and forever, obligated to my father."

Seligman smiled, sizing up Stone anew.

"Why did my father move the money?" Stone asked.

"Tell me," Seligman replied, "what does Zohar believe is going to happen?"

"I need to know," Stone said. "Why did my father cut you off from the account?"

"You're in no position to ask questions, Matthew."

"Maybe I'm in no position to answer questions."

Seligman laughed quietly to himself. "Matthew," he said, "do you understand what's going on right now? You're in no position to negotiate."

Though Stone was powerless, lying supine on the floor of the SUV, his ankles bound and Seligman palming his chest, he felt an incredible surge of confidence working through his entire being. Stone's duty was to do his father's bidding. Anything else was empty, useless. He had to know or else nothing mattered. "Tell me why he moved the money. You had a falling out with my father."

"Is that what Zohar told you? Now he's got you doubting."

"It wasn't Zohar," Stone said. "I can figure things out for myself."

"Falling out sounds so dramatic," Seligman said. "Your father was the closest thing I ever had to a brother. Let me tell you, even blood brothers bicker and quarrel. You know your father was hardheaded, and so am I. But it turns out your father was right. He knew we were being watched. Every time I landed at Kennedy Airport, the FBI was waiting. They've placed me on a watch list because of my activities in Judea and Samaria. They think I'm some sort of dangerous radical. Can you believe that? A rabbi, a man of the book, a grandfather of four. So your father moved the money and removed my name from the account in order to protect the money. He never expected he would die."

"But he did," Stone said, "and now you can't touch the money."

"Matthew, we thought we had all the time in the world. Growing old is the most unexpected thing for a man of substance. Somehow, we believe death will come only in some distant, theoretical future, but then it's upon us and it's too late. Your father was my best friend in the world, you know that. It hurts me nearly as much as it does you that he is gone, but we have the power to complete his legacy, you and I."

Seligman said what Stone needed to hear. Both Stone and Seligman wanted the same thing: to do right by the Judge and complete his work.

"Zohar thinks there's going to be a terror attack in Brooklyn."

"And you told him what?"

"Nothing. Nothing at all. He has a proven track record of targeting

Jews as radicals," Stone said. "He sees terror where we see justice. He sees violence where we see strength. I told him nothing."

"And what do you know about such an attack?"

"My father had ideas about violence and how it can be used to achieve goals which otherwise could not be achieved."

"That's all?"

Stone nodded.

"And your lowlife friend Michael Pinsky. How do you feel about what happened to him?"

"He got what was coming to him," Stone said.

"No pangs of remorse?" Seligman prodded.

"He deserved what he got," Stone said.

"Matthew, I don't need to remind you I've always thought of you as family, even when you were not able to see I was there for you. I could have saved you from all that mess with the Arab whore back in Israel, but I gave you the space to make your mistakes, because you were young and I knew your father would want to set you straight himself. But the time for mistakes is over now. You understand, Matthew, if you ever speak of what happened to your friend, the thief, you are implicating yourself as well. Do you understand that?"

"Yes," Stone said. "I understand."

"You'd never speak of this to anyone, no matter the punishment?"

"Never," Stone said.

"You are so sure of yourself now, but how can I be certain that won't change? Wouldn't it be wise to get rid of you, in case you have a change of heart?"

Stone couldn't tell what he heard first: his heart stopping or the driver's side door opening. The inside of the SUV was flooded with a melancholy gray light, heralding cooler days and the inevitable change of seasons, and Stone saw through the tint of Seligman's aviator glasses the cruelty in his annihilating eyes. The back hatch popped open and Moshe, the shapeless executioner, stood, black hat pressed down onto his idiot head, the thick, saturated afternoon light flowing all around his form like waves. Moshe grabbed Stone by the armpits and hefted him out of the trunk. He dangled from Moshe's powerful arms like a marionette as Seligman unfolded himself into the fresh air. "I'm sorry, Matthew. But you haven't proven anything yet, and we can't take the risk you'll talk."

"But what about Pinky?" Stone shouted. "I delivered him to the Rosh, I did the right thing! I am with you, not against you."

The weights tore at his ankles and Stone screamed out in pain. Moshe lifted Stone into a bear hug, squeezing him with unbelievable force, but somehow Stone found the strength to cry out, "Wait! I have the passcode to my father's account."

Moshe continued to walk through the high marsh grass as if he had not heard Stone's words, but Seligman bade him to stop. He dropped Stone to the ground where he came to rest in the dirt against his throbbing ribs. Seligman's scuffed leather shoes appeared before Stone's face. One of his shoelaces was untied.

"Are you lying?" Seligman asked.

"No, of course I'm not lying."

He pulled himself up into a sitting position, massaged his bruised ribs and got to his feet. Neither Moshe nor Seligman stopped him. "I know you want access to the account and I know you can't get at it without the passcode, and you can't get the passcode without me. We are talking millions of dollars. If you want to get what you want, you have to give me what I want."

"I'll have you know, Matthew, I'll survive without money. You on the other hand . . ."

Awakened by a strange sensation he could not pinpoint, Stone realized any lie he concocted could buy him time if he could just sell it to Seligman as fact. The lies flew from Stone's mouth as fast as he could invent them.

"I've left a notarized letter with my father's lawyer, C. T. Holland, founding partner at the firm Holland, Rowe and McKim, to be opened in the event of my death or disappearance. In the letter, I've named you, Zalman Seligman, along with Isaac Brilliant, Moshe Reisen, Dov Wexler, and the yeshiva boys, as responsible."

"You're lying," Seligman said, but his expression was uncertain. "You wouldn't do that."

"Yet," Stone said, "you believe I would rat you out to Zohar. I know you spoke with him yesterday. Whatever he told you is a lie. It's so transparent. Can't you see what he is trying to do?"

"Tell me what you told him, and you can save your life," Seligman said.

"Nothing. I told him nothing. I want to help you."

"All right. We're done," Seligman said, nodding his head to Moshe.

"I have the passcode numbers. They were in my father's books. I found them, I found them!"

"You're going under that water, Matthew, unless you tell me what you told the FBI. You've been inside the *beis*."

"The base?"

"The *beis midrash*. The study house. You've seen the operation. I know you talked."

"I told them nothing."

Seligman flicked his wrist in the air, his gold watch slinging out from under his sleeve.

Moshe lifted Stone off the ground, his brutal hands squeezing Stone's tender places. There was nothing else to say, but rather than panic and beg, Stone was overcome with a peculiar sense of relief; his trials were finally over, and the pain of being would be washed away by the brackish waters of the salt marsh. His life had been a relentless journey toward death, and now he had arrived. He had done everything he could to please the Judge since his death and he would be with his father soon. The Judge would know the truth about him, and that was all that mattered now. Suspended in the air, dry stalks of cord grass bending around him like supplicants, Stone began to laugh inexplicably, a manic machine-gun staccato, frightening in its strength.

Seligman appeared before Stone, a terrible look of distress on his face. "What is so funny?"

"You're going to die," Stone said through laughter. "We are all going to die. Do you think God can save you? Nobody can save you. The Book of Judgment is open now and you will not escape. Go ahead. Do it! Do it!"

Seligman began to laugh in return, low, baritone howls rising from deep within his belly. The two of them and their dueling laughters out there in the salt marsh must have looked like some mad tableau concocted within the padded walls of an asylum, because Moshe placed Stone delicately on the ground and stepped aside. "Matthew," Seligman said, wiping spittle from his beard with a handkerchief, "I must admit I am impressed. You're not the weakling I took you for. I believe you when you say you didn't speak to Zohar, that you didn't tell that mamzer a thing. How else could we have known whether you would or wouldn't crack? You've done good, Matthew."

Stone could not distinguish whether Seligman was telling the truth or whether he was toying with him, but Moshe had already walked away and was leaning against the side of the SUV, a blank look on his bearded face.

"I don't understand," Stone said, confused, a strange disappointment running up and down the length of his spine. He had prepared himself mentally to take the final leap into the void and have the delicious mystery of whatever was to come revealed at last. To come that close to death was simply too much to bear, and he broke into sobs, his body quivering with the indefinable combination of joy and grief and disappointment.

Seligman threw an arm around Stone and pulled him close. The strange masculine smell that was the signature scent of both Seligman and the Judge overpowered Stone's senses, and he stopped crying, shocked at the turn of events.

"When a Gentile wants to convert to Judaism, it is the rabbi's duty to turn him away. And if he returns again, it is the rabbi's duty to turn him away once more in order to test his level of commitment. The Rosh turned you away, and you brought him the *gonif*. You had your opportunity to shame yourself with lies to save yourself, but you were prepared to die for your truth. *Kol ha kavod*, Matthew! Your father would be proud of you, and I am proud of you."

Stone took a moment to gather himself before asking, "So, what happens now?"

Seligman flicked his toothpick into the grass. "Moshe drives me to the airport and I fly home to Israel for Yom Kippur. I'm not needed here any longer. In fact, now that I know Zohar has his eye on me, the whole operation is better off with me out of the picture. You, on the other hand, have a very important role. I'd like you to take over for Dov—"

"But Isaac, the Rosh—"

"Does as I instruct him to do. He may be the head and the hands, but I am the soul, and the soul dictates everything. Do you think those were his hands clutching your throat when you stumbled into the *beis*, or mine?" Seligman smiled a broad toothy smile. "When you go to the *beis* tonight, bring the passcode numbers with you and the Rosh will thank you and tell you what is needed next."

Stone had burned through all the infinite manifestations of fear and could no longer worry about what would happen next. He felt an odd kinship with Seligman, who had applied the harshest measures of tough love imaginable to test his worth, and Stone knew his father would approve. He wanted to hug Seligman to thank him for giving Stone the opportunity to succeed, to be a player in his father's operation, but Seligman was already walking back to the SUV, Moshe in the driver's seat, igniting the engine.

"Come on, Matthew, let's go," Seligman called. He reached into his wallet and pulled out a hundred-dollar bill. "We'll drop you on the way. You can take a taxi home."

22

When he got back to the apartment, Stone called Dasi, but Esther told him she couldn't come to the phone. After what had just happened with Seligman and Moshe in the wilds of Marine Park, Stone did not want to be alone. The solitude of Pinky's apartment was intolerable. Pinky's eyes, staring from Abi's half-finished painting, followed Stone throughout the apartment, around corners, penetrating locked doors, imploring Stone to save his sorry life. Stone turned the portrait around so it faced the brick wall, and that helped quiet his conscience. His father's books lay silent all around him and he couldn't find Pinky's stash of weed to help calm his nerves. Stone had to talk, had to feel human warmth and contact, and though he knew he could never speak precisely about what had just happened, Stone needed to be near Dasi, to hold her, to feel the softness of her self-affirming body pressed against his.

He showered, changed his clothes, and climbed into the Thunderbird. He drove toward Ocean Parkway with the windows rolled down, his mind troubled by the fact that Dasi had not returned any of his calls since they had last seen each other. They had connected in a most profound way and he could not figure out why she was silent now, in his time of need. He thought back to the night on the pier and how she had wanted him to hurt her, dominate her, assert his power over her as he finally blossomed into the man he was meant to be. He was not his father, but he was of his father. That was a powerful realization;

understanding that while he contained the same elements as his father, his creator, he was his own person, gifted with an untapped strength he was only now learning to draw upon.

Stone rang the doorbell, his nerves jangling like the car keys he tossed from hand to hand as he waited for someone to answer. Forget his unreturned phone calls—she and Stone were destined to be together. They might both have been imperfect, broken creatures, the provenance of their meeting dubious, but the Judge's iron endorsement forged an unbreakable bond between the two of them, and Stone was not prepared to accept otherwise. Someone was moving around in the dim vestibule behind the threadbare curtains. After a moment, Esther opened the door and greeted Stone, saying, "I'm sorry, Dasi's not feeling well."

She did not try to close the door, but she did not invite Stone inside either. "But," he stammered, "I need to speak with her."

"Dasi is not speaking with anyone right now," Esther said, her expression inscrutable.

He loved her, and she had to love him back or else everything he had learned, everything he had done to change his life, was for nothing. His breathing fell shallow and as he stared into Esther's watery blue eyes he managed to say, "I'm worried about Dasi. Is she all right?"

"I'm sorry," Esther said, "but I can't say any more."

She moved to shut the door, but Stone jammed his foot across the threshold, blocking it from closing. "I can help her," Stone said. "Just one minute. That's all I ask."

"I'm sorry," Esther said. "Dasi said she didn't want to speak with anyone."

Stone's body broke out in a sudden sweat and he was afraid if he didn't find something to grasp on to right now—Dasi, a few hits of a joint, some pills, booze—he would fall apart. He couldn't hold back the flood of anguish much longer. She was the culmination of everything he had learned and was the key to his sustained happiness.

"Please," Stone said, and though he was appalled by the pitiable sound of his voice, he repeated again, "please, please, please, please."

Esther's face remained still, showing no change in her features. Then Stone heard Dasi's voice from somewhere inside the house. "I'm warning you, Matthew, I look like a different person without my makeup on. And it's not a pretty picture."

A pair of worn ballet flats appeared as she descended the stairs, then her pale shins, her black dress, slender arms, and her face—drawn, melancholic, and no less beautiful. Her face had a soft, vulnerable look to it without the veneer of her makeup, and her lips, though thin, were pink and vibrant against her white skin.

Stone wanted to take her in his arms, to hold her and press his lips to hers, but he doubted it would be welcome. Seeing Dasi in front of him now made him realize she really was everything he ever needed. Though his breath still struggled to issue from his lungs, he could already feel the oxygen coming on in fuller drafts simply from the relief of being in her presence.

Dasi thanked her aunt Esther, said she'd be back soon, and turned her face toward Stone. "Let's take a walk."

They crossed the busy thoroughfare of Ocean Parkway in silence, Stone restraining himself from reaching for her hand. They arrived at the grassy island separating the two sides of Ocean Parkway. The street was alive with people enjoying a last taste of late summer, sitting on park benches chatting or playing chess, or out strolling at the end of a long day. Stone was thankful for the chance to be out among people with Dasi.

Dasi turned her attention to Stone and surprised him by saying, "I just wanted to apologize."

"For what?" Stone said.

"I know I'm being a brat, not returning your calls, but it's not easy," she said. They walked along the tree-lined path beneath the turning leaves. "Will you forgive me?"

"Of course," Stone said, "but for what?"

"I thought I was so ready to finally meet you after all this time, and then this horrible thing happens with Dov and just messes everything up. I'm not saying I don't want to be with you, because I do want to be with you very, very much, but you need to be patient with me because

I have so many mixed-up feelings right now that I don't know how to behave."

"What do you mean?" Stone asked.

"I never loved Dov," she said. "But he's a part of my life and I care about him. And now he's in the hospital with these awful injuries, and you're here, just the way I imagined you would be, and I feel I'm being forced to choose."

Stone offered no response. He just wanted Dov to disappear.

"I don't know what to do," Dasi said. "I think I need to be alone for a while, to concentrate on my studies, to sort myself out. I'm not asking you to wait for me, but I hope you do."

"How will being alone help you? I can be good for you."

"I know that," Dasi said. "But the timing, it's just . . ."

This sounded to Stone like a prelude to breaking up. Asking for space, to be alone, was just a gradual way of moving on, an attempt to inflict the least amount of hurt, usually with the opposite effect.

"But what if I need you now?" Stone said. "What about me? Don't you understand my father died? I'm in a lot of pain. I need you in my life."

"I just can't give you what you need right now. Maybe we both need to be alone for a while," Dasi said, her face painfully close to his, her breath peppermint fresh. "I'm sorry."

"So that's it?"

The sun had already moved far to the west, burning pink and orange and red over New Jersey, leaving the sky before them a dark, inky blue. A single star appeared in the sky over the Atlantic.

"You're not listening, Matthew. Don't be angry."

"How can I not be angry? You don't want to see me."

"That's not true," Dasi said. "I do want to see you, but I want to be at my best when I'm with you. And right now, I've just got too much uncertainty and confusion to be the person I want to be with you."

They arrived at a jostling crowd, pushing and clambering to get a better view of a young boy, no older than six, playing chess against an elderly bearded man in a black suit and kippa. Some men clutched bills in hand as if prepared to lay bets.

"But I don't care if you're at your best. Don't you understand?" Stone said. "You at your worst is better than most people at their best."

"Matthew, I'm sorry, but this isn't about you. It's about me, and I can't go into anything I care about with less than everything I can give. Please be patient."

"How long?" Stone said.

"I don't know," Dasi said. "I've got to get home now. Walk me home?"

"Not yet," Stone said, wanting to hold on to his time with her a little bit longer.

"I have to get back."

"I can't believe this," Stone said. "It feels so right."

"It's not," Dasi said. "Not now, it isn't."

"Is there anything I can do to change your mind?"

"No," Dasi said.

They walked back to Esther Grunhut's house in silence, Stone's loneliness amplified by the couples pushing strollers along the path, old men in hats laughing on park benches, children tossing colorful balls back and forth beneath the streetlights. Dasi walked a step or two in front of him, her straight black hair caressing the middle of her back, and for a moment he thought to grab a handful, pull her close to him and never let go, but the inimitable voice in his head told him to do no such thing.

They arrived at Esther's house. It was so painful to be this close to her and not touch her. She smelled of lavender or some sort of bath powder, and he imagined he would never see her again after tonight. Her dark eyes looked so sad as she turned to him outside her aunt's front door. He realized, looking at her now, that the freckle under her right eye was not a freckle at all, but rather a scar, and he wanted to ask her what had happened, but she spoke first.

"I know this has been horrible, Matthew. I'm really not trying to mess with you, I'm just—"

"I want to kiss you good night at least," Stone said, leaning in. "Just once."

Dasi withdrew and said, "Trust me, there's nothing I want more than that, but I can't." Her mouth twisted into a thoughtful frown. "I just can't."

"When can I see you again?"

"I don't know," Dasi said.

"Can I call you at least? Just to talk?"

"No," she said.

"Well, what then?" Stone said, drowning.

She must have felt his pain, as acute as it was, because her face brightened with the realization that she had found an acceptable compromise. "You know what? Why don't you join us for the break fast after Yom Kippur? I know it's not what you have in mind. Please come and respect the fact that you are coming as a dear friend. I want you to be part of the break fast. Just, no expectations, okay?"

"All right," he said. "I'll come to the break fast."

"Oh, that's so great," Dasi said, relief washing over her face. "You're not mad at me?"

"I'm not mad," Stone said.

"Thank you," Dasi said. "I have to go." She pulled open the door and disappeared inside, leaving Stone alone on the porch with a tangle of moths flickering in the light.

STONE JUMPED INTO the Thunderbird and drove as fast as he could to the *beis*. He rang the bell and waited, anticipation and fear mixed as one. After a few minutes, Moshe appeared at the door and let him in. He looked into Moshe's impenetrable face, trying to figure out what was going on inside his head. Had he really been prepared to drown Stone in the salt marsh? And, if so, was he bothered Stone was here now, alive?

"Nice to see you," Stone quipped, but Moshe said nothing in return as he locked the door and led Stone down the worn stairs to the mirror maze and through the darkness of the warehouse.

He must have been late, because he found Brilliant pacing back and forth before eight or nine of the yeshiva boys, surveying them in critical silence. Was Brilliant even expecting him? He was about to ask Moshe when Brilliant spoke, at last, to the group assembled before him.

"Self-discipline is more important than grand ideas, passion, righteousness. Self-discipline is everything. When you show up late, laughing like schoolchildren, everything crumbles."

Yossi, who stood no more than ten feet from Stone and Moshe, began to speak, but Brilliant cut him off.

"I know what you're going to say. But visiting hours for that waste of a human being is no excuse. You are giving in to the evil inclination. Distractions will destroy all of us in the end. Your friend Dov has already destroyed himself. Don't follow his lead. Yes, self-discipline is difficult with the daily obstacle of life getting in the way, but self-discipline is the only way. You may find it difficult to shower every day, eat three meals, but you do find a way. If you find it difficult to do what you have pledged, then you must force yourself with an iron will." Brilliant spoke with a profound inner conviction, staring hard at each face as he spoke. "You're still perfecting your ABCs, and time is short. Now tell me, what do I mean when I say ABCs?"

"Learn to shoot!" the group shouted in unison.

"Good," Brilliant said. "Why?"

The pear-shaped one took a step forward. "Because we cannot rely on the goyim to protect us; because blood will be shed as we reclaim our land."

"Good," Brilliant said. "Every day, like clockwork. Discipline."

Stone wondered whether this show was put on for his benefit alone as Brilliant dismissed them and they made their way in silence to the shooting range.

Brilliant approached and Stone feared he would be sent away. He wasn't certain he was welcome in the warehouse at all. Stone was aware of Moshe's looming presence behind him, and he expected at any moment to be manhandled by the silent giant. Had Seligman meant it when he said he would be welcomed or was he just passing him along to Brilliant so he could have his way with him? Stone's ears rang as the sound of gunfire began to issue from the shooting range.

Brilliant welcomed Stone with a small smile. He had to raise his voice above the gunshots, but Stone clearly heard, "We're very pleased you could come this evening. The Rav says you have something for us?"

Stone nodded his head in assent and showed Brilliant the card.

"Thank you for doing your part, Matthew. What is the passcode?"

Stone hesitated for a moment, fearing that once he gave up the numbers he would be of no use to Brilliant, and could just as easily end up dead like Pinky. He had felt such absolution and relief when he had called the bank the second time to verify the passcode was correct, and he knew he had a larger role to play in this unfolding drama than just supplying the numbers. He was in charge of the fund now, the fund his father ran, grown from a nest egg his grandfather built decades before Stone was even born.

"I can tell you the passcode, but you still need me," Stone said. "Any transactions from an account that size need to be done in person, at the bank. I can give you the passcode now, but it won't be any use to you without me."

"So what exactly are you trying to tell me?" Brilliant said.

"I want to be a part of this. I want to do what you wanted from Dov."

Brilliant laughed. "Have you even fired a gun before?"

Stone had never so much as held a gun, but seeing the yeshiva boys lined up at the shooting range, fringed *tzitzes* dangling from their pants, pistols held out in front of them, their fiery discharge deafening in the closed space of the low-ceilinged basement, Stone yearned to belong, to be one of them.

"I'll go to the bank and transfer the money wherever you need it, but you have to let me in on this."

"You're not going to dictate to me," Brilliant said.

A strange clarity filled Stone's head and he knew, if he pressed his case with force, Brilliant would give in.

"I'm telling you," Stone said, "I'm a part of this or you never see a penny." Was this what it felt like to be the Judge, to stand up to his adversaries without fear, knowing his will would win out in the end? Stone still had no idea what he was getting involved with, but he was prepared to go forth and do what needed to be done.

"All right," Brilliant said with a sneer. "But if you are lying about the account, I will cut your throat."

Brilliant signaled to the Israeli and pointed at Stone. "Boaz will show you the proper way to stand and how to hold a gun. Never point it at anything unless you plan to kill it." Brilliant laughed.

Stone realized he had barely taken a breath during the entire exchange, and now he breathed in a deep satisfying breath of air and released it as his rigid body relaxed. Boaz greeted Stone with a bright, easy smile, his tanned face relaxed. "You like to shoot?"

"I don't know," Stone said. "I've never done it before."

"Don't worry. I will pop your cherry, and leave you petitioning for more," Boaz said, his Israeli accent thick. "I am the best hired gun money can procure. And I am very committed to making money. I am expert marksman with many notches on my belt. I'm here to instruct you to shoot, so you will shoot."

They found an empty lane at the end of the range, beside Itzy, and Boaz instructed Stone to put on a pair of orange headphones. They were huge, noise-canceling headphones that muffled the sound enough that Stone was gripped by a woozy underwater sensation. Boaz already had a pair of Day-Glo foam plugs jammed into his own ears. He slipped a clip into the butt of the gun, checked it, and fired a shot at the target some thirty feet away.

Boaz's first shot hit the target, a keffiyeh-wearing Arab man, in the middle of the forehead. "Don't worry about the head," Boaz shouted, while miming a bullet to the torso with B-movie grace. "A shot in the chest will slaughter a man nine times out of ten."

He handed Stone the stainless steel gun. It was heavier than Stone imagined it would be, and far more beautiful. The work of a master craftsman, it fit perfectly in his hand. Boaz popped out the magazine and showed Stone how to load it himself. He did so without any difficulty.

"This is a SIG Sauer P226, 9 mm. It is a combat handgun used by US Navy SEALS, federal agents, and many law enforcement organizations. It is very easy to handle because of its superior balance. You will have no trouble becoming a killing machine with this in your hands."

Boaz positioned Stone, knocking his feet apart with his knees, squaring his stance, raising his arms out before him, lifting his chin with nicotine-smelling fingers. Stone tried not to look down the row to see how well the rest of them shot, but he could not help but notice their shredded targets flying back down the laundry line to be replaced with fresh ones.

Stone fired, and the kickback wrenched his shoulder. He missed the target completely.

"Hurts, yeah?" Boaz laughed. "Try easy—loose—but firm." Boaz shook out Stone's arm for him, lightly massaging his muscles. "Now, again. The pistol is your flesh."

Stone fired again and the recoil was less severe with his body relaxed. The bullet did not hit the target. He fired three more times and missed.

"Okay," Boaz said in a warm, avuncular manner, "think about the psychology of shooting, Matthew. You have to want to shoot a gun with the same enthusiasm you feel about fucking a woman. If you are not turned on by her, you can't get it up. The same is for shooting. You must long to shoot the way you long to make love to a woman. The gun is your dick; the bullets are your seed. Now, do you want to shoot your load?"

"Yes," Stone said, feeling foolish. "I do."

"You are fucking a woman in her wet pussy. If you can't hit target now, you are either homosexual or hippie pacifist. Or both!" Boaz laughed and slapped Stone between the shoulder blades.

Stone imagined Dasi, her slim legs spread for him as he hovered above her manicured landing strip, savoring the moment, and then thrust himself inside her. He fired again and hit the target, then again and again. His dick was as hard as iron and he didn't want to ever put the gun down. The pistol was an extension of his best self and he understood how he could overcome his own physical limitations to be equal or better than those around him. It would be so easy to kill now.

"*Tov maod*," Boaz said. "You're a fucking pimp with that firearm. You see what I mean?"

Boaz moved back along the row to instruct the rest of his peers.

Stone paused to watch Boaz strut with the sort of confidence unique to native-born Israelis, shouting advice at his charges.

"Watch it," Itzy shouted. "Your gun."

Stone's pistol was pointing directly at Itzy's feet. "Don't let Boaz see."

Stone righted his pistol and aimed it toward the target. He didn't fire. "What's his story? He's not like the rest of you."

"Yeah, well," Itzy said, shrugging, "he piled up quite a body count in Lebanon. I heard Boaz was in Grozny in the Chechen War laying waste to the Russians, maybe Kosovo, too. Don't ask to see his resumé, but, trust me, he's a stone-cold killer."

Itzy fired off a round to punctuate his words. The acrid smell of burned gunpowder hung in the air and a smoking shell casing rolled to Stone's feet.

Boaz was shouting at the pear-shaped one, their faces pressed so close together the pear-shaped one's kippa fell from his head as he angled his neck back for space.

"We're lucky you could step into Dov's place," Itzy said. "Otherwise we'd be shorthanded for the plan. We need all the good men we can get."

Stone had to know what had happened to Dov. He had never hated a person so much in his life; Dov's very existence intruded upon Stone's burgeoning relationship with Dasi.

"How is he doing?" Stone asked in the most neutral tone he could conjure. With guns firing all around it would be difficult to read nuance in his voice, but Stone wanted to be careful not to reveal his true feelings.

"He is messed up. Permanently," Itzy said.

"What do you mean?" Stone asked.

"It's bad," Itzy said. "And the Rosh is furious with him for acting without his permission."

Stone asked what he meant by that.

"He was trying to make a bomb on his own and it blew up in his face. We are only supposed to do as we are told by the Rav or the Rosh. We act as a team, not as lone wolves."

"So, what happened to him?" Stone asked.

"He punctured his eardrums and lost most of the hearing in one of his ears. Totally destroyed his leg; it may need to be amputated below the knee. It's horrifying," Itzy said. "I mean, I am committed to the cause, and I know this is a terrible thing to say, but sometimes I think I would rather die than be permanently maimed like that."

Fuck you, Dov Wexler, Stone thought, Dasi is mine.

"I mean he was never very nice to me, always called me Itzy-Bitsy Little Shitsy, but he shouldn't have to lose his leg." Itzy paused and gained his composure. "But, the important thing is you're here now and the plan will go forward."

Stone was literally stepping into Dov's life, stripping him of everything he had ever cared about—his girl, his place in history.

"What is the plan?" Stone said.

Itzy lifted up his safety goggles and wiped the condensation off on his shirt. "You don't know?"

"I have a pretty good idea," Stone said. "But not exactly . . ."

"The Rav said we had to be careful. But you're here, so I assumed you knew. The Rosh fills us in on a need-to-know basis. That way nobody can possibly compromise the plan without exposing himself."

Boaz signaled for everyone to stop shooting, but Stone wanted, needed, to hear more. He was so close.

It was time to train with the M16s, and two of the yeshiva boys were summoned to retrieve them. Stone removed his headphones and heard a crashing sea of white noise above the ringing in his ears.

"If you were in Munich in 1923," Itzy said, "at the beer hall where Hitler tried to seize power for the first time, wouldn't you shoot him, put a bullet between his eyes? Think about history. Everything would have been different; no war, no Shoah, six million Jews, rest their souls, would have lived out their natural lives."

A vague phantom stirred within Stone, and he knew for certain what he would have done.

Itzy continued, "The Rally for Palestine on Atlantic Avenue. There'll be all sorts of Arab bigwigs from around the world. A state assemblyman from Brooklyn who is a friend of Arafat, Winston

Haloumi, the terrorist professor, and R. R. Nation as the emcee, with his brown-and-black unity BS."

This was far more meaningful than what his father had demanded in his will. Killing Nation would be far more beneficial to mankind than another useless doctorate.

"If there's one thing we've learned from the Muslim Brotherhood, it is the way they shot down Sadat on the podium in Cairo. He wasn't expecting it, couldn't conceive of it. It was perfection. Only, we will come out of nowhere. We'll pop out of the manholes beneath the street and shoot them onstage for the world to see. This is a chance to get them all at once. Show them there will be no Palestine beside or in place of Israel and any Arab who facilitates it will have a target on his back and will not be safe anywhere in the world."

It all began to make sense now. Itzy's father had been killed in an attack by Arabs; this was his version of an eye for an eye. Stone's own father would still be alive today if it had not been for the hectoring and harassment of R. R. Nation in his speeches to the media, always hungry to anoint the latest villain.

Impatient excitement sweltered throughout Stone's body. He wanted to do it now. This very minute. Put a gun to Nation's head and pull the trigger. The two yeshiva boys wheeled a cart loaded with M16s down the row of the shooting gallery, exchanging the pistols for the semiautomatics. Stone asked Itzy how the plan was going to work.

"There's an old train tunnel under Atlantic Avenue. We've got it all mapped out from our property on Henry Street. All we have to do is pop out and it's like shooting fish in a barrel." He laughed a high, wheezing laugh.

So that was why the property on Henry Street was so important. There was never going to be a museum, and Stone was never going to live in a third-floor apartment. He was not upset he had been deceived by Seligman; he had not been ready to take up the fight, he had not earned Seligman's trust yet, but now he was ready. Stone realized this really was a plan hatched by his father before he had died, and the completion of this plan would be the ultimate fulfillment of his wishes, something he could never have considered requesting in his will. Stone thought back to his marathon reading sessions, his brain computing connections he had not made earlier. Time and again, his father had underlined passages on tunnels and their relation to the Jewish struggle for nationhood. Stone could not imagine how he could have missed this when it had been spelled out right before his eyes. But now, as if he were gazing at a photograph coming gradually into focus in a darkroom, Stone could never un-see what his father had intended.

Zedekiah, the last king of Judah, had escaped through tunnels running from Jerusalem to Jericho when the city was conquered by the Babylonian king Nebuchadnezzar. During the Bar Kokhba Revolt against the Romans six hundred years later, the Jews had hidden in underground tunnels until their ultimate defeat at Betar. During the Spanish Inquisition, Marranos, living as Jews in secret, conducted Passover seders and other religious rituals in underground tunnels. The Judge had marked all these passages in his books, as well as articles describing how weapons had been smuggled from Egypt to the Gaza Strip during the 1948 War of Independence and, recently, during the conflict with the Palestinians. Stone had even found a newspaper clipping from just two years earlier, written when rioting exploded in Jerusalem after the Israeli government opened a passage to a long-sealed Hasmonean tunnel running beneath the Dome of the Rock. Over eighty people died in the fighting that ensued, and another violent uprising began.

What really struck Stone, what connected his father's markings together and made him realize the tunnel was the key to the coming attack, was a quotation he had found in a book of nonfiction by Walt Whitman on the defunct Long Island Rail Road tunnel that ran under Atlantic Avenue, from Columbia Street to Boerum Street. His father had underlined: "The old tunnel, that used to lie there underground . . . now all closed up and filled in, and soon to be utterly forgotten . . . the tunnel dark as the grave, cold, damp and silent."

The Judge had written the single word "YES" in the margin.

23 The buzzer rang. It was either before noon or after noon, Stone had no idea, but he was loath to interrupt his reading to see who it was. He found himself deep in the pages of Josephus. The Judge had highlighted his own share of quotations and passages throughout the volume, but Stone believed, now that he had discovered the passcode, that he had earned the right to add his own annotations to his father's books, father's and son's thoughts blending into a unified viewpoint. His pen hovered in the air for a portentous moment before he underlined this passage: "<u>Now, my father Matthias was not only eminent on account of his nobility, but had a higher commendation on account of his righteousness and was in great reputation in Jerusalem, the greatest city we have</u>."

The meaning behind marking this passage had two purposes, the first being to acknowledge his own father's great deeds, particularly in relation to Israel, of which Jerusalem was the ever-beating heart.

The second reason behind underlining the passage was as surprising to Stone as anything he had ever considered. He had suffered from pain and distress for so long, loaded down with the weight of his own misery, that he had never truly imagined a future for himself in which he was present as a lucid, functional being. Now, as he ran his pen back and forth, thickening the lines beneath the words, he realized this acknowledgment was also aspirational in nature, not backward-looking toward whatever creature Fairuza had born, since he would never know it. He was reaching out across the years to a future son he could proudly call his, who would, one day, read the name Matthias and know Matthew, his father, was speaking about himself and his own accomplishments.

The buzzer rang again, a long drawn-out whine as omnipresent as a mosquito in the ear canal. Stone, aggravated by the distraction, relented, made his way down the long hallway, and pressed the intercom button.

"Matthew," his mother's tin-canned voice said through the crackling speaker. "I know you're in there. Open up."

Stone buzzed her in, and she appeared at the front door a moment later.

"Why didn't you answer? I was worried about you."

"I'm busy," Stone said, offering no salutation, no explanation.

Abi stood before him in paint-splattered jeans and a T-shirt emblazoned with Marc Bolan's miserable face, her hair pulled back into a casual ponytail.

"I wanted to pick up Michael's painting," Abi said, peering around the apartment. "You don't need me in your way while I finish it. Is he home?"

"No, he's not home," Stone said.

The idea that his mother thought Pinky could actually be in the apartment made Stone's stomach drop in a queasy free fall. Pinky was dead and he was never coming back. He no longer existed except on the canvas of his mother's painting. Abi noticed her unfinished painting turned against the exposed brick wall and said, "Now, is that really necessary?"

She acted as if Pinky were still alive, as if she would one day soon show him the finished product and receive his stamp of approval. Maybe he'd eat caviar and crackers and sip champagne at the opening at some TriBeCa gallery. How could she go on acting as if Pinky were still alive if he wasn't? This made no sense to Stone. He was dead, yet she wanted to know if that piece of trash was home?

Abi had stepped into the apartment and was already halfway across the living room, beelining for her canvas. The painting was an oppression. She picked it up and regarded it at arm's length. Stone knew it was a mistake to look over, but he did, and he saw Pinky's face, pale and bloated with the early stages of decomposition. His eyes were wild, penetrating, beseeching Stone to *do something!*

"What do you think, Matthew?" Abi said, turning toward Stone with a sly half smile on her face. "I think it's a very good likeness. Just a bit of shading here and there."

"Get out," Stone said.

A look of confusion swept across Abi's face as she stepped toward him, the painting still in her arms. "Matthew," his mother began.

"Take it and go. Now!"

"Matthew, what is happening with you?"

"Get out. Now," Stone shouted. His changes of mood were so rapid now, each rise and fall of his emotions a jagged, short-lived earthquake.

"What's the matter? I thought we agreed to get along now."

She still held that hideous painting in her arms, Pinky's face animated in death, a grotesque reminder that Stone was an accomplice to murder. Pinky's death had been a great triumph in Stone's evolution, but the implausible fact that Pinky still lived inside that painting, begging him, chastising him, set off a squall of emotions he could barely contain.

"Get out, get out, get out," Stone cried, in a voice that sounded to his ears just like that of his father. "Get out, or I will kill you."

"You don't mean that," Abi said. "I'm your mother."

"I do mean it," Stone said, propelled forward by some unseen force. He tore the painting from her arms. Abi looked so small and delicate standing before him; he reached out for her and found only empty air as she dodged his wild flailing. Abi ran out of the apartment in complete silence, as if she were too afraid even to scream. The painting lay on the floor, faceup, staring at Stone; Pinky's face gaped at him with the irreality of a hallucination. "And now you're all alone," the painting mocked. Stone collapsed to the floor, numb, keening with the inarticulate fervor of an animal. He lay on the wood floor, shrouded in his father's robe, feeling the grit tracked in on the bottoms of shoes against his fingers and cheek. These were people, Stone realized, this grit and dust and dirt were *people* atomized down to the basic element from which they came. Dust to dust to dust to dust. He was surrounded by the dead, by infinitesimal fragments of lives that once lived and breathed. He was alone but he was not alone, and he knew each one of those dust flecks at his feet was watching him, whispering, the whispering so dense and overlaid that he at last understood for certain the constant hum one heard amid silence was the voices of all the dead of the earth trying to be heard.

What had he done? What was happening to him? He needed his mother, needed to hear her voice, needed to feel her warm embrace, needed her in a way he had not needed her even as a child. He wanted so deeply to apologize to her, to fix what he had done. She was, after all, alive, and only the living had the capability to hold one in their arms.

He discarded his father's robe onto the floor and, a moment later, found himself on the sidewalk in front of the apartment. The homeboys were out there throwing dice again, and Stone asked if they knew which way his mother had gone. She wasn't at the bus stop across Myrtle Avenue, she would never have walked to the subway at Jay Street all by herself, and taxis in the neighborhood, forget it.

"She went thataway," one of the homeboys said, pointing a long, ringed finger up the street.

Stone turned his back to Myrtle Avenue and ran without saying thanks.

"Tell your moms I wanna date her, know what I'm saying?"

"Yeah, she a doll, Goldberg."

More and more these days, Stone imagined he was wearing a yellow star stitched to his chest, alerting the world that he was a Jew and fit for destruction. Everyone knew he was a Jew, his entire being screamed it. He put his head down and ran. Stone's ears burned all the way up Waverly until he turned right at the co-op, the homeboys out of earshot. He had a pressing need to make things right as he ran up tree-lined Clinton Avenue and past the nineteenth-century mansions of the robber baron Pratt children, tripping on a root that had pushed up the slate sidewalk. He wanted to apologize for everything he had ever said and done to hurt his mother; he wanted her to know he had space for her in his life and that she could exist alongside the memory of his father. And then he saw her, fifty yards ahead, shoulders stooped, head lowered, as she turned onto the bustle of DeKalb Avenue. She must have been heading to the Q or the R train.

DeKalb Avenue was a different world—just two blocks away from Myrtle Avenue and its barbershops and fried-chicken houses, dice games and drug deals—lined with newly renovated brownstones, chic restaurants, shops selling African crafts and clothing, a black equivalent of SoHo running from Washington to the park. The air seemed cleaner, fresher, the greenery more full, and as he closed the gap between him and his mother he wondered how beauty like this was allowed to flourish in one place but not another.

She was a bus length ahead of him, waiting absently at a red light, when a man appeared in Stone's field of vision, tugging her by the elbow. She did not struggle as they crossed the street together, and that was when Stone recognized it was Zohar. Had he been stalking her, too? Stone felt a sudden need to protect his mother. His anger just moments earlier had been misplaced. Stone felt his fists go heavy, bracing themselves for battle. It was Zohar who needed to die. Stone watched as they turned in to a restaurant, advertised on a sign hand-painted in pan-African red, black, and green as THE LONG DREAM. Young black professionals and artists sat out on a patio, drinking beer and eating before the chocolate facade of a newly renovated brownstone. Stone stopped outside the low wrought-iron gate and caught his breath.

The sun glared off the high glass windows, the stenciled phrase WORDS CAN BE WEAPONS AGAINST INJUSTICE haloed in the afternoon light. From where he stood by the PLEASE WAIT TO BE SEATED sign, Stone could not see into the restaurant. A pretty host with dreadlocks stationed at the entrance to the patio asked if he had reservations, but he brushed past her and walked inside.

His mother had her back to him, pulling out a cane chair to sit at a table for two. As Stone's eyes adjusted to the dim light of The Long Dream, he understood the magnitude of his mother's betrayal. Zohar sat across from her, an incongruous mask of concern spread across his self-satisfied face. Their body language said it all; they knew each other. This was not the first time she had spoken with Zohar, and the look of shock on his face confirmed Stone's worst fears. A vein pulsed so hard in Stone's neck he actually clutched at the throbbing in an attempt to make it stop.

Stone realized in that instant that his mother had found him after all this time because of Zohar. Zohar had recruited Abi to inform on the informant, had flown her out from California on the Fed's dime, and now they sat across from each other in a tony restaurant plotting their next move against Stone and his father's legacy.

If she had been working for Zohar all along, did all her apologies, her heartfelt declarations, mean nothing?

Zohar blanched, and Abi turned to face Stone, her eyes filled with tears.

Stone might have screamed out something or he might not have, he wasn't sure, and he had no understanding of how he arrived back at the apartment, tearing his mother's painting apart with a steak knife, Pinky's face shredding to ribbons beneath the blade.

He had left the door open, and Abi appeared in the threshold. "Please don't hate me. You have to understand, I was looking out for you."

"Is this supposed to be some display of maternal compassion, talking to the fucking FBI?"

"I was trying to help you, Matthew."

"You're not my mother. You're nothing," Stone said. "I don't know who you are."

"And I don't know who you are," Abi countered. "But you are my only son and I am afraid you are getting tangled up in something you don't understand."

"Did he call you? Is that why you dropped back into my life? As a snitch for the FBI? And to think I believed you actually cared."

"Matthew, you're sick. I am trying to help you."

"You are nothing but an aging narcissist with a hero complex."

"Your contempt is frightening."

"Then leave. I didn't ask you to come here."

"Please just leave here with me right now and never come back. We'll go right to the airport. Please, just trust me."

"And why would I ever do that now?"

"You need help."

"Not from you."

Her eyes flickered as she caught sight of her tattered painting, torn to postage stamp–sized bits and pieces, scattered all over the floor. A tiny sound issued from her mouth, sort of a broken *oh*. Then she saw the Judge's robe lying on the floor behind Stone, and she leapt past him before he could react, grabbed the robe, and began tearing at it with her hands.

"If you're going to destroy something, destroy this. Your father is nothing but a cult of murder and lies."

Stone grabbed the robe back from her and his fist raised itself like a hammer ready to strike.

"Stop your moralizing, Abi. What you did to me was worse than anything the Judge could ever have done to anyone. I inherit my father. You can crawl away and die."

And then it was over.

She stepped into the doorway, her gait stern and confident as if she were trying to force strength into herself through her steps alone. She turned around at the threshold, her black eyes hard again.

"I'm afraid for you, Matthew. Not of you, but for you."

"Good-bye," Stone said. "Never come back."

NOT KNOWING WHAT to do with himself in the apartment after Abi left him for the final time, Stone let his legs carry him instinctively to the *beis* for the Kol Nidre service. He needed something powerful to overwhelm the recent events between him and his mother, to push her deeper into his consciousness. He was done with drinking and drugs, and he vowed in the new year he would live like his father, by the spirit of *hadar*. The small sanctuary was filled with men lost in the haunting melody of *Kol Nidre*. The entire gathering of worshipers chanted as one and Stone recognized the tune instantly, though he could not decipher its meaning. It played on some ancient part of his being, hundreds of years old, thousands even, the strange Aramaic tune reaching across generations with crystalline clarity.

Later, as he recited the *Al Chet* prayer acknowledging the mistakes Jews had made in the past year, Stone realized he was not alone in his guilt. Others had degraded parents, used vulgar speech, committed *lashon harah*, rushed headlong into evil. Others had committed the sin of immorality, speaking harshly, wronging a friend, having a hardened heart. As he read along to the Hebrew acrostic, matching up the words with their English equivalents on the opposite page, the worshipers beat their chests with closed fists while they recited the forty-four statements of guilt. This communal act of repentance provided Stone with the purest form of release. He understood, in the manner so many before him had, that he was part of a community of sinners, and he would be absolved.

24

The next day was Yom Kippur and Stone slept late, as though he were hungover. He did not dream, but he awoke with a deep disquiet stirring within him. He threw himself at his father's books with renewed fervor, stopping only to eat Pinky's spoiling leftovers from the fridge. He tried to keep his mind clear, as he read about the organized butchery that was the Kishinev Massacre, the terror of Nicholas II and the Black Hundred, but his thoughts kept wandering back to Dasi. He imagined she had died overnight or that something awful had happened. He imagined he would never see her again, that she'd been carried off by a mighty hand, erased from the face of the earth, no remnant remaining.

The sun had gone down. He didn't know how it had gotten so late. He dressed in his nicest clothes, shaved the scruff off his face, and jumped into the Thunderbird, windows open to the cool air. It soothed and refreshed him as the deformations of loneliness uncoiled from his body, like a snake sloughing its skin. He had been alone too long, and his father's books possessed him, filled him with terrifying thoughts of annihilation and destruction.

When Stone arrived at Esther Grunhut's house, the door was ajar and raucous conversation was well underway. He knocked on the door; when no one answered he let himself in.

Stone scanned the room for Dasi, repulsed by his own intense need for her, but saw only an empty seat where she had sat the last time.

Dr. Cohen was seated at the foot of the table, his back to Stone, opposite David Grunhut at the far end of the table, their voices raised in hot debate. The aged doctor had risen out of his chair and his pant leg slid up, revealing an intricate network of black varicose veins.

"What kind of beast walks into a hotel banquet hall full of people, strapped with explosives and nails, and detonates himself?"

"An animal," David said.

"No animal could do this. Tables laid out for the Yom Kippur break fast: a massacre."

"Then tell me, Irving."

"Some *thing* that hates Jews more than it loves life. A thing, a nullification of a thing. Pure evil."

A radio blared in the kitchen, the Hebrew voice of the announcer speaking rapidly. Stone made out the word *Netanya*, a city by the sea between Tel Aviv and Haifa, and the word *Hamas*.

Hamas was an Arabic acronym for the most violent, rejectionist Palestinian terror group. Stone knew from his readings that *hamas* was also an ancient Hebrew word meaning "violence," dating all the way back to the scriptures. As much as the world had advanced with the civilized trappings of technology and liberal political philosophies, nothing had changed. The methods of murder had evolved, the justifications updated, but the goal remained: the total destruction of the Jewish people.

"Every time there is a suicide bombing," Dr. Cohen said, "I read the list of the dead and look for myself."

"Irving, you live in America."

"America," he laughed. "They will kill Jews wherever they can."

"I disagree," David said. "It's about the land. The Arabs are making a fallacious claim to the land we were promised."

"It's not about the land, it's about blood, Jewish blood." Dr. Cohen pulled his necktie loose and adjusted the clip on his kippa.

"Everything is about the land," Yossi said, catching Stone's eye and motioning for him to sit across from him. "Remove the Arabs from the land, and you remove the problems."

A wooden leaf had been taken out from the middle of the dining room table, lending a more intimate atmosphere than there had been at the Rosh Hashanah meal. From where he sat, Stone was able to see Dasi moving about in the kitchen. His heart clenched and he wanted to go to her, bury his face in her hair. She wore high, lacquered heels that tapped across the linoleum floor as she paced back and forth, her head cocked in concentration toward the radio report. He would have done anything to soothe that look of worry on her face.

Dov was not present, still laid up in the hospital, and Stone knew his path to Dasi was free. Eli, who had known the Judge at Kiryat Arba all those years ago, was also absent. Of course Seligman was gone as well, back on the secure iron hill of Giv'at Barzel. Itzy and another yeshiva boy to Yossi's left talked among themselves. Yossi sat beside Malka, balancing a sleeping Arieh on his knee.

"Look at your history. It is nothing but a roll call of death. Killing Jews is the oldest sport known to man."

"Irving, relax. Yom Kippur is over and you have been written into the Book of Life for another year."

Stone apologized for being late, and Dr. Cohen crossed his arms on his chest.

"Now Yom Kippur is just another day," he added. His eyes were pink and raw.

Finally, Esther said, "Matthew, you must be starving. Shmuel, help him get some food."

A man with a large round face and a tentative beard leaned over the table and piled the cold, runny salads onto his plastic plate with all the care of a unionized sanitation worker. "Here," he said, forcing the plate on Stone.

Stone was not hungry, and the talk of the suicide bombing did little to stir him to eat.

"Yes, the doctor is spoiling everyone's time again," Dr. Cohen said.

Dasi entered the dining room stricken, her face drawn and flushed. She had been monitoring the radio reports from Israel and the news just kept getting worse. "Thirty-two confirmed dead," she called out before emerging. "Over eighty-five injured." She looked delicate in her black dress, her skin so pale her blue veins were clearly visible, a softly pulsing road map to her heart. Stone wanted to take her in his arms and embrace her, crush her.

She put on a smile for him, but it was clear it took everything she had to do so. He couldn't speak to her here, amid Dr. Cohen and Yossi and Itzy and David Grunhut. What Stone wanted to hear from her, what he needed to hear from her, could be uttered only in the intimacy of their own private space. He had made a mistake in coming. What did he really expect anyway? That she would have changed her mind over just a few days and come to him with open arms? Nothing had changed with Dasi. She was a stranger to him again, a vibrant dream painfully dematerialized.

"I have to wash my hands," Stone said, to no one in particular. He stood up from the table, careful not to look Dasi in the eye. The conversation continued as he made his way to the bathroom.

"If you forget your history, then you will die because of it. Do you think the anti-Semites forget their history? Esther, you know as well as I do what they can take from you."

"Irving, let's not stir up the dead tonight," David said.

Stone felt a painful need to be alone. Dasi held both his happiness and his misery in her hands and he couldn't bear the thought of her confirming his deepest fear. How easy it was to fool yourself into thinking that you were worthy, that you had overcome all your worst inclinations, when you were what you were. A primitive loneliness overtook him as he locked the bathroom door behind him, that singular feeling of being either the first person in the world, or the last. He wished there was some way to wipe Dasi from his mind, strike out her influence over him in a single stroke. Love did not exist as anything more than a phosphene vision of a person's own madness; like the victim of a metastasizing sickness, the afflicted lost his senses one by one.

Yet despite these dark ruminations, he still wanted Dasi to love him, to remove once and for all the pain he had carried with him every day of his life since Abi abandoned him to the Judge. There was a soft knock on the bathroom door, and Dasi saying, "Matthew, it's me. Open up."

He was afraid to open the door and face the reality that Dov had had her while he had not. Seeing her up close would only remind him of all the places Dov had been.

"Matthew, please," she said, her voice flat and sad.

"What do you want?"

"Come on."

Stone opened the door and she stood before him in her black dress as if in mourning.

"I just want you to hold me," she said, locking the door behind them. She threw herself into his arms and embraced him with incredible force, pressing herself into the safe harbor of his body. Her heart pounded against Stone's chest, and just that simple intimacy alone caused him to soften, and caress the nape of her neck with his free hand.

"I have friends in Netanya," she said, her face buried in his chest, "from the army."

He wanted to be her protector, to prove to her he was everything she thought he was—strong, decisive, a man of action. He thought of learning to shoot at the *beis* under Boaz's tutelage, preparing for the day in which he would carry out his father's plan, striking fear into the hearts of those who would dare shed Jewish blood. If death was the great equalizer, then Stone knew payback would not be long in arriving, and that the dead and maimed of Netanya would be redeemed, here, in the streets of Brooklyn.

"This will be made right," Stone said, stroking her hair.

"What do you mean?" Dasi asked.

"You don't know what I'm talking about?" Stone said.

"No," Dasi said, offering a concerned smile. "What do you mean?"

Stone knew better than to say too much. He was new to this world, and Dasi had learned her lesson well not to speak. "Evil is always punished," Stone said at last.

They stared at each other in silence for a moment, and Stone knew she understood exactly what he was alluding to.

Then, as if to affirm his suspicions, she leaned in to kiss him, softly at first, and then hungrily, as if she were biting into a ripe plum, her lips firm and pliant. Dasi slipped her tongue into his mouth and he closed his eyes and kissed her. She pulled him closer, her hands gripping his hips, pressing herself up and down against him. They breathed together, exhaling slowly.

"I want to be alone with you," she said. Her eyes were so dark they almost looked black.

"So do I," Stone said.

"I'm sorry," she said. "I never wanted to hurt you. Will you forgive me?"

Stone silenced her with a kiss.

But she broke away from him and added, "It's just, I want to be with you, and it's scary to think about giving yourself to someone."

Stone told her he understood, but she could never fathom the terrors from which he suffered, standing at the edge of forever without her at his side. "You want to give yourself to me?"

"Yes."

"Say it, then."

She paused, bit her lower lip, and said, "I want to give myself to you, and only you."

"Really?" Stone said.

"I'm just so confused. But I don't know if there is ever a perfect time and I don't want to miss this chance."

"I want you," Stone said.

"I want you, too."

Down the hall, at the foot of the dining room table, Dr. Cohen pronounced, "But the Holocaust is never over chapter and verse. That book remains open."

Dasi looked at Stone, her eyes soft. "I'm wet."

He slipped his hand under her dress, his knuckles caressing her soft inner thigh as he found the damp spot between her legs.

"Matthew," she whispered, "not here," but she didn't move to stop him.

He pulled aside her sheer panties and slid his finger up inside her. She was slick with desire and he pistoned his finger in and out three or four times.

"Matthew, stop," she said. "I mean it."

He did as she said and removed his glistening finger from her. "Taste it," he said. "I want you to taste it."

She stared at his finger for a brief moment, lips upturned in a hint of a smile, then took it in her mouth, sucking up and down. "Want to know what it tastes like?" Dasi asked when she was done.

"Yes," Stone said in a small voice.

"I'll bet you do," she said.

Dasi turned, opened the bathroom door, and receded down the hall. Her dress was wrinkled at her hips, which shifted as she walked as if trying to work her panties back into place.

THE CONVERSATION AT the table evolved from one disaster to the next as coffee and cakes and pareve ice cream appeared. The doorbell rang and Dr. Cohen screwed up his face into an elaborate frown, as if the sanctity of his unending drumbeat of misery had been spoiled. Dasi stood up to answer it, and Stone watched her as she maneuvered around chairs and Arieh's scattered toys.

Yossi asked Stone something about the Yankees and their magic number, but there was only one magic number for Stone; he had found it and he wielded that number like a sword. He was important, crucial to his father's plan. No other numbers mattered anymore. Dasi had still not returned from answering the door, and Stone found himself listening to Yossi absently bantering about batting averages and winning percentages with the two yeshiva boys.

Then Stone heard Dasi cry out, "That's enough, okay? I'm done."

The entire table stopped mid-conversation, the clinking of serving dishes in the kitchen suddenly audible.

"You're done when I say you're done."

Stone recognized Dov's voice. He rose from his chair and headed to the door. Yossi and Itzy rushed to the door as well, as Esther called, "We still need to *bentsch*."

Dov stood on the porch, propped up by an aluminum crutch. A thin mist of rain fell, refracting the yellow light of the streetlamps into a diffuse, melancholy glow. He wore a backward Yankees hat and a loose hooded sweatshirt from which his fringed *tzitzes* hung raggedly. His right leg was mummified below his knee in a secure boot and he balanced himself precariously on his one good leg. His face was still swollen from the concussion of the explosion. With his skin still raspberried with scrapes and abrasions, he looked tough and rakish and full of the unwarranted braggadocio of one who has survived a tragedy.

The yeshiva boys greeted him, but Dov kept his focus on Dasi.

"I'm going to lose my leg and you don't even come to visit me."

"I did," Dasi said.

"Once. You visited me once. And I wasn't even conscious."

The image of Dasi intimately whispering in Dov's ear as he lay in a hospital bed flamed into Stone's mind and he stepped to Dasi's side and slipped an arm around her narrow waist.

"What's this?" Dov said, spitting his words like he'd eaten something rotten. "You can't even wait until I am gone. I can't believe you."

Dasi slid out from Stone's grip and said, "Dov, stop. You don't understand."

"What don't I understand? That you're a slut who can't make it on her own for five minutes without latching on to the first man who comes along."

"Whoa, whoa, whoa," Yossi said. "You don't need to speak like that."

"It's all right," Dasi said. "Dov, you know how I feel and nothing is ever going to change that."

Dov's eyes were wide with fury. "In front of him we have to do this? In front of them?"

He gestured to the dining room window; when Stone turned, he saw the curtains shift back into place where the observers had been.

Dov carried the medicinal smell of salve and unguent on his skin. Was he even in a condition to leave the hospital?

"I want to speak to you before I leave," Dov said, his tone recalibrated into something less aggressive. "My plane leaves for Israel in a few hours." He gestured to a battered blue Corolla idling in the street. The pear-shaped yeshiva boy stood sentry, arms crossed, in front of the vehicle, as if he were guarding the Holy of Holies. He was driving Dov to the airport. Dov was leaving the country.

"I'm doing rehab in Israel, but I'll probably lose the leg."

"I'm sorry," Dasi said. "I am so, so sorry."

Why was she apologizing to Dov with his repulsive sneer and arrogant tone, when he was the intruder, the interloper?

Dasi's shoulders were small and rounded, and her pale face looked birdlike against the screen of her black hair.

"I want to speak to you alone," Dov said. "I'm not a public freak show, okay?"

"Dov," Dasi said, "it's break fast. There are people here."

"I'm going back to Israel to lose my fucking leg. This is the last time you'll ever see me whole."

Dasi did not respond, but Itzy placed a hand on Dov's and said, "Relax. It will be okay."

"It won't be okay," Dov said. "Nothing will ever be okay again. Don't you get it? I'm ruined, a cripple."

"Dov, stop," Dasi said. "That's enough." Her voice broke and she dropped her chin to her chest in a gesture of defeat.

"Don't make me beg you," Dov said. His voice altered again to something resembling the boy he must have once been to Dasi. "Please don't make me beg you."

Dov's outburst was repulsive to Stone, in part because he knew he could just as easily be the one begging. He saw his own pitiful weakness in Dov, and that made him want to vanquish Dov once and for all so he would not be reminded of it.

"Don't you understand," Stone said, interjecting at last. "She doesn't want you."

"This is none of your damn business," Dov said.

"I think it is," Stone said.

Dov looked past Stone and fired his words into Dasi's face from just a foot or two away. "So this is your new love, huh? As good as the last one? Or the one before?"

"Dov, enough."

"I don't care," Dov said. "You always come back to me."

"Did you hear what she said?" Stone said, reaching for Dasi's waist again.

Dov edged closer, cutting the distance between them in half.

"Easy," Yossi said, stepping between Dov and Stone. "Easy."

"As a matter of fact, I'm having some trouble hearing, since one of my eardrums has been blown out, but I did it in service of a higher cause. You wouldn't know anything about that, would you, since you live in your father's shadow. Son of the Judge. Big fucking deal. I knew him, and you're nothing like the Judge."

How dare he use his father as a weapon against him! Stone was about to say something cruel and biting when Dov spat in his face. "You're nothing, you got it? Nothing."

Dov's warm saliva dripped down Stone's face, and he drew back his fist to bury it in Dov's jaw when Dasi shouted, "Stop. That's enough."

The front porch was silent and the rain fell all around, hissing in the air like something about to catch fire. Dov was crying, red-eyed, humiliation burning at his face. He looked strangely awkward, his Adam's apple jutting out from his thin neck. "I wanted to speak to you, not your latest boyfriend."

Even in the darkness of the front porch, lit only by the towering streetlamps, Stone could tell Dasi's eyes were full of pain. He wanted to take her in his arms, go back inside with her, and lock the door on Dov once and for all. He would soothe her, caress her soft skin, make her forget all about her sorrows.

She turned toward Stone, her humped nose prominent in profile, her lips, that just minutes earlier were his, downturned and thin. "Matthew, you'd better go. I have to talk with Dov."

Dov's spit had gone cold on Stone's face, and he absorbed Dasi's words like a punch to the kidney.

"What?" Stone said. "What do you mean?" He couldn't believe Dasi was choosing Dov over him. The vault of his stomach collapsed in on itself, Pinky's rotten leftovers rising up his esophagus, acid burning at his throat. "What?" he murmured as if he had lost the ability to understand language.

"I'll call you," Dasi said.

Before Stone had a chance to take possession of himself, Dov and Dasi were inside the welcoming warmth of Esther Grunhut's house, and he remained outside on the rainy porch with Yossi and the two yeshiva boys.

"You know they're engaged to be married," one of the yeshiva boys said.

"What?" Stone said, barely audible even to his own ears.

"Yeah," the other yeshiva student said, "in his own mind."

And they both laughed.

"Hey," Yossi said, "you've got your car, right?"

Stone nodded.

"Let's go to the *beis* and do some target practice."

Aside from bursting back into Esther Grunhut's house and pounding the living daylights out of Dov, Stone knew the firing range was the best solution to ease his aggressions.

"Fine," Stone said, his legs seasick beneath him, "let's go."

Stone drove in a silent rage, his foot heavy on the accelerator.

Yossi joked, "Buckle up boys, we're going for a ride."

Everything was upside down and backwards. He had been sent out in the rain so Dasi could be alone with her former lover. He had been rejected, not Dov. Dov claimed her as his and had been intimate with her body, touched her in ways Stone could only imagine. The thought that Dov could be pressed close against her right now, fingers and lips touching her most private places, overpowered Stone's mind. When he arrived at the *beis*, he would grab one of the pistols from the armory closet and then make up some excuse that he had to leave to deal with something important. It would be so easy to put a bullet in Dov's face and be done with him. The temptation was irresistible. He would be doing Dasi a favor, ridding her of him for good. She would cry at his death, but inside she would feel freed of an awful burden, and Stone would stand by her as she grieved appropriately before her community. He envisioned laying Dasi down on the soft, packed earth of Dov's fresh grave and fucking her in triumph. These vivid imaginings caused Stone's heart to rev with desire.

"You okay, Matthew?" Yossi asked.

He was back in the world now, slick hands clammy at the wheel. The Statue of Liberty stood tall in the distance, her torch raised high above her head, black water quaking around her. Manhattan appeared in the misty rain before them, strikingly close, as if its towers and spires would block their passage. Brooklyn was spread out below to their right, steeples and smokestacks and houses piled up into low hills. Beyond, the glowing face of the clock on the Williamsburg Savings Bank tower smiled sadistically, the building itself obscured by a gray, smoky mist. Stone eased up on the accelerator to take a curve, and knew the moment had passed; he would not go after Dov tonight. Dov was returning to Israel, leaving Dasi behind. Wasn't that punishment enough?

25 By the time the Thunderbird pulled up outside the *beis*, Stone was looking forward to the camaraderie and sense of mission he had missed the previous night. There had been no training scheduled on Kol Nidre and Stone's dark readings had caused him to feel isolated, paranoid, afraid that he, too, could fall victim at any moment to the eternal Jew hater. Every sound and shout in the street outside could have been the trigger for a pogrom, and even his father's robe, wrapped tight around his form, did nothing to ease his mind.

Stone realized now, seeing Itzy's soft face amid the others and Boaz, armed with his quick smile and sharp rejoinders, that he was proud to be part of something—no longer just a lone individual but a foot soldier in an ancient, intractable war, an interconnected piece to complete the puzzle that was his father's life.

A noisy debate was already well underway.

"One dunam equals one-tenth of an acre," a stocky kid with a neatly trimmed black beard said. He spoke with authority, as if he had cornered the market on truth.

"You're wrong, Federman," Yossi responded, jumping right into the middle of things. "One dunam equals a thousand square meters."

"It's the same thing," Federman responded, rolling his eyes comically.

"I think," Itzy said, carefully measuring his words, "a dunam of land is equal to one-tenth of a hectare."

"You think, or you know?" Federman said.

"I thought it was a quarter hectare and one-tenth of an acre," another one added.

"And how much is a hectare anyway?" yet another added.

Boaz, who had been sitting off to the side, picking his teeth with a shell casing, interrupted. "No, no, no. You are all wrong. One dunam is equal to one-quarter acre, which is the same as a thousand square meters, which is the same as one-tenth of a hectare. Four dunams equals one acre. Trust me, I know every hectare and dunam of Judea and Samaria like the inside of my head."

Fairuza had often used the measurement of dunams when she spoke of her many relations' olive groves checkerboarding the rocky hills of the West Bank. Stone, feeling curious, could not resist asking, "And how many dunams are there?"

"As many as we need," Federman answered automatically, "to claim all the land of Israel."

"All right, all right, the mathematics lesson is completed," Boaz said. "Are you prepared to shoot or do you wish to keep shooting your mouths?"

Brilliant appeared and everyone, except for Boaz, froze and stood at attention with martial precision. Brilliant asked the group to line up in front of the shooting range, saying he wanted to share something important. Stone's stomach stirred with anticipation as he took his place in line, overcome with pride that he had been invited to join this swashbuckling band of latter-day Maccabees.

Moshe appeared at Brilliant's side, materializing out of the darkness with his monstrous face slack and empty.

"Now that the Days of Awe are over," Brilliant began, "and we move closer to our objective, we must redouble our efforts to ensure everything goes according to plan. The digging is complete. We have tunneled all the way to Atlantic Avenue and have breached and secured the old train tunnel wall. We are moving to the next phase in our mission. It is too risky to coordinate our attack in the actual tunnel, even in small groups. We can't risk being discovered, so we will practice in the *beis* until it's second nature."

The actual attack would be launched from the basement of the house on Henry Street, using a storm drain Brilliant's men had reopened to reach Whitman's tunnel beneath Atlantic Avenue, some sixty yards south.

"To minimize risk, just four of you will carry out the attack and only those on the stage will die. This plan is an absolute good, and it is worth laying down your life. If you are martyred carrying out your mission, your place is reserved in the world to come, where you will reside in honor, eternally alongside the likes of the great Hebrew warriors Joseph Trumpeldor, Avraham Yair Stern, and our dear departed friend Dr. Baruch Goldstein, may his memory be a blessing upon us all."

The Judge had concocted the plan and Stone needed to be the one who helped carry it out, or else he had failed his father once again.

Brilliant continued, "You all know there is nowhere in the world in which a Jew is safe. We are killed as if there is no prohibition against the killing of a Jew, as if that is the natural state of the universe. The Romans; the Inquisition; hundreds of years of pogroms; the expulsion from our biblical heartland in Hebron; massacred by our own neighbors. You may think the Shoah is ancient history, but just recall in our own lifetime: eleven Israeli athletes murdered at the Munich Olympics, and yet the Olympics continued. Could you imagine the same outcome if another nation's athletes had been murdered? Of course not; it would be an abomination and an affront to all civilized humanity. Imagine, synagogues attacked in Rome, Brussels, Vienna, Paris; Israel's embassy and a Jewish community center blown up in Buenos Aires; a car bomb set off in London outside Israel's embassy just one day after high-level peace talks between Israel and the Hashemite king. Remember the massacre of innocent children at Ma'alot; the failed Entebbe operation; the attacks on Nahariya; Kiryat Shmona; rocket barrages from Lebanon targeting innocent civilians of the Galilee; suicide bombings in Afula; Hadera; Dizengoff; Beit Lid; Ramat Gan; Ramat Eshkol; Netanya just this week, and countless others. And what is the casus belli for all this ceaseless violence?" Brilliant paused for dramatic effect and then, at last, he said, "We exist."

Something ineffable, determined, bloomed inside Stone, the machinery of his organs shifting ever so slightly, like the delicate fluttering of a butterfly's wings—seemingly inconsequential, but powerful enough to change the entire world. He would be a part of this, even if it meant laying down his life.

Brilliant went on, "It is sickening to note, this is only a very partial list that will continue to grow in the years and decades to come. Perhaps, someday, one of you or your loved ones will be taken and forced to admit, before your execution, you are Jewish and your family is Jewish. The people being killed are real, and they could just as easily be you. Remember Leon Klinghoffer, an elderly Jew in a wheelchair vacationing with his wife, tossed from the deck of the cruise ship *Achille Lauro* into the Mediterranean as if he were a sack of garbage. Ari Halberstam, not much younger than you are now, shot and killed by an Arab gunman on the Brooklyn Bridge entry ramp; the killer, a Lebanese national, shouted, 'Kill the Jews,' as he made his escape. A one-hundred-and-forty-one-year sentence will not bring back one second of Ari's life. Even the great Rav Grunhut, forceful and fearless to the end, sits in heaven today, murdered by an Arab assassin. And now, those young boys kidnapped and murdered in the hills of Judea by bloodthirsty terrorists who hand out candies to celebrate the slaughter of Jews everywhere. The list goes on and on. Why should Jews fear for their lives wherever they go, knowing their murderers will not be prosecuted with the same vigor as those who kill the goyim? Why should an Arab who pledges the destruction of the State of Israel and Jews everywhere be free to walk the streets of Brooklyn with no fear for his life? The entire world runs through Brooklyn eventually. If they know we can hit them here, we can hit them anywhere. This is a balancing of the scales. The land of Israel belongs to us, to the Jews. This rally on Atlantic Avenue is a farce and an insult."

A few of the yeshiva boys muttered, "Hear, hear," while another began a slow clap that died a lonely death. Stone's heart jumped with a furious leap, and he nearly shouted, "It has to be me. I have to be a part of this."

"We have been victims for too long," Brilliant said. "But not

anymore. There was a Holocaust in the middle of the twentieth century, a time of progress surpassing in scope any that preceded it in
the history of the world. I am warning you, it will happen again if
we are not strong, if we don't take the land that belongs to us. The
Arabs have twenty-two countries in which to live and yet they cannot
even see fit to grant the Jews a tiny homeland, a small sliver along the
Mediterranean. Why? Because they hate us. Because they want us to
be annihilated. Jabotinsky saw the Holocaust coming long before the
cattle cars rolled, and he did everything he could to organize a Jewish
army to instill physical courage in the Jew, after centuries of abuse,
murder, and persecution at the hands of the Gentile. He did everything he could to acquire land in Israel for the Jew and to settle the
land as our own. He taught us as long as we can shoot a gun, there is
hope. And we, Jabotinsky's spiritual heirs, can see the coming Holocaust: the disaster of assimilation, the rise of a Palestinian terror state,
a resurgence of European anti-Semitism, United Nations favoritism,
the increase of weapons of mass destruction and the ease with which
they can now be acquired.

"The answer is Jewish power. We will make a show of strength
frightening enough to terrify the anti-Semite, wherever he lives, so
that no Jew hater anywhere in the world will ever again feel safe to
raise his head out of the muck.

"This is our credo and we will live by it. Now repeat after me: *We
are the will of Samson, the answer to all Jewish suffering and misfortune.*"

Stone chanted, full-throated, along with the others, filled with
immense pride to be a part of this vanguard movement.

When Brilliant was done, Boaz instructed the yeshiva boys to grab
a firearm from the cart and get in position at the firing range. Stone
was too keyed up to handle a gun, his nerves jangling with excitement.
He followed Brilliant back to the small box of an office where the
maps awaited further blue pushpins.

It was during those midnight sessions that Stone felt truly assured
of his purpose on earth, the way he imagined the Judge had, striding
through the world. With the pistol in his hand, sometimes a practice
.22, other times a powerful 9 mm, Stone slipped free of the apathy,

depression, and self-negation he had suffered for years. It had been Boaz's steady instruction and his blue humor—"Just pretend there's hair around it, and shoot your load"—that had instilled in Stone the belief he could possess the aim of a sharpshooter in short order. But something else was at play as well. The plan—hatched in the mind of his father, birthed by Seligman, guided by Brilliant, to be carried out by Stone and the others in the *beis*—was for something. He had never believed in anything before, but now he realized he was answering the call of his blood stretching all the way back to Julius, his grandfather. Julius had been instrumental in the formation of the State of Israel, and his participation had led to death as well. He had shed blood, but it was for something bigger, a homeland for the persecuted, harassed, murdered Jews, of whom Stone realized, increasingly, he was entirely a part. He understood he was a descendent of kings.

Jabotinsky had written of a race that was proud, generous, and fierce, who would rise again in all their strength and glory. Stone needed to be a part of that renewal.

"I would like to speak with you," Stone said, feeling an overwhelming desire to throw his arms around Brilliant and beg him to allow him to be one of the four.

Brilliant smiled a thin smile and invited Stone into the fluorescent icebox of an office.

"I just wanted to say I was very inspired by what you had to say, and I want to let you know I would like to be one of the four who carries out the mission."

"Why is it so important to you?"

"It's personal," Stone said, "but it means the world to me."

"Does this have anything to do with your father?"

"My father started this," Stone said, "and I need to finish it."

"That is quite a transformation. You have learned a lot in a short time," Brilliant said, "and I appreciate your passion, but this mission cannot be about egos and hurt feelings. Logistics come first, and I have not yet made up my mind who is going to go."

"But I need to be a part of it."

"You are a part of it," Brilliant said. "We are all a part of it. Tomorrow you will go to the Chase Bank on Montague Street and transfer the money into the appropriate accounts."

"You don't understand. That's not enough," Stone said. "That's just the beginning. I want to do more."

"I do understand," Brilliant said. "And there will be other opportunities."

"But this one," Stone pleaded. "I need to be a part of this."

"I know you believe you do, but this is a highly organized team effort. Everyone has an appropriate role."

"And why not me?" Stone said. "I shoot as well as anybody out there."

"At the range maybe," Brilliant said. "But killing a man is not the same as shooting up a paper target." He reached across the desk and produced a manila folder full of photographs, fanning the pictures out on the desk before them. "I want you to look closely at these faces and tell me what you see. I need to know with certainty that whomever I send can pull the trigger and get the job done. The whole mission is at risk if even one of you goes soft in the heart."

The first photograph was of Jordan Issa, a state assemblyman from Brooklyn who had visited Yasser Arafat at his compound in Ramallah and stood smiling for photos as Arafat, in Arabic, praised the perpetrators of suicide bus bombings in the cities and towns of Israel.

Next, Brilliant showed a campaign photo of US senator Joe Salem, who had called for a Palestinian state as well as a war crimes tribunal in The Hague to prosecute Ariel Sharon, Yitzhak Shamir, Shimon Peres, and two dozen other Israeli leaders for alleged crimes of genocide.

Brilliant moved from one photo to the next, providing his commentary for each as he went. Walid "Winston" Haloumi, Columbia professor and author of the landmark book *Irgunism: The Terror State of Israel*, de rigueur reading on liberal university campuses around the country.

Imam Rasul Taibe, of the Farooq Mosque on Atlantic Avenue, who had preached every Muslim must draw his sword and drive it through the heart of Jews everywhere to liberate Palestine.

Sheik Iyad al-Shuhada, author of a well-circulated fatwa declaring the killing of Jews an ennobling act to be celebrated in heaven and on earth. He was also responsible for a fund-raising campaign that sent hundreds of thousands of dollars to families of suicide bombers in Israel.

Hana al-Husseini, chairman of the Land Day Committee, who, on the eve of peace talks in Oslo, encouraged Arabs throughout the West Bank, Gaza, and Jordan to descend on the neighborhoods of Jewish Jerusalem, Jaffa, and other communities with papers they claimed were deeds proving their ownership of Jewish homes. A class-action lawsuit was also undertaken at the World Court to sue for compensation from Israeli Jews.

Yasser Ramadi, Palestinian Authority representative, who had been exiled to Tunis along with Arafat and his PLO cronies, and had Jewish blood on his hands going back almost thirty years.

Jerry Steinberg, head of the ultraliberal Upper West Side–based Free Palestine Movement, whose sole purpose was to purchase Jewish land to be "returned" to Arabs who had fled after the 1948 and 1967 wars. He spoke regularly on CNN about Jewish crimes of appropriation, and once compared the State of Israel to the Nazi regime.

The last photograph was of the Reverend Randall Roebling Nation, bejeweled Mr. Fat Cat himself, founder and head of the Brotherhood Ministries, spokesman for the Black and Brown Coalition, and former candidate for the head of the National Democratic Party, who had promised, if elected president, to withdraw American financial support for Israel in order to "balance the scales of equality."

A visceral bolus of hatred gathered in Stone's belly, like a tightly clenched fist ready to strike. He was certain Nation had driven the Judge to an early death with his speeches before the courthouse, the oratory, the television interviews, everything aimed at destroying his father's carefully built reputation. Nation had the charisma to match his righteous indignation. It was Stone's responsibility now to avenge his father against Nation, who had committed *lashon harah* against his father, not simply because it was an opportunity to advance his own career at the Judge's expense but also because he saw in his darkly shaded crosshairs "the man" incarnate, who had locked up nearly

40 percent of young black males in the country. He was not simply attacking Walter Stone, a privileged Jew with power; he was attacking all Jews who, he believed, rose at the expense of blacks, who succeeded on the backs of black failure. What could be better than to take down the Jew, publicly humiliate him in the heart of Hymietown?

Stone had failed to act on behalf of his father at the time, gloating in secret at his father's pain. He would not, could not fail him now.

"I am absolutely certain I can pull the trigger and get the job done," Stone said, his voice bright with confidence.

"Oh, are you?" Brilliant said, eyeing Stone with his impenetrable gaze.

"I have as much at stake as you do. This is my father's legacy and I need to be a part of this. You have to believe me when I say I wish it were me who killed Pinky. I would do it now in an instant."

"You say that now, but your resumé is slim to say the least. I have men out there who served time in the IDF, have known the whirlwind of the intifada, and understand how to handle themselves under pressure. But you're just a neophyte, a dilettante, trying his hand as a man of the sword, the gun, the bomb. I'm afraid you may not have the taste for it just yet."

"I do," Stone said, breaking into a chill sweat. "It's my birthright."

"You can't rely on your bloodlines alone. Your father and grandfather were extraordinary men, and you may be one day yourself, but you are only just beginning."

Stone was prepared to do whatever was necessary to humble himself before Brilliant. "Please give me a chance. I know I can do it. Let me prove it to you."

Brilliant laughed. "There will be other opportunities. This is only phase one. Be patient and the world will be yours."

Stone was afraid Brilliant considered the conversation over as he dropped the photographs onto his desk and turned his back on Stone, his eyes scanning the maps on the wall.

Stone's mouth was dry and he felt on the verge of falling to pieces. He had no doubt anymore about his ability to do what needed to be done, but he had to find a way to convey it to Brilliant. "And what about the Arabs who were shot in the head on Atlantic Avenue and in Jersey City and Dearborn? Which one of them did it? Was that Boaz? I can do that job if you want. Just give me a name and I will carry out your order. Any time, any place."

"The executions?" Brilliant laughed as if he had heard a joke.

"Yes," Stone said. "I will execute anyone you ask. Please, please just give me a chance to prove myself."

"Those Arabs were killed by their own," Brilliant said, "with Israeli weapons sold to them by the traitor whose name I will not mention."

Stone let out a cry of anguish. "What are you talking about?"

"More Arab propaganda. Another blood libel defaming Jews as murderers and Arabs as victims."

"But why?" Stone said. "Why did Arabs kill Arabs?"

"Because they were selling land to Jews in Eretz Ysrael."

Zohar had been wrong again, favoring the Arabs over the Jews to frame his self-hating personal narrative. Stone didn't know which was worse: that Zohar had deliberately lied to him, or that he was simply an incompetent company man. After discovering what Zohar had done with his mother, Stone understood him to be the most loathsome, repulsive human being he had ever encountered. But now, armed with this new knowledge, Stone needed to act. An idea flashed across Stone's mind, materializing in an instant.

"The FBI agent, Zohar, the one who has been following me, I'll kill him. I'll put a bullet in the back of his head. I'll kill him. You'll see. I will kill him and then you'll know that I am up to the task."

"Matthew, relax," Brilliant said, his tone steady and even. "You need to keep your personal grudges out of this. Your hatred will blind you."

"He wanted me to inform on you, to destroy my father's legacy. He wanted me to wear a wire, but I refused. I never told him a thing. He needs to be taken out."

"You've been watching far too many Hollywood movies," Brilliant said, laughing. "He is not a threat to us now. We don't want to draw any unwelcome attention."

"But I can do it," Stone said. "I can do it tonight!"

"Matthew, I'm warning you. Stay away from Zohar."

"But I can do it."

"Be smart," Brilliant said. "You're tired. You're not thinking clearly. You need to go home, get some rest, and go to the bank first thing tomorrow. That's what you should be thinking about. After you have transferred those funds, you will have paved the way for a dozen new operations to demonstrate the will of Samson is strong, well financed, and committed to destroying enemies of the Jews wherever they may be."

26 A deep uneasiness penetrated Stone's entire being. The apartment was a hollow abandoned place, joyless and full of recrimination. He could not imagine how he would make it through to the morning. After the bank opened and he transferred the money, he would need to find a way to appeal once again to Brilliant's sense of justice after proving himself crucial to the entire operation.

He found a slim volume about the Serbian assassin Gavrilo Princip, who had lit the spark setting off World War I, and read it in one sitting. Princip had only been a teenager when he shot Archduke Franz Ferdinand, and he had altered the fate of the entire world. Stone was a quarter-century old and found himself at risk of missing out on his chance to effect meaningful change. Transferring the money was a near invisible act, demanding no risk, no bravery; it would do nothing to quiet the ever-present voices of reproach in his head. Even his father's books mocked him; the young rugged Princip, who was dead by twenty-three, stared back at Stone vacant-eyed, deriding him for his failure to achieve. When Stone reached for another book, it fell open to a picture of Yigal Amir, the twenty-five-year-old assassin of Israeli prime minister Yitzhak Rabin, his handsome, arrogant face splashed across the page, underscoring Stone's disgrace.

Stone needed to do something to distinguish himself. If Brilliant would not grant him the opportunity, he would have to take it for himself.

Zohar was somewhere out there watching, waiting for his chance to destroy everything the Judge had worked toward. Stone paced the long hallway of his apartment, considering whether he should take the initiative to find Zohar and remove him permanently. He might be standing on the corner right now, or hiding in the thick shadows of the BQE, waiting to spring. The monstrous hulk of the Thunderbird had done it before, so why not again? It was as easy as stepping on the gas. He could do it; he knew he could kill Zohar. What was killing after all but hastening the inevitable? But Stone also knew, inexplicably, if he left the apartment in search of Zohar, he would find himself detained somewhere, untracked from his true purpose, and miss the bank's opening, so he resigned himself to staying put. There was nothing to do but wait.

He wanted so badly to talk to someone, to talk away the empty, falling feeling, the queasy, breathless sensation of drowning in air. He wanted to call Dasi, but the thought of her and Dov together made him want to throw up. It was too late to call anyway, and he was afraid of what she might say. Love was a disease, Stone thought. The only way to get rid of it was to conquer it or kill it.

His father's robe was the best curative for distress, and Stone slipped it over his shoulders and stood before the high wall of books, awaiting further instruction. The whispering undertones humming around him guided Stone to the Judge's books dedicated to Nazi Germany. There was something so insistent playing on Stone's senses he felt he had no choice but to obey. Stone selected a thick volume on the rise of Hitler, but the minutia of his life and ascent was so familiar, Stone read absently for almost an hour without so much as moving a muscle, drifting from page to page in a near trance state. It was when he arrived at a line regarding the 1933 Reichstag fire in Berlin that Stone's senses became sharp and alert. *Yes*, the whispers breathed, *this!*

His father had left no markings behind in this book, but the page went bright before Stone's eyes, nearly blinding in its whiteness, as he lit on a sentence about a tunnel running beneath the Reichstag through which inflammable materials and accelerants had been spread to start the fire. Book after book mentioned a tunnel under the Reichstag, sometimes using the word *flammable*, other times the interchangeable *inflammable*, but it was all the same. Stone mused on this singular detail and why it struck him as important. Some unseen urgency stirred beneath the robe, but his father had ignored the lines altogether. Stone scoured dozens of his father's books in search of notes or annotations that could explain why he was so drawn to the explosives in the tunnel beneath the Reichstag.

There were explosives in abundance stashed away in the *beis*, Stone knew. Dov had maimed himself playing with IDF-issue C-4, and they had been used as well to clear out blockages in the tunnel from the Henry Street house to Atlantic Avenue. What was it the books were trying to tell him about explosives, and why hadn't his father left notations behind for him to follow? Stone puzzled over this question until he drifted off into a dreamless sleep.

STONE WAS SWEATING heavily in his suit as he entered the squat, glowing, limestone building through a heavy wrought-iron gate woven with delicate filigreed vines and arabesques. It was just after nine o'clock in the morning, and he stood in the great hall of marble and gold waiting for an account manager to become available. In this grandiose temple of banking and commerce, Stone felt as if he had stepped back in time, the ostentatious display of wealth calling to mind not the Internet Age but the Gilded Age. He looked skyward at the richly adorned ceiling, the delicate mosaic tiles mapping out the constellations of the Northern Hemisphere. He craned his neck and was able to make out impressive renderings of Ursa Major and Minor. Stone was seeking out the North Star when his eye tripped across the dome of a security camera fastened to the ceiling precisely where Polaris should have been. Stone jolted his head down, suddenly aware he was being watched; cameras were everywhere. A quick scan of his surroundings showed no fewer than five cameras behind the bank tellers' windows. Stone had done nothing wrong. The account was legitimate and he was legally in charge of its funds. There was nothing wrong with transferring money from one account to another.

A young woman dressed in a conservative suit introduced herself to Stone and bade him to take a seat at her desk. She apologized for the wait and asked if he'd like a cup of coffee. Stone couldn't stop thinking of the cameras. He had called the bank just a few days earlier and had the wrong passcode. Sure, he had managed the security questions, but he wondered now whether the account was being flagged as a result. He decided on the spot to transfer just a token sum of fifty thousand dollars into the account Brilliant had provided him with, hoping to leverage his control of the rest of the money into a more vital role. He knew Brilliant would not be happy with the paltry sum transferred, but Stone had cover and would simply tell Brilliant he'd rather be careful than stupid.

When he arrived home, the answering machine in the living room was blinking. The last few times he had checked the machine, there had been breezy messages from one or another of Pinky's so-called friends asking where the fuck he was. He's nowhere, Stone thought, nowhere at all. Stone stood before the answering machine for a long time, wanting only to hear Dasi's voice piped through the cheap lo-fi speaker. The red light flashed and Stone's heartbeat picked up tempo to match the rapidly blinking light. His palms were wet with sweat, his mouth a desert. At last, he leaned over and pressed the play button, and the voice on the machine sounded as if it had been relayed from across the world, rather than a few miles across Brooklyn.

It was Dasi, and she spoke in rapid snippets of thought, apologizing for what had happened with Dov. "But he's gone now . . . I want to see you . . . first thing tomorrow." She hesitated, the magnetic tape crackling with the phantom undercurrent of old messages not quite erased, and then she said, "I really do want to be with you. I hope"—she paused again—"I hope you still feel the same way I do." The volcanic humors controlling Stone's moods shifted in an instant from deep despair to a levitating joy.

When the message was complete, Stone rewound the tape and played it again to assure himself he had heard exactly what he thought he had. The message remained the same. She had called him last night before he had even arrived home from the *beis*. How could he have missed her call? There was another message from 9:37 that morning. "I guess you're out or still sleeping. I'll try again later." She paused for a beat and said, "I hope you're not mad."

He dialed her number from memory and Esther picked up. She told Stone Dasi was at school and wasn't expected home until after dinner. He left his address and the nearest subway stations and asked her to pass the information along to Dasi if she called. He'd be home waiting, he said. He made his way to his room, head swimming in a disorienting fog. Stone was so overcome by all-encompassing thoughts of Dasi, he could not concentrate to read. He didn't know whether he wanted to punish her or embrace her. She had chosen Dov over him last night, but she hadn't really, had she? She wanted to be with Stone, and Stone wanted Dasi more than he'd ever wanted a woman before. Something was changing in him, little by little, like a clock's minute hand creeping ever so slowly toward the hour. Stone knew he needed to dominate her, take what he wanted, be the man he was born to be. He had spent too much of his life being weak, and Dasi was too important to ever let her slip away.

The phone rang a little after noon; Dasi told Stone she would come over after class. She sounded hurried, and as Stone tried to respond, he heard her say, "Okay, okay. Gotta go."

Stone didn't know when her class ended, but he knew she was coming and he wanted everything in the apartment to be just right. He rushed to the kitchen sink and washed his and Pinky's dirty dishes and glasses, scrubbing every remnant of scum down the drain. He swept the floor and found a vacuum that did not work—and spent the next twenty minutes tinkering with its guts in a hopeless attempt to fix it. Stone scoured the bathtub and the sink and wiped down the mirror with a lemon-scented cloth. No matter how much Stone cleaned, the apartment still looked squalid, the remnants of Pinky everywhere, from his New York Jets stickers pasted onto the fridge door to the burned-out light bulbs Stone could not reach.

The buzzer rang a little after four and Stone rushed to the door to answer it. Dasi stood before the chicken wire–crossed glass vestibule door, her hair pulled back in a tight ponytail, dark sunglasses over her eyes. Her lips were a deep pomegranate red. She chatted amiably with one of the homeboys hanging out on the sidewalk, and Stone swung back the door, a surge of jealousy thrumming in his nerves.

"Hey," Dasi said, unsure how Stone would receive her. He stared at her in silence, trying to sort out his feelings, which oscillated from a nascent rage at her careless words spent on the homeboys outside to a sudden flood of tenderness. She was, after all, there before him, her thin arms tentatively open for an embrace.

Stone threw his arms around her, the warmth of her body calming against his chest. He smelled fresh perspiration at her neck, his hands hitting off the side of her book bag strapped to her back.

"Oh, sorry," she said, slipping it off her narrow form and dropping it to the floor. "I think I cleaned out Butler Library. So much reading. My brain is so exhausted from studying that Bretton Woods and Cape Breton are starting to sound alike to me."

Stone hefted her backpack onto his back. There must have been thirty pounds of books in there.

Dasi thanked him and followed him down the faux marble hall to his apartment, her ballet flats skimming off the gritty floor. Now that she was here with him, Stone was gripped with the fear he would do something to Dasi he would regret, something out of his control. Some unseen force stirred within him as he recalled the desolation of Dasi inviting Dov into the house, closing the door in his face and sending him out into the rain. What had Dov done to her last night? Had he held her in his arms and cried, begging for one last fuck for old times' sake? And had she given in? Had she held him in her arms, falling back into familiar patterns, murmuring softly in Hebrew in his ear before he'd taken leave? Was she thinking about him now?

"So this is yours?" she asked, her mouth very close to his ear.

"Yep," Stone said.

"I love exposed brick. Do you live here alone?" She raised an eyebrow with a sort of flirtatious arch that made Stone feel queasy. "No roommate?"

Why was she doing this? Why was she reminding Stone of Pinky now, when he was not here, when he wasn't anywhere anymore? Did she know what happened? Had Yossi told her Pinky was dead? Stone didn't know what she knew and what she didn't know, but the question about him living alone was needlessly provocative.

"My roommate died," Stone said. "He's dead."

Dasi laughed as if she thought he was joking and the punch line was yet to come, but Stone offered no explanation.

The entire apartment was a miserable place now, a graveyard of unpleasant memories—of murdered Pinky, whose name was on the lease and whose voice Stone could still hear echoing through his head, and of Abi, who had betrayed him so badly as she stood on the threshold of the apartment, breathing heavily from the exertions of vandalizing his father's robe, telling her only son she was afraid for him, not of him. If Stone could have gone back to that moment, he would have struck her in the face and shown her he was someone to be afraid of.

Now Dasi was here, and the ground beneath his feet had been salted by the awful memories of his former roommate and mother, and he knew no joy could be had in this apartment, even with Dasi. But Dasi was oblivious, pacing around the bare living room as if she herself lived here and was taking measurements for a new couch and coffee table. "Very nice, very nice," Dasi said.

Stone needed to get to his room, where he would be in possession of himself once again, surrounded by his father's books, not so much a lone individual but a conduit of all worldly wisdom. From the kitchen cabinet he grabbed a half-full bottle of vodka he'd uncovered while cleaning up and said, "My room's down there."

Stone opened the bottle and took a hard slug, then offered it to Dasi.

"Matthew!" she said, but then softened her tone and added, "No thanks. It's four thirty in the afternoon."

In the comfort of his bedroom, Stone could be the best person he could be, connected intrinsically to each individual book on a near mystical level.

"Look at all these books," Dasi said. "Have you read them all?"

"A lot," Stone said. "I've read parts of most."

"Matthew, I am impressed," Dasi said.

There was nothing more attractive than a woman who loved books and spent her money on books rather than the latest fashion trends, who always had a book tucked away in her bag, who got excited by a trip to the library and could quote her favorite lines of poetry as easily as saying her name. But most of all, a woman who read understood the depths and possibilities of what it meant to be human with all its flaws and miracles; Dasi's effusive love of books made him want to whisper, Cyrano-like, the magic words of Shakespeare into her ear to seduce her, to make her understand in the most concrete fashion she belonged to him.

Stone was so familiar with the books and their contents that he knew the exact location of all seven volumes in which Shakespeare's Sonnet 116 appeared. It contained the lines, "Love alters not with his brief hours and weeks, / But bears it out even to the edge of doom." He was about to open a copy to recite the sonnet to Dasi, but she had already found a book of her own and was flipping through the pages of *Don Quixote*.

She read, "'The Delightful History of the Most Ingenious Knight.'"

Don Quixote was so silly, so ridiculous, so far from the erotic, Stone wanted to grab the book from her hands and toss it away. He wanted to undress her, throw her down on his mattress and have his way with her, but she was hiding behind this giant doorstopper of a book, avoiding discussing what needed to be said. She continued, "'There lived not long since, in a certain village of the Mancha, the name whereof I purposely omit, a gentleman . . .'"

Stone came up behind her, trembling, still unsure as to what he would do; he placed his hands at her clavicle, could feel the pulse of her neck.

"Here's one," she laughed. "Is this you . . . ? 'He plunged himself so deeply in his reading of these books . . . whole days and nights; and in the end through his little sleep and much reading, he dried up his brains in such sort as he lost wholly his judgment.'"

"Put the book down," Stone said, his hands at her neck. Her sweat-damp skin was almost hibernal in its whiteness, like a field of unspoiled morning snow, or the newly dead. Would he even have been attracted to Dasi physically if not for his father's endorsement? She wasn't quite as thin as a ragged starveling, and she dressed well with perfectly applied makeup, but Stone was used to larger-breasted women with a hint of color to their skin, not the pallid complexion of a wandering spirit. Her nose, too, though not large, was clearly broken and bent at the bridge, which made him wonder whether she was used to being a consolation prize. But that tiny fragment of a gem pierced into the side of her nose caused Stone to think otherwise; she had made peace with that flawed part of her anatomy and proudly drew attention to her nose. Despite everything about Dasi playing against Stone's usual type, he wanted her in the most intimate manner, because she was beautiful in her own unique way, painfully and profoundly so.

She read on, oblivious to Stone's touch. "'His fantasy was filled with those things that he read, of enchantments, quarrels, battles, challenges, wounds, wooings, loves, tempests and all other impossible follies.'"

"Just stop," Stone said, leaping back from Dasi as if he were afraid of her, his hands shaking at his sides. "Stop, okay? Why are you avoiding this?"

"What are you talking about?" Dasi said.

"Dov," Stone said. "I need to know what is happening with you and him."

"Oh, Matthew," Dasi said, her eyes soft, "I'm so sorry. I didn't even think. It's so obvious to me he means nothing. He's in the past. It never occurred to me to say anything. He only stayed for five minutes and sulked like a teenager. There's nothing between us anymore. It's over."

"But you told me to leave."

"It just would have been so awkward for everyone. That's why I called you right away last night after he left. Saying good-bye was easier than I thought."

"But he wants to marry you."

"Well, there's a saying by a great rabbi—you can't always get what you want."

She put the book down on a pile and embraced Stone tightly. He could feel the contours of her body fitting to his. "You were really worried?"

Stone said nothing, just squeezed her tightly.

"Tell me," Dasi said, "please."

But Stone was afraid, and he just wanted to remain holding her, smelling her hair, feeling her breathe in time with him. He never wanted her to leave him, ever, but he was afraid he didn't truly have the strength to command her to stay. Finally, Stone said, "Yes," and his voice cracked; he paused again to gain his composure. He was a muddle of contradictions and felt any move he made could send Dasi running. "I was worried," he said. "I don't want to lose you." It had been a long time since he exposed himself in words, and he knew that words, once uttered aloud, solidified emotion into fact.

"You won't," she said. "Losing you would hurt me just as much."

Stone kissed Dasi, and she kissed him back as if she had been anticipating it for a long time. She gasped as he pulled back on her ponytail and Stone opened his eyes to discover she had been kissing with her eyes open. A large black eye stared directly into his. Her lipstick was smeared around her face as if it had been applied in a fun house. They each burst out laughing and stumbled, still entwined, over to Stone's mattress on the floor.

He reached for the zipper at her back and she did not resist as he unpeeled her from her dress. Dasi stood before him, pale and haloed in the yellow light flooding in from the street. She was terribly thin; her breasts still hidden behind her bra were small, her prominent nipples extended behind the sheer fabric.

"Now your turn," she said.

Stone stepped out of his pants, tossed his shirt aside, his heart banging in his chest. He was afraid she would see his scars, his burned skin, and would be repulsed by the imperfections he had inflicted upon himself.

"I want to let you know I've done it before, but not today, okay? Maybe not for a while?" She phrased her statement like a question, as if Stone were the final arbiter. "Just so you know," she continued. "We can do other things." She kissed him, lightly biting his lips, his chin. "But I want to. I really, really want to, with you."

Dasi took his hand and placed it between her legs to demonstrate how ready she was for him.

They fell onto the mattress, their hands breezing the gentle topography of each other's bodies. Stone just wanted to lose himself in the sharp bowl of Dasi's hips, the soft plain of her belly, feel her shudder beneath him. Dasi ran her hand up the inside of his thigh, her painted fingernails scratching just hard enough to remind him pain and pleasure were often the same thing.

"What's this?" Dasi asked, her fingertips playing lightly at the edges of his scars.

"Nothing," Stone said, and he clapped a hand over her mouth and bit her sharply on the neck.

"No. Stop," she said, rolling away. "Your skin feels different there."

There was no point in hiding it, but he didn't want to explain what had driven him to mess up his skin like that. Those days were so far in the past now that Dasi was in his life. He had been a completely different person when he had burned himself.

"Let me see," she said.

Stone let her. He lay on his back, eyes closed, afraid to see her expression change from one of fascination to one of revulsion. He knew what she was looking at. The scars were clumped together, roughly assembled in the size and shape of an open hand. They were varying shades of purple, brown, beige, translucent white. The most recent wound still hurt to touch. Dasi pressed her finger to the edge of the latest cigarette burn.

"What is this?"

Stone was silent, but opened his eyes to see deep concern etched across Dasi's face.

"Nothing," he said.

"It's not nothing," Dasi said. "Tell me."

A drop of semen had gone cold on Stone's boxer shorts and he knew whatever he had hoped to do with Dasi would now have to wait until another day.

"They're just little burns."

"From what?"

Stone was silent as Dasi studied the raised edges with her fingertips.

"Do they hurt?" she said. And then, "Why would you do this to yourself?"

"It's a long story," Stone said at last. "And not a pleasant one."

"Tell me," Dasi said. They were both sitting up on the mattress, their bodies touching at ankle, hip, and shoulder, utterly unsexual, but very intimate still.

"I'd rather not say."

"You don't need to be afraid," Dasi said.

"You really don't want to know," Stone said.

"I want to know everything about you, good and bad, Matthew. You have to know I will never judge you. I want you to feel safe with me. I want you to trust me."

"I have others over here," Stone said, raising his left arm—under the armpit there was another assemblage of burns, a few more in the crease of his elbow.

Dasi let out a long breath. "Promise me you won't do this anymore. Promise me if you feel like hurting yourself you will call me."

"It doesn't hurt," Stone said. "It actually helped take the pain away."

"Just, please," Dasi said. "Don't do it anymore. It makes me too sad."

"I promise," Stone said.

The mood was broken and Stone had gone soft. There was no starting up again now. Dasi was already scrambling for her dress on the floor and he just wanted to hold her in his arms.

"You're leaving?"

"I have to get back for dinner. My aunt gets upset."

Stone could only imagine the expression on his face, reminiscent of an expressionist painting he might have pinned on his dorm room wall in college.

"No, no," Dasi said, correcting herself. "It's not bad at all. I only planned to come for a short while. With the high holidays, I'm over-loaded with schoolwork and I need to play catch-up."

Stone sat cross-legged on his mattress, wearing only his boxers, as Dasi dressed and reapplied her lipstick. He didn't want her to leave, but he knew saying so would only drive her further away.

"I want to tell you something."

Dasi clicked her compact mirror closed.

"Sort of a confession," Stone added.

Honesty was a strength, not a weakness, he thought. He could stand on his own without lies to hold him up.

Dasi's face showed no expression.

"I don't speak Aramaic and I never sent poetry to *The Paris Review*. That was all my father. I guess he was trying to impress you on my behalf, but couldn't think of anything I'd actually done, so he substituted himself."

Dasi smiled softly. "Your father was an amazing man in so many ways. But do you think it matters for one second? I like you. Don't you get it? I like you. *You*."

"I was sold to you on false pretenses."

"That doesn't matter," Dasi said. "I'm here and I'm not disappointed and I'm not going anywhere."

She kissed him.

"You know I'm doing important things," Stone said. "Things that will change the world. Things that no one will ever forget."

When she smiled softly and nodded her head, Stone knew she was fully aware of what he was speaking about.

"I've got an idea, just so you know I'm in this for real," she said. "I hope you don't think this is stupid, but there's a luncheon on Wednesday the twenty-first at Columbia. My professor is being honored and I want you to come and meet him."

That was the day of the Rally for Palestine—Dasi knew that. He had just alluded to it and she had acknowledged the fact with a smile.

"I don't mean to be presumptuous, I'm not assuming you are my boyfriend or anything," Dasi said. "But you know, I want to share this part of my life with you."

The Rally for Palestine and the attack on the Arab dignitaries would be a great moment in Jewish history; of course she would want to spend it together. But how did she know Stone would be available, how did she know he would not be participating in the attack? Had Brilliant told her, had Yossi? Perhaps Dov in a final parting shot had revealed to Dasi that Stone was too weak to carry out the attack and he would be home, drowning in shame for missing out on greatness.

"Wednesday the twenty-first?" Stone asked.

"Yes," Dasi said. "Don't torture me. You know you don't need a passport to cross over the river into Manhattan. Say yes or I'll think you just want me for my body."

"Of course I will," Stone said. "I want to be with you."

A bright smile broke across Dasi's face. "This means so much to me. Just imagine your father, seeing us together like that. He'd be so happy."

Now Stone knew for certain she was speaking in code. Yes, the Judge had gone to Columbia, was a proud alumnus, but he had barely set foot on the campus in years, since the tenuring of Winston Haloumi. No, this was her way of saying she knew the role his father had played in organizing this attack. She wanted a front-row seat with Stone to witness the shining pinnacle of Walter Stone's career, his final legacy.

"I can't wait," Stone said.

"Neither can I," Dasi said.

STONE WAS DRUNK when Dasi returned the next night after dinner. It was dark outside, and she had slipped away from her aunt and her studies for a few hours under the pretense of meeting a friend at a coffee shop in Carroll Gardens to discuss the International Monetary Fund and its heavy-handed use of conditions in order for certain nations to receive loans, aid, and debt relief.

Stone had spent the day rereading Jabotinsky's political philosophy, and as the day progressed, he realized sitting on the sidelines with Dasi was not enough. He needed to be an active participant in the attack even if it meant death. He had tried to speak with Brilliant the night before, but Brilliant was upset he had transferred just a token sum into the new account, and told him to stop playing games. The day of the attack was drawing near. Again and again, Brilliant ran them through an exhausting obstacle course that simulated the tunnel and its exit points before the stage, but this only upset Stone more; he was playing the hero in the sanitized environment of the warehouse, an understudy at best.

Stone took Dasi in his arms and kissed her, and he undressed as they stumbled their way down the hallway to his bedroom.

"Good day?" Stone asked.

"Yes," Dasi said.

But tonight was not for talking—it was time to make up for what they had not done the previous day. Stone was thankful his scars could not be seen in the dark. She took him in her hand and stroked him lightly as he kissed her breasts, Dasi gasping with the pleasure of his touch. Soon the pressure within him surged toward release and he asked Dasi to stop.

"Am I hurting you?" she asked.

"No," Stone said. "It's just—I'm going to get a condom."

"Why?" Dasi said.

"Why do you think?" Stone said.

She let go of him and backed into the corner against the wall as far as she could get from Stone without leaving the mattress altogether. "I told you, I'm not ready yet."

"Why not?" Stone said. He needed Dasi to prove she really did want him. A nauseating wave of jealousy washed over him. Was Stone, in reality, less than just a replacement for Dov, but rather a cheap, sexless facsimile?

"I don't want to talk about it."

"Why? Because you're thinking about Dov, because you used to sleep with Dov and now you don't want to do it with me."

"Matthew, stop," Dasi said. "You're drunk."

"Why not me? What's the matter with me? I'm every bit as good as he is. I'm better, even."

"Please stop talking about Dov, it's not about him, and it's not about you."

"Then what is it about? How can I believe you actually care about me when you won't even—"

"Stop, Matthew. Please."

"You still love him."

"I told you I never loved him. You have to believe me."

"Then why?" Stone asked. "Why not me?"

Dasi was silent, and in the darkness, lit only by the streetlights out-side, her skin looked almost blue. "This isn't easy for me to say. But I will tell you, because I care about you, and because I don't want you to think for a moment this has anything at all to do with you. If you have to know, Dov and I never had sex."

"But you said—"

"It was a lifetime ago. I was too young, fifteen, with a soldier from Be'er Sheva who was guarding our school bus. I don't even know how it happened. Maybe it was rape, maybe it wasn't. I don't know. I wasn't in my right head. There was nothing pleasurable or erotic about it, okay?"

"That's it?" Stone said. "Just once."

"Yes, just once. Now you know everything. I'm not holding back because of you. It's not you. You have to trust me when I say I want to. It's just I can't yet. I have to be sure because you can never take it back."

Stone didn't know how to respond. The fact that Dov had not slept with Dasi only made him want her more, so he could claim her once and for all and vanquish the memory of Dov.

Dasi asked Stone where the bathroom was and excused herself.

"Keep the lights off," she said.

After a few moments, he heard Dasi enter the room, saw her approach in the dark, but something was different about her. She was a black mass moving toward him like a storm cloud, not a slim, waifish knife of a girl he needed to possess. A car passed by in the street and its lights played through the high windows, splashing across Dasi's form. She was wearing the Judge's robe.

"What are you doing?" Stone said. Nobody else could wear the robe and be close to his father. It belonged to him now. His father belonged to him.

"I was cold," she said, laughing.

"Take it off," Stone said.

"I want to wear it," Dasi said, turning a pirouette in the middle of the room. "I won't hurt it. Promise."

"Take it off," Stone said again, his heart crashing in his chest. "It was my father's."

"He was very strong, wasn't he? Very powerful. He was such a big man, I'm drowning in it."

"Stop," Stone said.

Her voice had changed to something grotesque, coquettish. Dasi was getting off on wearing his dead father's robe. The Judge's presence filled the room at once, and Stone was awash with shame, the same impotent sensation that had stirred within him as a child, when he'd stood naked in the shower at the YMHA, his father's impressive pubic beard reminding him of royalty, mocking his pale, grub-like offering.

"I can still smell him in the fabric," Dasi said. "That masculine tobacco smell."

"Take it off now," Stone said, his voice rising.

"He had such broad shoulders, and huge hands—the kind that would make any woman feel safe." Dasi rubbed the fabric across her cheek. "Your father was very handsome, charismatic."

"That's enough," Stone said, pulling himself off the mattress, his pitiful half erection slapping ridiculously at his thigh. "Take it off."

"Why?" Dasi said. "Do you want to wear it?"

"Take it off now," Stone shouted, and in his anger he heard the voice of Walter Stone.

"Fine," Dasi said. She slipped a bare leg out the side and then unzipped and let the robe pool at her feet. "There," she said. "Think of me when you wear it."

Her nipples were hard and her chest heaved with excitement, and Stone was afraid he was going to hurt her. "You have to leave."

"What?" Dasi said, surprised.

"Now," Stone said. "You have to leave now, or else." A terrifying rage surged through Stone's veins and he did all he could to restrain himself from obeying his impulses to choke the life out of her. That's what he was being ordered to do, in that ineffable language of the blood.

"But I didn't mean to."

"You have to leave," Stone said again.

"Why? I just—"

"I'm afraid I might have to hurt you."

"What do you mean?" Dasi said, eyes wide, the shock of his words darkening her features.

"That's my father's robe," Stone said. "Nobody wears it but me."

Dasi dressed in silence, and Stone wished she had never found the robe.

She looked as if she were about to break down in tears, her mouth clenching to hold back a torrent. As Stone watched the pitiful scene before him, he realized the compulsion to harm her had passed as swiftly as it had arrived and he felt the need to explain.

"When I want to be close to him," Stone said, breaking the long silence, "I wear the robe. When I read his books, when I'm sad, when I wish he were still here with me."

"I'm so sorry," Dasi said, keeping her distance as he moved closer. "I crossed a boundary. I'm so, so sorry. I was just trying to spice things up. It was a terrible mistake. Please forgive me." She stood completely dressed before his naked body. "Matthew, you are very special to me. But you worry me. You are hurting so much. Just know, I would never do anything to deliberately hurt you. It was wrong of me, presumptuous. I'm, I'm sorry."

"I know you are," Stone said.

27 For the next two weeks Stone continued to train nightly with the discipline required by the spirit of *hadar*. When Federman turned to him once at the shooting range and sneered, "Where did you learn to shoot like that? The FBI?" Stone held his tongue because the spirit of *hadar* required nobility, chivalry, and tact.

Boaz taught Stone and the others how to fashion a small bomb out of a nine-volt battery and liquid nitrogen, which was held in an empty film canister. They were taught how to assemble a bomb using a simple wristwatch as a timer.

"It may be small," Boaz said, "but so was David."

The bomb could kill; it was strong enough to rip a man to pieces if placed under the seat of his car, but it could also blow a man-hole cover or knock a door down. "But this is still child's play," Boaz added.

Stone returned home from the *beis* tired but exhilarated, the acrid stink of the ferric oxide, nitric acid, and methylamine clinging to his hair and skin, coating his body with the irresistible force of their elemental strength. Stone, the burgeoning warrior, showered in a thick haze of steam, imagining himself popping up alone in front of the stage and firing into the bodies of the Arabs; they deserved such a fate and Stone would oblige. He washed every suggestion of the noxious chemicals down the drain without a trace and imagined the limitless possibilities of what he could accomplish with his newfound knowledge. He could not sit on the sidelines and live with himself. To come this close to redemption and then fail was unthinkable.

Back at the *beis* that night, Brilliant announced he had decided who would take part in the operation. Four men would enter the tunnel through the Henry Street house, emerge before the stage through loosened manhole covers, fire their shots, and disappear in the ensuing chaos. Moshe would be waiting on a side street with the escape vehicle. Stone kept silent, his nerves roiling. It was his house on Henry Street, he had furnished the money, he needed to be one of the four.

"Only four?" Federman said.

"With four, you'll have enough firepower to kill a hundred men," Brilliant said.

A bearded student named Miller said, "What about innocent bystanders? They could be killed too."

Brilliant appeared quickly in his face. He was nearly a head taller than Miller and he stared down into the student's shrinking face and said, "You have to be as strong as iron. Forget about bystanders. Nobody is innocent."

"But what about—"

"The children?" Brilliant laughed and said, "If you want to be good, then let yourself be killed. Give up everything that means anything to you." He shook his head and added, "Die like a good Jew. Jewish blood has always been cheap."

"But I don't want to die."

"Good," Brilliant said. "Then you'll stay home."

"What do you mean?"

"If you are afraid to die for your principles, you can leave now." Brilliant called Moshe to usher Miller out of the *beis*.

Miller considered protesting, but instead walked away, sheepishly, glancing back at Moshe's approaching figure. After he was gone, Brilliant said, "Make sure someone keeps an eye on him."

Stone pitied Miller and his hangdog expression, if only because he knew how much it would hurt if he had been left out, but this was no time to get sentimental; the loss of Miller meant Stone's chances of inclusion among the four had just grown significantly.

"I have confidence in each and every one of you that you are capable of doing what needs to be done," Brilliant said. "Only four can carry out the operation without increasing the risk. The rest of you are reserves, ready as needed."

Stone, more than anyone else in the *beis*, deserved to be chosen, needed to be selected, lest his life become an empty monstrous joke. Brilliant had to know this and accommodate.

"Now I want to reiterate, you are all soldiers and I'm proud of each of you. The work we have done, are doing, and will do brings redemption closer."

Brilliant called Itzy forward. He did the same for Yossi and Federman and someone named Brenner. Federman pumped his fist and shouted, "Yes!"

The other three smiled and shook hands quietly.

"So it's set," Brilliant said. "These four warriors will carry out our mission."

Stone shivered in a feverish rage, unable to comprehend his misfortune. Was this actually happening or had he found himself, inexplicably, in someone else's lucid nightmare? His burns itched and he ached to pick them raw.

The pear-shaped student with the watery eyes groaned audibly at his own exclusion, but he stepped forward and managed to say, "We are the will of Samson, the answer to all Jewish suffering and misfortune." The rest of the group followed gamely, repeating their credo. Stone could barely force the words out, his disappointment ran so deep.

After they had dispersed to take their places at the shooting range, Stone caught up with Brilliant. It was the money, wasn't it? He had been too clever by half, holding back the bulk of the money, providing the illusion of leverage, when in fact he had shown Brilliant he could not be relied upon. What a terrible mistake. He had panicked there in the bank with the cameras on him, afraid his machinations would be discovered. But that was simply paranoia, and now he realized paranoia was another form of weakness. He asked Brilliant for a moment of his time and Brilliant said, "I know what you're going to say, Matthew. But I've made up my mind. There will be other opportunities."

"It's about the money, isn't it?" Stone asked.

"You've done your part," Brilliant said. "I've given my reasons and I will not discuss them anymore."

"But I still have access to the rest of the money."

Brilliant's face took on a hard cast as he stepped close to Stone. "I know you want to be one of the four, but I hope you are not suggesting what I think you're suggesting. How do you think your father would feel about you playing games like this? Your father was a great man. Greatness, you should know, seeks out the man who runs away from greatness. Your eagerness will destroy you. Show some humility and good things will come to you."

"I just want to be given the chance to prove myself."

"Then do what I have asked you to do and transfer the rest of the money," Brilliant said, his voice brittle, like an icicle.

"But, such a large amount, I'm afraid—"

"Figure it out, Matthew."

"I belong," Stone said. "I need to be a part of this."

Brilliant's patience was at an end; he took Stone by the arm and asked him, "How long have you been with us?"

Stone started to say something about his father, but was cut off.

"How long have you, Matthew Stone, been with us?"

"Not long," he began, "but—"

"No but," Brilliant said. "The Jew-hating rally on Atlantic Avenue has been in the works for over two years, meant to coincide not just with the anniversary of the unrest on Court Street but also with the completion of the Al Salaam Mosque five miles away, at the end of the parade route. We knew the activists organizing this modern-day Nuremberg Rally would eventually gain approval after they had jumped through every hoop City Hall threw at them, cut through every piece of red tape the Immigration and Naturalization Service had to offer. This is not some plan concocted out of thin air. It took a lot of work. I don't see how you can think you have done anything to deserve a front-row seat."

"I understand," Stone said. "But there has to be—"

"You want to get ahead with me?" Brilliant said. "Stop shooting your mouth off and start shooting."

So, there was still a chance.

The next morning marked the second week of October, and an early frost threatened, fogging Stone's bedroom window. Yossi rang the buzzer and called Stone out to the street. He couldn't bear the thought of seeing Yossi and the others, but he knew the books would only oppress him, drive him to despair, remind him of the emptiness that was his life. He needed to get away from the books, from Princip and Amir and King David, from all the prodigies who had written their names eternally in blood.

Federman sat, scowling, in the passenger seat of Yossi's car, and Stone was glad to see Itzy in the back seat. Stone got in and sat next to Itzy. He didn't ask where they were going and he didn't really care.

"Didn't see you this morning," Federman said, lifting his Yankees cap off his head and wiping his brow. "You still with us?"

There was something mocking in his tone, and Stone chose not to answer. He had made sure he was at the bank the minute it had opened, transferred precisely half of the available funds, and come right back home.

"Aw, leave him alone," Yossi said. "He forgot."

The car turned onto Myrtle Avenue, the windows fogging.

"That's why he's out and we're in." Federman punched the dashboard. "Where's your fucking defrost?"

The car stopped at a red light, and Stone could tell Federman was nervous every time a black person passed close to the idling car. Yet somehow Federman was chosen for the attack. Fucking coward, couldn't handle a couple of homeboys in the 'hood. On the sidewalk, a makeshift shrine of candles and flowers lay before a gaudy portrait of a young man painted on a redbrick wall with the words WE'LL NEVER FORGET YOU, BLUE. PEACE.

They drove on, and soon the Williamsburg Savings Bank tower receded behind them like a stiff middle finger in the rearview mirror. Then they were driving down the broad industrial stretch of Fourth

Avenue, passing used tire shops, gas stations, and dark, squalid doorways.

"Don't worry about this morning," Yossi said. "You can say Kaddish tonight."

But Kaddish meant nothing to Stone anymore. He had done his duty and was ready to act on his conviction. His father must be remembered in more than just the spiritual world.

The car ride was doing Stone good. He was glad to be out in the cool fall afternoon, the changeable landscape of Brooklyn passing by out the window. They drove through Sunset Park, a neighborhood just now being slowly occupied by the gentrifying hipsters of Manhattan. Soon, they reached the fringes of Bay Ridge. In another few blocks Stone anticipated the Verrazano Bridge coming into view against the slate sky. The car came to a stop before an intersection. An R train stop was on the corner and schoolkids bustled past.

Federman rolled his window down. The cool autumn air felt fresh on Stone's face.

"Here they come," Federman said, leaning out the window. A clutch of about a dozen young schoolgirls, probably middle schoolers, dressed in their dark winter coats, white head scarves bright against their brown faces, laughed and moved as one, as if each girl were connected to the same nervous system of a central body. Stone stared at them with fascination. Imagine laughing so easily, so freely.

"Hey," Federman called out the window. "Going home to fuck your fathers, or your brothers?"

The girls laughed and stopped, but their smiles quickly disappeared.

"You, with the mustache, they let you out without a leash?"

Some of the girls gave Federman the finger and moved on.

What the hell was going on? This was beneath their sacred mission. But Stone said nothing, watching Federman with interest.

Federman jumped out of the car; so did Yossi. They were two heads taller than most of the girls. Yossi said something in Arabic that was obviously a curse word.

"Bitch cunts," Federman called, as a few of the girls disappeared down into the R train station. "Run, you monkeys."

"This is crazy," Itzy said. "I thought we were picking up supplies for the *beis*." He popped out of the car and was restraining Federman in an instant. Federman pushed him away.

One of the girls shouted back, "Fucking Jew."

Federman threw a piece of garbage he found on the ground and she called out, "Nice throw, asshole," and disappeared with the rest of the girls into the subway station.

Stone watched the farce before his eyes with disgust. This was a violation of all of Jabotinsky's principles. This was nothing more than small-time street thuggery, which would only end in trouble.

"I'm going to get her," Federman said.

"Enough," Itzy said.

"You heard what that Arab called me."

"Leave her alone," Itzy replied.

Stone stepped out of the car and helped Itzy direct Yossi and Federman back. Inside, Federman turned to Itzy. "What are you, some kind of fucking goy? An Arab? This is payback for the double suicide bombing in Tel Aviv."

"They're just girls. They had nothing to do with it."

Stone liked Itzy more and more for standing up to Federman, the schmuck, and he knew if he supported Itzy against Federman, Itzy would do the same in supporting Stone's claims of Federman's reckless disregard for their mission when he spoke to Brilliant that night.

"One day, they'll be mothers," Yossi said. "And their sons will be martyrs of their genocidal fight. They are nothing but psychotic suicide machines."

"Oh, come on," Itzy said.

"Do you want Jewish blood to be on your hands?" Yossi said. "An Arab killed your father."

"That's a low blow," Itzy said, screwing his face up against the painful memory. "But this is not how we do it."

"You're a fucking goy, a weak, converso goy," Federman said. "You should be ashamed."

"I'm ashamed of you."

"Oh, are you," Federman said. "Then go convert to their gutter religion and get it over with."

"Itzy's right, you know," Stone said. "You are a disgrace."

"Shut up," Federman said, turning in his seat. His hard eyes flashed with a blind conviction that would lead nowhere but destruction.

"Hey," Yossi said. "Lay off him. He didn't do anything."

"That's right," Federman said. "He didn't do anything. He'll never do anything. He can sit home and pick his ass for all I care."

An NYPD cruiser slowed near their car; Yossi pressed his foot to the accelerator and turned right when the light changed.

"I know he's the Judge's son," Federman said, "but where has he been all this time? He's not like us. He doesn't know Torah, yet he's called up to read at Simchat Torah. He didn't study with the Rav. I don't know who he is. I don't trust him." Now he turned to Stone. "I'm keeping my eye on you. You'll fuck the whole plan up. You'll blab your mouth."

Federman was jealous of Stone, threatened by his quick entrée into the group, like an insecure child. Federman's actions, rather than illustrating his strength, were an unconscious act of self-abnegation, proof of his own weakness. He didn't understand that Stone was critical to the success of the mission; it was Stone's birthright after all. He had been selected for this approaching moment many decades before he was even born. The Judge would want Federman, and his barely suppressed rage, eliminated. He could not be trusted to control himself. Thucydides had written about the importance of discipline; so had Jabotinsky, Clausewitz, and others. The Judge had marked passages on the subject again and again.

"I don't care if you don't trust me," Stone said. "I have two witnesses here who can attest to your reckless behavior today. You are a threat to the plan. My father's plan. You are a danger and this bullshit with the girls was a fucking sideshow. What do you think the Rosh would say if he knew you were out on Fourth Avenue calling attention to yourself? What do you think would happen?"

"You're going to tell on me?"

"No," Stone said. "You're going to tell the Rosh what you did."

"Over my dead body," Federman said, his eyes wild with adrenaline. "I know what this is all about. You're not taking my place."

"You're going to tell him what you did today," Stone said.

Itzy nodded approval. "I agree completely. This sort of behavior is beneath us and our mission."

Federman's eyes glazed with a film of tears. "But what about Yossi? It was his idea."

"You're going down for this, Federman," Stone said. "It's over for you, and you know it."

Yossi looked into the rearview mirror and raised his eyebrows, a soft look of gratitude on his face. He was as guilty as Federman, and he had to know supporting Itzy and Stone's claims against Federman was the only way he would escape this fiasco with his position intact. He might have been every bit the fanatic that Federman was, but Yossi's testimony would protect him, even as he destroyed Federman. Three voices against one was all it would take, and Stone would be in. How could Brilliant deny his participation after this?

After a moment of determined silence, Yossi tried to lighten the mood with a joke. "Who won the Arab beauty contest?"

The car hummed along in silence for an awkward moment, then, finally, Yossi said, "No one!"

But nobody laughed.

28

Dasi agreed to meet Stone beneath the glowing green globe announcing the entryway to the G train station. He could barely contain his excitement waiting for her, knowing Federman was out and he, by rights, would be in. Stone knew he was not supposed to speak of such things, but he regretted how he had treated Dasi the last time he had seen her and he wanted to take her into his confidence, share a part of his secret life with her. Stone was approaching the final stages of his redemption—tonight Brilliant would tap him to execute the plan in place of Federman and he would, finally, be worthy of his father's robe, not as an imposter, but as an equal.

Dasi climbed the steep stairs that smelled of urine and human waste, her school bag humped on her back.

"Sorry I'm late. Train stalled in a tunnel."

Stone absently muttered something about the MTA meant only to acknowledge he had heard her words.

She wore a pair of round, steel-rimmed Emma Goldman glasses that made her look thin-lipped and professorial.

"Reading anything good?" Stone asked.

"Yeah, a real page-turner on the World Bank."

She smiled but looked tired, drawn—her skin wan and waxy beneath the streetlamps. It was a crisp autumn evening, and colored leaves crunched beneath their feet as they walked. There was a part of Stone that believed an apology was required following his behavior the other night—the robe had ignited something within him he could barely control—but it didn't feel right to prostrate himself before Dasi when his mood was so bright. This was a night for celebration, not regrets.

"I've got some exciting news," Stone said.

"Really?" Dasi said. Her tone was flat, guarded. Stone was too keyed up to take her demeanor into account as he said, "Yes. I know I probably shouldn't say anything, but I know I can trust you."

She took his hand in hers and they walked quietly down the slanted slate sidewalk toward his apartment. "I wanted to talk to you about something as well."

"All right," Stone said. "So, we're even."

Dasi did not respond.

When they arrived at his building, Stone was surprised to see the homeboys had gone, leaving their milk crates tipped over in the middle of the sidewalk. Stone barely considered what Dasi wanted to tell him as he was busy plumbing for the precise words to tell her what had happened with Federman and what he expected Brilliant to tell him when he went to the *beis* later that evening.

As he fumbled for his key, he saw, out of the corner of his eye, an impossibly tall, thin man approaching. The man was white and balding and wore beige chinos and a light navy windbreaker. "Excuse me," the man said, "got a minute?"

"No," Stone said, brusquely.

"Just a minute," the stranger pressed. "Okay, Matthew?"

"What did you say?"

"I just need a minute of your time."

He was not a stranger; he knew Stone's name and was far too purposeful for this encounter to be a coincidence. He was perhaps a journalist or an undercover cop, nobody Stone was interested in talking to, but Stone sensed by the way the man hovered with a quiet intensity he would not give up so quickly.

Dasi dropped her book bag to the ground and sighed.

Stone turned to Dasi and said, "Why don't you go inside? I'll buzz you when I'm ready."

"Are you sure?" Dasi asked. She looked exhausted after her long subway ride from 116th Street.

Stone slipped her the keys and she took them, wordlessly, the door swinging shut behind her.

"That's a fine-looking girl you've got there," the stranger said.

"Who are you supposed to be?" Stone said.

"I'm Agent Gargiulio of the JTTF." He had a long, thin face with deep, worn creases in it. "And you are Matthew Stone."

"Did you figure that out all by yourself?" When Gargiulio didn't bite, Stone asked, "What happened to Zohar?"

"He wants to speak with you, but figured he'd be doing you a favor if he sent me."

"So you're just his errand boy? You can tell Zohar I almost got killed for talking to him."

"Matthew, we would never have let that happen. We take care of our assets."

"*Assets*," Stone muttered. "Well, thank you very much and good night. I have nothing to say to you." Stone spun toward the door and remembered he had given Dasi his key.

"I have authority to take you in right now if that's the way you want it. Now you either agree to speak with him or . . ."

A vein throbbed in Gargiulio's neck. He produced a card and a badge and Stone accepted who he was on face value.

". . . I take you down to Federal Plaza right now and leave that skinny piece of tail inside to worry. What's her name again? Hadassah Grunhut? With the dead fanatic uncle? Boy can you pick 'em. Now, what's it going to be?"

"I have nothing to say to you," Stone said. His will was being tested, challenged by this empty suit. The entire street was motionless—not a car, not a wayward shout, not a breath of cool air stirred—just Gargiulio, sunken-eyed Gargiulio, the skeletal structure of his face hard and steady as he stared at Stone. This government-issued death's head was supposed to scare him? "You tell Zohar to go fuck himself, and while you're at it, you can do the same."

"All right," Gargiulio said, reaching for his handcuffs. "But you need to know up front that when I take you in, everyone, from Zalman Seligman to Isaac Brilliant, Yosef Grunhut to Moshe Reisen, will know for certain that you are and have always been an FBI informant."

Stone's breath caught in his throat. He heard a sudden cacophony of pigeons roosting precariously on the spiked window ledges above.

"Fine," Stone said, "I'll meet him. When and where?"

"Tomorrow. First thing. Nine a.m. in the Green-Wood Cemetery Chapel. It's a safe place. No need to worry about being spotted by your brethren." With that, Gargiulio stalked off, his long shadow stretching up the brick wall of Stone's building and then around the corner.

Dasi sat on the couch reading a book. In her glasses, she looked like a stranger to Stone. Her lips were pale, wiped clean of her ever-present red lipstick, as if she had consciously washed away her power to provoke desire. Her eyelids looked heavy, and Stone knew he could not tell her about Federman and Brilliant, not after Gargiulio. How could he have believed that Zohar was finished with him, after all he had done to bring Abi back as a tool to bend Stone to his cynical will?

Dasi glanced up from her book, and she could tell Stone was shaken, his nerves still vibrating a dissonant coda to his encounter with Gargiulio.

"Are you okay?" she asked.

Stone said he was fine and went to fix a drink. "Guy was lost, wanted to know how to find the Belt Parkway."

Stone offered Dasi a drink and she declined.

"Listen, Matthew, I want to talk to you about something."

There was something in her tone that alerted him immediately he wasn't going to like what she had to say.

"Sit down." Dasi patted the couch next to her.

Stone swallowed the vodka in one burning gulp and sat beside her on the couch. A long silence hung between them. Stone noticed she wore sheer black patterned stockings on her pale legs. He wanted to take her right there on the couch.

"You know how I feel about you, Matthew, and how happy I am that we finally met, but . . ."

His heart rattled in his chest and he needed to do something to hold himself together, to forestall the inevitable. "Wait a minute," he said, and disappeared into Pinky's room, where he found a disposable lighter and a half-finished pack of Marlboros. He returned to the couch and lit a cigarette.

"You don't smoke," Dasi said.

"There's a lot you don't know about me," Stone said, blowing a thick, petulant cloud of smoke as punctuation. How could he even for a minute have considered telling her about Federman, sharing the good news that he would be a frontline participant in the upcoming attack? She was going to break up with him. He'd been on this side of the conversation before, and it was always the same. He was thankful now Gargiulio had been sent to remind him, once and for all, to keep his mouth shut. He couldn't tell anyone what was going to happen, not even Dasi.

"I like you a lot," Dasi said. "But it feels like things are going too fast. I think we need to slow down. I need to be careful not to rush into things."

Stone stared hard at Dasi and took a long pull on the cigarette. She fanned away the smoke with her long, slender fingers.

"I'm not sure I'm ready for this yet, and I'm not sure you are either."

"Of course I'm ready," Stone said.

His life was riding such an intense upward trajectory; he knew if Dasi wasn't there beside him to keep him grounded, he might explode like a supernova, alone at the edge of the universe.

"You're still mourning your father. You are in so much pain."

"But you are helping me with that pain. I want you. I need you. I need you so much. Life without you in it is not worth living."

"Don't say that, Matthew. You have so much to live for, and I can't take away your pain."

"But you can, you do. We're meant to be together. Can't you see that?"

"I thought so too, but I don't know anymore."

"What is that supposed to mean?"

"The other night, with the robe. This isn't a healthy thing we have. It's so dark, so full of menace, and, yes, there is an appeal in danger, but

I was just playing, trying to have some fun, and your reaction, it really shocked me. I was afraid you would hurt me."

"Just forget about the robe," Stone said, moving close on the couch. He placed a hand on her thigh—it was warm and he wanted to tear the stockings from her. He lifted the hem of her dress. "I would never hurt you. You know that, right?"

"I don't know that, Matthew. I don't," Dasi said, rising from the couch. "I have to go."

"But it's early," Stone said. "Have a drink. Relax. We can read my father's books together."

"I don't think you understand," Dasi said. Her eyes looked sad and bruised and tired.

"Don't you care about me?" Stone grabbed her arm more forcefully than he intended. She twisted her arm and wrenched herself free.

"I do," Dasi said. "But things are complicated. I don't always know what I want. It's scary."

"This doesn't make any sense. You're breaking up with me?"

"I'm not," Dasi said. "That's not it."

"Then don't go."

"I have to."

"Don't leave me. Please!"

But the panic was already in his veins. He took a deep drag of the cigarette, pulled his shirt over his head, and pressed the cigarette into his skin, just above his heart. He felt a jolt of pain like he had never experienced before, an elemental shock constricting the valves of his heart.

"What are you doing?" Dasi screamed. "Stop it!"

He relit the cigarette, drawing deeply on the filter, and pressed it into his skin again. He could smell the acrid odor of his own flesh burning, and a sense of power and control gathering itself within his chest. She would have to stay now, take care of him, tend to his wounds. Only a monster would leave him in this condition.

"Stop it. Stop it. Stop it," Dasi cried, fat tears rolling down her face.

"I just want to be with you," Stone said, through gritted teeth. "You make me feel everything is all right. Without you, the world is shit."

"I have to go. I'm sorry."

"Did you forget who I am? Walter Stone was my father. I am the Judge's son and I'm going to show the world what that really means."

"Stop it, Matthew. You're scaring me."

"I am his only living son. Do you understand what kind of power he has passed down to me? Soon the entire world will know. You're going to walk away from that awesome legacy?"

"That's enough!" Dasi said.

"Why do you hate me?"

"I don't hate you. Don't you understand anything I've said to you?"

"You said you don't want me."

"That's not what I said!"

"You said you're leaving. Didn't you?"

"Yes. I have to."

"Then get out," Stone shouted.

Dasi froze in the open doorway, precisely where Abi had spoken her last words to Stone. "Promise me you won't do anything stupid," Dasi said. "Please don't hurt yourself."

The burns hurt so much he felt like slamming his head into the brick wall just to dull the pain. He must have pressed the cigarette harder and deeper than he was accustomed, held it longer, as Dasi stared at him with a look of plain horror in her eyes. It had been wonderful at the time, such a high, the power he wielded as she looked on, helpless to stop him. But then she was gone and he was alone in the empty living room, out of his mind with pain. It didn't make any sense that she would leave. Their coming together had felt like destiny fulfilled, an integral piece to the puzzle that was his life. There would be plenty of time to win her back later, once she understood he was not just a man of substance, but a man of action, willing to do whatever it took to alleviate Jewish suffering and misfortune.

Stone fumbled through the silverware drawer and found a cleanish steak knife, determined to cut out the inferno in his chest. He took two long shots of vodka from the bottle, then washed the knife with it for good measure. He edged around the raw hole in his chest, counted to five, closed his eyes, and dug the knife in, levering against the charred skin in the hope of scooping out the wound.

His blood was everywhere—coating the knife, his hands, his pants, the floor puddling with it—but the pain persisted. He took one more slug of vodka, and this time had the courage to cut out the entire burn, slicing his tender skin away until he had reached the pink flesh beneath it. He knew he should cauterize a wound this deep or risk bleeding without end, but the thought of pressing fire to his skin so soon made him nauseous, and he dry-heaved into the sink as hot blood ran down his chest. The second burn was easier but no less bloody. He found one of Pinky's old T-shirts, cut it into strips, and applied pressure to each wound until he passed out on the couch. He woke with two bloody rags in his hands, but he had succeeded in stanching the bleeding. The vodka had taken full effect as well and he was drunk. It was nearly time to go to the *beis*. Stone changed into fresh pants, applied half a dozen bandages to each wound, and slipped into a clean shirt.

By the time he arrived at the *beis*, Stone had bled through his bandages, the wounds blossoming like rose petals on his chest. Moshe opened the door and let Stone inside. Stone knew he must have been a terrible sight, spots of blood blooming at his chest, and he looked even worse than he imagined, reflected back to himself stumbling through the mirror maze. He had to speak to Brilliant at once, before Brilliant had the chance to select someone else for the job.

When Stone emerged from the mirrors, Federman was nowhere to be seen among the yeshiva boys gearing up at the firing range, and Stone took that to mean he was going to be anointed as his replacement. It never occurred to Stone that Brilliant would think otherwise. When he asked Brilliant for a moment of his time alone, Brilliant knew what Stone was going to ask and said, "I'm sorry Matthew, but Stupp is going to be replacing Federman."

Stupp? Who the hell was Stupp? Then he realized with a sudden shock that Stupp was the pear-shaped kid prone to asthma attacks and bouts of intense coughing. He could not be less suited for the job at hand. Stone's wounds throbbed at his chest and he wanted to tear at them with his hands to demonstrate for Brilliant how overwhelmed he was with hurt and pain.

"I don't understand," Stone said. "I transferred the money. I need to be a part of this."

"For the last time, Matthew, you are part of this."

"You don't understand. I need to be the one. I need to be out there."

"You want to shoot Amalek?" Brilliant said. "You want to fire the gun?"

"Yes," Stone said, hope surging through his innards. Brilliant could still be convinced with the right words, the right argument.

"Matthew, I just want you to understand we are all a part of this. We are all brave Maccabees. Everyone has a role to play, and you have done so well in yours."

"I haven't done anything," Stone said.

"You brought us the traitor roommate of yours, you transferred the money, you exposed Federman as unfit for our mission. You have done so much. Your father would be so proud of you."

This was bullshit. His contributions were nothing but half measures. His father would never have celebrated such a slight offering. Stone could feel his body devouring itself from the inside, his organs rebelling against Brilliant's decree. This was how people got cancer, the diseased cells metastasizing inside them, overwhelming the healthy ones with their irresistible force.

"You don't trust me. You don't think I can pull the trigger. But I can. I can do it. I'm supposed to do it."

"Calm down," Brilliant said.

"My father would have wanted me there. Why would you deny me this chance?"

The boys were at it now all along the firing range and Brilliant had to raise his voice to be heard.

"You are a quick study, Matthew. But you are still green. There will be other opportunities."

"No," Stone shouted, realizing his performance now endangered his future status with Brilliant, but he could not resist. "I need to be part of this. I have to be part of this. Federman is out, and Stupp is nothing but a punch line. Put me in or else I'll . . ." But he could not finish the sentence without disqualifying himself forever.

Brilliant was done listening to Stone's tantrum, and the last hint of kindness disappeared from his eyes. "It's too late. The team has already had a test run down in the tunnel. They know the landscape."

Stone refused to understand it was over, searching for any logical loophole he could use to his advantage. "It was Zohar, wasn't it? You saw him talking with me. I swear, I said nothing. Please, please, please consider me. Don't let him ruin this for me as well. You have to understand. I will do whatever you ask of me. I'm prepared to do anything. Just give me the chance."

Brilliant laughed his arrogant laugh and said, "Look at you, covered in blood, drunk, raving. Go home and get some sleep. I understand the enormous pressure you have been under, but there's nothing else you can do. You've done your part, and you should be proud."

"But—" Stone began.

Brilliant was already walking away. "On Wednesday afternoon, you can sit back in front of the television and watch as the fruit of your labors ripens, for the whole world to see. Good night, Matthew."

Moshe appeared at Stone's elbow to escort him out of the beis. Those hands reminded Stone that Moshe had been prepared to kill him simply because he had spoken to Zohar, because Zohar was a threat to the entire operation, and Zohar was still alive and on alert and poised to ruin everything. He had one last chance to convince Brilliant to let him participate, and that would be to kill Zohar.

29

A black sedan was following Stone. He knew he was a dead man if it was someone from the *beis*. The driver would be armed with strict orders from Brilliant to terminate Stone for the good of the movement. It wasn't Moshe's familiar SUV and it wasn't Yossi's broken-down beater, he knew, but through the glare of its windshield, Stone could not make out the driver of the car pursuing him. He raced lights, turned down one-way streets, pulled sudden U-turns and fish-tailed away, floored the gas, tires smoking on the concrete, but he could not shake the car on his tail. It could have caught Stone's hulking Thunderbird half a dozen times if it had wanted, passed him or forced him off the road, but it was content simply to ride his bumper and withdraw, teasing, revving its engine and then slipping back a length or two, keeping Stone firmly in its sights.

Stone's adrenaline was up, his head burning with fever, his wounds throbbing, the bloody steak knife wrapped in newspaper slipped inside the leg of his pants. At a red light, Stone took his eye off the side-view mirror and glanced at the dent in the hood of his car, the collision point that marked the end of Emile Alcalai's sorry life. What a monument that dent was, what an inspiration! Zohar would understand too late that Matthew Stone was every bit as dangerous and powerful as Julius and Walter Stone had ever been.

Stone believed he was possessed by a new strength bordering on the supernatural. Some vital trace of his father and grandfather lay

coiled within him, ready to spring. Stone was more certain than ever
he had the taste for blood and it was only a matter of proving his bona
fides to Brilliant; then it would be impossible for Brilliant to deny him
any longer.

After one last unsuccessful attempt at losing the sedan in the confusion of rush hour along Fort Hamilton Parkway, the Thunderbird
turned onto Fifth Avenue and passed under the arch of the elaborate
Gothic gate of Green-Wood Cemetery with Stone's pursuer right
behind him. Electric green parakeets roosting in the nooks of the
ornate spires squawked as Stone blew past, and then he was greeted
by the turning autumn trees and peaceful statuary depicting winged
children, mourning women, and angels. He raced through the honey-
comb streets of the cemetery, winding up and down hills, passing
narrow footpaths, great obelisks, hunched stone tombs, and majestic
family crypts, still trying to shake the black sedan. He could not afford
a confrontation now, not with Zohar this close.

He wound his way through the cemetery in which many of Brooklyn's famous and infamous had been laid to final rest: Samuel Morse,
inventor of the telegraph; toy magnate F. A. O. Schwarz; Louis Comfort Tiffany; Charles Ebbets; the Brooks brothers; Henry Ward
Beecher; Leonard Bernstein; even Albert Anastasia, former mob
boss, and Gambino family hit man Crazy Joe Gallo. The black sedan
remained close behind.

When it seemed Stone would never lose the black shadow trailing
him through the rabbit-warren streets of Green-Wood, a grounds-
keeper's tractor managed to slip between the two cars, blocking the
path of the sedan as it chuffed and idled in the middle of the narrow
road. Stone let go of the steering wheel and pounded the horn in
celebration, his knuckles white from clenching so tightly. He slowed
down to a moderate speed, knowing the sedan had little chance of
finding him among the graves and monuments of over a half-million
dead. He parked the Thunderbird far from his actual destination, near
the statue of Athena overlooking New York Harbor, and took off by
foot through the graves toward the chapel.

The heavy wooden door to the chapel was closed but not locked, and Stone entered the marble and stained glass sanctuary breathless with anticipation. The knife was still tucked against his thigh, held fast by the elastic waistband of his boxer shorts. Zohar sat alone on the front bench before the altar, running his hand pensively over his trimmed goatee. Stone watched him, imagining what it would feel like to kill him; would Zohar struggle or go easy under the blade? The time had come at last for Stone to act, and he reached into his waistband. All Stone had to do was steal up behind Zohar, grab him by the hair, and slash the blade across the perfect canvas of his throat. Zohar looked to be musing on the stained glass tableau of Jesus. He did not turn his head when he said, "You're late, Matthew."

Stone was surprised to hear his voice, dry and flinty, devoid of emotion, spoiling the ecstatic illusion Stone held in his mind. Zohar's words echoed off the high, ornamented ceiling and fell hard on Stone's ears.

"Do you know how stupid you are?" Zohar said, staring straight ahead, as if he were chastising the mute representation of the son of God.

Zohar still had not turned his head to look in Stone's direction, but he was alert to Stone's presence; the opportunity for a surprise attack had passed.

"You called me here to insult me?" Stone asked. "Is that it?"

Zohar turned around to face him, his eyes full of rage. "A terrorist attack is going to happen at the Rally for Palestine tomorrow and you know how it is going to go down."

"I have nothing to say to you," Stone said. If Brilliant knew he was here, he was finished, unless he did what he came for.

"You're not one of them," Zohar said, rising to his feet. His abdomen looked tender and exposed, helpless against the flash of a knife blade. "You are not a part of that world. You are part of civil society with your liberal education, your urbane upbringing, your values."

"You know nothing of my so-called values," Stone said.

Zohar approached Stone—arrogant, careless, his arms loose at his sides. His entire torso was exposed. The blade vibrated against Stone's leg with the electric will to kill. All he had to do now was draw and close the narrow gap between them, sticking him again and again in the abdomen. But what would happen if he failed, if Zohar managed to swat the knife away? A tight band of pressure formed around Stone's head, the Judge's incomparable voice telling him to draw, *draw the fucking knife, you coward*, but he hesitated as a sudden burst of angelic choral music flooded out of speakers hidden on high, and the moment was lost. He recognized the music at once as one of his father's favorites: Hildegard von Bingen's *Symphony of the Harmony of Heaven*.

"What goes on inside that warehouse?" Zohar said.

"Get a search warrant and see for yourself."

"I'm asking you," Zohar said, "so we don't have another Waco."

Stone was silent beneath the soaring voices of the canned choir, observing Zohar, this unscrupulous thing who had used Abi, conned her like some carnival barker into believing she was doing Stone some good by parachuting back into his life, when in fact she had only exposed herself once again as a fraudulent mother. Now Stone was going to destroy Zohar for making him believe, however briefly, in the impossible illusion of maternal love.

"I'll bet it's an armed camp," Zohar said, shaking his head.

"Why do you think I'd tell you anything after what you did?"

Abi had offered Stone hope that the past could be fixed, and Stone had foolishly begun to believe it was possible.

"So this is what it's all about?" Zohar said.

"You disgust me," Stone said. They stood an arm's length apart, their eyes fixed on each other.

"She cares deeply about you," Zohar said, searching Stone's face for some sort of reaction. "Any mother would do anything to keep her son out of trouble if she had the chance. And you are in a world of trouble."

"You don't know what you are talking about," Stone said.

Zohar seemed to be counting his teeth with his tongue, holding off a long moment before offering, "NYPD found a badly decomposed body washed up in Wallabout Bay. It had been shot in the back of the head, execution style. We found a wallet on the body; the fingerprints confirmed it was your roommate."

Stone said nothing, showed nothing. The triumph of victory was

close at hand. Pinky was dead and Stone was on the cusp of something
great. Soon, Zohar, too, would be dead. If only he could have taken
a pistol from the *beis* without being discovered, Zohar would be dead
already. Even a .22 would do the trick at this range.

"Michael Pinsky sold five pounds of military-grade C-4 explosives
to an undercover agent and then he was off our radar, gone. You could
be next. You know what I'm talking about."

Stone's only answer would be the blade. He silently calculated
angles, approaches, the possibilities of what it would take to pierce
Zohar's pathetic armor—an off-the-rack suit jacket, a blue Oxford
shirt, his olive skin. A furious squall of voices layered one on top of the
other in Stone's head demanded he do it, do it now. *Don't be a spine-
less hands-upper . . . c'mon kid, stick it in his breadbasket . . . do it and you
will become my greatest invention.* Jabotinsky, Julius, and Walter Stone
had never had such doubts, Stone was certain. None of them allowed
room for pity or hesitation; they simply followed the plain power of
their wills without a wasted thought. But Stone had already wavered
for too long, and when he reached for the handle of his knife, Zohar
had stepped behind the safety of a wooden pew and launched into a
lecture aimed at changing Stone's mind.

"As we move into the twenty-first century, it is us against them,
the extremist against civil society. The biggest threat to our society is
ideologically motivated groups heavily armed with weapons, explosives, and a nihilistic desire to destroy the foundations of our civi-
lization. We saw it at Oklahoma City, we saw it at the World Trade
Center, and we will see it again and again unless people like you wake
up and do what is right. You are a rational person. Tell me you will not
fall sway to this madness." Zohar held Stone's eyes with his to ensure
he was paying attention.

It didn't matter what Zohar had to say, no matter how reasoned,
because he had permanently disqualified himself from consideration.
There was no human being on earth more loathsome to Stone than
Larry Zohar. His words might as well have been wind blown from the
ass of a chimpanzee. Stone would never consider his pathetic appeals.

"Matthew, there is going to be a catastrophic terrorist attack in

Brooklyn. You can help me, or you can choose not to help me, but I'm going to stop it. I'm appealing to your sense of right and wrong one last time. Don't let yourself become an accessory to mass murder. Are you listening to me? Do you hear a word I'm saying?"

"What makes you so sure there's going to be an attack?"

"Well, look at that. He's awake from his trance," Zohar said, slapping his thigh.

Stone wished he had not responded, had shut Zohar out without a word. Now his blood rose and he wanted to take down Zohar in the manner he knew best.

"Matthew, I'm connecting the dots."

"The assassinations?" Stone said, setting Zohar up. "In Brooklyn, Jersey, and Dearborn? Are those all dots?"

"Part of the big picture," Zohar said.

The morning light flared behind the stained glass and Stone believed he could devastate Zohar with just the simple use of logic.

"I know and you know the killing of those Arabs was carried out by other Arabs, not Jews. It's true, isn't it?"

"It's true," Zohar said after a moment.

"There you go again. Blame the Jews for everything," Stone said. "Another blood libel. You are a liar, yet you expect me to help you. You are inept and incompetent, and, worse than that, you think you are actually good at what you do. The power of self-delusion has rarely been on display so boldly."

"Matthew, listen," Zohar said. "When I spoke to you, all the evidence pointed toward—"

"The Jews," Stone said. "Just like you tried to pin the World Trade Center bombing on the Jews."

"You don't understand. Two days after I spoke to you about it, an Arab man, a Palestinian in his midtwenties, reported his rental car stolen and was foolish enough to provide his real identification. We found gunpowder on his clothes, and he broke down, admitted to everything."

"And yet you point your finger at the Jews. Why are you always looking for Jews to be the villains?"

"Matthew, you know I'm not."

"Blue-blooded G-man in a cheap suit. Do you think becoming like them will save you?"

"Do you?" Zohar said.

"At least I'm not ashamed of being Jewish," Stone said.

"You've come a long way," Zohar said, chuckling.

"Fuck you."

"Do you want to know what happened to Fairuza Freij?"

"She means nothing to me," Stone said. "The past is past."

"The past is never the past for a Jew. The Jew lives forever in the past even as time moves forward. Why do you think the Jew is so possessive of his past?"

Stone said nothing, anticipating more of Zohar's poker-faced prevarications.

"Because it grants him a power, a strength bigger than the individual. He is empowered by the bookish, pious, martyred history connecting him personally to God. How vain is it that Jews believe God chose them out of all the people of the world to be his chosen?"

The door creaked open behind Stone and a white spear of sunlight slashed across the cool marble floor. An elderly couple stood in the sunshine, smiling, as if waiting to be invited in.

"You hate yourself," Stone said. "You hate yourself because you are a Jew and there's nothing you can do about it."

The door swung shut and the couple was gone.

"I'm Jewish," Zohar said, "but I will not be ruined by history."

Stone laughed. Everything was so clear now. He thought of Jonathan Pollard, the US Naval Intelligence analyst who had been arrested by the FBI for selling top-secret military intelligence to the Israeli government. He had been sentenced to life in prison and his plea for clemency had been denied by President Clinton. But this had not been the first time Jews were accused of having split loyalties, of being a nation within a nation. He remembered the nightmare tales the Judge had told him about Alfred Dreyfus, the nineteenth-century French artillery officer who had been accused of passing secrets along to Germany simply because he was Jewish, and of his exile to Devil's

Island. Stone thought of the Rosenbergs, Ethel and Julius, who had been executed for handing nuclear secrets over to the Soviets. But it was Pollard specifically, Stone knew, who had driven Zohar to seek out Jews as his target so he would not be suspect in the eyes of the conservative FBI establishment. Zohar had found a way to adapt, carve out his niche, and save his skin. But at what cost?

"If the future of Israel was at stake," Stone questioned, "and you had the ability to help Israel at the expense of the United States, would you?"

"I'm an American first," Zohar said.

"That excuse would never have mattered to Hitler. Assimilate all you want, but you know when the time comes and Amalek is hungry for Jewish blood, your head is on the chopping block. Holding an American passport won't make a difference in the world. The suicide bombings in Tel Aviv; don't they mean anything to you? You are the target as much as I am, as much as Jews everywhere are marked for death."

Zohar slapped his thigh with the palm of his hand and let out a loud whistle. "You've drunk the Kool-Aid. They actually got to you, Matthew," Zohar said, his voice soft, choked with astonishment. "What happened to you?"

"I woke up. I realized I didn't have to be weak and neurotic and afraid of everything. I understood I was every bit as powerful as the great Maccabee, Mattathias." The knife hummed in his waistband, calling him to destroy Zohar, following in the footsteps of his warrior namesake who had killed rather than offer up a sacrifice to false Greek gods.

"You're sick, Matthew. You need help."

"I've never been better in my life," Stone said, reaching for the handle of the blade. "Are we done? Am I free to go?"

Zohar moved in front of Stone, blocking his way, and crossed his arms. "What do you think happens to an unmarried pregnant woman in Beit Jala?"

"It's not my problem," Stone said.

"What if it was your friend, Fairuza Freij? Would that make a difference? Would it matter that she had to rush into marriage with a man she barely knew, someone her parents chose, just because she would not be able to explain away the growing bulge in her belly?"

"That's not my concern," Stone said. "You can't hurt me anymore."

Zohar let out a sadistic laugh. He had one card left to play and he threw it down with the intent to wound. "And what do you think Dasi Grunhut would feel about this, her boyfriend, father of an Arab child?"

Mention of Dasi's name made his heart jump. His arms shook, his muscles electric beneath his skin as he shouted, "Dasi is gone. Say what you like." Stone's eyes were blinded by a scrim of tears as he vocalized that most painful reality.

"Really?" Zohar chuckled. "That was quick."

Stone had to kill Zohar. Killing Zohar would prove to Brilliant he was up to the awesome task of pulling the trigger in the heat of battle, and that would set off a whole domino effect of positives in Stone's life—the completion of his father's wishes crowned with Dasi begging, on her knees, for him to take her back.

"There's going to be an attack at the Rally for Palestine on Wednesday. Information I've gathered tells me lives are at risk."

"Arab lives," Stone spat.

"Human lives," Zohar responded. "That is all that matters."

"Well, good luck, then. But I can't help you," Stone said. "I'm done."

Zohar didn't see Stone slip the knife from his pants, the crumpled newspaper dropping to the floor. He gripped the handle tightly in his right hand, prepared to puncture Zohar's kidney. That would be enough to take the fight out of Zohar, then Stone would be free to have his way with him, to cut his throat as Zohar looked him in the eye, to know he had been defeated by a better man.

"His name is Salem," Zohar said. "Peace."

Stone froze in place, imagining a brown child who was half him and half Fairuza, both a bookish scholar and a wild jackal. He knew this child would forever feel the emptiness created by his absence, just as Stone had known the void left behind by both his parents. But the child's pain was his own pain to bear, and he would find his own way to salve his psychic wounds.

Stone was a father, just as Julius and the Judge had been fathers, neither perfect, both estranged from their sons, intense, distant, but deeply connected. And the sons had made it. Both the Judge and Stone himself had survived and found success in the world. One day his own son would come looking for him, and Stone knew he would face his son as an enemy.

"Do you want to contribute to this hundred-year conflict?" Zohar asked, his back still turned. "Help create a more violent and divided world for your son to grow up in?"

"That's not up to me," Stone said flatly. "Put out your snipers and barbed wire and Jersey barriers. You won't find anything."

"Oh, I will," Zohar said, flashing Stone one final look of disgust. "I'll be there with my eyes wide open."

Zohar swung the door open and stepped out into the fresh autumn air. He was just a foot or two ahead of Stone, oblivious to the danger behind him, his thoughts overtaken with useless fantasies of heroism.

Stone imagined the first time Julius had killed a man, strangling the Cuban bootlegger with a piece of scrap metal. He imagined his father, gunning the engine of the Thunderbird as Emile Alcalai pedaled at his bicycle to be crushed and killed beneath the wheels of the Judge's car. Now the moment had arrived for Stone to join his father and grand-father, true blood relations at last.

The blade was four, maybe five inches long and serrated along the stainless steel edge. The tip was sharpened to a fine point. Stone had already made use of it on his own flesh, and now he thrust it toward Zohar with a shout of triumph.

Something blurred into Stone's vision, smashing him in the ribs, as a man's charging head knocked all the breath out of him. The knife flew up into the air and, as the blade rotated like a windmill against the sky, Stone was crashing to the pavement, his ribs battered against the concrete, a voice at his ear growling, "You stupid, stupid fuck." Then Gargiulio yanked him to his feet, frog marching him toward the waiting black sedan.

This isn't happening, Stone thought, his lungs crushed inside his rib cage, empty of air. I want a do-over. I want to try again. He was so close to killing Zohar that his mind still hadn't caught up to the reality that Zohar was approaching him now, a quizzical half smile on his face. Gargiulio tightened his grip on Stone's arms, pulling back so his shoulders hurt.

"Let him go," Zohar said with disgust. "He's useless to us."

Zohar slipped on a pair of suave sunglasses and then, without warning, sucker-punched Stone in the face. Stone went snow blind with pain, his nose broken. He dropped to his knees and was able to make out, beneath the roaring in his head, "This piece of shit is all talk. He's nothing. I'd be surprised if he could even blow his nose."

30

He awoke late Wednesday morning from a restive sleep in which the ceaseless ringing of the telephone kept him from drifting fully under into the restorative embrace of REM-cycle sleep. Too exhausted to lift his battered body off the mattress, he let the phone ring out in the empty hollow of the living room. There was nobody in the world he wanted to speak to; he was a man alone, a man poised for greatness, and he could tolerate no distractions.

A clutch of chattering pigeons had gathered outside on his window ledge, their bobbing heads crowned by the morning light. Stone's swollen nose throbbed, his chest wounds seethed with a grotesque, ocher-hued pus. The pain did not bother him. He was overcome with anticipation for the great event, and nothing could derail his mounting excitement. Though a part of him wished he could take part in the execution of the act, he took comfort in the fact that he had stood up to Zohar, called him out as the turncoat disgrace he was, told him nothing, wasted his time. He knew he was a good soldier, and his face would forever bear the mark in commemoration of his deeds. What was a broken nose after all, compared to the elation Stone would feel after the body count was tallied, after the message had been relayed: *The only permitted blood is the blood of Ishmael*. He had done his part. Now he needed simply to pass the time and wait.

The pigeons, too, seemed filled with expectation, even awe, as they observed Stone spread out on the mattress, absently fingering his raw sores. A blue-gray pigeon fixed its nervous eyes on Stone, and Stone stared back for a long moment, startled by the beauty of the thing, how the iridescent green patch at its neck turned from emerald to azure to aquamarine with the infinitesimal gradients of the light. If only it were so easy to transform oneself, to turn toward the sun and then away, and find oneself changed. Stone had worked hard to make himself the man he was meant to be, and here he was, nearly complete. The pigeon performed a single mindless peck at the window ledge and then took off into the sky, followed by its brothers and sisters.

Stone dragged himself up off the mattress so he could watch the pigeons in flight, mesmerized by the occult geometry of their effortless configuration. The day was bright and sunny and chilled with autumn, but Stone was content to remain inside the apartment, watching the proceedings on television. He went to the bathroom to regard his face in the mirror. That erstwhile alien emotion of pride crept into his mind as he considered the fact that these were war wounds, that he had sustained the crack in the bridge of his nose while standing up for something he believed in, something all brave Jews must believe in. Stone punched at the air with a combination of cunning lefts and devastating rights. His optimism peaking, Stone dropped to the ground, pressed out seven agonized pushups, and collapsed to the floor. His breath came hard and his heart thumped behind his wounds. He was the brains, not the brawn, Stone thought with certainty. His mind was more dangerous than a dozen bloody knuckles, more frightening than a loaded gun. After a few quiet minutes of solemn congress with the wooden floorboards during which his telephone rang unanswered, he stood up, poured himself a drink, and turned on the television.

The rally was broadcast on a local cable station known best for its low-budget studio panel shows *City Hall This Week* and *Close-Up on Broadway*. Stone sat in his boxer shorts and sipped his drink, listening to the chatter of the newscasters. "Security is tight for today's Rally for Palestine, described by organizers as a gathering of hope in support of self-determination and equal rights for the disaffected around the world and in Palestine."

Palestine was not even a thing anymore, Stone thought, shaking his head. Even Merriam-Webster knew Palestine was just a tiny strip of land wedged between the Mediterranean and the Jordan River, a backwater administrative district under the sultans of the Ottoman Empire and, later, during the British Mandate. The so-called Palestinian people were just a convenient fiction, an excuse to murder Jews.

The reporter continued her live feed from the crowded corner of Court Street and Atlantic Avenue. "Traffic is snarled throughout downtown Brooklyn. The NYPD has closed off many streets running off Atlantic Avenue and Fourth Avenue, where the procession will make its way to the newly completed Al Salaam Mosque in Bay Ridge. Tension is high in the wake of twin suicide bombings in Tel Aviv Sunday morning, and Jewish leaders have pledged to demonstrate against the rally."

The screen transitioned to a taped interview with a silver-bearded man in his early fifties who wore a large black kippa on his head and a gold Star of David on a thick chain resting against his bearish chest. "Blood is on their hands. It's not time to celebrate when people are dying."

This attack was justified more than ever. Sound bites and picket signs were one thing, but now was the time for action. Stone gulped the rest of his drink, secure in the knowledge that Jews were waking up at last to Jabotinsky's clarion call of self-defense.

Next, a moon-faced young woman dressed in the colors of the local Quaker school spoke in counterpoint. "The colonial occupation of Arab lands must end. As long as there is one Arab child living in a squalid refugee camp, the resistance is justified." She spoke with fervor and deep earnestness, but lacked nuance and understanding. She was a naive dilettante at best, a hack political operative in pigtails and John Lennon glasses. Stone was tempted to change the station until she had finished disseminating her libel, but the reporter was back on screen announcing the mayor's office had issued an eleventh-hour appeal to organizers to postpone the rally until the political situation abroad stabilized. The mayor himself even threatened to issue an injunction, but organizers cited the annual Salute to Israel rally that ran down

Manhattan's Fifth Avenue as precedent that gatherings such as these had not been canceled in the past, despite political turmoil.

Roiling crowds of people pressed close to the elevated stage, chanting *hey-ho, something, something, something!* and flying homemade banners above their heads. A stomach-turning placard featuring both the Israeli prime minister and Adolf Hitler flashed across the screen and then was gone, as the camera focused in on the empty stage. A lectern draped with the Palestinian colors stood downstage, a row of folding chairs lined along the back. Stern-faced plainclothesmen and regular officers held back the crowd. When would his comrades appear and put an end to this spectacle?

"And here they come now," the reporter said, her voice rising in excitement as the speakers took their places on the stage. "There's state assemblyman Jordan Issa, followed by US senator Joe Salem. And there's Winston Haloumi, writer and Columbia professor." Haloumi nodded his head solemnly to the crowd, looking just like the egotistical shit on his book jackets. "And now, Brooklyn's own Reverend Randall Roebling Nation, today's master of ceremonies, is ascending to the lectern."

And there he was, the man most responsible for the death of Stone's father, a race man opportunist with a Bible, a media whore, a cynical phony with a matchbook college degree, bent on self-promotion through sanctimonious pronouncements. No, you are not the voice of the oppressed, thought Stone, you are a ruthless hypocrite who cares only for yourself and your ever-important wardrobe.

The crowd cheered as Nation, dressed in a finely tailored, gasoline-blue suit, clasped his hands together above his head and shook them in a gesture of friendship and solidarity. He wore stylish sunglasses and a braided gold chain around his neck. His conked hair was brushed back on his head and shined in the sun. He was about the same age as the Judge had been when he died, but here was Nation bursting at the seams with life. He wouldn't be for long. Nation stood in silence, smiling a straight-toothed smile as the crowd cheered. He calmed the mass of people, gesturing with his flattened hands horizontally pressing down on air.

"Thank you, my friends. Thank you." His voice was rich and sonorous and studied. "I stand before you today not far from the spot where a nine-year-old boy was tragically run down by a speeding truck, his life taken from him before its time. I stand near the very epicenter of the awful riot that took the life of one man, injured dozens, and stained the very soul of this peaceful neighborhood. I stand before you on the spot that has marked division and hatred ever since. But I'm not here to speak about rage or hatred. No. I have seen enough to last me ten lifetimes, a thousand. I come to you with a message of hope."

The crowd cheered, and Stone felt the overwhelming desire to shout at the TV screen.

"As many of you know, I grew up in Jim Crow's South, where a black man was considered a fraction of a man, less than human. We were slaves and remained so, long after Emancipation, long after the birth pangs of Reconstruction had receded into the shadows of our collective memories. In my own lifetime black men and women continued to be raped, lynched, terrorized, denied their God-given rights during one of the most ignominious and ignoble periods in human history.

"My mother, God rest her soul, was chosen. When I was nine years old she took my brother and me and our two sisters on a bus ride that would change our lives forever. My mother was chosen, and we went to the Promised Land"—Nation paused a beat—"to New York City, to a place with the grand-sounding moniker of Bedford-Stuyvesant. It sounded like paradise to me, and that paradise was right here in Brooklyn, where I was enrolled in a public school and given the same opportunities as every other child, regardless of race, creed, faith, or nationality.

"We came to a city where a man could fly as far and as high as his hard work would carry him, freed from the stinging yoke of history. My mother was chosen, and I was chosen. But wait, let's not stop there. We are all chosen by the Almighty, each and every living soul. No one is a favorite child, not the white-collar workers of Wall Street who live in their tall glass towers, or the poor blacks of East St. Louis, Bushwick, or Watts, not the Serbs or the Croats, not the Japanese or the Germans, not the Pakistanis or the Indians who aim their missiles at each other's hearts, not the Hutus or the Tutsis who have massacred each other in God's name. The sons of Abraham, *both* Isaac *and* Ishmael, sit side by side in heaven. There is no favorite child. We are all God's children. We are all chosen."

Pure hypocrisy, Stone thought. He'd co-opted the mantle of chosen people from the Jews, not to bring peace and harmony to the world but to bring the Jews down, to strip them of their rights to a land of their own. This was the time to bring down the iron will of Samson, cut Nation off before he could further delegitimize the Jews and their God-given rights to the land of Israel. "Now," Stone shouted at his TV, "do it now!" But Nation continued.

"You might ask me, Reverend, if we are all chosen, then why does one suffer while another does not, why does one drink the sweet wine while the other is parched? I'll tell you, it's because one must choose one's fate. You are the chosen, but you must choose. If my mother had not *chosen* action over defeat, if she had not *chosen* to be brave, if she had not *chosen* to be chosen, all those years ago, would I be standing here before you today, a reverend with ministries in every borough of the greatest city in the world, former Democratic candidate for the president of the United States?"

The crowd roared again.

Nation stood on the dais, smiling, calming the crowd with his well-practiced gestures. He didn't know it, but he would see his God sooner than he knew, as death, the great equalizer, lay just beneath, in the old train tunnel under Atlantic Avenue. The boys from the *beis* would see to that.

Nation continued: "And when our brothers and sisters over in Palestine find themselves detained, harassed, imprisoned, shot down in the streets of their towns and cities, their land taken from them, their homes demolished by immaculate bulldozers of hate . . ."

Stone's buzzer rang and he jumped up as if he'd been stung. He couldn't take his eyes off Nation, but he couldn't stand to watch him lie and dissemble another minute.

Through the intercom Stone heard Dasi's worried voice, pleading to be let in. "Matthew, are you all right?"

I don't need your pity, Stone thought, but he buzzed her in anyway.

A moment later, Dasi tapped at the apartment door. When Stone opened up, she was dressed in warm fall colors, high chestnut boots, pumpkin-colored stockings, and a vintage-looking dress, her black bangs sharp against her pale forehead.

"I was worried," she said. "You didn't pick up the phone."

"Listen to him incite the crowd," Stone said, by way of greeting. He offered nothing else.

Dasi gasped. "What happened to your face? You look terrible." She approached him to examine the damage to his nose, but Stone turned his back to her so he could better observe Nation on the television.

"Matthew, tell me what's going on. You look like you've been beaten up. What's wrong? I've been worried sick about you."

It was a mistake opening the door. Stone did everything he could to block Dasi out and direct his focus toward Nation.

"If only dark days appear to lie ahead, we must always remember we must choose to be chosen. We must rise up and choose to be free, we must rise up and choose our destiny, we must rise up and choose to be strong, we must rise up and choose to be chosen. Rise up and choose to be chosen, rise up and choose—"

Dasi clicked off the set and stood in front of the screen.

"Turn that back on," Stone shrieked. "Turn the fucking TV back on."

"What is going on with you?" Dasi stared at Stone with a look of weary bewilderment.

"We're going to miss it," Stone said, reaching for the remote. "Turn it back on."

"Miss what?" Dasi said, narrowing her dark eyes. A deep vertical line had formed between her eyebrows. "What are we going to miss?"

"The rally," Stone said. "I've got to watch until it happens." It could be happening right now and he was missing it because Dasi insisted on pleading ignorance about the attack.

"Matthew, I don't know what you are talking about."

"You don't know?" Stone said.

"Don't know what?" she said.

"You don't know? I thought you knew. Dov was part of it, Yossi, the others, Rabbi Seligman. I thought you knew what was happening."

"Matthew, you're scaring me. Tell me what's going on."

Stone was silent for a long moment.

"What's going on, Matthew?" Dasi was shouting now. "Tell me, please. What is happening? Tell me!"

An icy sweat appeared on Stone's skin like beads of quicksilver. It was true he had never flat-out asked her, but if Dasi didn't know about the plan, what exactly did that mean to Stone?

"You really don't know? Really?" Stone pressed. "Really?"

Dasi looked beautiful to Stone, for what would be the last time, as she chewed on her lower lip, her left eye screwed shut to hold back a tear. "Tell me, Matthew," her voice a pleading whisper. "Tell me what you've gotten into."

"This is supposed to be the greatest moment of my life, the culmination of my father's life work."

"All right," Dasi said. "I'm calling the police."

Stone lunged for the phone, ripped it out of the wall, and dashed it to the floor.

It lay broken in a dozen jagged pieces.

"Matthew, please," Dasi said. She was begging, but this was not the type of begging he had hoped for. "Just tell me."

He told her everything from Seligman to Brilliant to Zohar, to the bank account and the passcode and the transferred money. He told her about the Judge's books and the whispered voices and the narrative about the tunnels he had pieced together from his father's marginal notes and underscored words and phrases. He told her about the shooting range at the *beis*. He told her he had never felt stronger and more in control in his entire life. He was fulfilling his father's final wish, completing his legacy and laying the groundwork for a new generation.

"My father thought I was weak, incompetent," Stone said. "I could never do right by him. But, now . . ."

"But now, what?" Dasi said. She wore a face Stone did not recognize—stricken, blanched of all definition, her face slack with terror. "You

were just going to sit here in front of the television and watch people
die?"

"They're our enemies. You know that! You were in the army."

"I was in the army to protect my family and my country," Dasi said.
"That doesn't make me a terrorist."

"Dasi, the entire world is against the Jews. We are not terrorists.
We have to show the world we are strong. There can be no permitted
blood. There are known terrorists and enemies of Israel on that
podium."

"Don't tell me you've bought into the paranoid delusions of the
Diaspora Jew. This is insane."

"This is what my father wanted. This is my last chance to obey his
wishes. Nobody innocent will die."

"Who gave you the power to decide?"

"The Judge did, my father. He started this plan and I helped bring
it to completion."

"How can you talk like that?" Dasi said, retreating in horror. "I
spoke to your father during his last trip to Israel, on Tu B'shvat, when
he knew he was dying. Matthew, he was a broken man. You know how
devastated he was, how embarrassed he was he had to step down as
a judge after the Riot trial. He was humiliated. He was dying and he
was afraid he would only be remembered for that after all the good
work he had done, after working so hard to make a name for himself
not connected to Julius Stone. Your father could never have agreed to
this plan, knowing it would tarnish his reputation. Yes, he had strong
feelings about the Arabs. But he had stronger feelings about his name,
his reputation. Do you know what he was reading when he came to
visit? *Othello* by William Shakespeare. He said he wanted to reread all
of his plays one last time. And I remember him reading me Cassio's
pitiful lines after he was punished by Othello, stripped of his honorable position."

"'Reputation, reputation, reputation,'" Stone murmured. He had
burned those lines into his heart, his father's credo.

"'And what remains is bestial,'" Dasi said. "Your father was deeply
concerned with his legacy after the disaster of the trial." She ran her

fingers through her hair. "Who put you up to this? Was it Rabbi Seligman?"

Stone nodded his head. "Yes."

"You trusted him? You know he's an ideologue and an extremist, Matthew, just like my uncle was before he was killed. Neither of them made it a secret they wanted the Arabs transferred out of Israel."

Stone recalled something soothing about Seligman's presence, as if he had a special connection to his father, as if through him he had found a facsimile of his father, a lucky chance at a second chance. "They were best friends," Stone offered.

"A long time ago, Matthew."

"What do you mean?"

"Your father and Rabbi Seligman had a terrible falling out and had barely spoken in years, just what was absolutely necessary to run the Eretz Fund. After my uncle was murdered, they each expected the other to do whatever they could to take control of the money."

"Why didn't you tell me this?"

"I thought you knew."

Stone was falling from a great height, a drop with no bottom and no end, his stomach pinwheeling and effervescent with nausea. A wide empty space opened up around him and he shrank into its depths, plummeting farther and farther away from everything he had ever desired.

His father's dying words made sense now. When the Judge said Seligman's name, he was not directing Stone toward him but warning him away from him. When he mentioned numbers, he had wanted Stone to keep them *out* of Seligman's hands. His stubborn father had kept that vital information to himself until the very end, safe from his incompetent son in the event he managed to live. And then, when it became clear he would die, it was too late, his voice was gone, the death rattle scraping in his throat.

Dasi stood before him, tears streaming down her face. "How could I have ever thought I could give myself to you?"

Stone imagined the palm of his father's massive hand slapping him across the face again and again, forever.

"What have you got to say?"

But Stone had nothing to offer, nothing that could ever make things right with Dasi, nothing that could undo his mistake.

Dasi kicked at him with her high boots, beating on his face and chest with her clenched fists. "Stupid! Stupid! Do something. There has to be some way to stop it. How did you ever get such a crazy idea in your head? Did you think I would love you for this? I'm sick," she said.

In that instant, Stone realized he would drag the bodies of the dead with him for the rest of his life. A great cry tore through Stone's belly. "I've made a mistake. I've made a terrible mistake."

Dasi turned to him, her wet eyes full of hate. "Get out of here," she screamed. "I can't look at you. Get out! Get out!"

A stabbing pain shot through his chest, but he found the strength to run. Stone sprang out the door in his bare feet, burst out onto Waverly Avenue, and ran as fast as he could toward the *beis*. Maybe it wasn't too late. If only he could speak to Brilliant, maybe he would call it off. He dodged traffic, ran through bits of broken glass, tripped on a traffic median under the BQE, but arrived at the *beis* in no time at all.

A familiar black SUV idled in the street behind the warehouse, its hatchback open. Moshe, carrying two suitcases, appeared in the opening of the service door slid wide on its tracks. Brilliant emerged after him. He wore a freshly pressed black suit that lent him a grave, funereal air.

"Matthew, I'm surprised to see you here."

Stone pushed Brilliant back into the warehouse, his vision blurred with rage. Brilliant fell to the floor, but Moshe was there, his leaden forearm across Stone's windpipe.

"Let him go," Brilliant said, getting to his feet.

Stone gasped for breath, his throat and sinuses aflame. "You've got to stop this."

"What?" Brilliant laughed, wiping the dust from his pant leg. "It's too late for cold feet."

"You're a murderer."

"Suddenly you have a social conscience, Matthew? I'll have you know you are a murderer, too."

"I'm not a murderer," Stone shouted. "I'm not!"

The mirror maze had been taken down and the warehouse was barren, cleared of all signs of habitation. The floors were swept clean and a chemical smell of industrial cleaner hung in the air.

"Save it," Brilliant said. "Moshe and I have a plane to catch."

"I don't understand."

"We'll be safe on the runway ready to take off for home. It'll be over soon. You didn't think we were going to stay as Atlantic Avenue is blown up beneath their feet? We have to get to Israel before the investigation starts. You understand, don't you?"

"What do you mean blown up?"

"A remote-controlled detonator that can be set off from a timer will ignite four drums of compressed hydrogen to be used as accelerant for seventy-five pounds of C-4. There will be an immense explosion, the likes of which this nation has never seen."

Stone stared, blank-faced, at Brilliant's sparkling eyes. Moshe slammed the trunk shut outside. Then Moshe's shadow lengthened across the floor as he filled the doorway.

"No," Stone muttered. "No, no, no, no, no."

"I know you've done a lot of reading, in school, your father's books. Did you ever come across anything about Israel's extradition treaty with the US? Let me explain: Israeli law prohibits extraditing Israeli citizens when they're accused of a crime in a second country."

Stone's throat clenched, as if plugged by a stopper. He tried to ask Brilliant what he meant, but could not get the words out. He had been sleepwalking his entire life, and now, at last, he was awake.

"If one understands, one has everything." Brilliant laughed. "Matthew, we're dual citizens. Citizens of both Israel and the US. Moshe's Israeli, I'm Israeli, Yossi, Itzy, everyone from the *beis* is Israeli. Except you."

Dizzy, deflated, overcome with the terror of what he had done, Stone gasped for air and managed to say, "This will be the worst terrorist attack in US history."

"You knew what you signed up for."

"No," Stone said. "No."

"You knew people would die. What's the difference?"

"They'll come looking for you."

"Why would anyone cause an international mess like that when they have a suspect right here in America? Is Washington going to withhold aid packages and loan guarantees when they have you to blame?"

"Nobody will ever believe I did this by myself."

Brilliant laughed again and so did Moshe. "The only thing to do with an idiot and a thorn is to get rid of them both. Remember, you transferred the money from your father's account. No one else had access to it. As well, you are undoubtedly all over the bank's security tapes. And you were quite a capable shot at the range. I'm sure the police will find it interesting that a gun with your fingerprints all over it is the same gun that killed your foolish roommate."

"No," Stone gasped.

"Yes," Brilliant said. "Moshe dropped it in a mailbox just this morning. It'll be found in the afternoon pickup."

"This is impossible."

Brilliant continued, "Just as your grandfather smuggled weapons from New York to Tel Aviv, you and your roommate smuggled weapons from Tel Aviv to New York. It's a perfect circle. A convincing narrative for the media to polish and sell to a scandal-hungry world."

Stone fell to his knees. "Why? Why me?"

"Your father just died. You were in terrible pain and we offered you heaven. You were an apple waiting to be picked. That's the trick of the evil impulse, it's sweet in the beginning but so, so bitter in the end."

"My father saved you when you killed Al-Bassam."

The sun streamed in through the open door, which Moshe had vacated, and merged with the artificial lights overhead to form a disorienting, hazy screen between him and Brilliant.

"We have to go," Moshe said.

Stone did not want them to leave. He wanted them to stay forever, as they were, just the three of them alone in the warehouse, outside of time.

"Matthew, when the history is written, people will remember

one name when they think of this attack, this spectacular attack that maimed and killed Arabs so far from their corrupt terrorist states. People will remember the name Stone."

"No," Stone cried.

"You are just the end of this story. It began more than fifty years ago, with your grandfather strangling his victims to line his pockets, his midnight hits and shakedowns, his contributions to the Irgun. He's a great antihero. People are fascinated with him. Yes, he helped with the establishment of the State of Israel, but he will always be remembered as a killer. And your father, the Judge, who fixed a jury to save a killer, a Jew, me. He always lived with the taint of your grandfather hanging over him. Now that his son has released such incredible carnage on the streets of Brooklyn, and on the very anniversary of the riot, to avenge his father, what do you think people will remember? They will remember the blood the Stone family spilled across more than half a century."

"I'm not a killer," Stone cried.

"When you are called before the Throne of Judgment, tell that to the Heavenly Father. Here on earth, you and your father are, and will remain, killers in the great collective memory, the worst in the history of this country. Good-bye, Matthew."

Brilliant turned to walk away, and Stone rushed at him, flailing his arms wildly.

Moshe grabbed Stone by the hair and pulled him off Brilliant, lifting Stone from the ground. Stone tried to protest, but Moshe was having none of what he had to say, and threw him across the room with incredible force. Stone flew through the air and crashed, shoulder first, into a bare concrete wall.

When he came to, Stone was alone in the darkness. His head and neck ached and he imagined he had died, but then he smelled the cleaning solution and heard the muttered voices of students at prayer sifting down from the second-floor study house. His tongue screamed where he had nearly bitten it in half on impact. Had this really happened? He looked at his watch, but it had stopped. Lying on the cool floor, Stone realized he had not understood anything in his life, and all the wisdom in the world from here on would be of no use. He pulled himself to his feet with difficulty and felt each and every bone in his body bruised, misaligned, from the force of his crash. He stumbled in the darkness, feeling his way with his hands, and unlatched the door. He slid it open. The day was bright and blue, the sky deep, expanding outwardly forever. He stepped out into the cool air and saw the city beyond, its buildings and towers sparkling, each one created with man's ingenuity, strength, and will. They rose into the sky and fit seamlessly into the space created for them.

A group of pigeons loitered nearby and Stone called to them. They flapped their wings and ascended into the sky, circling in formation in the sunshine. They rose higher and circled, the entire city spread out beneath them, the dazzling waters of the East River catching the sun just right. The birds were beautiful to watch, moving as one synchronized body through the air. It occurred to Stone that perhaps the day had stood still, time had somehow stopped, caught in the languid web of the warming sun. Then, as the pigeons circled above for a second time, something shattered the still of the day, something distant, but distinct, and they dipped, looped, and tumbled dizzily from the sky, scattering in all directions like a fractured dream, to be lost forever.

ACKNOWLEDGMENTS

I am grateful to my wonderful, tireless editor Michelle Caplan for seeing the best in me as a writer and challenging me every step of the way to make this novel everything it should be. Every writer should be as fortunate to have the opportunity to work with Michelle. I'd like to thank Fredric Price, Erika Dreifus, and everyone else at Fig Tree Books; you are doing important work. Thank you Mitchell Waters and the folks at Curtis Brown. Thank you Charlotte Strick and Claire Williams for the kickass cover. Thank you Stephanie Goldenhersh for lending me your giant brain and your eagle eyes. Thank you Gary Alpert for making me look presentable in my photos; you are a magician. This book would never have come into being without Josh Lambert, who remembered me and helped to rekindle my creative fire. Thank you Caroline Leavitt, Dara Horn, and Sara Nović for your undying support. Thank you Sara Lippmann, for your cheerleading and literary *shidduch*-making; if everyone felt the same way as you about my writing, I would be famous. Of course, thank you to Eve for being you and for giving me the space I needed to complete this book; I know it wasn't always easy. I love you all.

PRAISE FOR *THE BOOK OF STONE*

"Equal parts thriller and literary epic—a smart, haunting novel that entertains as it apprises. Papernick writes with impressive breadth, in turns crafting the minute details of a psychological profile and dissecting the vast sociopolitical complexities of religious zealotry pushed to its outer limits. *The Book of Stone* is an important read for our historical moment."

—SARA NOVIĆ,
author of *Girl at War*

"Jonathan Papernick's *The Book of Stone* is a psychological thriller with a complex soul. In the tradition of writers like Robert Stone and Ian McEwan, Papernick describes the quest to save oneself by redeeming history, and the perilous consequences that arise from confusing the two tasks. It's a harrowing, distinguished book."   —STEVE STERN,
author of *The Wedding Jester* and *The Angel of Forgetfulness*

"*The Book of Stone* is many amazing things: a searingly-told father-son story in which profound estrangement is tenuously and dangerously bridged through the intermediaries of books and ideas; a modern family tale that is itself embedded in the never-ending, violent tribal drama of the historical conflict between Jews and Arabs. In all its layered psychological intensity, Jon Papernick's new novel is riveting."
—ARYEH LEV STOLLMAN,
author of *The Illuminated Soul* and *The Far Euphrates*

"*The Book of Stone* is going to have everyone on the planet talking. Blisteringly smart, provocative, and passionate, Papernick's astounding novel layers a complex father-and-son story onto the Jewish-Arab conflict, where fierce loyalties and stunning betrayals are about to detonate. Nothing is as it seems in this divided American world: the political becomes personal, religious faith overrides family, and fear can shatter the possibility of love. An astonishing achievement that's sure to ignite dialogue—and, as the best works of art do, push us to see the world differently."   —CAROLINE LEAVITT,
New York Times best-selling author of *Is This Tomorrow* and *Pictures of You*

"Devastating, gripping, and beautiful. *The Book of Stone* is about fathers and sons, how the past haunts the present, how trauma transcends generations, and how wrong we can be about those who made us who we are. What will haunt you forever is how Papernick brings you right up to the border of justice and terror and then makes that border disappear. Open this book carefully. You will close it changed."   —DARA HORN,
award-winning author of *The World to Come* and *A Guide for the Perplexed*